Deserves to Die

Bonzi appeared, his caramel-colored coat dappled with snow, his lips snarling, showing teeth. His eyes were trained on the creek, just beyond the brush. As Jet shied, the hairs on the back of the dog's thick neck raised. Tail stiff, he snarled and barked, his eyes focused on a bend in the creek.

What was it? A wildcat or puma? Maybe a wolf?

Shivering inwardly, Eli followed the dog's gaze with his own.

"Trouble?" his father shouted from somewhere not far behind.

The last thing he wanted was his dad to think he couldn't handle his horse. Eli's gaze scoured the wintry banks of the creek, searching the exposed rocks and tangled, snow-covered roots. "No," he said, shaking his head, "It's just—"

His words died in his throat.

His stomach dropped.

Fear cold as an Arctic blast cut through him as he saw what the dog had sensed. Ten feet ahead in a deep pool, a woman's arm stretched out of the water, fingers wide as if supplicating the heavens.

About the author

Lisa Jackson's books are number one bestsellers in America. She now has over twenty million copies of her books in print in nineteen languages. She lives with her family and a rambunctious pug in the Pacific Northwest. You can visit her website at www.lisajackson.com, become her friend on Facebook or follow her on Twitter @ readlisajackson.

LISA JACKSON

DESERVES TO DIE

MULHOLLAND
BOOKS

HODDER

First published in Great Britain in 2014 by Mulholland Books
An imprint of Hodder & Stoughton
An Hachette UK company

1

Copyright © Lisa Jackson LLC 2014

A CIP catalogue record for this title is available from the British Library

Paperback ISBN 978 1 444 79325 3
eBook ISBN 978 1 444 79326 0

Printed and bound by CPI Group (UK) Ltd, Croydon, CR0 4YY

Hodder & Stoughton policy is to use papers that are natural, renewable
and recyclable products and made from wood grown in sustainable forests.
The logging and manufacturing processes are expected to conform to
the environmental regulations of the country of origin.

Hodder & Stoughton Ltd
338 Euston Road
London NW1 3BH

www.hodder.co.uk

DESERVES TO DIE

Prologue

She wasn't quite dead.

Though her eyes seemed fixed as they stared up at the night sky, her breathing was shallow, her heart still faintly beating as she lay, faceup on the tarp. She was still alive, but barely, only inches and seconds from meeting the grim reaper, which was a good thing, he thought. No longer could she taunt or ridicule anyone. No longer would she ever smirk again. Comatose, so near death that it would take little for her to cross over, she lay on the marshy bank of the bayou, an easy victim.

Crouching over her, he grinned at her ultimate vulnerability. If he wanted to, he could slice her throat and watch drips of blood accumulate over the grotesque smile he would carve into her white flesh.

He considered doing the deed with his knife, a slim switchblade that felt heavy in his pocket.

But no, she was close enough to death already and he had another, more intimate way of slicing her.

Something jumped into the murky water not ten feet away. A bullfrog maybe? It reminded him to get back to work; he didn't have much time. A full moon was rising, casting silvery shadows through the white-barked cypress, their roots exposed, Spanish moss draping over the dark water. Crickets chirped, fish jumped, and the water lapped gently in the isolated stretch of Louisiana.

Beads of sweat dotted his brow and ran down his face, creating salty tracks that passed over his lips and dropped onto her still body as he took her left hand in his, splaying her fingers easily. Antique diamonds winked in the pale moonlight, their brilliance seeming to mock him. Oh, what those icy stones had meant, the promises that had been vowed, the secrets they held.

A deep, smoldering rage ran through him as he eyed the stones. Using his free hand, he pulled a slim, automatic pocket knife from his pocket and clicked the blade open. It too reflected the moonlight. Without hesitation, he went to work, holding her fingers wide, then cutting quickly, nearly seamlessly slicing her finger off at the knuckle.

She didn't so much as flinch.

As her blood pumped, he yanked the ring from its ugly stump and felt a welling satisfaction at a job well done.

Straightening, he looked down at her, nearly a corpse, her gauzy dress filthy, her beautiful face condemned to death.

He held her finger in his open palm, the ring now his.

Exquisite diamonds.

So easily removed.

So easily pocketed.

Satisfied, he kicked the body off its mound, watching it roll down the short bank. With a soft splash, she slipped into the murky water to float for a second, catching the slow moving current, heading downstream and out of sight.

"Good riddance," he whispered.

He took in several deep breaths and wiped his brow before pocketing his treasure. As he turned back toward the dense foliage, he heard another sound over the chorus of crickets and bullfrogs, a quiet, ominous splash, the sound of a large reptile sliding into the water.

Perfect, he thought as the creature swam noiselessly under the water's surface. He smiled as he hurried to his hidden truck, knowing that she was already gator bait.

As if on cue, there was a loud splash, a frantic, sickening roiling of water, a flash of a white belly as the reptile rolled to make its kill, jagged teeth sinking into her skin, vise-like jaws gripping and pulling her under the water until the last bit of air escaped her lungs.

Then all went quiet for a second as the stillness of the bayou surrounded him and only the barest of ripples spread to the surrounding water. The chorus of insects, momentarily silenced, began again.

A fitting end, he thought. It served the cheating bitch right.

CHAPTER 1

This has to be the place.

Jessica Williams stared at the dilapidated cabin and her heart sank. Of course she'd been hoping for an isolated place to live, one without the prying eyes of nosy neighbors, but this little cottage went far beyond *rustic*, with its mossy roof, sagging porch, and rusted downspouts. At least the windows weren't boarded over, and there was a garage of sorts, but it was all piled under nearly a foot of snow. She doubted very strongly that there was any central heat within the building. If she'd expected a haven, she'd been sorely disappointed.

Too bad.

For the foreseeable future, this little eighty-year-old building nestled deep in the forested foothills of the Bitterroots was going to be home, whether she liked it or not.

"*Not*, is what I'm thinking," she said as she hopped from the cab of her ancient SUV, a Chevy that had over two hundred thousand miles on its odometer, and into the pristine snow. The air was crisp and cold, the snow crusted over and no longer falling. For the last fifty miles of her long journey the Tahoe's engine light had been blinking on and off and she'd ignored the warning, praying that she would get there before the damn thing overheated or gave out completely. Somehow, subsisting on energy bars, bags of Doritos, Red Bull, and bottled water, she'd arrived after nearly thirty-six hours on the road. She was tired to the marrow of her bones, but she couldn't stop. Not yet.

She glanced behind her vehicle to what could barely be called a lane where there was the merest break in the trees, just wide enough for her rig to pass. Twin ruts broke up the pristine mantle of snow, evidence that someone was occupying the cabin.

Jessica Williams, she reminded herself. *That's who lives here. That's my name now. Jessica Williams.* The name felt uncomfortable, like a scratchy coat that rubbed her bare skin, but it had to be worn.

Before she started unloading, she broke a path to the rotting porch and trudged up the two steps. Snow had blown across the porch, a couple inches piling near the door, dark dry leaves poking up through the thin layer.

She inserted her key into the lock. If it were rusted, which she half-expected, she'd be in trouble. *More trouble,* she reminded herself. She tried the key and it stuck, unmoving, in the lock. She rattled it. "Come on, come on," she muttered under breath that fogged in the air.

She'd rented this place online, and struck a simple deal with the out-of-state owner. She paid him up-front, in cash, no questions asked. She only hoped he held up his end of the bargain.

With a final twist, the lock gave and she was able to push the door open.

"Oh, man," she said, peering inside. She flipped a light switch near the door and nothing happened, so she headed back to her SUV. She found her flashlight and a roller bag that worked only so-so through the snow as she returned to the porch and the open door. Snapping on the flashlight, she swept its harsh beam over the interior that looked as if no one had been there for a decade. It smelled musty, the air thick with dust. She ran the beam across an old love seat with faded, lumpy cushions and a scarred wooden frame. A coffee table sat in front of it and a rocker, with most of its stuffing exposed, was situated by a river rock fireplace where she suspected birds might roost in the summer. Old nests were probably clogging the flue and that didn't begin to count the bats.

"Fixer Upper's Dream," she said aloud. The ad certainly hadn't lied about that, nor, probably, "A Hunter's Paradise." The terrain and the building were beyond rugged. From the looks of the cabin's interior, mice and other rodents had been the last house guests and she half-expected a raccoon or worse to be cowering in a kitchen cabinet.

On that she was proved wrong. There were no cabinets. Just a table near an antique wood-burning stove and an empty spot where a refrigerator, or maybe an icebox, had once stood. All the conveniences of home, which had been advertised, were sorely lacking. She'd asked for running water, electricity, a septic system, and cell phone access, if not the ability to connect to the Internet. It seemed she might have none of the basics.

"Great." She reminded herself that the most important aspect of the cabin, her tantamount request, was isolation, and that had been provided. "La-di-frickin'-dah," she said, then caught herself.

She tested the toilet. Of course it didn't flush, but once she twisted the valves underneath the tank, water began to flow. A good sign. She'd been afraid that the pipes had rusted through or were frozen. "Will wonders never cease?" She flushed again and water swirled down the stained fixture. It worked and when she tested the sink, water ran through the faucet, all of it ice cold.

Good enough for tonight.

She toured the rest of the cabin, which consisted of the kitchen, a bedroom, the bathroom, and a small loft tucked beneath a sloping roof. A back porch overlooked a small stream that ambled through the hemlocks and firs that lined its shores. It was nearly frozen over, just a trickle near the middle indicating that the water was still running some.

There were no visible signs of a furnace, nor duct work, just a kerosene space heater tucked into a gun closet, and of course the river rock fireplace with its charred and well-used firebox. "Home sweet home," she said as she walked through the interior and out the front door. She needed to unload the Tahoe, clean the place up if she could, dare start a fire and settle in for the night.

As she walked outside again, she noticed dusk was settling in, twilight casting deep shadows across the small clearing. A soft snow began to fall again and, of course, cover the tracks her rig had made when she'd turned off the county road twenty miles into the hills surrounding Grizzly Falls.

Good.

Surely I'll be safe here, she thought, her gaze scouring the woods. There was no way he could find her. Right? She'd covered her tracks completely. Again, she looked at the ruts her SUV had dug into the unbroken snow. If ever there were red arrows pointing to a target, those ruts were it. Worse yet, she felt as if she had been followed, though she'd seen no one in her rearview for miles.

Paranoia crept in with the night stealing across the snowy landscape. She always felt as if someone were only a step behind her, ready to pounce and slit her throat. Absently, she touched her neck and reminded herself that she had friends in Grizzly Falls, people she could trust.

And what good will they do, if he finds you? They can't save you, Jessica, *and you know it. No one can.*

Despair threatened her just as a stiff breeze kicked up, rattling the branches of trees and swirling around the thin walls of the cabin.

Get over yourself. The law in Grizzly Falls was supposed to be different from what she was used to, the sheriff a thinking man with deep convictions and an ability to sort fact from fiction.

Dan Grayson would help her.

He had to.

Setting her jaw and tamping down her fears, Jessica hauled in her sleeping bag, a pillow, a backpack, her empty thermos, and a single bottle of water, which, along with half a bag of jerky and a banana that was turning brown, would be her dinner. She eyed the living room, searching for any kind of hiding spot. There was a vent in the back corner of the firebox that allowed for the dropping of ashes and intake of air when opened. That would work for the items she wanted to keep safe but wouldn't need handy and also act as a decoy if the house were ransacked. In that little niche, she'd hide one set of fake identification documents, the ones she'd used in Denver. But that little hidey-hole wasn't enough, so she looked for other spots and decided her best bet was to pull off a section of the baseboard, tear out a hole in the wood wall, then replace the board. It was where she'd hide the other ID and money she wanted to stash. She spent the next hour at a spot at the edge of a built-in bookcase. Once she'd whittled out an area large enough, she stuffed her valuables inside and replaced the baseboard.

She thought of her weapons—a small switchblade that fit in her palm she'd keep with her, hidden inside the padding of her bra during the day and up her sleeve at night, and a gun. She'd carry it as well, in her SUV, under the seat, and at night, tucked beneath her head on a pillow. Not very imaginative, she knew, but the tiny pistol would be close enough to grab should an intruder burst in.

Her heart pounded at the thought.

Could she do it?

Pull a trigger?

Take a man's life?

Absolutely. In a flash, she remembered him, how cruel he was, how he'd enjoyed torturing her. She wouldn't think twice about blowing the bastard away.

After tucking the Kel-Tec P-32 under the pillow, she let out a slow breath and found her meager dinner.

Bon appetit! she thought as she peeled the banana and cracked open the bottle of water. Spreading her sleeping bag over the ancient love seat, she took a long swallow from the bottle, then checked her cell phone. So far, she had service. Maybe the Internet wasn't an impossibility. But not for tonight. No. After a double check to make certain she wasn't locking any creatures into the cabin with her, she threw the deadbolts, ate two bites of the banana and, lying on her makeshift bed with the wind keening down the mountainside, decided she'd never fall asleep.

Within two minutes, she was out like a light.

Detective Selena Alvarez sent up a prayer, one she'd learned in catechism, then added a personal request to God that he spare the life of Dan Grayson, who lay comatose in the hospital bed. Tubes and wires were attached to him, monitors tracking his vital signs, the room sterile and utilitarian. A tall man who barely fit on the hospital bed, Grayson was the sheriff of Pinewood County, one of the best men Alvarez had ever known, one she'd once fancied herself in love with. But the person lying under the crisp white sheets and slightly rumpled blankets was a shell of the man she remembered, the vibrant, slow-talking lawman whose eyes twinkled when he was amused and darkened dangerously when he was serious. His skin had a weird grayish tinge under the fluorescent lights, his gray mustache was untrimmed, his breathing labored.

She touched his fingers with the tips of her own, willing him to open his eyes, wishing he'd never stepped out of his cabin and been the target of a crazed assassin. The bastard who had wounded Grayson had been caught and was behind bars and awaiting trial for a variety of charges including murder and attempted murder.

"You hang in there." Her throat clogged and she chided herself as she was usually in control, her emotions under tight rein.

"A cold bitch," she'd heard in the lunchroom of the sheriff's office. It had come from Pete Watershed, a deputy who was quick with crude jokes and thought of himself as an expert when it came to the opposite sex.

"Ice water in her veins," Connors, the buffoon, had chimed in, sliding Alvarez a sly glance as if he hoped she'd overheard.

She had and had retorted with, "Better than carrying the double I-gene like you, for impotence and idiocy." Afterward, she'd kicked herself as she rarely let herself be goaded, had prided herself on keeping cool and collected. It was just that Connors was such a dick sometimes.

But the man before her in the hospital bed, Dan Grayson, was one of the best.

She glanced out the window to the still winter night. Snow was falling steadily, covering the parking lot and the scattering of cars parked beneath tall security lamps. She trusted Grayson was safe, but she wasn't certain he'd survive. Releasing a pent up sigh, she leaned forward and brushed a quick kiss against his cool cheek. Though she was in love with another man, one she hoped to marry, a part of her would always cherish this sheriff who had taught her humility, patience, and empathy.

She left the room quickly, nodding at the nurse on the night shift who opened the electronic doors. They parted and there, on the other side, waiting patiently, probably understanding how conflicted she was, stood Dylan O'Keefe, the man who had been in and out of her life for years and whom she loved.

"How is he?" O'Keefe asked, knowing full well how Alvarez felt about her boss. His eyes, a penetrating gray, were filled with concern.

"Not good." She flung herself into his arms as tears burned the back of her eyelids. "Not good."

Strong arms held her close. "Shh. He'll be fine," O'Keefe assured her and she took comfort in his lies. "He's strong. It takes more than a bullet or two to knock that cowboy down."

Squeezing her eyes shut, she wished to high heaven that she could believe him. And she had to. Despite all of her efforts to bring his assailant to justice, Dan Grayson still had to fight this battle on his own. She'd done all she could, even going off the rails and becoming a bit of a rogue cop—totally out of character for her—to arrest the man responsible for Grayson's injuries. But she couldn't help him now. He was fighting for his life and it was all down to the strength of his body and his will to live.

Sniffing, forcing back her own dread, she finally took a step back. "You're right. He is strong."

"Ready?"

She nodded and O'Keefe pressed the elevator call button. When a soft *ding* announced the car had arrived and the elevator's doors whispered open, they stepped inside, and once more, Alvarez silently prayed for Dan Grayson's life.

When Jessica woke up, she was disoriented, her bladder stretched to the breaking point, the darkness in the cabin complete. She found her phone in her pocket and first checked the time. Nearly five AM. She'd slept almost around the clock and had a crick in her neck to prove it.

But she'd survived.

At least one more night.

A quick glance through the window showed her that her footsteps were still visible, but quickly disappearing with the night's snowfall, as were the Chevy's tire tracks.

Good, though it really didn't matter. She couldn't stay hidden away. She had to go out today and would in the days after, as she needed to secure a job and fast. The cash she'd taken with her was running out and though her expenses were little, her dollars could only be stretched so far.

She relieved herself in the barely functioning toilet, then using her flashlight, followed its beam to the back porch where she'd seen a stack of wood the night before.

The split fir had been in its resting spot for years, judging by the nests of spiders within and the fact that it was dry as a bone. It would ignite easily. A small axe had been left, its blade stuck in a huge round of wood that had obviously been used as a chopping block. She carried in several large chunks and stacked them in the grate, checked the flue, opened the damper, then went back outside and, with her flashlight balanced on the porch rail, split some kindling.

Thank you, Grandpa, for showing me how to do this, she thought, conjuring up the old man with his bald, speckled pate, rimless glasses, and slight paunch. He'd been the one who had taken her hunting and camping, molding what he'd considered a pampered princess into a self-sufficient woman.

"Ya never can tell when you'll need to know how to shoot, or build a camp, or make a fire, Missy, so you'd best learn now," he'd told her. Smelling of chewing tobacco and a hint of Jack Daniels, he'd set about teaching her.

Of course he was long gone, but his memory and advice lingered.

She set up one piece of fir, raised the axe, and brought it down swiftly. A bit of kindling split off. She repeated the process again and again until she'd made short work of three fir chunks and, despite the freezing temperatures and her fogging breath, was sweating profusely.

Once back in the cabin, she used her lighter and soon a fire was burning in the grate, smoke drawing through the chimney, heat emanating. There were still a couple hours of darkness, so she hoped to warm the little space and use the firelight as illumination. Once dawn broke, she would let the fire die so that no smoke was visible.

She made a list of essentials she'd need, then checked the online connection on her phone, which she used with a device she'd bought on the black market, along with a new identity.

"Jessica Williams." She eyed the driver's license from California and the social security number she'd been told wouldn't raise any red flags. Coupled with her disguise, she might just blend into the local Montana landscape for a while.

My life as a criminal, she thought, checking the help wanted area of a website dedicated to finding jobs in western Montana. She'd posted her resume two days earlier, indicating that she was moving to the area and only had a temporary address, so that anyone interested would have to contact her through the site. *So far, nothing,* she noted as she finished the rest of the banana.

She found the website for the Grizzly Falls newspaper and located the want ads where there were two opportunities to hire on as a waitress. Betsy's Bakery and the Midway Diner. She made note of them, then ate a couple bites of jerky and washed them down with her water.

Wasting no time, she cleaned up as best as she could with the cold tap water, changed her clothes, and examined her reflection in the cracked mirror on the medicine cabinet over the sink in the bathroom. Dawn was just breaking, light filtering through the falling snow and cloud cover.

Her features were still in shadow as she applied her makeup with the aid of the flashlight's harsh beam. Contacts to change her gold eyes a dark brown, tweezers to contour her arched eyebrows flat, a dull blond wig that hid her auburn hair, and removable appliances that made her jowly enough to match the padded body suit that seemed to add at least thirty pounds to her athletic frame.

Over it all, she dressed in too-tight jeans and a sweater under a jacket, then again, surveyed her image in the mirror. She was unrecognizable to anyone who knew her.

Maybe today she'd get lucky.

Lucky? Really?

Who would have ever thought she would end up here, the daughter of privilege, a woman who'd showed such promise, one with a damn master's degree, no less, and now on the run?

God help me.

For a split second, she was back in that swamp. In her mind's eye, she saw the glinting image of a blade, heard the lap of water, saw the blood flowing. . . . She felt the pain, the despair, the utter bleakness of that moment and remembered the fleeting feeling that if she just let go, if she finally gave up, she would be free.

But she'd fought.

And had miraculously survived.

So far.

Reaching up, she fingered the scar on her nape at her hairline, made sure the wig covered it and then headed for the door. She wasn't about to let *him* win.

Ever.

CHAPTER 2

The new guy was a prick.

At least in Detective Regan Pescoli's estimation.

She doubted she was alone in her viewpoint that Hooper Effin' Blackwater, until recently, commander of the criminal department, now acting sheriff, was a poor replacement for Dan Grayson.

Then again, Grayson's size twelve boots were damn hard to fill.

She crossed the department's parking lot and headed for the back door. It was cold as hell, the night still lingering enough that the street lamps were just winking off, the wind fierce enough to snap the flags and rattle the chains of the poles near the front of the building.

As she walked through the department's back door she shook the snow from her hair and brushed several melting flakes from the shoulders of her jacket before stomping whatever remained from her boots. Opening the vestibule door into the department, a wave of heat hit her full in the face, the old furnace rumbling as it worked overtime.

Already, the office was bustling with the sound of jangling phones, clicking and sputtering printers, and bits and pieces of conversation.

Unwinding her scarf, she headed past the lunchroom where some of the officers lingered, either before or after their shifts. A few straggling members from the night crew were gathering their things, having a last cup of coffee, and scanning the headlines of the latest edition of the newspaper. The morning workers were beating a path to the coffeepots already percolating on the counter, the rich aroma of some South American blend scenting the air.

Pescoli's stomach turned a little at the thought of coffee, a morning cup she once considered one of life's greatest pleasures. A cup of black coffee and a cigarette, what could be better? Now, of course, she indulged in neither, at least nothing with a jolt of caffeine in it. And zero nicotine.

A shame, really.

Sometimes being healthy and a role model to her children was a major pain in the ass.

Speaking of pains, she returned her thoughts back to the man in charge of the department, if only for the time being. The change didn't sit well, nor did sipping a caffeine-free Diet Coke. It just didn't hit the spot, but she dealt with it. She had to.

Because, surprise, surprise she was pregnant.

Again.

The baby was unplanned.

Again.

Would she never learn?

Bypassing the lunchroom, she nearly collided with Joelle Fisher, the department's receptionist and head cheerleader, at least in her own mind.

Bustling toward the cafeteria in pink, impossibly high heels that matched her suit and the little heart-shaped earrings dangling from her earlobes, Joelle caught herself before tripping. "Excuse me, Detective," she said a little sharply, her voice accented by the staccato rhythm of her footsteps. Balancing a huge white box that no doubt held dozens of cookies or cupcakes, she was, as always, in a hurry. Her platinum hair was piled into a high beehive, not a single strand waving as she moved with lightning speed toward the lunchroom.

It was Joelle's mission to ensure every member of the force was filled to the brim with whatever holiday goodies were in season. From her great-great-great-grandmother's recipe for fruitcake at Christmas, to the "witch's tarts" she created for Halloween, Joelle ensured that each officer of the Pinewood Sheriff's Department had his or her sweet tooth satisfied and blood sugar levels elevated.

Maybe all those sweets were a good thing. She had to be around sixty, but she appeared a full decade younger, despite her nod to 1960s fashion.

"I'm . . . I'm not drunk," a loud voice insisted from around the corner. "Ya hear me? Damn Breathalyzer is broke, I tell ya! Issus . . . it's who? Ten in the morning?"

"A little after eight, Ivor." Deputy Kayan Rule's voice was firm. "Time to sober up."

"But I am . . . I am sh . . . sober. I'm tellin' ya."

"You've told me a lot of things. Let's go." Just as Pescoli reached her office she caught a glimpse of Rule, a tall black man who looked more like an NBA power forward than a county road deputy, shepherding a cuffed and unhappy Ivor Hicks to the drunk tank.

"Bastard!" Hicks said angrily.

Pescoli had no love for the man or any member of his family; in fact she had a personal, deep-seated loathing for Ivor's son, but she tried not to think about that particular nut job. Nonetheless, her skin crawled as Ivor was shepherded along the hallways.

"You'll get yours," Ivor predicted with some kind of sanctimonious malice, the joy being his ability to predict Rule's dire future. From behind thick, owlish glasses, he glared at the deputy. "Mark my words. That son of a bitch, Crytor? He'll get you, y'know. Damn general of that pod, he'll come for you like he did for me. And he'll plant a damn invisible chip in you, too!"

"He'll have to stand in line. I've got lots of folks out to get me," Rule said and tossed Pescoli a *what're-ya-gonna-do* look. Then he guided tipsy Ivor Hicks, still ranting about the leader of the army of reptilian aliens he'd believed had abducted him, around a corner at the end of the hall. Ivor was convinced that the extraterrestrials had done a vast array of medical experiments on him years before and that his memories of the terrifying event had nothing to do with his fondness for whiskey.

Just a normal day at the office.

As they passed out of sight, Pescoli stepped into her office and stripped off her jacket and scarf. Outside it was freezing, a raging storm from Canada passing through, but inside the building, the heat was almost stifling. The temperature was set above seventy and in Pescoli's current state, the department felt like a sauna. She was sweating by the time she kicked out her desk chair and sat at her computer.

God, she thought, logging onto her e-mail, *I'd kill for a Diet Coke* with *caffeine.* But it was not to be. She was going to have to opt for decaf coffee, instant, no less.

Waiting for the screen to come up, she made her way back to the lunchroom and found the carafe marked HOT WATER and poured a cup. It steamed as she returned to her desk. She didn't want any of her coworkers to note that she'd switched from "high-octane" to "unleaded" because she hadn't shared her secret with anyone, including Nate Santana, her fiancé and the father of her unborn child. He had no children of his own, and she wasn't sure how he would react to the news. She trusted him, loved him, and had agreed to marry him, though she'd been reluctant as she'd walked down the aisle twice before, once to Joe Strand, her son Jeremy's father. A cop like her, he had died in the line of duty. Theirs had been a rocky, if passionate union. The same could be said for husband number two, Luke "Lucky" Pescoli, a sexy trucker who had swept her off her usually grounded feet. She'd married him on the fly and the results were their daughter Bianca and a divorce. Lucky had remarried Michelle soon afterward who was, in Pescoli's biased opinion, a life-sized, walking, talking Barbie doll, barely older than her stepson Jeremy and a whole heck-of-a lot smarter than she let on.

As she carried her mug back to her desk, Pescoli heard Blackwater on the phone, but she didn't peer into the sheriff's office as she passed, not like she used to when Grayson was there. She couldn't stomach the thought of Blackwater leaning back in Grayson's chair, feet on the desk, receiver to his ear as he kiss-assed the higher ups; or, more likely, sitting ramrod stiff in the chair and doing isometric exercises as he restructured the department.

Maddening.

Once seated at her desk again, she shoved aside a stack of papers, then added freeze-dried decaf coffee crystals to the steaming water in her mug and stirred with a spoon she kept handy in the top drawer. She caught a glimpse of one of the pictures she kept on her desk and felt a tug on her heart. The shot was of Jeremy at nine, his smile stretched wide, his teeth still a little too big for his face, his hair mussed. He was standing on a flat rock near the banks of a stream and proudly holding his catch, a glistening rainbow trout.

Her heart squeezed. The years since then had flown by and he was nearly an adult who, despite her protests, was going to follow in his parents' footsteps and become a cop.

Lord help us, she thought, though the truth was that her son had saved her life recently, and it seemed, in so doing, had finally crossed the threshold into manhood.

After taking a sip of her coffee, she felt an instant souring in her gut. From the coffee? Or Blackwater, whose voice still carried down the hall. Irritated, she rolled her chair to the door to shut it and thought, again, of the new life growing inside her.

Pregnant.

And pushing forty.

Now *that* had been a surprise. She had near-grown kids already. Jeremy was almost out the door . . . well, that had yet to be seen, but he'd made a few futile attempts in the past. Bianca was in the last years of high school and deep into teenage angst.

So *now* a baby?

Starting all over again with diapers, sleepless nights, shifting schedules, and juggling a full-time job?

She wasn't ambivalent about the baby, not really. She just knew how much work and chaos a baby brought into the home, especially a home that wasn't exactly picture-perfect already. And she wasn't married. Not that being unwed and pregnant was such a big deal these days, but Santana was already pushing for them to tie the knot.

She had the ring to prove it, even if the band with its diamond was currently tucked into a corner of the top drawer of her bureau. She'd had it on briefly, but with everything that had happened recently, she didn't feel like bandying it about quite yet.

She took another sip of the coffee, found it too bitter, and put the half-drunk cup aside on her already cluttered desk.

A sharp rap on her door sounded, then Alvarez stuck her head inside. "Busy?" she asked as Pescoli swiveled in her chair. "Or do you have a minute?"

"Something up?"

Alvarez shook her head and slipped into the tiny room, leaving the door open a crack. "I just wanted to see if you'd gone to visit Grayson."

"Not for a few days. I was going to drop by the hospital after work. Wanna go with?"

"I was there last night." Alvarez was grim as she shook her head.

"And?"

"Not good."

"It's only been—"

"I know. But I expected him to, I don't know, come around by now." Compressing her lips together, Alvarez gave her head a quick shake as if dispelling an unwanted picture in her mind. Though it had been Pescoli who'd found him lying in a pool of blood at his cabin, Alvarez had been the most shaken up by the attack on their boss.

"They're moving him out of ICU, into a private room," she added. "That's what one of the nurses told me before I went in to see him."

"I thought he was going to be transferred to Seattle, a neurological unit specializing in brain trauma or something."

"That plan's been scrapped and I don't know why," Alvarez said, obviously frustrated. "The doctors seem to think he's stable enough that he doesn't need round-the-clock observation, that he'll get better with time, but I don't know."

"He'll be okay."

Alvarez looked up sharply. "How do you know? Everyone keeps saying that, but really, it's just words." Her mouth was pinched, her eyes flashing.

"I . . . well, you're right. I don't really know, but that's a good sign, isn't it? That he's being transferred out of intensive care. Come on, Alvarez, have a little faith."

"You, the self-professed agnostic? You're telling *me* to have faith?"

"I'm just saying that if anyone can pull through, it's Dan Grayson. He's a big, strapping man and . . ." Pescoli let her voice trail off. "One of the good guys."

"Yeah—"

"Detectives?" Hooper Blackwater's voice preceded him as he took the time to stick his head into Pescoli's office.

Pescoli looked up at him.

"Reports?" His eyebrows raised, a nonverbal reminder that there was work to be done that bugged the hell out of her. "The Haskins suicide? Armstead domestic dispute?"

"Both done," Alvarez said.

"Good. E-mail them to me." With a quick, sharp nod, he was off, boots ringing as he strode down the hall, probably searching for his next Red Bull or a spot where he could drop and do twenty quick push-ups. Just because he could.

"I can't stand that guy," Pescoli said under her breath.

"I know," Alvarez said. "And he knows. For that matter, we all know." Her dark eyes were without reproach, though, as if she silently agreed. "Maybe you shouldn't make it so obvious."

Pescoli didn't respond. She knew she was being bitchy, but she didn't really care.

"Try it," Alvarez suggested, her professional mask slipping back into place. "I'll catch you later." She was out of Pescoli's office quickly.

Once more, Pescoli rolled her desk chair to the door and pushed it firmly shut, a practice that was new to her. Since Blackwater had grabbed the reins of the department, she felt she needed privacy, at least for now and the foreseeable future.

She wasn't kidding herself. Grayson, if he ever returned, was a long way off from regaining his rightful place as sheriff. She and the whole damn office were stuck with Blackwater, the go-getter who let everyone know it.

"Shit," she whispered.

Grayson, forever with his black lab Sturgis at his heels, his Stetson squarely on his head, was soft-spoken and thoughtful, yet quietly firm. A tall, rangy man who looked more cowboy than lawman, a sheriff elected by the people of Pinewood County, his quiet command was effective. He had strong opinions and all hell could break out when he was angry, but for the most part, he was in control and steady, a rock-solid force Pescoli could depend upon.

Blackwater was all action—fast-paced and guns blazing as if he had to prove himself. He made sure that everyone who worked for him knew he was an ex-Marine who had served two tours in Afghanistan. Pescoli had heard that he ran every morning, three miles minimum in all kinds of weather, and three days a week he spent hours in the gym, boxing and lifting weights to reduce his stress and stay in Marine-proud shape. At work, he downed Red Bull, Rock Star, or Monster energy drinks the way an alcoholic tossed back martinis. Part Native American, he appeared perpetually tanned, his eyes an intense brown bordering on black, his nearly six-foot physique all compact muscle.

Pescoli admitted to herself that he was handsome enough, if that mattered, with a slightly Roman nose that looked as if it had been broken at least once, bladed cheekbones, and black hair without a trace of gray, cut short, again, a reminder of his military background. Blackwater was smart, too, Pescoli allowed, and had the law degree to prove it. He attacked each problem head-on with the ferocity of a wounded bear, no excuses, and had already made it clear that he expected every member of his staff to do the same.

It wasn't his work ethic that got under her skin. It was his style that rankled. All his terse sentences, orders, and damn meetings indicated that he'd come to not only play but to stay.

Pescoli had been toying with the idea of quitting, or at the very least, cutting back her hours to part-time, and her pregnancy had only reinforced her plans. However, there was that little matter of making sure Grayson's would-be assassin spent the rest of his life behind bars. She wasn't going to do anything until she was certain that son of a bitch never walked free again.

She'd have to suck it up for a while. Yes, the entire atmosphere in the department had changed and it bothered her, but so what? A lot bothered her these days.

Deal with it, she told herself as she clicked on her mouse and focused her attention on her e-mails. She sure as hell didn't want to be late with any damn reports.

Her life had become a pathetic good news–bad news joke, Jessica thought as she drove past the snow-crusted fields of a farm on the outskirts of Grizzly Falls.

The good news? She'd landed the job at the Midway Diner.

The bad news? Dan Grayson, the man she had thought just might be her savior, was in the hospital fighting for his life, so her plans to enlist his help would have to be put on hold. Indefinitely. Her spirits were low; she'd counted on the even-tempered sheriff's help. Her plans would have to change.

Taking a corner a little too fast, she felt her wheels slip on the icy road and eased off the gas. The tires gripped the road anew and her SUV straightened. The radio was blasting over the rumble of the engine and the clock on her dash indicated it was a few minutes after midnight.

Fiddling with the Chevy's finicky heater, she considered her options. With the temperature having dropped below freezing, the heater was blowing lukewarm air, its rattle nearly drowning out a country song about the pain of love lost that filled the interior. Snapping off the radio, she noticed the defroster was fighting a losing battle with the condensation that was crawling inward over her viewing angle. She gave the glass a swipe with an extra sweatshirt that was lying on the passenger seat, and squinted, trying to find the turn off to the long lane that wound to her cabin. "Home," she reminded herself.

Snowflakes danced, swirling as they were caught in the headlights' glare, piling along the fencerows and frosting the branches of the evergreens that rose in the foothills.

She could continue to lie low, retaining her disguise while keeping her ear to the ground, or she could bolt again, heading farther west or north. Or, she could seek her own revenge, try to turn the tables on the bastard from whom she was running, lure him in, and then destroy him. The thought of taking another human life had always repulsed her, but she'd never been so scared before, had never been fighting for her own existence. She'd always had the luxury of naiveté. If she came face-to-face with him again, she had no doubt she could shoot him dead or plunge a knife deep into his black heart and give the blade a little twist.

"Sick bastard," she whispered.

As the wipers of the old Tahoe slapped snow from the windshield, leaving streaks upon the glass, she checked her rearview mirror for the hundredth time.

No one was following her.

No menacing pickup's headlights appeared over the last rise. Still, she could sense her pursuer.

Letting her breath out slowly, she noticed an old No Hunting sign posted on the massive trunk of a giant hemlock that caught in the headlights. She was close. The engine groaned a little as the incline grew steeper, and less than a quarter mile up the hill, she spied the spot where the trees parted a bit and the old lane ambled off the county road. Of course, there were tracks from her Tahoe, enough to be visible despite the snowfall, but so far, he hadn't appeared.

Had she finally lost him?

Most likely not. Several months had passed from the moment she'd stared up at the moon and gasped for air as she'd lain on the soft banks of the bayou. It was there she'd fought the battle of deciding whether to live or die.

Life had won out, and she'd started her journey of two thousand miles down a desperately crooked path that had finally ended up in the wilds of western Montana.

Was she safe?

She doubted it.

He was nothing if not dogged and deadly.

Shivering a little, she nosed her Tahoe through the stands of hemlock and fir to the tiny clearing where her cabin, after a call to the owner, was finally equipped with electricity and hot water. There was still no furnace, but she'd picked up a used space heater at a second-hand shop, along with a few other essentials.

House Beautiful the old cottage was not, but at least it was functioning, the utilities in the owner's name and billed to him. She parked near the garage, locked her SUV, and made her way inside where the smell of wood smoke and last night's microwave popcorn greeted her. On a makeshift coffee table was the local paper, where she'd first learned of the attack on Dan Grayson and his subsequent hospitalization. There was a new sheriff in town, if only temporarily, a man by the name of Hooper Blackwater who was rumored to be a strict, by-the-book officer of the law, a person she was pretty certain she couldn't approach.

So who, then, would help her?

The simple answer was Cade Grayson, Dan's brother, the man from whom she'd heard about the sheriff. But she wasn't about to go running to that rangy cowboy, at least not right away. Unfortunately, he was the man who had started all her trouble and as such would only be her last resort.

CHAPTER 3

Troy Ryder rolled into Grizzly Falls, Montana on a wing and a prayer. His old Dodge truck was wheezing by the time he pulled into a service station and mini-mart where he filled up his tank, added antifreeze to the radiator, and bought a prewrapped ham and cheese sandwich, bag of chips, and two bottles of beer.

He'd spied a motel on his way into town, one of those long, low buildings with a shared porch, empty parking lot, and a sign proudly announcing Free Wi-Fi and Cable Television right next to the Vacancy sign. Good enough. His back ached a bit, his stomach was growling, and he needed to settle in for at least a few hours to study the lay of the land and figure out if Anne-Marie had landed there.

It seemed unlikely, but then stranger things had happened.

Hell, didn't he know it?

He drove back to the motel. After locking his old pickup, he crossed the icy lot and pushed open a glass door to a small, brightly lit reception area that smelled of bitter, overcooked coffee and a hint of cigarette smoke. A second after he approached the counter, a heavyset woman of fifty or so appeared through an open doorway leading to the inner sanctum of the River View Motel. Wearing a uniform that was on the tight side, she took one look at Troy and smiled widely enough to show off a gold crown on one of her molars. "What can I do ya for?"

"Lookin' for a room."

"That we got. How many nights?"

"Just one to start with." After all, he wasn't certain that Anne-Marie had stopped here. "Then, we'll see."

"Got a double-double or a king. What's your pleasure?"

"One bed'll do. 'Round back, if you've got a room there."

"You're in luck," she said, then her eyebrows drew together as her hands clicked over the keyboard of a computer that looked as if it had been built before the turn of the millennium. "Well, I mean, if you call room thirteen lucky. It's the only one that's ready on the back side, where, you know, you get a river view. You're not superstitious, are you?"

"Not much." He filled out the required paperwork, listened to her drone on about the beauty of that part of the country, then snagged the key from her hand and returned to his truck where he drove to the far side of the building and parked in front of room thirteen, an end unit with what only an optimist could describe as a "view" of the river. Not that he cared. He hauled his gear inside, flipped on the lights, and closed the door.

A big bed that looked as if it sagged in the middle, a television on a stand, two night tables with matching lamps, and one chair positioned near the window were the extent of the furniture.

Good enough.

The place was showing its age. The carpet near the door was discolored, the comforter on the bed fading a little, the smell of disinfectant not quite masking a lingering odor of cigarettes, but all in all, it would do.

After cracking open a beer and taking a long swallow, he took a short shower, then changed into fresh clothes and went to work. One way or another, he was going to find Anne-Marie Calderone and haul her tight little ass back to New Orleans.

Alvarez was right.

Okay, she was right *again*, Pescoli thought as she drove down a winding lane that led to the partially built home where she and Santana were planning to live once they were married. Two days earlier, her partner had informed her that Dan Grayson was being moved from ICU and sure enough, when Pescoli had gone to visit him, the sheriff was in a private room, hooked up to all kinds of monitors, not too far from the hub of a nurse's station.

She had expected him to be recovering a lot faster than he was, but she told herself to be patient. So he hadn't woken from his coma, that didn't mean anything. If it were a problem, certainly the doctors and nursing staff would do something. And Grayson's family, his two brothers, Cade and Big Zed, had been at the hospital, along with Hattie, their deceased brother's wife, every day since the assassination attempt.

At least, she thought as she drove around the edge of an icy pond, *Grayson's attacker had been rendered harmless.* Injured during his capture, he was in custody, a bullet lodged against his spinal cord, his ability to walk in question. Though still under doctor's care, the son of a bitch who'd nearly taken her boss's life was no longer a threat.

No armed guard needed to be posted at the hospital any longer.

As she drove along the lane, she tried to be positive. She wasn't certain how she felt about moving as she already owned her own little cabin in the hills, a place that was finally paid off and the home where she'd raised her kids. It wasn't much to look at, but it was cozy, and she'd been proud that she'd been able to pay it off early by doubling up her payments whenever she was able, and finally claim it as her own.

She caught a glimpse of the lake on which the new cabin was built. It would be roomier than her little house, everything within it new enough that she wouldn't have to rely on her questionable plumbing and electrical skills, and it would provide a fresh start with no reminders of the other husbands she'd been married to. She and Santana planned to start their life together there. *It sounds perfect*, she thought as the house erected on the shores of the icy lake came into view.

And yet . . .

She didn't know if she was making the right choice. Jeremy had graduated from high school a couple years earlier and Bianca had one more year, so wouldn't it be smarter to wait?

"No time like the present." Santana's advice echoed through her mind as she cruised along the lake's snowy shores. *"May as well let the kids claim their rooms and feel like they are a part of this."*

That made sense, she supposed, or at least it had until she'd realized there was a new baby on the way, another child who would need his or her own room eventually. She seemed to be involved in revolving door parenting—as one kid was leaving a new one was coming to take his place.

The house came into view and she swallowed hard, wondering if she would ever think of it as home, *her* home. Two stories of raw cedar with a pitched roof covered in snow. With a gray stone fire-place, the house was nestled in the trees on the shore of the lake, picture-perfect. The garage was attached by a short, windowed breeze-way and had private stairs that led to an area overhead where Santana planned to make his office. Considering everything, she wondered if Jeremy might tag the spot as his own, insisting the baby needed its own room as much as he needed his own privacy.

"Not gonna happen," she said under her breath, then decided she was borrowing trouble. Besides, Jeremy was working, taking classes, planning to enroll full-time spring term, and finally appeared to be on a path going forward. He'd been through his own trauma the last few weeks but wouldn't hear of her trying to help him in any way. She didn't want to do anything that would impede his progress, like maybe telling him he was going to have another sibling soon . . .

But she was getting ahead of herself, far ahead of herself, she decided as she pulled into the parking area and cut the engine.

Nikita, Santana's husky, appeared in the open doorway to the main house and gave a quick bark before bounding through the snow to greet her with his back end wiggling wildly.

"Hey, Detective!"

She looked up to see Santana standing on the upper floor deck, off the bedroom, looking every bit as sexy as the first time she'd met him, in a bar no less. Wearing a faded shirt that stretched across his shoulders, he folded his arms over his chest and leaned a shoulder against the frame of the French doors as he stared down at her. One side of his mouth drew into a lazy smile. "About time you showed up."

"Always the bastard," she threw out at him, trying to hide her own amusement.

His grin widened, showing off white teeth against his bronzed skin. Like Blackwater, he had more than a trace of Native American blood in his veins, visible in his high, bladed cheekbones, ink-black hair and dark eyes, the kind of eyes that seemed to sear to her soul, eyes that were twinkling with that sexy kind of mischief that she found impossible to ignore.

What had started out as a white-hot attraction and equally hot af-fair hadn't flamed out as she'd expected. No, she thought, petting Nikita's furry head before heading into the house, that first spark of interest had burned through all her barriers to the engagement and, she hoped, marital bliss.

"Third time's the charm," she told herself as, with the dog on her heels, she walked through the open door and found her way up the stairs that would remain open, offering a view through the glass walls of the living room to the lake visible between each free floating step.

The staircase had been designed before she had any inkling that she would get pregnant, or that in the not-so-distant future a toddler would be trying to climb up and down the steps. At that thought, she paused, imagining a child with Santana's dark hair running through the hallways.

She almost smiled and decided the staircase would need to be boxed in, at least for the next few years.

Sooner, rather than later, she'd have to break the news to Santana.

But not today.

She just wasn't in the mood.

Eli O'Halleran couldn't believe his good luck. Though his father, Trace, had always taken him with him when there were chores to be done around the farm, until today he had never said, "Yeah, son, come with me. You can be the lead dog on this one. Let's see if we can find any other holes in the fence."

"All right!" Eli had said, thrilled. Within a matter of minutes, he'd ignored his breakfast, run to the barn and, with his dad's help, saddled and bridled Jetfire, his black gelding.

While his dad was still cinching his bay mare's saddle, Eli rode Jet through the barn's big roller door and into a back paddock. Both dogs, Dad's shepherd and Bonzi, Kacey's dog, which was at least part pit bull and probably yellow lab, were milling around, anxious to be a part of the action.

"Hold up!" Trace called, but Eli kept going through a series of corrals as the snow fell, all the while feeling like a real cowboy, though he was not quite nine years old.

"Come on," he urged the horse as they reached the open gate to the final field. Glancing over his shoulder, he caught a glimpse of his father leading Mocha from the barn and swinging into the saddle. The dogs, of course, had already escaped the barn and were sniffing and running in the fallen snow, while a cold wind was blowing, snowflakes falling from the gray Montana sky.

"Eli!" his father called, just as Eli leaned forward, eased up on the reins and let the horse go.

Jet surged forward, speeding into a full gallop and tearing down the long, tractor lane covered in snow. Eli's hat blew off, but he didn't care, loving the feel of the wind slapping his face and blowing his hair as he caught sight of the dogs bounding through the drifts and giving chase. Jetfire, after being cooped up in the barn, was eager to run. As Eli hung on, Jet tore up the field, a black blur streaking toward the foothills.

Breathless, Eli didn't care that his dad would probably be mad at him for taking off. It just felt right.

The ground sloped up to a small rise and the gelding ran eagerly upward, breathing hard, racing toward the crest. Eli clung like a burr, his nose running and feeling numb in the cold.

On the far side, the ground dropped off, sloping downward to the creek where the fence separated O'Halleran land from that of the federal government. It was where the problem had started, his dad had told him, a broken spot in the fence where five calves had found the break and gotten through. The strays had been rounded up, and the major hole in the fence had been repaired, but they were just making sure there weren't any more areas where those idiot cows could get through.

The truth was that Trace was tired of being cooped up, too. Otherwise, why would he have decided to survey the fence line in the middle of a near blizzard? It didn't matter, though. Eli was just glad to be out of the house as there was no school.

Plowing through the snow, kicking up powdery clods, Jet crested the hill and raced downward to the meandering brook that cut like a sidewinder back and forth beneath the fence. The field gave way to woods that, on the government side of the property, covered the foothills of the Bitterroots.

Nearing the creek, Eli pulled back on the reins and Jetfire slowed easily, cantering down to a walk just as his dad and Mocha appeared over the rise behind them.

"Didn't you hear me?" Trace demanded as he reined his horse to a stop once they'd reached the corner of the property. He held the reins with one gloved hand and in the other, Eli's stocking cap.

"Sorry," Eli mumbled, though he really wasn't. For the first time, he felt a jab of the cold piercing his jacket.

Trace glared at his son for a second, then let out a sigh. "No harm, no foul, I guess." He still wasn't smiling. "Believe it or not, I was your age once. Broke my arm, being bucked from Rocky. That was my horse at the time."

Eli knew better than to say "I know," even though he'd heard the story before.

Leaning forward, Trace handed Eli his hat. "Think you lost something."

"Thanks." Eli pulled the hat down over his ears as they were starting to freeze, but he didn't dare complain. After all, he'd begged to be a part of this. But as snowflakes slid under the collar of his jacket and the wind blew bitter cold, he was starting to second-guess himself. Not that he would admit it.

"You still want to do this?" his father asked.

Though much of Eli's enthusiasm had faded, he wasn't going to admit it. Nodding, he swiped the back of his gloved hand under his running nose.

His father raised one eyebrow, then gave a quick nod. "Okay, then. You ride up ahead and I'll follow. We'll see if there are any more breaches."

Eli did as he was told, riding along the fence line, growing colder by the second, while his father, more thorough as he scrutinized the wire from atop his mount, lagged behind.

Sometimes being a cowboy really sucks, Eli realized belatedly, his gaze trained on the wire mesh that cut a straight line through the thickets of hemlock, fir, and maple. The stream, nearly frozen, wandered back and forth, a thin trickle in the middle gurgling softly.

Another blast of wind rattled the branches of the surrounding trees and he shivered, tired of the adventure. He just wanted to return to the house, so he urged Jetfire forward through the icy woods. The sooner the job was done, the sooner he could go back inside.

Though he'd begged his father to let him come, Eli began to wish he'd never said a word, just stayed in his pajamas and played on his iPad until breakfast was ready, because inside the house there was a hot fire, a warm cup of hot cocoa, and Kacey, his soon-to-be step-mom. She would be getting ready to go to the clinic where she worked. But instead of being seated at the table, sipping hot chocolate and eating peanut butter toast while watching television, he was out in the cold.

Jetfire stepped quickly through the drifts and Eli swept another quick glance over his shoulder to make certain that his dad was following on the rangy bay. Sure enough, he saw Trace easing his horse through a stand of pines about twenty yards behind him. The two dogs were following, Bonzi with his head lifted as if he were testing the air, Sarge farther behind, exploring a bend in the creek.

Eli wished his dad would hurry.

Through the veil of snow, man and rider were partially obscured, blending into the wintry landscape, appearing almost ghostly. Even the dogs seemed to disappear.

Eli waved at his father, but Trace didn't notice, his concentration and gaze steady on the fence as he appeared and disappeared in the wind-fueled flurries. It worried Eli a little that he was so far ahead of his dad, but he reminded himself to be cowboy-tough. He had a job to do. Once more, Trace and the bay vanished for a second and Eli wondered what he'd do if his father didn't reappear, if he became lost somehow.

But that was nutty.

He knew where he was and his dad was right behind him. Squinting, Eli searched the grove. But no. He couldn't see his father. Nor the dogs.

About to call out to him, Eli caught a glimpse of the bay stepping through the trees again, a phantom horse, barely visible just like in the cartoons he watched or the video games he played.

Feeling a little better, he leaned over the saddle horn, shifting his weight, urging Jetfire forward. Man, it was cold. Too cold. The sooner he found the dumb hole in the wire mesh, the sooner he could go back inside. Jetfire picked up the pace, threading through a copse of saplings as Eli peered through the shifting snowflakes. The fence crossed the stream again as it cut through the trees, heading in a crooked path to the river a few miles to the west.

The fence looked a little different, not as much ice building up over the wire, no snow sticking to the posts. Maybe the cattle had rubbed up against it when searching for a way through. After all, he was near a deeper part of the stream. A particularly stubborn calf with just enough curiosity and no darned brains could wade in and, if he tried hard enough, maybe duck under the wire where the fence spanned the creek. There was no guard there, no floating cattle panel that moved with the current. Squinting through the snowfall, Eli encouraged Jetfire forward, closer to the creek, but the horse snorted and balked.

"Come on," Eli insisted, giving Jetfire a nudge with his knees, urging the gelding to walk closer to the creek.

Instead, Jetfire started backing up.

"Hey!" Eli said sharply. "Let's go!"

But the gelding was having none of it. Tossing his head and snorting, Jet shied away from a thicket of maples.

Eli took a firmer grasp on the reins. "What's got into you?"

From somewhere nearby, a dog growled low and warning, the sound causing the hairs on the back of Eli's neck to lift. Jet reared up.

Eli fought the reins. "Whoa. Stop!"

Bonzi appeared, his caramel-colored coat dappled with snow, his lips snarling, showing teeth. His eyes were trained on the creek, just beyond the brush. As Jet shied, the hairs on the back of the dog's thick neck raised. Tail stiff, he snarled and barked, his eyes focused on a bend in the creek.

What was it? A wildcat or puma? Maybe a wolf?

Shivering inwardly, Eli followed the dog's gaze with his own.

"Trouble?" his father shouted from somewhere not far behind.

The last thing he wanted was his dad to think he couldn't handle his horse. Eli's gaze scoured the wintry banks of the creek, searching the exposed rocks and tangled, snow-covered roots. "No," he said, shaking his head, "It's just—"

His words died in his throat.

His stomach dropped.

Fear cold as an Arctic blast cut through him as he saw what the dog had sensed. Ten feet ahead in a deep pool, a woman's arm stretched out of the water, fingers wide as if supplicating the heavens.

Eli yanked hard on the reins as he stared at the hand. Reaching upward, one finger severed, the hand seemed to be grasping into the empty air for help.

"Oh . . . Oh . . . God . . ." he whispered, horrified. The horse, feeling his fear, minced in a tight circle, tossing up snow.

Eli forced himself to look harder. There, under a thin layer of ice, lay a woman. She was staring straight up, the current below her rippling around her, feathering her long brown hair, causing her blouse to billow around her midriff. Set in a death mask, her face was a grayish hue, and beneath the glaze of ice, her eyes were wide and fixed, seeming to stare straight into his soul.

"Eli?"

His father's voice barely registered. He felt as if he might be sick. "No . . . oh . . ." His insides turned to water. "Dad!"

Screaming before he could stop himself, Eli nearly toppled out of the saddle as Jetfire, nostrils distended, reared, then spun and took off at a full gallop, racing through the trees and across the pastureland, his hooves throwing up clods of snow. Over the rush of wind in his ears, Eli heard his father shout and the dogs begin to howl and bark, but all he could do was hang on to the reins and saddle horn as the horse tore up the rise toward the house. The world went by in a blur of white, but all Eli saw, indelibly etched in his brain forever, was that mutilated hand reaching for the sky.

CHAPTER 4

You're a chicken.

That irritating voice inside Pescoli's head wouldn't leave her alone, even though she'd tried to immerse herself in the autopsy report she'd found on her desk this morning.

She'd had the perfect opportunity to tell Santana about the baby after he'd met her at the top of the stairs, kissed the damn breath from her lungs, and for the first time in their new house, made love to her right on the hard subfloor of their master bedroom. Okay, there *had* been a sleeping bag, but still. . . . The sex had been intense, maybe even a little rough, but filled with the passion she found exhilarating. Afterward, as she'd snuggled up against him, both their naked bodies shining with sweat, she should have screwed up her courage and let him know that he was going to be a father later this year. But she hadn't, content to hold him tight, feel his strength, and listen to his heartbeat as she stared through the open French doors and watched the nightfall.

Every time she moved in her desk chair, her rump ached and she was reminded of Santana and how animal their union had been. Their lovemaking had always been that way—playful and utterly primal. And yet, before, during, or even after, she hadn't uttered a word about the pregnancy.

With an effort, she focused on the autopsy of a man in his late forties, who may or may not have been the victim of a homicide. Derrick "Deeter" Clemson had died of wounds he'd received after a fall off a cliff. The question was whether he'd made a mistake and his death was accidental, if he'd leaped intentionally down nearly one hundred feet of timberland, or if he'd been helped in the fall by his bride of six months. The autopsy report didn't give any clear answers, and she was slightly distracted by the noise filtering through her doorway, that of Blackwater on the telephone in Grayson's office.

She hadn't shut her door yet and could hear Blackwater. Undoubtedly at his desk down the hall, he was having a one-sided phone conversation with someone it sounded like he was trying to impress. Either someone higher in the department or a reporter, she guessed. Maybe even that cockroach Manny Douglas, of the *Mountain Reporter* or, worse yet, Nia Del Ray from KMJC in Missoula.

Blackwater was making noises as if he were about to hang up, so she rolled her desk chair to close her door. She didn't need him poking his head in again and giving her another gung ho speech.

Her hand had just come off the knob when the door was flung open and Selena Alvarez burst in, her expression grim, her jaw set. "Let's roll," she said without preamble. "Looks like we've got a DB at the O'Halleran ranch."

"Dead body?" Pescoli rolled her chair back to her desk, got to her feet, and reached for her jacket and sidearm. "Who?"

"Jane Doe."

"What happened?" Sliding her arms through her jacket's sleeves, she was on Alvarez's heels as they walked crisply down the hall toward the doors leading to the parking lot. Blackwater, whose door was ajar, looked up as they passed, but was already punching out numbers on his phone for his next call.

"No one knows. Trace O'Halleran and his kid were checking the fence line and found her dead in a deep spot of the creek that runs through their property."

"What is it with that place?" Pescoli asked, digging in her jacket pocket for her keys. "Don't those people ever get a break?" She was thinking of the last shootout that had occurred on the ranch where O'Halleran and the local GP in town, Kacey Lambert, had been targets of one of the many madmen who seemed to have discovered their part of Montana. Once a sleepy little town set in the Bitterroots, Grizzly Falls seemed to attract psychos like magnets.

"I guess lightning really does strike twice," Alvarez said as they walked through the back door.

A gust of wind hit Pescoli full in the face. Ducking her head against the weather, she touched the remote for her keyless lock and her Jeep beeped from the spot in the parking lot where she'd parked it not an hour earlier. By the time Pescoli had settled behind the steering wheel, Alvarez was buckled in and already on the phone, talking to the deputy who'd first taken the call and was on the scene. Pescoli fired the engine, snapped on the heater and backed out of the parking spot as the police band crackled. She hit the wipers and lights, then nosed her Jeep into the sludge of traffic that seemed crippled by the storm.

Lights flashing, she eased around slower vehicles, then pushed the speed limit. She was used to the storms and worsening driving conditions in winter and had little patience for those who weren't.

As a van from a local church pulled over to let her pass, she hit the gas and sped through the outskirts of town, her Jeep whipping along a road that skimmed the edge of Boxer Bluff, which offered a view of the Grizzly River and the falls for which the town had been named.

From the corner of her eye, she saw Alvarez click off her phone, letting the edge rest against her chin for a second as if she were lost in thought. "Anything?"

"A crime scene unit is on the way, might beat us there. O'Halleran's kid Eli was out riding the fence line with his father, as I said. They weren't side by side and the boy saw the victim first. His horse spooked or something and he took off. O'Halleran was riding to the spot where the commotion occurred, spied the woman, and pulled her from the stream, tried to revive her, but she was dead, the body nearly frozen."

"ID?"

"None. But she was dressed. Only mark on her is a missing ring finger. Left hand."

"What? Missing? You mean, like a birth defect? Or?"

"Severed. Recently."

"Oh, Jesus."

"Yeah, it doesn't sound like she was just out walking, fell and hit her head, and drowned."

Pescoli glared through the windshield where her wipers were

doing battle with snow that had been falling for hours. "I'm amazed O'Halleran and his kid were out in this."

"Ranchers. Just about as crazy as cops, I guess."

Pescoli harrumphed. "They can't let the weather beat them, either." She turned onto the county road that cut through snowy fields where drifts piled against the fences and icicles hung from the few mailboxes that guarded long lanes leading to farmhouses surrounded by barns and outbuildings.

The O'Halleran place was no different. The big, square two-story farmhouse set upon a small rise far off the road was barely visible through the falling snow. A county-issued Jeep with its lights flashing was parked near the garage.

As Pescoli slowed at the end of the drive, they were met by a deputy for the department. Pete Watershed was tall and good-looking, something he'd never quite forgotten. She didn't like him much. That whole lady-killer attitude rankled her, and his jokes, sometimes with a misogynist twist or teetering on bigotry, put her off. Not that she was a prude, but she could do without the slightly sexual remarks. Watershed tended to push it. If he weren't a good cop, dedicated and all business when on duty, she would have been in his face more than she already was.

"What have we got?" she asked, the wind rushing in when she rolled down the window.

"DB found in the creek out back," he said, pointing to the area behind the house. "You can drive down there. Just follow the tracks. I'll come with." Leaving his partner in the other vehicle, he climbed into the back seat and pointed out the makeshift road. "This is the lane O'Halleran uses for his tractor and hay baler and other equipment," Watershed explained.

She drove through a series of paddocks where the gates had been left open and followed the tire tracks that wound their way onto a huge field where the pristine blanket of snow had been broken into a thick trail of tire tracks running along one fence.

"This butts up to government land," Watershed explained. "O'Halleran and his kid were out checking for holes in the fence." As the Jeep powered through six to eight inches of snow, he went on to tell the same story Alvarez had relayed earlier, finishing with, "So once the kid spooked and took off for the house on his horse,

O'Halleran investigated and found the woman, obviously dead. Still, he pulled her from the water and checked for a pulse, listened to her lungs, but she'd been in there a while, her body half frozen. You'll see."

"And the missing finger?" Alvarez asked.

"Ring finger, left hand. Not found. So far. Sliced off pretty cleanly at the first knuckle. Don't know if it was pre- or postmortem."

"Lovely," Alvarez said. "A finger fetish?"

"Just a freak," Pescoli said as they reached the end of the field near a meandering brook bordered by stands of trees. Officers were already on the job, a tarp laid out across which a partially clothed body of a woman lay. Her skin was blue, her hair wet, the finger missing, but Pescoli noted there were earrings visible in her earlobes. "O'Halleran didn't see anything out of the ordinary?"

Watershed shook his head. "Nope. And no tracks have been found around the area. Don't know if she was killed here, or brought here and the body dumped. Could have come from the federal land. There's an access road about a mile west."

Pescoli asked, "What about the neighbors?"

"Haven't talked to them yet."

"Let's do it," Pescoli said, scanning the area. "She had to get here somehow." Squinting through the falling snow, she added, "Not much chance of finding any trace." The frigid weather was working against them, but then it always did.

"You don't know what we'll find." Alvarez was always more optimistic than she, a woman who believed that with today's technology, anything was possible.

At the edge of the trees, parked helter-skelter, were a rescue vehicle from the fire department, another department-issued Jeep, a crime scene van and a banged-up pickup with two dogs locked in the cab, their noses pressed to the window. Officers dressed in heavy outerwear were already scouring the creek bed and surrounding area. Crime scene tape stretched from one sapling to the next, roping off the area that was to be searched.

Pescoli parked the Jeep close to the rescue van. "O'Halleran here?"

"Yeah, out talking to Cabral," Watershed said as Pescoli cut the engine.

She noticed the rancher standing near another deputy, Rosetta

Cabral, new to the force, all of twenty-four years old. Just a girl in Pescoli's opinion, though she was a college graduate, divorced, and a single mother of a two-year-old. Cabral was blessed with the same gung ho fire as Blackwater and was currently engaging Trace O'Halleran in conversation.

"The kid?" Pescoli asked.

"In the Jeep with Beaumont." Watershed nodded toward the other Pinewood County vehicle. "Came back down here with his mom after he ran back to the house. She's a doctor, you know. Drove like mad down here in that truck," he said, hitching his chin toward the beat-up Chevy. "Brought the kid with her 'cause she wasn't sure what was going on. She thought that maybe she could save the Jane Doe, but nah, it was . . . too late."

They climbed out and trudged between the vehicles to the tarp where a woman, maybe thirty or thirty-five, lay stretched onto a tarp, another sheet of plastic tented so that the body was protected and couldn't be viewed from the vehicle where the O'Halleran boy was keeping warm.

"We got statements from everyone?" Pescoli asked, and Watershed nodded.

Mikhail Slatkin, a forensic scientist, was kneeling on the edge of the tarp, examining the body as they waited for someone from the coroner's office to arrive. Over six feet and rawboned, the son of Russian immigrants, he was one of the best forensic scientists Pescoli had ever worked with.

"What happened to her?" she asked, studying the victim.

She'd been short, around five-two, Pescoli guessed, with long brownish hair on the curly side that was stiff and riddled with tiny ice crystals. The woman's face was heart-shaped, with a straight little nose and blue eyes that were fixed, seeming to stare blindly upward. Neatly plucked eyebrows and thin cheeks lay above cold, blue lips. She was wearing a dress, gray and fitted, earrings that looked like diamond studs, and fingers and toes that were polished a matching cranberry hue. Unbroken fingernails, neatly manicured, suggested there had been no struggle. Well, except for the ring finger of her left hand, most of which was missing.

What's up with that? The killer's trophy? Or an accident that had sent her running here? Pescoli regarded the wooded foothills where snow was covering the ground, boulders and snags protruding from the thick white blanket, the nearly frozen stream softly gurgling as it wound between the trees.

Slatkin glanced up, his blue eyes finding her gaze. "Don't know yet. Maybe drowned. Or could be head trauma. Got a few bruises." He frowned thoughtfully, eyeing the woman's slim throat. "Possible strangulation." His thick eyebrows drew together over his cold-reddened face. "Won't know until the autopsy."

Nodding, Pescoli stared down at the dead woman and wondered what had happened to her. How had she ended up in this creek? Had she made it under her own power, or had someone left her here? And why here? She glanced around the stretch of ranch land where field met forest. Why had this place been chosen as either the killing ground or dumping spot? Eyeing the creek, she saw that it was deep enough for a body to submerge, despite the encroaching ice. Where was the woman's coat or jacket? Her shoes? Her purse and, especially, her finger?

What kind of whacked-up freak would cut off the finger?

Of course, Pescoli reminded herself, *we don't know one hundred percent that the woman has been murdered.*

The missing finger certainly suggested that something violent had gone down, maybe even some kind of accident. She had learned over the years not to make quick assumptions, though oftentimes her gut instinct proved right. Until all the facts were in, however, she wouldn't make a final decision.

Once more, she looked at the left hand where a finger had been severed, the bone and flesh visible. Her stomach turned a bit and she drew her eyes away for a second, nausea building.

She'd never been queasy at a crime scene, except years before . . . Oh, God. Another roll of her guts, and saliva gathered in her mouth. *For the love of—*

At that moment, she knew she was going to be sick. She turned away, took a few steps from the creek, and just managed to get behind a fir tree before she upchucked into the snow. She hadn't thrown up at a crime scene since . . . she was pregnant with Bianca. Morning sickness. *Perfect.*

"Hey!" Alvarez said. "You okay?"

Pescoli heaved once more, then straightened, a sour taste in her mouth. "Fine," she lied, running her tongue over her teeth.

"Jesus, Pescoli! Look what you're doing to the crime scene," Watershed admonished. "It's not like you haven't seen a dead body before."

She didn't dignify his remark with an answer. To Alvarez, she said, "I'll talk to O'Halleran. You take the boy. See what he has to say. Maybe he saw something he doesn't realize might help."

Alvarez was already on her way to the idling car where an officer was staying with Eli O'Halleran, and Pescoli walked over to where Trace O'Halleran was deep in conversation with Cabral.

Nurse Amy Blanchette was dead tired. Thankfully, her shift was nearly over. In five minutes, come hell or high water, or even a damn plague, she was "outta here." Northern General Hospital wasn't her idea of a dream place to work, but since Johns Hopkins and the Mayo Clinic didn't seem to be calling, she'd stick it out and collect her paycheck, at least until she could figure out if she was going to stay in Montana near her parents, who lived in Hamilton, or venture out into the much bigger world. God, she'd love to get out of the miserable weather and try somewhere a little warmer, or exotic, or at least, somewhere that had a little more mystique. A place by the ocean, maybe.

LA sounded good. Or maybe San Antonio or somewhere in Florida. Anywhere she didn't have to wake up to piles of snow and freezing temperatures would be nice. Better still, a hospital where she didn't work with her damn ex-fiancé, who'd decided to bail six months into the engagement. Thankfully, she'd only lost her heart, not her life savings on a wedding. But even though she tried desperately to work opposing hours, she ran into Dr. Dylan Stone—yes, he sounded like he was one of those fake doctors on an old soap opera—too often. The fact that he was dating a handful of her coworkers made her working environment all the more caustic. By summer, she swore, she'd have that job elsewhere.

She had a few more minutes of her ten-hour workday to get through. A few nurses and orderlies on her shift were starting to leave while the nurses for the next ten hours were arriving. The hub was a little chaotic with the switch. Nurses who were leaving exchanged patient information, a few jokes, and a little bit of gossip with the nurses coming on duty. Worse yet, the flu had not only infected several patients on the wing, but the staff as well, devastating some of the teams. Her floor in particular was short-handed and the staff was forced to depend upon recruits from other areas of the hospital, sometimes working for the first time with newbies. Just today, Amy had shared her area of the wing with a couple orderlies, two doctors, and a nurse she'd previously never met.

But it was about over.

"One more patient," she reminded herself as she responded to the call light for room 212. The patient, Reina Gehrig, was a real pain in the butt. Amy wasn't one bit sorry that she would be able to pawn the older woman off on Mona Vickers, the nurse scheduled to take over Amy's patients. Mrs. Gehrig in particular, seemed to believe she was the only patient in the entire hospital.

Most definitely a pain in the backside.

Forcing a smile, Amy slipped into the room where Reina Gehrig was propped in her hospital bed, television tuned to a game show, her head swiveling expectantly as the door opened.

"How're you doing?" Amy asked, turning off the call light.

"Oh, not so good, I'm afraid," the small woman said. She was a frail thing with a lined, narrow face and a halo of thin white curls that didn't quite hide the pink of her scalp.

She's lonely, Amy thought and felt a little ashamed for thinking badly of her.

Barely a hundred pounds, with hazel eyes that snapped behind the folds of her eyelids and thick glasses, Reina said solemnly, "I think there's something wrong."

"Well, that won't do." Amy gave the woman a smile. "Tell me, how do you feel? Rate your pain." She indicated the chart that hung on the wall that showed caricatures of faces in varying expressions of discomfort.

" 'Bout an eight, maybe a nine, I'd say," the patient said. "And it doesn't just hurt in my leg, but all over." Frowning a little, she added, "I think I might be coming down with something. The flu's going around this year, you know. And my neighbor Elsa, she caught it. Nasty stuff."

"Hmm. Well, we can't have that," Amy said. "Let me check your vitals again."

The patient's chin suddenly thrust out. "I need to see Doctor Lambert."

"She didn't do your surgery." Amy checked Mrs. Gehrig's temperature, blood pressure, and pulse again, noting that everything was in the normal range, right where it should be. "Dr. Bellingham says you can go home tomorrow."

"Oh, I don't think so. I'd feel a lot better if Dr. Lambert had a look at me." Mrs. Gehrig was nodding in her bed as if agreeing with herself. Her thin hands, with veins visible, plucked at the edge of the sheet covering her.

"I'll let her know," Amy promised, " and mark it on your char—"

"Room two-o-six STAT!" Polly, another floor nurse, poked her head into the room as she passed the open doorway just as Amy heard the Code Blue announcement from the speakers in the hallway.

"What?" Mrs. Gehrig was confused.

Amy was already reversing toward the door. "I'll be back."

"No, please—" Mrs. Gehrig's face folded on itself in disappointment. "Wait! Where are you going? I need—" The rest of her request was cut off as Amy rushed toward the room a few doors down.

"Mr. Donnerly's coding!" Polly called to her as they entered 206.

Already, the room was bustling with staff members. The patient had recently had heart surgery and had been improving enough to be released from ICU to his private room. One nurse was handling his chest compressions while another had a bag valve mask in place over the patient's mouth and nose. A doctor was giving orders as the defibrillator cart was rolled quickly inside and another locking cart with narrow drawers for medications followed. Amy stood at the ready should she be required to administer the epinephrine or whatever other drug the doc ordered.

"How long?" the doctor asked.

"Coded under two minutes ago," a floor nurse who had been attending Benson Donnerly said as the rest of the team continued working.

"Pulse?" the doctor asked and another nurse pressed against the patient's neck, checking the patient's carotid artery.

"No pulse."

"Code Blue!" another page called over the loudspeaker, adding to the tension.

We're here already, Amy thought, refusing to be distracted in case she was needed.

"Code Blue! Room two-twenty!"

"What?" The doctor turned his head.

"Has to be wrong," Polly said, surprised.

"Double-check," he said, nodding at Amy, who quickly slipped out of the room and caught up to two nurses headed rapidly down the hallway.

"Let's go," Reba, a tall RN with a single braid falling down her back said to Amy. She was hurrying, the braid swinging side to side as she tried to keep up with Brad King, a male nurse with a trimmed beard and long, athletic stride.

Avoiding an orderly heading in the opposite direction, Amy hurried to fall into step with Reba. "Wait," she said, trying and failing to keep up. "The patient who's coding is in two-o-six." She hooked her thumb in the direction of Mr. Donnerly's room.

"Yesterday's news," Brad said over his shoulder as he broke into a jog and Reba followed suit. "We've got another patient coding."

Two cardiac arrests on the same floor at the same time? It happened, of course, but very infrequently. "But—Hold up." Amy was processing what the senior nurse had said. "Two-o-six?" she repeated, hoping she'd misunderstood. "Isn't that the sheriff's room?"

"That's right," Brad confirmed as he pushed open the door of the room where the patient lay unmoving, his chest no longer rising and falling, his pallor weak, his eyes closed.

Oh, no.

His heart monitor was visible from the doorway and the green line moving across the screen remained level, not so much as bumping the slightest as a piercing sound that should have been softly beeping was a steady, ominous warning.

Brad moved to the patient's side and started compressions on his chest as Reba found the bag valve mask to force air into the patient's lungs.

"Make sure the doc knows that we've got a second cardiac arrest. We need a defib cart ASAP!" Brad was still working over his patient as he barked at Amy.

"The cart's in Mr. Donnerly's room—"

"Order another one."

"There's only one on the floor."

"Then get one from another floor. STAT!" he ordered as he worked over the patient who, so far, wasn't responding. His heart monitor showed a flat green line, its high-pitched whine piercing. "For Christ's sake, move it!"

Amy was already turning into the hallway to get more help, but her own heart was pounding double-time at the thought of losing this patient, who just happened to be the sheriff of Pinewood County.

CHAPTER 5

Hearing the sound of another vehicle approaching, Pescoli looked up and squinted through the curtain of falling snow. She and Alvarez were about to leave the O'Halleran ranch as they'd already taken statements and looked around as much as they could in the frigid conditions. The victim's body had been taken to the morgue, the emergency workers had left, and the O'Hallerans had returned to their house. A guard was still posted near the front gate and the crime scene team was still finishing up gathering trace evidence, but her work was done.

A Jeep emerged, twin headlights cutting through the gloom, big tires kicking up snow. The driver parked next to the crime scene van, cut the engine, and emerged swiftly. Blackwell.

"Just what we need," Pescoli said under her breath. Half expecting to see the KMJC news van following in his wake, she glanced to the ruts cut into the snow where half a dozen or more vehicles had come and gone, mashing the snow beneath dozens of tires.

But Blackwater was alone, no entourage of reporters following.

A first. Well, that wasn't really the truth, but she wasn't in the best of moods after losing her breakfast and dealing with the bitter cold as, potentially, another nutcase of a killer was making his presence known in this part of the Bitterroots.

Blackwater's expression was grim as he strode through the powder to her vehicle.

"We're just about done here. Wrapping things up," Pescoli told him.

"Good. I need to talk to the both of you. In person." A muscle worked in his jaw.

"Something up?" Pescoli asked as Alvarez's eyes narrowed a fraction.

He hesitated, glanced at the woods for a second, then forced his gaze back to the two detectives standing before him. "Bad news," he said,

Pescoli felt her back muscles tighten. "What?"

Beside her, Alvarez drew a sharp breath as if she guessed what was coming.

"It's the sheriff," he said solemnly, the corners of his mouth twisting downward. "He didn't make it."

"What?" Pescoli exploded. "What the hell are you talking about?"

"I'm sorry."

"Oh, God." Alvarez leaned hard against the front panel of Pescoli's Jeep, her knees buckling. Her face had washed of all color and she was shaking her head. Even as she did, she made the sign of the cross over her chest.

"No!" Pescoli stared down Blackwater and fervently shook her head. "Not Dan Grayson. There must be some mistake."

"I wish there was." Blackwater seemed sincere, holding back his own emotions. "Grayson's heart stopped. A Code Blue was issued, and as I understand it, the team was there in seconds, trying to get him going again. Spent nearly forty minutes trying to get a pulse—defibrillation, epinephrine, whatever it is they do to bring someone back, but it was over. They couldn't revive him." He glanced from Pescoli who'd gone numb with disbelief to Alvarez who turned her head away, probably to hide her tears.

"What the hell happened?" Pescoli demanded, gesturing angrily. "He was getting better. Stable, that's what the hospital and his damn doctor said. They even moved him out of ICU because he'd improved, right?" She didn't wait for an answer. "He was shot in the head, not the heart, for Christ's sake! His heart was fine. Strong." She swung back to look at Alvarez for confirmation, but her partner didn't respond. To Blackwater, she snapped again, "What the hell happened?"

"The hospital is checking. Could be that the injuries he sustained were too much for him and his heart just stopped," Blackwater said without his usual bluster. To his credit, he seemed genuinely disconsolate. "I don't know. No one does. Yet. He'd been through a lot."

"Through a lot and out the other side!" Pescoli insisted, though the truth, like the steadily falling snow, was cold and bleak as it settled over her. "Oh . . . oh Jesus," she finally said in a rush as she started to believe what Blackwater was saying.

"I came out to tell you myself, so you wouldn't hear it on the police band or the news or from someone else."

Alvarez let out a soft moan.

"They told us he would be all right," Pescoli said. "And those bastards lied." Turning to Alvarez, she said, "Let's go."

"Where?" her partner asked and even as she did, she seemed to stiffen her spine, to gain control, her mask of always cool detachment slipping back into place.

"To the hospital to get some damn answers. To find out what went on, why they lost him." As she said the words, the full truth hit her like a ton of bricks. Grayson was gone. Forever. She'd been there when he'd been shot and in her mind's eye, it was Christmas morning once more and she watched in horror as the bullets from a hidden assassin's rifle had struck the tall man with kind eyes and a thick moustache.

Grayson's body had spun with the first bullet, his ever-present Stetson flying off his head, the split kindling he'd been carrying flying end over end to land on the snow-covered earth. With the second shot, his head had snapped back and he'd fallen to the snowy ground and lay inert. Pescoli, who had been driving to his house to ask about cutting back her hours, never got the chance.

She'd been the first responder, viewed his blood, prayed like she'd never prayed before and then had sworn vengeance on his assailant, that coward who had hidden in the snowdrifts with a high-powered rifle aimed straight at Dan Grayson.

"Son of a bitch!" she said angrily and kicked one of the Jeep's tires in fury.

"You're not going anywhere," Blackwater said. "You've got a new case to investigate with the Jane Doe found right here, so I suggest you start." He frowned. "Hell, I know this is a blow for the two of you and the whole department. That's why I came out, but that doesn't mean we still don't have jobs to do." Snow was collecting on the brim of his hat and shoulders of his jacket. Though there was a trace of compassion in his eyes, he remained rigid, ever in charge. "The

Missoula police are on the scene and the hospital is double-checking every procedure, all of his vital signs records, every report and notation. Of course, there will be an autopsy."

"Fuck the autopsy!" Pescoli said, her anger exploding. "I'm going to the hospital, whether you like it or not!"

"Detective," he warned.

But Pescoli was already around the Jeep and behind the wheel.

Alvarez slid into the passenger seat. "Let's go," she said in an out-of-character display of disobeying her commanding officer.

"What?" Hattie Grayson dropped the jar of jam she'd been holding. The small container shattered on her kitchen floor, shards of glass flying, sticky strawberry jam spraying in thick clumps. "No. Not Dan. Not Dan!"

She stared into the tortured gaze of Dan's brother Cade, who had just driven over to give her the news that cracked her world in two. Disregarding the spilled jam and shards of glass, she fell into his arms. Tears welled and she felt as if they'd started in the center of her soul. She'd known Dan all her life, been married to Bart, one of his brothers, and had half-fancied herself in love with him before reuniting with Cade. The Grayson brothers—all four of them, including Big Zed—had been the center of her universe.

Now two of the brothers were gone. Bart's death had been ruled a suicide, though she was certain that he'd been killed. Dan had been murdered by a maniac as well, someone he should never have trusted.

"I don't want to believe it."

"Me neither."

"The bastard who did this—"

"Will pay."

That much was true. Dan's assailant was already captured and behind bars, fighting his own injuries.

Still, the rage at the man who'd snatched Dan's life away burned deep. "I hope he rots in hell."

Cade's strong arms folded her tight against him. "I know."

Thank God he didn't say "it will be all right" or any other platitude, because deep in Hattie's heart, she knew that it would never be. With Dan Grayson's easygoing strides no longer walking the earth, the planet would be an emptier, colder place. He'd been so good to her, to her twin daughters, to everyone in Grizzly Falls. At least she had time to pull herself together before she told her girls. Mallory and McKenzie would be as devastated as she was. A coldness settled over her and she shivered in Cade's embrace.

"First Bart, now Dan," she whispered, drinking in the smell of the man holding her so close. The scents of leather and horses clung to him and filled her nostrils. "I don't want to believe this, Cade. I just . . . I just can't. There's got to be a mistake."

"I wish, darlin'," he said, his own voice rough, his warm breath ruffling her hair. His jaw was scratchy with beard-stubble, his eyes a deep, somber gray, all of the carefree, bad-boy attitude gone. He squeezed her a little more tightly and his voice cracked as he said, "God, don't I wish."

The hospital was remarkably calm, Alvarez thought, almost as if the whole world surrounding Grizzly Falls hadn't changed drastically with the passing of Sheriff Dan Grayson. Yes, there was a news camera crew outside. Nia Del Ray, a reporter for KMJC, was standing near the sign at the entrance of Northern General Hospital, snow catching on her short black hair as she was probably reporting on Grayson's demise, unless some other story had trumped his, which Alvarez doubted.

Inside the wide hallways, the floors gleamed under bright lights, conversation hummed, and people went about their work as if nothing monumental had just gone down within the hospital's walls. Near a placard that listed those who had donated to the hospital, she and Pescoli stepped around a woman with a cast on her leg, being wheeled down the hallway by the orderly, after which they nearly ran into an elderly man who had suddenly stopped for no apparent reason.

"Sorry," he apologized, blinking as if he'd been in a daze.

They moved past him to the elevators. "You know what this means, don't you?" Pescoli said, slapping the call button just as the doors to one of the cars opened and a group of three women emerged.

"Tell me." Alvarez walked into the car.

Once they were inside and the elevator doors had whispered shut, Pescoli pounded her fist on the button for the second floor. "That the son of a bitch who took down Grayson just lost his GET OUT

OF JAIL card forever. No more *attempted* in the charge. He's going down for murder."

The doors opened and they stepped into the wide hallway, again brightly lit and complete with alcoves, benches and chairs, and a wide nurse's station at the center of it all.

They walked up to the desk and a woman seated at a computer looked up. Pescoli showed her badge and said, "Detective Regan Pescoli, Pinewood County Sheriff's Department. This is my partner Detective Alvarez. We have some questions about . . . about the sheriff . . . Dan Grayson . . . and what happened to him. We'd like to talk to the supervisor of the floor and his doctor, whoever was in charge of his care."

Alvarez's gaze shifted to Pescoli, whose green eyes shifted in hue with the light.

Under the glare of the hospital's illumination they were a light jade color and hard as stone. Athletic and tall, with sharp features and a penetrating gaze, she was intimidating. An ex-basketball player, Pescoli wasn't afraid to get into anyone's face and bore more than her share of battle scars as a no-nonsense police officer and single mother. She was glaring at the small, nervous-looking nurse behind the desk as if the poor woman was a hardened criminal.

"I'll get Rinalda, uh, Mrs. Dash. She's in charge," the girl behind the desk said.

Before either of the detectives could thank her, a booming female voice carried up the hall. "Is there a problem, Stephanie?"

In her peripheral vision, Alvarez caught a glimpse of a slim woman quickly approaching. Tall, African-American with close-cropped hair and an expression that was as stern as Pescoli's, she stopped at the desk. "I'm Rinalda Dash." With her height, she actually looked down at Pescoli. "What can I help you with?"

Again, Pescoli flashed her badge and introduced them both. "We're here about Dan Grayson, who was your patient. We'd like to know what happened."

"We all would," Nurse Dash said solemnly. "And we're looking into it as we do with all unexpected deaths. There's a place where we can talk more privately," she said, indicating a small niche near a bank of windows. Complete with a square of carpet, a coffee table, bench, fake ficus tree, and two side chairs, the spot offered little privacy, but it would have to do.

To the nurse behind the desk, the supervisor said, "Stephanie, page Dr. Zingler, please. See if he's still in the building. I'm sure the detectives would like to speak to him, as well." She gave Pescoli a patient but firm smile as she led them into the alcove. "Believe me, we will find out what exactly caused the sheriff's death."

Blackwater held a meeting in the conference room, which not only opened from the hallway but from his office as well. Everyone who worked for the department and currently not on the road was required to attend. One person in each department was to man the phones and he expected the meeting to be short, but he owed it to the officers, those who had worked under Dan Grayson, to explain the situation as best he knew it. He stood before the deputies, secretaries, volunteers, detectives, and various officers and met all of their solemn gazes with his own.

"This is a bleak day for the Pinewood County Sheriff's Department," he began at the podium. "A difficult time for all of us, most of you more than me, as you had the honor of working with Sheriff Dan Grayson much longer than I did. We all respected him. He was a man who walked tall among men, a fair and just man, a man with a steely determination balanced by his compassion and quick wit. He would want, no, he would expect, all of us to continue working here for the good of Pinewood County, to protect and serve its citizens, and so we shall.

"That doesn't mean that I, as the acting sheriff, will not expend every effort to find out what happened at the hospital, and if there were extenuating circumstances regarding his death. I promise each and every one of you that the person responsible for sending Dan Grayson to Northern General Hospital will be tried and convicted for his crimes. The district attorney is already updating the charges against the suspect." He glanced around the room, letting his words settle, then added, "The best way we can honor Dan Grayson's memory and years of service is to continue with our jobs as officers of the law. Sheriff Grayson would have expected as much, and so do I. We have cases that require our immediate and undivided attention and I expect each and every one of you to give a hundred percent in ferreting out those responsible for the crimes under our jurisdiction and bringing them to justice."

He paused for effect. "For an as yet undetermined amount of

time, I'm lowering all of the building's flags to half mast. Everyone, please, keep the sheriff's memory alive by continuing to provide the citizens of Pinewood County with your best service. Thank you."

He thought about saying more, even including a quick prayer, but decided short and to the point was all that was necessary. Each officer would grieve on his or her own terms. Hopefully, the meeting would provide some closure until a funeral could be arranged and business could go on as usual.

It wasn't that he was just a hard-ass. He believed that the work of the department couldn't be interrupted for anything, even a commander's death. He would back off a bit, allow a few tears and conversations, let those who were closest to Grayson have a few days to grab hold of their emotions, but he had a department to run and a sicko on the horizon, if the body discovered on the O'Halleran ranch was any indication.

That case bothered him in its brutality, but he knew that it would also raise the community's awareness of him as the sheriff. It was an opportunity to show that he was up to the task, and was also a test of his mettle and skills. The Jane Doe whose body had been found in that near-frozen creek could be his ticket to the kind of fame he needed to be elected sheriff.

As he strode to his office, the one so recently occupied by Grayson, he considered that there could be an outside chance that a perfectly sound explanation existed as to why a healthy-looking thirtyish woman had ended up dead in a near-frozen pool of a creek, her ring finger recently severed. *Not much of a chance*, he thought, *but one that had to be explored.*

Walking into his office, he ignored the feeling that he was stepping into another man's boots. More than one, if he were honest with himself. Yes, Grayson had worked here. Yes, he was beloved by the staff and citizens, but he wasn't the first exalted leader, nor would he be the last. The long row of eight-by-ten photos in the lobby proved the point of how many had gone before Dan Grayson. The empty wall invited those who would follow.

Blackwater settled into a chair that was too big for him in more ways than he wanted to consider. He only hoped that he could finish out Grayson's term and be elected to sheriff on his own merit, so that one day his own picture would grace the wall of the lobby.

Of course, in order for that to happen, he had to prove himself.

Show the citizens of Pinewood County that he was the logical choice for sheriff.

He thought about the detectives on his staff and wondered how long he'd be able to deceive them. Alvarez with her master's degree in psychology. A beautiful Hispanic woman with jet-black hair, full lips, and dark, suspicious eyes, she did little to enhance her looks, but she took her job seriously. She was dedicated, he'd give her that. A natural Type-A who worked out in the gym, she kept her body tight and her mind sharp, and usually reined in her emotions. Called an "ice princess" or "bitch with a heart of stone" behind her back, she was harder on herself than anyone else was.

Blackwater related to her, knew she was a good cop, and that she played by the rules. With the news about Grayson, she'd fallen completely out of character, though he supposed it was understandable given her staunch belief in him and her loyalty. But she'd defied his orders to join her partner.

That one. Pescoli. She was as out of control as her partner was in. Married a couple times, with kids who gave her fits, she was a wild card. A good cop, yes, but she relied on gut instinct and adrenaline, more than Blackwater liked. He had little doubt that she'd take him on if given half a chance. Wearing one's emotions on one's sleeve was never a good idea in his opinion, and for a cop, it was worse.

She was a rogue. Period. Didn't respect the rules one iota.

He leaned back in his chair and glanced through the door he'd left ajar. Pescoli's office was just down the hall, which was perfect.

Because he planned to watch her like a hawk.

CHAPTER 6

"Sheriff Grayson is dead? He . . . he . . . passed away?" Jessica repeated, stunned as she loaded the order for table five—three coffees and a tea—onto her tray in the kitchen of the Midway Diner.

"That's what everyone's saying." Misty, a tall, leggy redhead, frowned down at the platters warming under the lights on the counter ready for pickup. She was at least five foot ten. With her hair twisted into a knot on the top of her head, she probably brushed six feet. "Hey! Armando!" she shouted at the cook manning the grill where burgers and strips of bacon were sizzling. Her lips, colored the exact shade of her hair and fingernails, were pursed in disgust. "I said, 'no onions' on one of these burgers."

"*Sì,*" he said, pointing to the middle platter. "No onions."

Misty picked up the top half of the bun and surveyed the patty. "Okay. Sorry. My bad."

"*Sì.* Next time, maybe you check first," Armando grumbled as he plucked one of the dual baskets from the deep fryer and gave the pale French fries within a quick shake before letting the basket descend into the boiling grease again.

Satisfied that her order was complete, Misty picked up the three platters and, as if they'd never been interrupted, went on with her gossiping. "I had two deputies in from the sheriff's department at table nine earlier today and they were talking all about it. How some of the people on the force are really upset and speculating about what will happen to the department." She headed for the swinging doors complete with portholes that separated the kitchen from the dining area but kept talking. "Sounded to me that nobody really likes the new guy, but he was promoted from the higher-ups, or something. I couldn't really hear everything. It was busy and the woman at table eleven was a real piece of work, complaining about every darned thing. Anyway, what I got out of it is that Grayson died. Maybe a heart attack. Maybe not. No one knows." She pushed the doors open with her shoulder and spun around as she entered the dining area.

Misty was a gossip, one of those people who practically licked her lips when she heard something "juicy" about someone else, and she had no qualms about embellishing that bit of information and passing it quickly along. Jessica had figured that out from the moment she walked through the back door, tied on an apron, introduced herself, and said she was ready to work. She thought back to that first day.

"I'm Misty," the older woman introduced herself. Smelling of a recent cigarette, she was sorting coffee cups and glassware that had been left in the dishwasher. "You'll be sorry you ever decided to take a job here, let me tell you. The boss, Nell, is a real piece of work, always thinks the employees are stealing her blind, got her nose in the damn till every hour or so. And Armando can't cook his way out of a paper bag."

"I heard that." The sour-faced cook was slicing onions, working quickly and efficiently with a butcher's knife not six feet away from where Misty had been complaining.

Jessica, as always, felt her stomach curdle as she caught a glimpse of the long blade glinting under the harsh overhead lights.

"Good. You should hear it. You know it's true," Misty said, unrepentant.

"Perra," he muttered, his knife making a quick tattoo with the rapid fire motion.

Jessica said, "You know, I make it a policy not to insult anyone with a weapon in his hands."

"Meh." Unconcerned, Misty lifted a shoulder.

"Idiota!" Flashing Misty a condemning look, Armando turned so that his back was to her, effectively shunning her as he concentrated on his work and muttered something unintelligible under his breath.

Undaunted by the cook's disregard for her, Misty continued with her litany of complaints. "Marlon. He's the busboy? Always late. Considers himself some kind of Romeo and is out tomcatting, so he can never get here on time. A real pain in the ass, let me tell you." To emphasize the fact, she rattled the silverware tray, then started wrapping table knives, forks, and spoons into paper napkins, creating individual settings and stacking them neatly near the glassware. "Besides all that, the tips are lousy and this"—she pointed to the dishware she'd carefully prepared—"is not my job." With a glance over her shoulder to the back door, where a boy who looked as if he'd just rolled out of bed was striding through, she pasted on a false smile and said, "Good morning, Casanova."

"What's good about it?" he countered.

"Well, now that I think about it, nothing. But you owe me half an hour's wages!" She quit stacking the silverware to glare at him, one hand on a hip.

"So I owe you. Sue me." The kid, like Armando, seemed inured to Misty's barbs and went about rummaging in the linen closet near the back door, where he found a clean apron and began cinching it over his black jeans and once-white shirt. His hair, a bristly brown, had been gelled into unruly stiff peaks, his face clean shaven, his build that of a middleweight wrestler, not an ounce of fat on him.

"Yeah, you owe me all right," Misty agreed. "The way I figure it, you're up to about a year's salary, but I won't hold my breath. You can finish with the silverware and you'd better hop to. We're opening the doors in fifteen and you know the regulars, they don't like to wait."

"Yeah, yeah." He dismissed her, but had taken over the duties of organizing the flatware and dishes.

Satisfied, Misty whispered to Jessica, "He's hopeless," then pushed through the swinging doors to the dining area where tables were scattered between a long L-shaped counter and the windows. Behind the counter was a walkway with a scarred floor covered with rubber mats. Along one wall was a narrow ledge that housed the coffee and milkshake machines, the soda dispenser, tubs for dishes, and rows of condiments like soldiers beside them.

Misty's waitressing lessons began then. "Okay, so let's start with the coffee since the customers that are already driving here will expect it to be ready. Fresh every day. Every hour. You think you can handle that?" She was teasing. Sort of, but she thought she was the only person capable of running the diner. "We need two pots of regular brewed and ready to go by the time we open the doors, oops, in less than twelve minutes." She eyed the big schoolhouse clock positioned near the door. "I always have a pot of decaf ready, too, for the wimps who want to start their day with 'unleaded,' for whatever reason. Then I check the pots every fifteen minutes during the rush. Marlon is supposed to be on top of it, but I don't trust him. He's too busy flirting with the customers or checking his cell phone for his next hot date. If Nell gets here and finds the coffeepots empty, there will be hell to pay, but Marlon doesn't care. 'Cause he's Nell's nephew. Doesn't think he'll ever be fired. Punk kid. Once the crush is over, like I said, every hour."

Jessica watched Misty measure coffee into the pots.

"Gotta be careful here. Don't put too much in, y'know. We're famous for our weak coffee, but if I make it any stronger, Nell's all over me. Cuts into profits, y'know."

"I think I can handle this." Jessica started filling the basket for the decaf. "But if it's so miserable, why do you stay?"

"Good question." Misty took an empty glass pot and carried it to a nearby sink for a refill. As she shut off the water, she pretended to think for a second. "Must be because I'm a masochist."

As she carried her tray into the dining area, Jessica couldn't help but think about Dan Grayson and the fact that he'd died. She'd been prepared to talk to him, to confess, and when she'd discovered that he was hospitalized, she'd decided that she'd have to deal with Cade instead because she couldn't spill her guts to just anyone. It was more imperative than ever that she ask Cade for direction. A once-upon-a-time lover, Cade Grayson was one of the few people in the world she could trust. Well, at least she hoped so. Truth to tell, she and he hadn't parted on the best of terms.

Cade would be deep into mourning and, if she bared her soul to him, she would take a chance that he wouldn't believe her, wouldn't trust her, or give her the benefit of the doubt.

But who else?

At least Cade was a person who could understand deception, even twisting the law a bit.

He was her last chance.

That is, if she decided to stay in Grizzly Falls.

But what else could she do?

Run, she supposed as she pinned a smile on her face and started distributing the coffee and tea to her customers seated at table five. "Your orders should be up in a minute," she told them.

"Oh, could I please get a little honey for my tea?" the round-faced woman at the table asked.

"Sure. No problem." Jessica turned back to the counter where the packets of condiments were kept and vowed to herself that she was done running, that she was through looking over her shoulder and always having one foot out the door.

Finding the honey packets, she grabbed several and as she carried them back to the table, prayed she could keep that promise to herself.

"What happened?" Jeremy, who had been staring into the refrigerator, swung the door closed as Pescoli walked into her house and Cisco, her dog, went into his usual frenetic routine. The little terrier mix was dancing circles at her feet as she unzipped her jacket and left her boots on the patch of linoleum by the back door. From the living room, the television was tuned to a reality show.

"Bad day," she said, and bent down to pet the excited yapping dog. Cisco's tail was wagging in a blur, and he licked Pescoli's cheek as if he hadn't seen her in years rather than hours. Sturgis, Dan Grayson's black lab, climbed out of his bed and stood at her feet as well, his tail moving side to side, his dark eyes looking up at hers as if he understood. "I'm sorry," she said, scratching him behind his ears. "Oh, buddy." Her voice cracked. "I've got bad news." Sturgis's long tail slowed and he stared straight into her eyes as if he understood. Her heart fractured and she felt near to tears.

Hormones, she told herself . . . *and grief.* Sniffling, she straightened and found her son staring at her.

"Then it's true," Jeremy said. "About the sheriff?"

"Yeah, it's true." She cleared her throat. Willed her tears away. "He passed today."

"Shit. I mean . . . damn . . ."

She didn't bother saying anything about his language.

"I can't believe it!"

She nodded in silent understanding.

Jeremy's expression grew dark and he swore again, under his breath. Then he leaned hard against the counter where the remains of breakfast—two empty bowls and a half-eaten piece of toast left on a napkin—had spent the day.

"That bastard really killed him?" His jaw was set, reminding Pescoli of her first husband, Joe Strand, Jeremy's father. As her son matured, he looked more and more like his dad and the funny thing was he even displayed some of Joe's mannerisms, though he'd never really known his father, surely couldn't remember him. They shared the same build, though Jeremy topped his father's six-foot frame by about two inches and his features were still slightly softer than she remembered Joe's were, but the way he threw a ball, or looked over his shoulder? Pure Joe Strand. That part didn't bother her. No. The bad news, at least in her opinion, was that Jeremy had decided to follow in his father's footsteps by becoming a cop. Just like his dad. Even though his father had lost his life in the line of duty.

Don't blame Joe. You're on the force, too. A cop's life is all your son has ever known.

Some of the blame definitely rested on her shoulders.

Though Pescoli loved the fact that he was enrolled in school again and was thrilled that he finally seemed to have some direction, she hated the idea of him becoming a member of the police force after seeing what the dedication to protecting and serving had done to their own family.

How often had she rued her vocation? Yeah, she loved being a cop, but she'd be a fool if she didn't admit that the stress and long hours of her job hadn't taken their toll on parenting her kids.

And now there's going to be another one. Oh, Lord.

"But didn't you say he was improving?" Jeremy asked. "How could this happen?"

"I guess he was more fragile than anyone, the doctors included, realized. The doc in charge, Zingler, he's double-checking everything," she said but didn't add that what really bothered her was that there were two patients who had flatlined about the same time. The first, just seconds before Grayson, happened to a patient named Donnerly who had over thirty years on Grayson. But he'd survived.

Of course, he hadn't suffered the same kind of attack as the sheriff, but Pescoli couldn't help but wonder if the heart stoppages had happened in the reverse order, if Grayson flatlining had been the first emergency, would the hospital staff have been quicker to respond? Would he have survived? It just didn't sit well with her.

"So, what happens now?" Jeremy wanted to know.

"I'm not sure," she admitted. "It's not good down at the station. Morale is at an all-time low, and that's saying something." She hung up her jacket on the hall tree and noticed the snow on her boots was already melting, making puddles. "Everyone's upset. Even Joelle isn't interested in decorating for Valentine's Day, which is probably a good thing, because Blackwater definitely isn't into it." She scowled remembering his recent edict about keeping the offices spotless and professional at all times. That would be a trick considering the drunks, suspects, informants, criminals, and general scum of the earth who were dragged through the hallways of the Pinewood County Sheriff's Department on a daily basis. "Hopefully he's only temporary."

"You don't like him because he's taking Grayson's job," Jeremy pointed out.

"That's not it. Well, not *all* of it."

"I don't think he's all that bad."

She glared at her son as if he'd uttered sacrilege, which he had. "You're only there part-time. *Very* part-time. As a volunteer. You don't really work for him."

"Yet." Jeremy caught his mother eyeing the dirty dishes on the breakfast bar and actually picked up the two bowls and placed them into the sink with the stack of ever-mounting pots, pans, and plates. Of course, he couldn't quite seem to find the dishwasher, but, Pescoli reminded herself, *baby steps*.

Not that long ago, her son was adrift, playing video games all day, smoking weed on the side, and chewing tobacco. Things were improving. He was growing up. Yeah, he still chewed. And of course, he continued to play video games, but even that had slowed down a bit and she thought his pot smoking had abated. Thinking about it, she unconsciously crossed her fingers.

As far as she could tell, Jeremy's general "hanging out" with some of his suspect friends had tapered off and his steady girlfriend of the past few years had moved away, thank God. It had only been a few weeks, but without Heidi Brewster as a distraction, Jeremy already seemed more focused.

His job at Corky's Gas and Go coupled with volunteering at the station kept him busy and he was talking about moving out with a friend. Again. So far, he'd bounced back after a couple half-assed attempts at living on his own. She'd already suggested that he move into the room over the garage in Santana's new home, but Jeremy had balked. Residing in any building attached to his mother's place of residence obviously didn't qualify as "moving out."

Considering her own rebellious history as a teen, she wasn't about to argue.

He saved your life.

That much was true. If it hadn't been for Jeremy taking aim at Grayson's killer during an attack, she wouldn't be alive.

"Give Blackwater a chance," Jeremy suggested, opening the refrigerator door and hanging on it again, as if somehow the contents within had changed in the last five minutes. "I think he's a good guy."

"We'll see." She wasn't convinced.

He discovered a previously overlooked slab of pie that had to be a week old and pulled it from the depths. "Since we can't have Grayson back," he said soberly.

She nodded, swallowed, then checked her watch. "So where's your sister?"

"At Lana's. Studying," he added dryly.

"Ahh. Well, you know, they could be."

He grabbed a fork that had been left near the sink, then carried the pie into the living room and plopped onto the worn couch. "They *could* be," he allowed. Both dogs, hoping he might drop a bit of food, followed at a brisk trot and positioned themselves at his feet, their ears cocked, their eyes beseeching.

"You know something I should?" Pescoli asked, following him into the living room.

"Just a gut feeling. Kinda like your cop instinct."

"Does she need a ride?"

"What she needs is a car."

"So she tells me. Every day." She found her cell phone to text her daughter.

"Lucky says she can have one. He'll buy it for her."

"And the insurance? And the gas?" Pescoli hated the fact that her ex could offer up extravagant gifts with no strings attached and, when they didn't work out, leave her to pick up the pieces and deal with the fallout.

"That, you'll have to talk to him about."

When hell freezes over, she thought darkly, relieved to feel something other than grief, if even for a moment, as she texted Bianca. Briefly, she considered having a beer, then immediately banished the thought. A "cold one" after work, one of life's pleasures, was out the window for around seven or eight more months.

"Have the dogs been fed?" she asked.

"Do they look like they've eaten?" Taking a huge bite of chocolate and whipped cream, he found the television's remote and switched stations.

"Hey, guys!" She found the opened bag of dog food in the pantry, scooped kibblets into two metal bowls and turned to find both animals waiting expectantly. "Hungry?"

Cisco spun in tight little circles while Sturgis swept the floor with his tail.

"Here ya go." As she fed the dogs, she received an incoming text from Bianca saying she had a ride and would be home within the hour.

Good. In time for dinner, whatever the hell that was going to be. Spaghetti out of a jar? Tuna casserole or cheese sandwiches and tomato soup from a can? Something Bianca would eat. She was beyond finicky and Pescoli was keeping an eye on her because she was obsessed with her weight, her body, and wearing the tiny bikini her stepmother had bought her for Christmas. At her stepmother's encouragement, Bianca was talking about becoming a model, so there were all kinds of comments about nutrition and exercise, carbs and fat, calories and workouts falling from her daughter's lips. Eating healthy would be great, but the operative word was eating, not starving. Working out, again, a great idea, but not to the point of passing out. Pescoli wished Michelle, a smart enough woman who was fixated by her own looks, would just leave her daughter alone and quit putting weird ideas into her head. As a teenager, Bianca already had enough of those.

So what could she whip up in the kitchen that her daughter

would find palatable? Nothing she'd already considered and, anyway, the thought of cooking made her already queasy stomach turn over. Maybe takeout, she thought, opening the drawer where they kept pencils, note pads, out-of-date telephone books, and menus for their favorite restaurants in Grizzly Falls. She'd just pulled out the menu for Wild Will's when her cell phone bleeped and she saw Santana's name and picture on the screen.

"Hey," she greeted him.

"I just heard about the sheriff." Santana's voice was grim.

"Yeah. Not good."

"You okay?" he asked.

"Not great," she admitted. "But I'll be fine."

"You sure?"

"Yeah." That was a lie.

"I'm coming over."

"No. Don't. Look, Santana, uh, I need to deal with the kids first." He hesitated and she sensed he thought she was shutting him out. "Seriously. I'm fine. The kids will be, too, but we have to deal."

Again silence.

"I need you to understand," she said.

"Okay. But, I'm here."

"I know. I . . . thank you."

"Tomorrow?"

"Yeah, I'll call. It's crazy at the station. Weird. I . . . just give me a little space to sort this all out."

"I always do," he said and she squeezed her eyes shut so she wouldn't shed a tear.

She hung up quickly. Afraid he might tell her he loved her and want to talk about their upcoming wedding. She just felt too raw and uncertain. It wasn't that she didn't love him. She did. Totally. But it was hard for her to be vulnerable, and uttering those three little words could break the dam of her emotions. "I'm sorry," she whispered as if he could hear her and was so glad he couldn't.

Jeremy called from the living room, "Hey, Mom. Maybe you wanna see this."

Still holding the menu, she walked from the kitchen and saw Hooper Blackwater's image on the screen. In full uniform, standing ramrod straight in front of the half-masted flags that were snapping in the wind, snow blowing around him, he was a somber and solid officer of the law. Looking directly into the camera's lens, he vowed to prosecute Dan Grayson's killer to the maximum extent of the law.

"This is what I was talking about," she said, glaring at the screen. "It's called grandstanding." She slid a look at her son. "And for the record? I don't like it."

CHAPTER 7

Talk about doom and gloom. The sheriff's office couldn't have been more somber if it were draped in black and a funeral dirge was playing throughout the hallways. Everyone was grim, feeling Grayson's loss, going about their business in whispered tones, not smiling, just getting through the day. Joelle had toned it down to a long charcoal-colored dress with a lighter gray sweater. Though she still wore three-inch heels, their clip was decidedly less sharp as she made her way down the hallway. Now that he'd spoken to the press and made his position clear, Blackwater had even holed himself into his office.

Pescoli hated the department's vibe as well as the empty feeling that had stayed with her throughout the night and followed after her like a shadow. She tried burying herself in work, but found herself distracted.

When Alvarez stuck her head into the office, Pescoli looked up, rolled back her chair, and said, "Come on, let's go," before her partner could utter a word. "I'll drive." She yanked her keys from her purse.

"Where?"

"To the morgue." Pescoli was already standing and reaching for her jacket and sidearm. "I can't stand this place another second."

"Okay."

"Maybe the ME can tell us about our Jane Doe. Any luck IDing her yet?"

Alvarez stepped out of the doorway to let Pescoli pass. "I talked to Taj in Missing Persons and so far no reports of anyone resembling our victim have been filed."

Pescoli's bad mood didn't get any better. As she waited for Alvarez to grab her own jacket, scarf, and gloves, she wondered about the woman found in the frozen creek. Though it wasn't conclusive that foul play had occurred, it seemed likely.

Once Alvarez slipped her cell phone into her pocket, they were on the move again, working their way to the back door, skirting a few solemn-faced officers walking in the other direction.

"It's personal," Alvarez said as she pushed open the door to the outside and a gust of frigid air swept inside. "If our vic was killed, I mean."

Squinting against the snow flurries, Pescoli shot a look at her partner. "I'm betting a year's salary that she didn't slice off her own finger, find a way to the O'Halleran ranch, and fling herself into the creek to commit suicide." They reached the Jeep just as Pescoli hit the button twice to unlock all the doors. Across the snow-covered roof, she added, "That's not how it's usually done. And an accident? With a recently lopped off finger?" She opened the driver's door and got behind the wheel.

"I'm just saying all the evidence isn't in yet."

"Sometimes evidence only proves what you already know." Pescoli started out of the lot, but waited for a snowplow to pass. Moving slowly, it piled a berm of snow and clods to the side of the road, impeding the driveways of the surrounding businesses but freeing up the street.

Rather than follow the slow-moving plow, she turned in the wrong direction for a few blocks, then circled back and headed for the main road leading to Missoula, and the basement of the very hospital where Dan Grayson had drawn his last, weak breath. "So *if* our Jane Doe's a homicide victim, why do you think it was personal?"

"The ring finger. That makes a statement."

"Could be we have a nutcase who collects fingers," Pescoli said.

"And possibly rings? Wedding rings? Engagement rings? What's the significance there?" Alvarez was thinking hard, absently rubbing her chin between her finger and thumb.

"Maybe just the handiest finger."

Alvarez splayed the fingers of her left hand in front of her. "Nope. One of the hardest to lop off. It's significant."

"So we've got ourselves another psycho. You know, we've been getting more than our share."

"Uh-huh." She was still staring at her hand and seemed lost in thought. "And why the creek? Was she taken there? Drowned?" Her lips compressed as Pescoli slowed for a light. "I'm getting a bad feeling about this one."

Pescoli actually laughed. "Like Grace Perchant?"

Alvarez shot her a pissy look.

Grace was one of the local nut jobs. She swore she held conversations with ghosts, could commune with spirits from the other side of life, poor trapped souls who hadn't completely passed. She also owned a couple wolf hybrids and had come into town with them in tow to warn some of the citizens about their murky futures. It was a little unsettling.

"More like you and your gut instincts."

The light changed and Pescoli held herself back from pointing out that Alvarez had always dismissed her sometimes unscientific approach to a case. "Here we go," she said, spying a coffee kiosk, then making a quick turn to pull behind a dirty red Jetta that was just pulling out. As she found her wallet, she asked Alvarez, "Want anything?"

"Sure. Tea. Hot. Some morning blend. Whatever they have."

"Got it." Pescoli turned to face the girl who was standing within the kiosk, waiting. Quickly rolling down her window, Pescoli repeated Alvarez's request and added a decaf latte for herself.

As the barista turned away, Alvarez asked, "What happened to black coffee?"

"I'm hungry this morning. Thought a latte would take care of it."

"A *decaf* latte," Alvarez reminded her. "Aren't you the same woman who drinks yesterday's Diet Coke when you find it in your Jeep's cup holder and orders double or triple espresso shots if your morning gears aren't revved?"

"Sometimes."

"All times. 'Coffee and a cigarette—a working woman's breakfast,' to quote you not so long ago."

"A loooong time ago," Pescoli disagreed as cash and cups were exchanged. "I'm jazzed enough today, okay?" She handed Alvarez her cup and placed her latte into the drink holder of the console.

Alvarez took an experimental sip. "Just wondered if you were feeling okay. Or coming down with something, considering that you lost your lunch."

"Weird that, huh? Guess all the changes in the department have gotten to me." Pescoli cringed inwardly, uncomfortable using Grayson's death as an excuse. But it was true enough, and she wasn't willing to admit to Alvarez just yet that she was pregnant. *First,* she told herself, *I have to give Santana the news.* She owed him that much. Then, when she felt the time was right, she'd explain it all to her partner.

But not now.

Though the snow was still coming down, it seemed lighter, the windshield wipers keeping up with the flakes. The interior of the Jeep smelled of coffee, the police band crackled.

"The department's never going to be the same," Pescoli observed, keeping emotion out of her voice with an effort as they drove past snow-crusted fields. "I mean, without Grayson."

Alvarez sighed, frowning into her cup as she obviously struggled with a wave of grief. Then, as if she'd convinced herself that she had to face the inevitable, she took a deep breath and said, "We'll all just have to adjust. It'll be difficult, but that's the way it is."

"It sucks."

"Amen."

Pescoli drove onto a curving bridge, a semi heading in the opposite direction. "I was thinking about cutting back on my hours anyway and since we've got Grayson's killer in custody, I'll probably put in a request. See what happens."

"Today?"

"Probably in the summer," she said.

Alvarez was looking through the passenger window. She nodded as if she'd expected this conversation. "You sure that's what you want?"

"My kids need me."

"Okay, but they're nearly grown."

"Then there's Santana."

"You're marrying him. Is that a reason to be semiretired? You're not even forty, for God's sake."

"I'm not talking retirement. Just cutting back a little."

"What're you going to do? Take up knitting? Join a wine club? Try out new Crock-Pot recipes?"

"Give me a break."

"Then what? Racquetball? Save mankind by joining some cause for world peace?"

Pescoli actually laughed. "Yeah, that's it."

"You'd miss it. Whether you know it or not, Pescoli, you live for this. Being a cop's in your blood."

"Now you sound like some B movie from the seventies."

"I'm serious, damn it."

"So that's it? You think we're destined to be together, riding in these Jeeps in the snow and ice, chasing bad guys, risking our lives and bowing to the likes of Hooper Blackwater?" She finally took a sip of her latte and scowled. "Jesus! People really drink this stuff?" The milky-sweet coffee hit her stomach and seemed to curdle. Dropping the cup back into its holder she added, "I don't need working eighty hours plus some weeks in my life."

Alvarez sent her a sharp look. "This is *all* about Blackwater and we both know it." When Pescoli didn't respond, she added tautly, "I don't like the new sheriff either, but he's what we're stuck with. For now. You're not the only one missing Dan Grayson."

Pescoli should have left it alone, but she was too raw, too bothered. "Yeah, well, I didn't fancy myself in love with him, either," she snapped and saw her partner's lips tighten. "What the hell was that all about?"

"Nothing."

"Oh, come on." She hit the gas and sped around a tractor inching down the highway, the driver huddled against the elements in a thick jacket and hat with ear flaps. "Jesus. Why the hell would you pull your John Deere out in this weather?" she grumbled.

Alvarez, obviously stung, didn't answer. She pulled her cell phone from her pocket and turned her attention to her e-mail and texts, scanning them quickly "Got reports from the O'Halleran neighbors. The Zukovs, Ed and Tilly, who live on one side of the O'Halleran spread. They told the deputy they saw nothing, were inside all day because of the blizzard."

"Smart."

"Same with the Foxxes, who are on the other side of the Zukovs. The husband ventured out to his barn, but took care of his cattle and that was it. Haven't heard from the ranch across the road or the one on the other side of the O'Hallerans yet." She tucked her phone into her pocket.

"I'm thinking whoever did it came in from the back," Pescoli said.

"A team checked the nearest access road."

"Tracks?" She felt a little ray of hope.

"Some. Maybe hunters."

"In this?" Pescoli said, staring out the windshield.

"Or cross-country skiers or snowshoers. People don't necessarily stay inside just because it's cold or snowing."

"Then they're idiots."

Alvarez gave her a long look. "What's going on with you?"

Oh, shit. She'd hoped that since the conversation had turned to the case at hand it wouldn't circle back to her. "What do you mean?"

"Don't play dumb. You're even more out of sorts than usual."

"Nice," she said, gripping the wheel more tightly as the farmland gave way to the outskirts of Missoula, but she silently admitted Alvarez had a point. Pescoli's emotions were all over the place. Since there wasn't much she could do about them, she shut up. Alvarez again buried herself in the information flowing through her phone and they drove the short distance to the hospital in uncomfortable silence.

Each lost in her own thoughts, they parked, hurried inside, and took the elevator down to the morgue. Pescoli tried not to dwell on the fact that Dan Grayson had given up his tenuous grip on the world, because, like it or not, that part of her life was over.

Ryder's breakfast consisted of black coffee from the machine in the motel's lobby and a burrito of sorts from a vending machine in the mini-mart located at the intersection half a block from the River View's front entrance. Even with the addition of hot sauce from a couple free packets he'd gotten at the store, the meal was tasteless, but he didn't much care. Along with the burrito, he'd picked up a newspaper, a bag of chips, a packet of jerky, and a six-pack of Bud, which he'd tucked into the tiny insulated cabinet the River View's management had optimistically dubbed a refrigerator.

Despite the fact that the bed had sloped decidedly toward the center of a sagging mattress, he'd slept like a rock. "The sleep of innocents," his grandmother had said, though, in his case, that assessment was far from the truth. He'd learned to catch his winks wherever he could, whether it be wrapped in a thin sleeping bag on some ridge under the stars, or in his truck in broad daylight, after he'd spent a night huddled in his pickup on a stakeout swilling strong coffee and holding his bladder until it felt like it would burst. Either way, he'd learned to drop off and catch whatever sleep he could. So the River View's sagging mattress hadn't bothered him any more than the meal of processed mystery meat—beef, if the label on the plastic-wrapped burrito was to be believed—trapped inside a tortilla that was probably several weeks past its pull date.

"So where are you?" he asked aloud as he pulled several ziplock bags from his duffel and laid them on the table that sufficed as a desk in the room. From each bag, he pulled out pictures, eight by tens, all in black and white, which had been taken of different-looking women, but whom, he believed, all were one and the same: Anne-Marie Calderone, the object of his search.

If he was right, and he'd bet his truck that he was on the money, she'd taken a crooked path from New Orleans to Grizzly Falls, Montana.

She'd become a master of disguise. Each photo was different; her style of dress, her hair color and cut, the shape of her body, whether she wore glasses or not, the curve and thickness of her eyebrows and lips. In one case where he thought she was wearing a short blond wig, she appeared seven months pregnant. In another, her bare leg was exposed by a short skirt and a tattoo was visible on her calf. In still another, her eyes appeared dark, almost black, though through the gray filter it was hard to determine the shade. Makeup accentuated her high cheekbones, or an appliance stuffed beneath her cheeks sometimes stole them from her. Her teeth were never the same, sometimes crooked, sometimes straight, but always longer or wider or with odd, gaze-catching overlaps than usually graced her smile. He found one where she'd placed a mole above her lip, and another where her fingernails were impossibly long, still another where her hair was stringy and dull. There were all kinds of distractions to catch the eye so that the viewer wouldn't take in the whole picture of her face and be able to say for certain that she was the woman in the first photograph, the one in color, of the real woman.

Picking up that photo, he studied the details of Anne-Marie's oval face—straight, aquiline nose dusted with fine freckles, naturally arched eyebrows, wide gold eyes, and full lips that, he remembered, stretched into a sexy and secretive smile. Her teeth were straight, incisors a little longer than the others, and the glint in those incredible eyes had caused more than one male heart to beat a little faster. A natural athlete, her hips were slim, her breasts small, her legs long.

She was far more clever than he'd given her credit for. Twice, he'd nearly caught her and just as many times she'd given him the slip.

"No more," he vowed as he found his iPad where he'd stored most of his notes on her. The pictures were on the device as well as his phone, but he liked the photographs as they were easier to pocket and pull out when necessary if he came across someone who might have run into her. They were easier to give to the person rather than let anyone handle his phone with all of its stored data.

Also, it seemed more likely to him that if he were "her brother," or "her cousin" or "a friend," all claims he'd made while tracking her down, that he would have an old photo. Bringing out a gallery of different shots stored on a computer file might be off-putting.

He checked his notes again. Her connection to Grizzly Falls was frail at best. Then again, when it came to the chameleon that was Anne-Marie Calderone, what he knew about her was about as solid as quicksand, the lies soft and shifting, hiding the solid footing of the truth.

His jaw grew tense at the thought of how she'd duped him.

All too easily.

Because he hadn't been thinking with his head when he was around her.

He felt the same cold fire burn through him as he gathered up her pictures and stuffed them back into the plastic bags.

Time to get moving.

He didn't know where she was. But he knew where to start looking for her.

Cade Grayson.

He shouldn't be too hard to find. Grayson was an ex-rodeo rider. Hard drinking. Womanizing. Trouble. The kind of man Anne-Marie had found irresistible. So of course, she'd come to seek him out.

From what Ryder had read in the local newspaper, Cade was one of two surviving brothers of Dan Grayson, recent sheriff of Pinewood County and the victim of a homicide. Cade and Zedediah still owned and maintained the Grayson ranch outside town, the place their ancestors had claimed as a homestead.

It seemed the likely place for Anne-Marie to show up. Ryder grabbed his heavy jacket and tucked his pistol and knife within. In a small case, he put the iPad, night-vision goggles, some various spy equipment, and his camera with all of its lenses.

After double-checking that everything, including the packs of chips and jerky, were in place, he zipped up the case and tossed on his jacket.

As he locked the door of the shabby room behind him, he thought of her again. How she'd once been. Without the makeup and disguises. Stripped bare. A natural beauty, a woman of privilege, smarter than most people knew.

He threw open the door of his truck, tossed in his gear, climbed inside, and fired the engine, her visage with him still. He'd trained himself not to think too much about her but sometimes he couldn't help himself. All his practiced self-control slid away and the door of his memories cracked open. When that happened, as it did as he backed out of the icy parking spot, he couldn't help but remember her naked body, shining with perspiration, flesh warm and smooth, eyes a smoldering shade as she stared up at him, almost daring him to give in to her.

She had been as erotically sensual and emotionally dangerous a woman as he'd ever met; a deadly combination he'd been unable to resist.

It wasn't a big surprise that he'd decided to hunt her down, he thought, driving out of the lot and joining a slim stream of traffic heading toward the town of Grizzly Falls.

It was the least she deserved.

Usually nothing about the morgue got to Pescoli. She could deal with the sight of a dead body, blood, and organs, and the cooler temperature in the room hardly registered. The clinical aspect of it was a comfort, if anything, and the smell, though unpleasant, wasn't a big deal. Even watching the pathologists work, examining and weighing organs while making notes on computers, was more interesting than troubling to her. She'd been there enough times, most often to collect the fingerprints off dead bodies. Nothing about the tiled room with its refrigerated coffin-like drawers, scales, stainless steel tables with sinks, or mutilated bodies really ever bothered her. She figured the dead were dead. Unfeeling.

It was her job to find out why, and if a crime had been committed, to bring the lowlife who'd perpetrated said crime to justice. Knowing the trauma a victim had gone through burrowed under her skin and increased her determination to nail the son of a bitch who'd committed the crime. Her emotions were often volatile, while her partner exuded a cool, almost icy detachment, but Pescoli wasn't particularly sensitive to the nuances. She just did her job.

At the moment, her senses were all out of whack. The smell alone was awful, that dead, sickly-sweet odor seeming to cling to her nostrils as she viewed the dead body of their Jane Doe lying faceup, her skin a grayish tone, her hair pushed away from her face, her eyes wide open and seeming to stare straight up at the huge body lift suspended over her gurney. Also, Pescoli couldn't help but let her gaze wander to the refrigerated drawers. Morbidly, she wondered if Dan Grayson's body was lying within one.

Her lungs constricted for a moment, but she told herself there was no reason to speculate. Forcing her gaze back to the victim, she tried to concentrate on the case.

Obviously, Jane hadn't been autopsied yet, no Y slice cut into her torso, no thin line sawed across her forehead and into her skull.

"I assume the autopsy has been scheduled?" asked Alvarez. She was standing at the side of the gurney. Her gaze had moved from the vic to the forensic pathologist who had pulled Jane from her resting spot in the refrigerated drawers lining one wall.

"Tomorrow, right after lunch."

Pescoli's already queasy stomach turned. "Ugh."

Alvarez glanced up at her quickly, obviously wondering at the comment that just slipped out.

Dr. Esmeralda Kendrick didn't even look up. She was one of those women who was all business. Somewhere in her early thirties, she could have been pretty, but made no effort, at least not for work. Pescoli appreciated that. Everything about Dr. Kendrick was professional. Her manner, her speech, her body language. As usual, her blondish hair was scraped back into a no-nonsense ponytail. She wore no makeup, not even a trace of lipstick, and her blue eyes, behind huge glasses, were serious. Though barely five-three, she managed to appear commanding. She wore scrubs, tennis shoes, a lab coat, and the air of someone who was very busy and didn't like to be interrupted.

The little bit of a tattoo, a shamrock it seemed, peeked from beneath her ponytail, so Pescoli guessed that Dr. Kendrick might not be as straightlaced and cold away from the morgue as she was while doing her job. Maybe.

"You've got her personal effects?" Pescoli asked her.

She nodded. "Not much. Just her clothes that have been examined and are laid out and drying, and a pair of earrings. Look like diamonds. Could be cubic z. Not sure yet. Nothing else."

Pescoli glanced down at the fingers. "Fingernail scrapings?"

"Done at the scene. And an officer came and took prints when the body was brought in," Kendrick said, looking toward the door which led to an underground parking area where bodies could be brought in discreetly. Across the wide room and through another doorway was a hallway that led to a viewing area, waiting room. Farther along was the staff area, much like the lunchroom at the station.

In the sterile-looking examination room, the feel was decidedly different. An operating room without the intensity, as no anesthesia was being forced into lungs to keep the patient under during surgery, no anxious relatives relegated to a waiting area to hear the outcome of the procedures, no life being saved. No, the lives here had already been lost, sometimes violently.

Pescoli eyed the surroundings, computer monitors, metal cabinets for equipment, scales, and three long stainless steel tables equipped with faucets, hoses, and gutters, the kind that reminded her of working in the cannery as a youth, where the detritus from the berries on the belt merged with the water running in the gutter to unknown drains, or as the gossip mill insisted, was used in wine making. Sticks, bees, rotten fruit, even a snake once, were pushed into the ever present stream of water flushing out the berries to be canned and sold in markets across the country.

The difference was that in the morgue the gutters were primarily for blood.

Observing the dead usually wasn't a big deal, just part of her job, until today, when the smell kept causing her stomach to roil uneasily and she'd had to fight to keep the nausea at bay.

"So what do we know about her?" Pescoli asked.

"We'll X-ray the body, look for anything out of the ordinary in the results, of course. There's not much in the form of distinguishing marks, other than a scar on her right forearm, probably from an accident when she was a kid, and a small tattoo of a flower—a daisy—on her ankle.

"She may have drowned," Dr. Kendrick said, her eyebrows pulling together thoughtfully. "Again, we won't be certain until we examine her lungs. There is a little bruising at her throat, but I can't be certain that the hyoid was crushed. We do know that she wasn't sexually assaulted, she wasn't pregnant, and the only serious and outward sign of trauma is her ring finger, which was sliced off cleanly and neatly."

Pescoli's gaze went to the hand in question where the stump was visible, then, once more, she looked at the woman's face. Serene in death. *Who are you?* she wondered. *And what the hell happened?*

CHAPTER 8

Jessica adjusted the padding around her waist, hips, and torso and stared at her reflection in the mirror she'd purchased at a thrift shop and mounted on the bathroom door. The suit wasn't comfortable, but necessary, she knew, hiding her otherwise slim frame. She'd already donned the dark contacts and wig, then eyed her reflection in the mirror. Not bad. She added a little more makeup, far more than she ever wore, changing the contour of her lips and eyes, then slid a mouthpiece over her natural teeth, changing her smile before pushing a pair of glasses onto the bridge of her nose. From a distance, the transformation would hide her identity. Close up, if anyone really knew her and was on to her disguises, she might not be able to get away with denying who she really was.

Hopefully, she wouldn't have to; not until she talked to Cade and decided upon her next move. She struggled into her uniform, a gold-colored dress with a front zipper, gingham trim, and red piping, like something waitresses wore in a 1950s diner, something Nell Jaffe had decided would attract customers. Slowly, she was converting the bland interior of the diner into a copy of something straight out of *American Graffiti*, a movie she outwardly adored.

After locking the cabin, Jessica drove into town and kept one eye on the rearview mirror. So far, she thought she was safe. But she wasn't going to let her guard down. She'd been in Grizzly Falls only a few days so she was still on pins and needles, fearing that, at any moment, she would run into him again, that he would find her. Her stomach twisted at the thought and her chest became tight, feelings she battled by breathing slowly and relaxing her muscles, even stretching her fingers rather than holding on to the steering wheel in a death grip.

The falling snow had abated and the plows had been at work, ruts being replaced by smooth roads where pavement was visible in some spots. Even the diner's lot had been partially cleared. After parking in the rear of the restaurant, she grabbed her backpack and hurried inside where the furnace was working overtime and already the smells of warm coffee and sizzling bacon greeted her.

Near the storage closet where fresh linens were kept, she yanked off her boots and stepped into the shoes she'd brought in her backpack, then exchanged her jacket for an apron and started sorting silverware. She was scheduled to work through the noon crush, then have some time off before dinner. Nell had asked her to return as two other waitresses were out sick. Nell had pulled a face and made quotes with her long fingers as she'd mentioned the flu, but as they were shorthanded, Jessica was fine with it. The more work, the better, though she'd probably have to put off tracking down Cade Grayson.

"Leave that for Marlon," Misty advised as she swept through the swinging doors and caught Jessica wrapping napkins around sets of knives, spoons, and forks. "Coffee's already on and, okay, the first of the local yokels who need their caffeine fix should be here in . . . uh"—she glanced down at her watch—"eleven minutes. Hear that, Armando? Kip Cranston will be pounding on the door soon. He'll want the usual."

"Already got it going," Armando said, not even looking over his shoulder as he tossed some onions onto the grill. They sizzled and filled the kitchen with their sweet aroma. Jessica's stomach growled and she realized she'd forgotten to eat her usual container of yogurt.

"Toast ready?" Misty called. "You know Kip likes rye and Jimmy is always looking for a stack of pancakes. And Patch wants his sausage cooked all the way through, no pink."

"*Sì.* I told you! I got this." Armando flung the words over his shoulder then turned away and muttered something in Spanish under his breath.

None of it, Jessica suspected, was good.

"I'm unlocking the door." Misty found the keys in a drawer and tucked them into her pocket.

"*Sì, sì.* I heard you. *Dios! ¿Te crees que soy sordo?*"

"No, I don't think you're deaf," Misty replied, her lips pursing, her eyes, with their iridescent lilac lids, narrowing. "Just stubborn."

"Like the bull. *El toro.* Yes?" With a snort, Armando returned to his work.

Over his mutterings, the roar of the fan, and the popping grease, Jessica heard the thrum of heavy bass and loud rumble of exhaust pipes announcing that Marlon, in his tricked-out Honda, had arrived.

"The Dashing Dishwasher has decided to make an appearance," Misty said before heading into the dining area. "Now, it's officially showtime."

Jessica followed her inside and sure enough, a group of men in their sixties and seventies were huddled under the portico. As Misty unlocked the door and pulled it open, they walked briskly inside. With red faces, stocking caps, bulky jackets, and gloved hands in their pockets, they streamed to the two tables that she had already pushed together.

" 'Bout time you opened the damn doors," a grizzled old fellow said good-naturedly. "I was like to freeze, and Ed there, he claimed he'd have to go warm up in the cab of his truck where he keeps a bottle of Jack handy."

"No need for extreme measures," she said, falling into an easy banter. "Coffee all around, except for you, Syd? You want decaf."

"Yeah," a short guy said, showing a wide girth matched by a grin that stretched from one side of his bearded face to the other. "Not what I want, but I'd better if I don't want my ticker to start racing."

"You got it." Misty flitted around the table like the pro she was, juggling two pots of hot coffee while the regulars turned up the cups on their tables indicating they'd like a little morning jolt. She poured and chatted while a couple showed up and took a table by the window, away from the crowd in the middle of the room where the group of eight was talking, several conversations buzzing at once.

As Jessica brought water and tea for her table, she heard snippets of gossip. Dan Grayson's name was mentioned several times but there was another topic of interest, a woman's body found in a creek on a ranch several miles out of town. She told herself not to make more of it than it was, that it had nothing to do with her, but as she brought an order of a farmer's breakfast and a veggie omelet to a middle-aged couple near the door, she heard the word *mutilation*.

Her heart stopped for a fraction of a second.

"What do you mean *mutilation*?" the woman asked as she found Jessica hovering near the table. In her mid-seventies, she turned her face upward and lifted a hand, catching Jessica's full attention. "Oh, dear, sorry to bother you, but could you get us a fresh bottle of catsup? This one"—she indicated the small, full bottle resting near the napkin holder and salt and pepper—"is a little, well, you know. It's got a little bit of gunk around the lid."

Jessica picked up the offensive glass bottle though she saw nothing other than fresh red catsup within. "Certainly."

"And could I bother you for another knife? I see a spot on this one's blade." Smiling, the woman held up the flatware in question and yes, there was a bit of a water stain on the stainless steel.

"No problem. I'll be right back."

"Wait! Please bring some hot water, would you be a dear? My tea's already gone cold." Her smile was beneficent, but a little malicious gleam shone in her eyes, as she narrowed her gaze on Jessica through rimless glasses. "If you wouldn't mind."

"Not at all." Jessica was off and the woman turned to her husband again.

"Harry?" she said, catching his attention. "I asked you what you mean by *mutilation*?"

Though he answered, Jessica couldn't hear the conversation, whispered as it was. When she returned with the requested items, the woman ended her conversation quickly, then eyeballed the new knife and bottle skeptically.

She took a sip of her tea after Jessica poured hot water into her cup and teabag, then let out a satisfied sigh. "Aaah. Much better," she intoned, finally sated, probably just because she was able to get someone to do her bidding.

Jessica had the sneaking suspicion that the little errands she ran for the fussy woman were more for the old lady's amusement than from any real need, but she kept her thoughts to herself and tried not to panic over the bits of information she'd overhead. A dead body had been found? It was a woman? There was mutilation? Oh. God. Jessica's stomach clenched and she nearly stumbled as she was carrying water glasses to a booth where a man and a woman in uniform had taken a seat.

Pull yourself together.

Fortunately, as they were at one of her tables, she was able to overhear their conversation, or at least snippets of it, as she waited on them. What she hadn't expected when she placed the ice water on the table was that the man was wearing a badge marked Sheriff.

"Coffee?" she asked, reading his name. Blackwater. The man she'd heard was taking over Grayson's position, at least until the next election.

"Black," Blackwater said, his eyes cool, his expression without the hint of a smile.

"Sure," said his compatriot, a woman whose name tag read Deputy Delanie Winger. "With sugar."

Nodding, Jessica slid menus onto the table, then, her knees trembling a bit, motioned to the whiteboard hanging near the swinging doors. "We've got some interesting specials today," she said by rote, though she felt the sheriff's gaze upon her. "Marionberry waffles, a BLT with a fried egg, and a peanut butter and chocolate smoothie. I'll give you a few minutes." She was sweating nervously, her hands nearly shaking under his piercing glare, almost as if he could see through her disguise. *Impossible.* She'd never met Blackwater, nor the deputy he was talking to.

Servicing the other tables near the booth where they were seated, she heard bits of "shop talk", but nothing more than general information.

"Waiting on the autopsy," the sheriff told his colleague. "No, nothing yet from Missing Persons . . ." and "checking other jurisdictions."

That conversation, Jessica figured, was about the woman they'd discovered.

Then, very seriously, he said, ". . . a shame . . . yep, a good man . . . irreplaceable, but I've got to try." Words for Dan Grayson.

There was other talk about what she assumed were open cases, but she couldn't hear much as they spoke in low tones, and became quiet as she served a breakfast burrito to the deputy and a spinach and egg white omelet to the sheriff.

"Refills?" she asked on a second go-around when they were nearly finished.

The deputy said "Yes," and Blackwater nodded, so she started pouring the coffee.

Crash! The clatter of silverware rang through the building and Jessica jerked, slopping hot coffee as a stream of angry, rapid-fire Spanish emanated through the pass-through to the kitchen.

"Sorry . . . oh, I'm so sorry," she said, seeing that she'd sloshed coffee onto Blackwater's wrist.

"It's fine," he said shortly.

"I'll get a towel."

His eyes turned on her and she quickly withdrew her hand. What the hell had she been thinking? She never touched a customer, and especially not a cop.

"Sorry," she repeated and turned away, carrying the coffee back and retrieving a clean towel from the linen storage inside the kitchen where Marlon was busily picking up knives, forks, and spoons, then loading them into the dishwasher haphazardly.

Armando shook his head over the grill. *"Por el amor de Dios. ¡Qué idiota!"*

Breathing fire, Misty flew through the swinging doors, her mouth set in a red bow of disgust. "What the hell do you think you're doing?" she demanded of the busboy.

As Misty unleashed the reaming out, Jessica hurried back to the dining area where a few of the patrons were craning their necks toward the kitchen and Blackwater was reaching for his jacket.

"It's fine," he told her as she offered up the towel.

"No no no. I'm so sorry."

For the briefest of seconds, his eyes, dark as obsidian, seemed to look through her facade, past her disguise. In the brightly lit diner, she sensed that he could see deeper into her soul, which was absolutely ludicrous. It was all she could do not to take a step backward.

"Of course, your breakfast . . . both of your meals," she added with a quick look at the younger deputy, "will be comped. I'm really sorry."

To her surprise, he flashed her a smile, white teeth against darker skin. "I think I'll live."

In an instant, the awkward moment had dissipated as if it hadn't existed and Jessica told herself that she was jumping at shadows, reading more into the situation than there was,

Blackwater, even though she slid the plastic receipt holder back into the pocket of her apron, left enough money on the table to cover the cost of both meals and include a decent tip. "Accidents happen," he said and shrugged into his jacket.

"Miss?" a man in another booth said, flagging her down and holding up his coffee cup for a refill.

"Be right there." To the sheriff, she said, "Thanks for coming in," and turned her attention to the man in the baseball cap with the empty cup.

From the corner of her eye, she saw Blackwater give her another once-over as he held the door open for his deputy, and that look chilled her to the bone.

As acting Sheriff, Hooper Blackwater had a lot of responsibilities. No problem. He easily shouldered most tasks assigned him. In fact, he welcomed them. *The more the better*, he thought as he drove his Jeep along the older section of Grizzly Falls, where the town sprawled upon the shores of the river as it had for well over a hundred years. Traffic moved slowly past the storefronts with their western "Old Montana" flair. He noticed the county courthouse, an ancient brick building where he'd often given testimony, and nestled beside it, a bank building that had the appearance of the Hollywood stereotype of buildings robbed in old black-and-white movies set in the late 1800s.

Ahead of him, in her own vehicle, Deputy Winger was heading toward her assignment as one of the road deputies who patrolled the county. She was one of the few people in the department he completely trusted, and so he'd initiated their breakfast meeting, which, he reminded himself, was *not* a "date." One thing was certain, he wasn't going to mix business and pleasure again. The women on his staff were off-limits. Period.

He'd made that mistake once already and wasn't about to do it again. Besides, aside from Deputy Winger, he didn't trust anyone working for him. It wasn't that the other men and women on the force weren't good officers. Just the contrary was true. But nearly every one of them was so loyal to Sheriff Grayson that they weren't as yet swayed to the inevitable fact that he was the right man to step into the job as acting sheriff.

I'll have to change that, he thought, pausing at the railroad tracks as a long freight train barreled through the town, blocking his route up the steep hillside. He watched the cars hurtle past, just on the other side of the crossing's flashing arm, and tapped his fingers on the steering wheel. An ambitious man by nature, he looked upon

Grayson's passing as a tragedy, but an opportunity, as well. Not that he would have ever wished his predecessor ill will or an early death. But since Grayson had passed on, Blackwater wasn't a man to let a chance like this slip through his fingers.

He believed in the old adage his great-grandmother had conveyed to him when he was very young. "Where there's a will, there's a way," she'd told him on more than one occasion and he'd used that saying as his personal credo from the time he'd entered school and sensed that he was different from his peers. He'd been able, from an early age, to know when someone was lying or hiding something, even if that person was adept at concealing their feelings. It was an ability that had served him well in his job. That waitress at the diner, Jessica, according to the pin on her uniform, had definitely been afraid of revealing something about herself. He'd known it as if she'd suddenly announced it to the world. When she'd recognized he was "the law", she'd been all thumbs, as evidenced by the coffee splatters on his clothes.

The last rail car shot by in a clatter of steel on steel, the train heading underneath a tunnel on the south end of town. As he half listened to the crackling police band, Blackwater watched the signal's flashing blade lift slowly. He eased onto the gas while on the opposite side a girl in an older Ford Mustang was looking down, no doubt paying attention to her phone and unaware the signal bar had lifted. On the road behind her, the irritated driver of a huge Suburban laid on the horn, startling the girl. She hit the gas and the Mustang lurched forward, the woman in the Suburban scowling darkly as she followed close on the blue car's bumper.

Road rage. Never good. A part of him wanted to pull over both drivers, one for possibly texting, the other for tailgating, but he had other fish to fry, specifically solving the cases that would help him be elected at the end of Grayson's term. He snapped on his wipers as the snow began to fall again. He was probably ambitious to a fault, but so what? Even though this job had just fallen into his lap, he wasn't going to let it go. In his thirty-eight years, he'd already learned that real opportunity knocked only once on a man's door, and sometimes passed by a person's house altogether.

The engine strained a little as the hills steepened, the road slicing into the hillside and skimming the top of the ridge.

Blackwater had been a poor kid growing up. His dad had loved baseball, alcohol, and other women more than he did his family and had bailed on his wife and kids when Hooper was a sophomore in high school. From that point on, he'd been the "man of the house", and he'd reveled in the responsibility . . . and yes, power. And he wanted the power that came with the job of sheriff.

He drove his Jeep into the lot for the station, and with a sense of rightful ownership, parked in the space marked SHERIFF. First up on his to-do list was make certain Grayson's killer was prosecuted to the full extent of the law, convicted, and locked away forever. He had limited control on that one. His department could only provide testimony and evidence to convict, but he'd been in talks with the DA ever since hearing the news of Grayson's death and that office was definitely on the same page. A couple other potential homicides would keep his staff busy and the public concerned, and that didn't begin to touch the normal crimes involving robbery, drugs, domestic violence, and such. Yeah, the department would be busy.

He loved it.

As he yanked his keys from the ignition, just for a second, he thought of the waitress again. Along with her anxiety at slopping hot coffee on him and the fact that he was a lawman, he'd sensed there was bone deep terror that she was definitely trying to conceal. He'd been left with the feeling that covering things up and hiding were all a very integral part of who she was. A mystery, the waitress.

Not your problem. You have more than enough to deal with.

After locking his Jeep, he jogged through the lightly falling snow, past the poles where the flags were drooping at half-mast, to the front door. It was cold, but he found the change of the seasons invigorating, the winters bracing after spending so much of his life in the Southwest. Inside, the bright lights and gleaming floors didn't match the somber atmosphere. Even Joelle, usually bubbly to the point of being ridiculous, was subdued, her demeanor sober as she looked up and told him that several reporters had already stopped by for interviews.

"Not this morning," he said. "Maybe a press conference, later. If necessary."

He started to turn away, but she held up a beringed finger. "Sheriff, I mean . . . Sir, I was thinking," she said.

He noted that the black stones of her ring matched her earrings, part of her mourning attire, he presumed.

"Maybe we should dim the lights for the rest of the week, make a little shrine here, beneath Sheriff Grayson's picture"—she motioned to the wall where the past sheriffs were displayed—"and, you know, have a moment of silence every day?"

"No."

"But—"

"This is the sheriff's department. Our business is the public's and we'll remain open at full staff, with the lights on. No shrine. I've got the flags at half-mast and we'll run the department with a skeleton staff for the funeral so any and all officers who want to go can attend. Sheriff Grayson will get a full-blown law enforcement funeral, motorcade, three volley salute, the whole nine yards, but the department will remain open, uncompromised, ready to handle any and all calls and emergencies. We owe that to Sheriff Grayson's honor."

Though her lips were pursed in disapproval, she didn't argue, just nodded tightly and turned to a ringing phone.

If Blackwater had to be a hard-ass as commander to keep the county safe and well protected, so be it.

Noting that the offices seemed quieter than usual, he walked briskly along the hallway to the office marked SHERIFF. No doubt about it, he felt a twinge of satisfaction as he hung his jacket on the hall tree near the door. This, he sensed, was where he belonged.

CHAPTER 9

The last thing Pescoli needed was Hattie Grayson seated across her desk bringing up the same damn topic she had in the past. When it came to the subject of her ex-husband's death, the woman was a broken record. Worse, she'd come in with Cade Grayson who, rather than take a seat, decided to stand, leaning against the file cabinets, looking enough like his brother to give Pescoli a weird sense of deja vu.

"So you don't think it's odd that two of the brothers are dead?" Hattie asked, her eyes red-rimmed, her face drawn. She'd been close to her brother-in-law and had, according to the local rumor mill, dated not only Cade, but Dan, too, before marrying Bart, or some such nonsense. The timeline seemed skewed to Pescoli, not that she cared. She did know that Dan, in the past couple years, had spent a lot of time with Hattie and her daughters. Then Cade had returned, and Hattie had turned her attention to Dan's younger, wilder brother. It seemed, them being together, that Hattie and Cade were a couple.

Pescoli gave a mental shrug. What did it matter? Considering her own love life, she wasn't going to judge Hattie on hers. But the obsession about Dan and Bart's deaths being connected was nonsense. Bart had committed suicide; Dan had been shot by an assailant.

"I think it's tragic that we lost the sheriff and that his brother died before him," Pescoli said neutrally.

"Bart did *not* kill himself," Hattie insisted, as she had ever since her ex, supposedly despondent over their split, had walked into the family's barn, tossed a rope over a crossbeam, and hung himself.

"I know that's what you think, but his death was ruled a suicide." There it was. The bone of contention.

"He wouldn't do that to . . . to the girls," she insisted, then more softly, "or to me."

"We know who killed the sheriff," Pescoli reminded the distraught woman seated on the edge of one of the visitors chairs positioned near her desk. The detective's gaze moved to that of Cade Grayson to include him in the conversation. "There's no argument. That man's behind bars. He'll be prosecuted and convicted."

"Are you sure?" Hattie asked.

Dear Jesus, yes! I saw Dan go down, I witnessed him take the bullets. And I was there when the son of a bitch who killed him was arrested. I almost lost my own damn life to that psycho. Though her emotions were roiling, she managed to keep her voice calm. "Of course."

Hattie squeezed her eyes shut and held up her hands, fingers spread wide as if she knew she'd stepped over the line. "Yes, I know that you got Dan's killer, but you told me you'd look into Bart's death again. Reopen the case." Blinking rapidly, she swiped under her eyes with a finger.

Pescoli located a box of tissues under an unruly stack of papers. Nudging it around two near-empty cups of decaf to the far side of the desk, she said to Cade, "You think someone killed Bart, too?"

"Don't know." His jaw slid to one side and Pescoli remembered that Cade had been the unlucky person who had found his brother's body hanging from a crossbeam in the barn.

"Could be." A couple years younger, Cade looked a bit like Dan with his long, lean body, square jaw, and intense eyes. The Grayson genes were strong enough that a family resemblance was noticeable, though he was a couple inches shorter than the sheriff had been, and, from all reports, a lot more of a hellion in his youth. He'd ridden the rodeo circuit, only recently returning to Grizzly Falls. "Bart was having his problems," Cade said, his gaze drifting to Hattie for a second. "We all know that."

Hattie's face grew more ashen.

"But she's right," Cade said, hitching his chin toward his ex-sister-in-law. "Bart loved those girls and it seems unlikely that he would take himself out, denying McKenzie and Mallory from knowing their dad."

Pescoli felt trapped. "Look, I said I'd look through the files, and I will. But I didn't mention reopening the case."

"Semantics," Hattie said.

"More than that. A major difference." Pescoli wanted to make certain they understood her position.

"Just, please." Hattie swallowed and plucked a tissue from the box to wipe her eyes. Too late. Mascara was already beginning to streak her cheeks. Clearing her throat and standing, she said, "I know you were a good friend to Dan, and your partner Selena . . . she and Dan were close."

Pescoli waved a dismissive hand indicating that she didn't understand but accepted Alvarez's romantic fantasies about their boss.

"Dan would want whoever killed Bart to be brought to justice," Hattie said determinedly.

That much was true. Pescoli reminded, "If he was murdered, but—"

"He was murdered!" Hattie leaned over the edge of the desk so that she could meet the doubt in Pescoli's gaze with her own conviction.

Pescoli rose from her chair and said firmly, "We don't know that."

"That's because when he died, everyone just assumed the worst," Hattie stated. "So, you're right, we don't know, but it's your job to find out."

"His death was investigated at the time. Even his brother—"

"Dan was never satisfied about the outcome," Cade put in, straightening. They were all standing in the room, regarding each other tensely.

Hattie lifted her chin. "If it makes you feel any better, Detective, don't do this for me. Do it for Dan." With that she walked away, her sharp footsteps echoing along the hallway.

Cade said, "She's serious about this, you know. And Dan wasn't happy with the outcome of the investigation, though, of course, he wasn't sheriff at the time. I know you weren't involved then, either, but if you've got the time, I'd appreciate it."

Something in his eyes reminded Pescoli of his older brother. For a second, she imagined the sheriff standing in front of her. But then Cade squared his hat onto his head and followed after Hattie.

Pescoli looked at the case files stacked on the corner of her desk. Deeter Clemson's fall to his death, Jimbo and Gail Amstead's domestic violence case where each had ended up in the hospital, Ralph Haskins's suicide, as well as the new, deceased Jane Doe. Throw her personal life into the mix, and she really didn't have time to dig into a long-closed suicide just because the ex-wife and beneficiary of the life insurance policy wanted her to. As Pescoli understood it, the insurance company had balked at paying the benefits to Hattie and her twin daughters as it was determined that Bart had taken his own life.

Pescoli really shouldn't bother with Bart Grayson's death. The case had been investigated and closed, but Hattie's final words echoed through her mind. *If it makes you feel any better, Detective, don't do this for me. Do it for Dan.*

"Oh, hell," she muttered and knew that she'd dig through the case file. Just a cursory look, then maybe her guilty conscience would be assuaged.

Then again, probably not.

Ryder gassed up his truck at a station-convenience store with the unlikely name of Corky's Gas and Go. *Sounds bad any way you cut it,* he thought as he replaced the nozzle and, hands deep in his pockets, dodged a minivan and a Prius parked beneath the broad canopy covering several pumps. A fuel truck had pulled around back, ready to refill the underground tanks, and a woman in a long coat and boots nearly ran him down as she pushed open the glass door to the market about the time he was walking in.

"Watch where you're going," she said as she hurried outside.

Ignoring her, he walked past her to where the heater was cranked to the max, a wall of hot air meeting him as he strode down the aisles to the back case and grabbed a beer and a couple bottles of water as the H_2O that flowed from the tap of his room at the River View wasn't exactly pristine.

A girl in her early twenties was manning the register in a tank top; it was that warm inside. "Hire anyone yet?" he asked, motioning toward the HELP WANTED poster taped to the glass just inside the door.

"Nuh-uh. Don't think so." She rang up his purchases. "You get gas?"

"Pump six. Any applicants?"

"Corky, he's the owner, just put up the sign this mornin'. It's still pretty early."

"What's it for?"

"You interested?"

"Maybe."

"Well, you have to take a drug test and submit to a background check." She rolled her eyes, indicating that was a pain. "Then, you start helping out at the pumps. Some people don't like to pump their own, y'know?" Another eye roll. "Corky's a stickler," she said.

Ryder decided Anne-Marie wouldn't take a chance on a background check. No, she'd find a job where the owners of the establishment weren't as conscientious as Corky.

Of course, there was always Grayson.

Ryder could go right to the source.

But he didn't want to spook her and there was more than a little bad blood between Cade and himself. And there was that little problem about Cade just losing his brother. The man might be hair-trigger touchy and who knew how it would go down if Ryder just showed up and Grayson was harboring Anne-Marie. If she caught wind that he was on to her, no doubt she'd bolt again.

For now, Ryder needed the element of surprise, so he had to be careful.

He bought a couple maps of the area that he'd study then keep in his truck, as the Internet service was often spotty, especially when he was driving in the hills. Besides, sometimes he got a better feel for the land with an old fashioned map rather than wireless Internet service. Climbing into his truck, he drove through town again.

Three times already he thought he'd caught a glimpse of Anne-Marie in the small town, and three times he'd been wrong. He'd gone through Craigslist, the want ads, and any Internet Web site that listed houses, rooms, and apartments to rent. He'd scoured through ads from a few weeks earlier, but had come up with nothing. At the same time, he'd gone through the motions of checking listings for job opportunities, marking off those that he thought would require background checks.

In the past, he'd always been one step and three or four weeks behind her, nipping at her heels, only to reach the town in which she'd landed to realize, after a week or two, that she'd taken off again. It always took a while to discover her next move.

This time, though, he believed he'd gotten the jump on her.

Of course, he'd missed her by several days in Denver, but had gotten lucky and found a bar where she'd poured drinks for six weeks before getting spooked. Wanda, one of her coworkers, had recognized her, even caught her adjusting a dental appliance and had figured out she was on the run. "Anne-Marie? Huh. I knew her as Stacey."

"Not Heather Brown?" That was the name she'd used in Omaha.

Wanda had shaken her head. "She's Stacey Donahue. She go by somethin' else, too?"

"Yeah." *A lot of something elses,* he'd thought

"That happens a lot, y'know. People changin' their names and runnin' from their pasts. Husbands, ex-boyfriends . . ." She'd skewered Ryder with a suspicious glare, then shrugged as if she'd determined he wasn't dangerous. "As I said, happens all the time."

Ryder had then interviewed all the workers at the establishment and discovered no one had really known where she lived. He'd ended up in a confab with Wanda and a couple other employees.

"Rented a room, I think. Somewhere not too far because she walked to work most days," Wanda offered. "I think she said she had family in San Bernardino that she was hoping to see . . . that was it, right? No, wait, maybe it was San Jose, oh, hell all those towns in California sound the same to me. Donella, you knew her better. Where did Stacey say she had family. San Jose?"

"I didn't know her that well," Donella denied, giving a quick shake of her head, her ponytail wagging. "I thought she said . . . San Jacinto. Maybe."

"No, that ain't it." Wanda let out a frustrated sigh. "All I know was it wasn't San Diego or San Francisco, but it started with San . . . wait, or maybe Santa. There's a lot of those, too."

"Talk to Tanisha," Donella declared. "She's the one who talked to her the most."

He'd thanked them, then, hours later, had shown up for Tanisha's night. The place was rockin' by then, a band coming on at nine, but he hadn't been thinking it would make any difference as Anne-Marie had told everyone she worked with a different story about heading out to somewhere in California, or Las Vegas, or Phoenix. Diversions to hide her true destination.

However, Tanisha, who happened to be one of the bartenders, had given him his first real clue.

"Yeah, I talked to her, but she kept to herself," she confided in a smoky voice that hinted at too many cigarettes. A short, black woman with a hard stare if a customer was getting too rowdy, she added,

"Said she was from Texas somewhere. Maybe Houston. I can't really remember."

Encouraged, Ryder had stuck around, ordering drinks and placing healthy tips in the jar on the counter.

Finally, Tanisha remembered. "You know, she did say something once about looking up an old boyfriend. When I asked her who he was, she clammed up and said she'd thought better of it. Didn't say his name, but I think he was some kind of cowboy. But y'know, we're in Colorado. Everybody's a cowboy here." She'd laughed then.

But Ryder had known Anne-Marie must have been talking about Cade Grayson. "Did Stacey ever talk about Montana?"

Tanisha was polishing the long wooden bar with a cloth and a man at the far end raised a finger, indicating he'd like another drink. Ryder had been impatient, wishing he had the bartender's attention all to himself, but then she said, "Y'know, that's about the one damn place in these United States she didn't mention."

Bingo.

He'd then canvassed the area and found a rooming house where the landlady who, for a little cash, admitted that her last tenant, a woman she "never trusted," had moved on and told her to forward any mail to a post office box in LA. Ryder hadn't taken that bait. He'd been fooled by Anne-Marie too many times. Instead, he'd followed the only clue that had made any sense to him—that she was going to hook up with an old boyfriend. Maybe that had been her plan all along, to go to Cade, or maybe it was a move out of desperation. Whatever the case, one-time rodeo rider Cade Grayson was Anne-Marie's ex-boyfriend and a bona fide son of a bitch.

And he'd returned right to his hometown of Grizzly Falls, Montana.

CHAPTER 10

Seated across the table from Santana in a booth at Wild Will's, Pescoli frowned at the screen of her cell phone.

"Bad news?" he asked, taking a swallow of beer as he eyed her.

The restaurant was crowded and noisy, most of the tables filled. Waitresses and busboys flitted through the cavernous dining area decorated with rough plank walls, wagon wheel chandeliers, and the heads of game animals mounted on the walls beneath the rafters.

"Depends on your perspective, I guess," she said and managed a perturbed smile.

They'd left on bad terms the other night when he'd called to offer his condolences about Grayson, and true to form, she'd been a stone-cold bitch, icing him out and pushing him away. Sometimes she wondered why he put up with her. They'd met in the parking lot after a brief phone call where Santana had suggested they have dinner at the familiar restaurant on the banks of the Grizzly River, just under the falls.

They hadn't met in person since Dan Grayson's death, only spoken on the phone. Seeing Santana again had brought tears to her eyes. Standing by his truck, he'd opened his arms wide and she'd stepped into them, letting him pull her close. He'd whispered, "God, Regan, I'm sorry."

She'd felt like a heel for how she'd treated him and had let herself be wrapped in the warmth of his embrace. He'd smelled earthy, of leather and horses and a bit of musk. With the snow beginning to fall around them and the rush of the river tumbling over the falls in her ears, she'd closed her eyes and forced herself not to cry.

"I am, too," she'd admitted. "Not just for Grayson, but for the other night. You wanted to come over and I . . . was dealing with a lot."

"I know," he'd said, but he hadn't told her that her behavior was okay, because it hadn't been.

But he did allow her to be herself and she knew he would never try to change her. Santana, more than anyone, understood how devastated she'd been with the loss of Grayson, that she had witnessed the horror of the sheriff being shot, and that she'd woken up screaming in the middle of the night, reliving the experience. She hoped the nightmares would cease or at least abate soon. Always before, whether it had been dealing with her grief after Joe had been killed or handling the aftermath of her own terror at the hands of a psychotic killer, she'd spent several weeks, even months reliving the horror in her dreams. With time and effort, she had shed the need to replay the awful scenes in her subconscious.

She only hoped the same would happen this time.

"So?" he said, nodding at the phone. "Work?"

With a quick shake of her head, she said, "Bianca's a no-show. Again." Pescoli didn't want to think what that might mean. "Third time this week." She glanced down at the text one more time. At Lana's. Homework. Be home later. A frowning emoticon followed the word *homework*.

She couldn't help feeling that she was being played. Never before had one girlfriend taken up so much of Bianca's time. Pescoli had considered this new friendship a good thing, as Lana was a more studious girl than those Bianca usually hung out with, the more boy-crazy crowd. However, she was second-guessing her daughter.

When she'd told Bianca about Grayson, her daughter's face had clouded briefly. "I heard. Lana's mom said something and Michelle called. It's too bad." Then she'd gone to her room.

Too bad?

It was a helluva lot more than that.

Irritated, Pescoli tapped the edge of her phone on the table then slid it into her pocket.

"You think she's lying," Santana stated.

"Not think. Know. Just don't know why."

"Maybe you're being too much of a detective."

Pescoli gave him a look. "I was a teenager once, you know. Not *that* long ago. So were you."

His mouth quirked and his eyes glittered. "I remember."

"So."

"Maybe you should have a beer."

"Not tonight. I need to be clearheaded."

"To deal with your daughter?"

"Amen. She's sharp. And then, unfortunately, I have to catch up on some work. At home."

"Then you definitely need a beer."

"Rain check," she said and he lifted a shoulder, cool with whatever she wanted. God, she loved him. She did want to spend the rest of her life with him though she hadn't yet slipped the engagement ring back on her finger. Santana had asked her about that, too, and she'd answered truthfully that she hadn't wanted to deal with all of the questions at the department, or the ribbing from her coworkers, especially after Grayson had been attacked. Those who had noticed her engagement ring had been few, and no one seemed aware that she wasn't wearing it anymore, or at least they weren't saying anything. She'd assured Santana that she wasn't backing out. She wanted to marry him. She just needed to do things her way.

He asked, "What about Jeremy? He coming?"

"Legitimate excuse. He's working."

"Then I guess it's just you and me." Santana's smile stretched wider and the twinkle in his eye turned a little wicked as the waitress brought a loaf of sourdough bread to their table and asked for their orders. "Ladies first."

"The stew and a house salad," Pescoli said, then Santana ordered the special—chicken fried steak and mashed potatoes with country gravy. All of it sounded like heaven.

"You could come to my place after this," he suggested once they were alone again.

"You mean 'our' place?" She sliced off a chunk of the bread.

"Not really ours until you move in."

"I don't think I'll do that until you, er, we have heat and running water. Furniture, too."

"Fair enough."

As she slathered the bread with butter and held it up to him, a peace offering of sorts, he shook his head and said, "I thought you were going to cut back on your hours."

"I was, but now we've got this new case."

"There's always going to be one, you know."

"Yeah." She bit into the bread.

"Maybe you need a long vacation away from everything for a while. See how it goes."

She almost choked. That's exactly what was going to happen, whether she wanted it to or not. Pregnancy leave.

Something in her expression must have showed because he became deadly serious. "You'd tell me if we weren't okay, right?"

She reached over and clasped his hand. "We're okay," she assured him.

He heard the sincerity in her voice and nodded.

By the end of her second shift, Jessica hadn't learned a lot more about the dead woman found on the O'Halleran ranch. She'd heard plenty of gossip, just snippets from customers that had peppered into the conversations about work, family, kids, school, friends, or grandkids. One item was about a preacher approaching retirement age who was leaving his wife for a young parishioner. There was also a missing dog, an apparent suicide, and a homicide investigation of a man who was either pushed, or fell, from a mountain trail around these parts. The biggest news stories by far rippling through the dining area over the clink of flatware and the endless loop of songs from the fifties and sixties was the county losing Dan Grayson as its sheriff and the discovery of the body of an unknown woman found in a creek winding through the O'Halleran ranch.

Unfortunately, Jessica heard nothing substantive about the dead woman and though she told herself it was just coincidence—a woman's body found in a deep pool of a local creek—she couldn't help the tide of panic that rose within her.

He's here, she'd thought frantically. *He's here somewhere in Grizzly Falls.*

By sheer will, she'd forced herself to remain calm as the hours wore on. Even if he really had found a way to chase her to Grizzly Falls, she hadn't sensed anyone following her. So far. Several times during the day, she'd scanned the dining area, but he hadn't been inside the diner, she was sure of it.

Yet, she reminded herself.

She considered her options. *Slim and none.*

Except for Cade.

God help her that her fate was dependent on the cowboy who had put her in danger in the first place. It was pure hell to think she needed to depend on him.

At the end of her shift, Jessica glanced outside to the parking lot in front of the diner. Empty of vehicles, the security lamps casting blue pools of light over the snow-covered asphalt, the area looked a little surreal. Again snow was falling, softening the edges of ruts made by earlier vehicles. From inside the diner, with its bright lights and wide bank of windows, she felt as if she were in a fish bowl, that anyone hiding in the shadows could watch her every move undetected. Feeling a sudden chill, she told herself she was imagining things. She was safe. For now.

Nonetheless she squinted, trying to peer through the veil of snow.

"Hey, hit the switch for the sign that says we're open. Just turn it off, so we can go home. It's that one there, the one with the piece of black tape on it. Yeah, over there." Misty was shouting her orders from behind the counter and waggling a finger toward a toggle switch near the door. "Then flip the sign on the door for the morons who can't figure it out even when the neon goes dark."

"Got it." Jessica pushed on the switch, then twirled the two-sided hanging placard on the door so that it read COME IN, WE'RE OPEN to anyone looking at it from the interior and SORRY, WE'RE CLOSED to potential customers peering through the glass.

Misty slapped at another switch near the doors to the kitchen and half the interior lights turned off. "That should do it," she said, one hand on the swinging doors. "You'd think people would understand that when we're closed, we're goddamn closed." She was in a bit of a snit as the last customer had come in fifteen minutes before closing, idled over her meal, texting and playing some game on her phone before asking for a doggy bag and leaving half an hour after the restaurant was supposed to close.

Nell was a stickler for attending to each person who walked through the door and so, though the doors had been locked, the customer was not hurried out the door.

A bare fifteen minutes since the customer had left, almost forgetting the leftovers she'd asked to be bagged, the floors had been quickly mopped, chairs squared around each table, booths brushed off, each station cleaned. All the tables were sparkling, coffee mugs turned face down on the Formica surfaces, condiments refilled and standing at the ready for the morning crowd that was due to arrive within eight hours.

With one last glance through the windows, Jessica started untying her apron as she walked through the swinging door to the kitchen.

Armando and Marlon were long gone and Nell was in the office with the door shut, where, as each night, she was counting the day's receipts and balancing the cash register.

Connie, one of the teenaged bus girls, was swabbing the kitchen floor with a mop that had seen better days, while sterile glasses were still steaming in the open dishwasher. The warm room smelled of pine-cleaner that didn't quite mask the lingering odors of deep-fryer grease and coffee.

"I can't believe this," Misty said, digging through the purse she'd retrieved from her locker area. Shaking her head, she crumpled the empty cigarette pack she'd located and tossed it into the trash. "Anyone got a ciggy?"

As Jessica shook her head, Connie gave a quick nod, reached into her pocket, and withdrew a pack of Marlboro Lights. To Jessica, she said, "I'm eighteen, okay?"

"I owe ya," Misty said, shaking out a filter tip, then flipping the pack back to the girl, who slipped the pack quickly into her pocket.

Jessica tossed her dirty apron into a bin with other laundry and unlocked her locker to grab her purse.

Misty, still clutching the cigarette, was shrugging into her jacket.

Jessica asked, "So did you hear anything about the woman who was found in the creek?"

"Just bits and pieces, same as you." Misty zipped up the jacket. "I did catch it on the news as I passed by the office. Nell had it on. It was that woman from the station in Montana. Oh, God, what's her name? Nia Something-Or-Other, not that it matters. All I heard was that they haven't IDed her yet. Kinda sounds like they suspect foul play and I don't blame them. You wouldn't believe the nutcases that have blown through here lately." Her lips, faded now as most of her makeup had worn off, twisted downward. "Not too long ago, Grizzly Falls was a sleepy little town, no trouble other than a drunk getting into a fight or shootin' up the WELCOME TO GRIZZLY FALLS sign. Now, though, it seems we get more than our share of psychos. And I'm not talking about our local weirdos like Grace Perchant. She's the gal who owns wolf-dogs and thinks she talks to ghosts." Misty shook her head. "Or that idiot Ivor Hicks who still claims he was taken in some kind of spaceship or something and experimented on by lizard people. No, those are our usual Grizzly Falls oddballs. That's not what I'm talkin' about. Nuh-uh."

Connie stopped mopping for a moment and nodded to Jessica, letting her know she should listen up.

Misty went on. "Just a little while back some lunatic killed women and then displayed them in the snow or some other fucked-up thing. Damn serial killer, that one was. And he wasn't the first. Right, Connie?"

"Sure thing." Slightly heavy, Connie was sweating as she leaned on her mop. "My mom is thinking about moving away and she's lived here all her life. But she had faith in Sheriff Grayson. He always caught the nutcases. Now—" She shrugged, indicating who knew what the future might bring, then carried her mop and pail to the back door.

Misty jabbed the unlit cigarette between her pale lips. "The trouble is, the way things are going, another psycho's probably coming down the pike."

Jessica's gut tightened. "You think that the woman found on the ranch is the victim of a serial killer?"

"Maybe. Who knows? Around here you have to go there, whether you want to believe it or not."

Connie opened the back door and threw the dirty water from her bucket into an area that, beneath the snow, was graveled.

"Watch out! We don't want that to freeze and end up being slippery as snot," Misty said. "The last thing I need is to break my leg, or wrench my damn back."

Connie said, "I tossed the water right where you told me to. Not in the damn parking lot or near the steps. It's in the effin' garden. Your idea."

"Last summer it was, when the temperature was in the eighties." Misty caught the girl's angry glare and lifted a hand. "Yeah, okay. Sorry. It's fine."

"I know it's fine." Connie peeled off her apron and stalked to her locker.

As the locker door slammed, Misty and Jessica walked outside together and Jessica asked the question that had been nagging at her ever since she'd heard the first whisper of a rumor about the victim. "Did you hear that the woman they found on the O'Halleran ranch was mutilated?"

Misty was clicking her lighter to the end of her cigarette. "Mutilated? Shit, no." Positively stricken, she drew in hard on her filter tip. "Oh, Jesus." She shook her head as snowflakes caught in her hair. "I didn't hear that, but I was too busy to pay much attention. You sure about that?"

"No. Just something I overhead."

"Well, I hope to heaven it's not true. Mutilated, how?"

"I don't know."

"Who was talking about it? That new sheriff? I saw you waiting on him. He should be careful about talking in public. That is, if he wants to get elected."

"No," Jessica said quickly, remembering the intense look he'd sent her way. "It was the woman who came in about the same time, the one who asked me for a million additions."

Misty's eyes narrowed through the smoke. "Oh, God, that's right. Lois Zenner, she was with her husband. Such a pain. Left you one dollar for a tip, right?" she asked. "One lousy buck. Well, she's a gossip and a prig and tight as ever, but she does have a niece who works at the department, I think. An underling, but usually Lois's gossip is right on."

Jessica's heart stilled. *That information had come out of the department?*

"But mutilated? Christ, what is the world coming to? The sickos sure find us, don't they?" Misty walked to her car and slid inside as Jessica made her way to her own vehicle. If she were lucky, she could get home and still catch the late-night news.

This has nothing to do with me.

But as she drove away, trying to deny that he had found her again and convince herself that he wasn't nearby, she couldn't stop her heart from beating a little faster, nor could she keep her fingers from nervously clenching the wheel. At the first stoplight, she slowed, let the car idle, and eyed the surrounding area nervously. The town was quiet, no one on the streets, no other sets of headlights behind her, no taillights in front. The traffic light blinked an eerie red upon the powdery streets and every muscle in her body was tense.

He's not here, she told herself, turning on the radio. Stepping on the gas, listening to Adele's voice, she wondered if she'd ever feel safe again.

Of course not. Until he's locked up or dead, you'll always be looking over your shoulder. You'll never have peace. You know what you have to do, don't you? Either find a way to send him to prison forever, or kill the son of a bitch.

That thought was unsettling and she checked the rearview mirror often on her drive home. No one followed her, at least no one that she could pinpoint in her mirrors. No tracks of any kind had broken through the snow to her cabin, it seemed, since she'd left.

Good. She let out a breath and walked inside, found the cabin just as she'd left it. "There's no place like home," she said, and wished she had a dog or a cat or even a parakeet. Something living to greet her, something she could talk to. Maybe a dog. One that would guard the place and put up a ruckus if anyone was lurking outside, one that could smell if an intruder had been inside. She warmed to the idea. Maybe.

After locking the door, Jessica threw her keys onto the scarred coffee table and tried to shake off her case of nerves. She turned on the television, then as it started glowing, the volume low, she double-checked the tiny rooms in the cabin to make certain she was alone. Once she knew the place was secure and the stained shades were drawn, she stoked the fire and space heater, then quickly stripped out of her uniform, body suit, wig, and contacts.

Earlier, she'd cleaned the phone booth-sized shower with liberal amounts of bleach and Pine-Sol though some stains refused to fade. She didn't care. The tiles were disinfected. She was bone tired and felt the diner's grease clinging to her skin. She stepped under a weak spray of lukewarm water, then lathered her body and her hair. For a second, she remembered another shower where the hot steam fogged the glass and the wide stall was equipped with multiple sprays and glistening tiles.

"A long time ago," she said aloud. "Another lifetime." She rinsed off and cranked hard on the handle. Old pipes groaned as she threw her one towel around her and dried off quickly. Shivering, she reminded herself that giving up creature comforts was a necessity. For now. Until she figured out what to do.

She threw on a pair of sweats, then combed out her hair. When she looked into the mirror, her face washed of makeup, her body no longer laden with extra padding or a wig, dental appliances, contacts, or glasses, she caught a glimpse of her younger self and remembered the woman she'd thought she'd be. She felt a pang in her heart as she remembered her dreams of a career, a marriage, and a family— all dust in the wind—foolish fantasies from a privileged girl who'd naively thought she could be anything she wanted to be, do anything she wanted to do, that success was dependent only on her desire.

That's where she'd made her mistake, thinking her wants and needs were so damn important.

Now, of course, she knew better.

She walked back to the living room. The television caught the local stations, so she watched while searching the Web, hoping for more information about the body that had been found. She sat on the edge of the couch, her gaze flicking back and forth between the bubble screen of the TV and the laptop's flat monitor. She was nervous about the discovery but wouldn't have thought that much about it except for that whispered word *mutilation*, one that caused warning bells to clang wildly in her head. Was he back? Was the dead woman a means to frighten her?

It's not about you. Remember that. A woman is dead. Killed, possibly. Murdered. It's just gossip, after all. Unproven. A rumor. Nothing to get upset about.

What are the chances that he's followed you all the way from New Orleans? You've covered your tracks. Relax.

And yet, she couldn't stop the paranoia that had been chasing her for months. Even now, she walked the perimeter of the small rooms, checking door locks and window latches, then peering through the blinds and the falling snow expecting a dark figure to shift in the shadows or the reflection of eyes to catch in the light.

Shuddering, she walked back to the fire and stoked the flames again, hearing the soft crunch as a log fell apart and sparks glowed brightly. She carried the poker with her to the couch and kept it nearby, within reach if she couldn't reach the pistol for some reason.

Until this madness ended, she would be forever looking over her shoulder, hiding, worrying that he was out there, bird-dogging her, waiting to strike.

That was the worst part, knowing that he enjoyed her terror, that he got off on it.

No more, she thought, dragging the sleeping bag around her. *No more*.

CHAPTER II

Pescoli sipped decaf coffee and avoided the lunchroom where there was talk of Grayson's funeral.

Another two days had passed and Joelle had come alive again, taking the bull by the horns and making plans for the service. It was something to do, to keep her busy. Blackwater was involved as well, along with some higher-ups, but Joelle was coordinating with the family—Grayson's brothers and two ex-wives. He had no children, but had kept up friendly relations with his first wife, Cara, married to Nolan Banks with whom she had a daughter and a couple of stepkids. Dan Grayson had also been divorced from his second wife, Akina, to whom he'd been wed briefly. She, too, had remarried and had children.

The kicker was that Cara Grayson Banks was a half sister to Hattie Grayson. They shared the same mother, and it seemed, the same fascination with the Grayson brothers.

It was all a little incestuous in Pescoli's estimation.

She turned her attention to the new case involving the unidentified victim and searched the incoming reports. Jane Doe's fingerprints weren't registering, at least not according to the information Pescoli had received. AFIS had reported back on the nine prints that were taken, but the victim's identity remained a mystery. She was not a known criminal with a record and her prints hadn't been recorded for any government job, either.

"Great," Pescoli said, tapping the eraser end of her pencil against the desk. Feeling a pang of hunger, she realized she was suddenly starving, despite upchucking in the bathroom before she'd driven to work. That was the trouble. She was either unable to think because she was battling nausea in the morning or so suddenly hungry in the afternoon that eating became priority number one. As if reading her thoughts, her stomach rumbled, and she said, "Quiet," as if the baby, or her insides, could hear her. Ridiculous. The baby was probably about the size of a kidney bean. She knew. She'd checked on one of those Web sites dedicated to pregnancy, something she'd not been able to do with either of her earlier pregnancies.

Things had changed a lot in the past sixteen plus years, she decided as she found a protein bar in her desk drawer and unwrapped it quickly. Macadamia and white chocolate and billed as "healthy" when she doubted it was all that different from the Snickers candy bar she'd hidden deeper inside that same drawer, for "an emergency."

Taking a bite, she let out a contented sigh. *I hope you're satisfied now,* she thought, mentally communicating with the minuscule baby growing inside her. A part of her was worried sick about having a child this late in life, another part was a little giddy at the idea. Three children with three different men. Who woulda thunk? Not exactly brilliant family planning nor how she'd expected her life to play out twenty-odd years ago when she was desperately in love with Joe Strand. But there it was. And damn it, the new little addition to her unconventional family would be worth every gray hair she would undoubtedly grow.

She just had to convince her existing near-grown teenagers of the fact. She tossed her pencil onto the desk and noted that the ring on her finger caught the light. She'd finally decided to wear the diamond Santana had given her. She was going to get some guff from her coworkers. *So what?* She was engaged and that was that. She'd show the kids tonight, not that it would be a big surprise; they'd already had many discussions about moving into the new house and the very real possibility of their mother remarrying.

With one foot out the door, ready to move out and get on with his life, Jeremy hadn't said too much, but Bianca had thrown a hissy fit, taking the opportunity to turn the whole thing around so that Pescoli's involvement with Santana was all about her. Pescoli thought about that drama-infused argument at the dinner table.

* * *

"You're only marrying him because Dad's married to Michelle!" Bianca charged.

"My relationship with Santana has nothing to do with that."

"Oh, come on, Mom. You've been jealous of Michelle from the minute she and Dad started seeing each other." Bianca reached up and fiddled with the rubber band holding her hair on the top of her head in a curly, seemingly careless knot that Pescoli figured took a minimum of fifteen minutes to create.

"Jealous?" she repeated with a derisive snort as Jeremy had reached for the bowl of spaghetti on the table and spooned out a second huge portion. "I don't think so."

That, of course, had been a lie. Any bit of envy she felt for his second wife at the time Lucky had taken up with her had rapidly disappeared. The more she knew Michelle, the less she cared. As for him, Pescoli realized how lucky it was that they'd split. Not that he still didn't have the ability to push all of her buttons. As long as they were parents, they would always have to deal with each other whether she liked it or not, so she tried to get along with him, even though most of the time she would have preferred to hit him alongside the head with a two-by-four. Not to do any permanent damage. Just hard enough to get his attention.

"Lay off Mom, Bianca." Jeremy defended her as he pronged two meatballs with a long fork and dumped them unceremoniously onto the mound of pasta on his plate. At their feet, Cisco whined for a treat while Sturgis regarded them from his dog bed in the living room. "She's entitled to her own life, you know." From a pitcher on the table, he poured a liberal amount of sauce over his plate while Bianca pursed her lips, her eyes flashing rebelliously as she picked at her dinner.

"Like you have it all figured out," she muttered.

"More than you." Jeremy had forked a huge wad of saucy pasta into his mouth, then met her churlish stare with his own as he'd chewed.

"You're an animal, y' know?" she declared.

He shrugged.

"Enough," Pescoli intervened. "This is dinner time. Family time."

Bianca's head snapped up so fast that her over-sized bun wobbled. "Right. The three of us." Using her fork, she made a circular motion to include them all. "We don't need any more."

"Tell me that when you want to get married. Or have a kid," Pescoli rejoined, thinking of the baby again. "Or Jeremy does. Families evolve, Bianca. That's why we count Michelle as part of ours. And now Santana will be."

"Awesome," Bianca said sarcastically. "So what if Jeremy and Heidi get married? Huh? What about that kind of evolution? Will she be part of the family?"

"They're broken up and Heidi's in California," Pescoli said.

"Like that means anything," Bianca muttered.

Pescoli's gaze flew to Jeremy, who was suddenly paying his undivided attention to slicing a meatball. "Right, Jeremy? You and Heidi aren't together anymore."

"We're friends," he mumbled, not meeting his mother's eyes. "She's in California," was his unsatisfactory answer.

Pescoli saw Bianca's smirk and wondered what she'd missed.

Thinking her mother wasn't looking, Bianca slid part of a meatball from her plate toward the floor where Cisco gobbled it up. "Heidi's thinking about coming back to Montana to go to college after she graduates high school in San Leandro."

"Is that true?" Pescoli asked as Sturgis stretched out of his bed and wandered over to the dining area.

Jeremy dropped his fork and glared at his sister. "Maybe."

"Hasn't she applied to University of Montana?" Bianca put in sweetly.

Pescoli's stomach lurched. "Jer?"

Jeremy snapped, "Pre-applied."

"What does that mean?" Pescoli asked.

"It's an option. That's all. She's still got family here. One of her sisters is going there." Jeremy tried hard to act as if nothing was the least bit out of place,

Pescoli tried to sort out what it all meant. She'd hoped that Heidi Brewster was out of her son's life. Beautiful and manipulative, Heidi had twisted Jeremy around her little finger for the past several years. When the decision was made to move from Montana to California, Pescoli had prayed that the two teenagers' fascination with each other would fade away.

"Why didn't I know about this?" she asked, only vaguely aware that Sturgis had seated himself next to her chair.

Jeremy turned to face her. "Because I knew you'd freak, Mom, and it looks like I was right."

"I'm not freaking."

"Don't worry," Bianca interjected. "Jeremy and Heidi aren't married . . . yet. They just can't stand to be away from each other. Besides, it's not really a big deal. Families evolve, you know."

Pescoli had wanted to wipe the "gotcha" grin off her daughter's face and send her to her room. Instead, she'd forced herself to remain calm. "Glad you understand. So, Santana and I are getting married and we're all going to move to the new house. Better start thinking about what you want to pack. And please, don't feed Cisco from the table. It makes him worse. Look, even Sturgis is getting into the act." At the mention of his name, Sturgis wagged his tail.

Like the lingering scents of garlic and tomato sauce from last night's dinner, the argument still hung in the air. This morning, Pescoli had left the house before either kid had bothered to get up and thrown herself into her work rather than dwell on the problems with her ever-growing family.

Heidi Brewster? Her daughter-in-law? *No way.* Angry at the thought, she bit into the energy bar. As she plopped the last bit into her mouth, she heard rapid footsteps in the hallway and Alvarez nearly slid into her office.

Pescoli looked up sharply.

"Taj might have something," Alvarez said. "Possible ID on our Jane Doe."

"About damn time." Pescoli tossed the wrapper into the trash can near her desk and was out of her chair in one swift motion. They needed a break on this one.

In the missing persons department, Taj Nyak was waiting for them. She stood on the other side of a long counter covered in some kind of wood veneer that was popular in the 1970s. An exotic looking African-American woman with features that hinted at some Asian ancestry in her genealogical mix, she flashed them a quick smile. "That was quick."

Alvarez asked, "What've you got?"

Taj turned her computer screen around so that they could see the image thereon, a clear picture of a female who appeared identical to the woman they'd seen in the morgue the day before, the woman found on the creek at the O'Halleran ranch.

"Ladies," Taj said, "meet Sheree Cantnor."

I know how to handle death, Alvarez thought as she sat in the interrogation room.

Dealing with those who had died was all a part of her job. She made her living trying to find justice for the dead. Death was business as usual except in the case of those near to her. Dan Grayson's death had leveled her, made her question her decision to be a cop, caused her to lose sleep at night. There were no platitudes nor soft words of encouragement that would assuage the pain she felt when she thought of the sheriff and how cruelly and needlessly he'd died. She'd toyed with quitting or transferring to another department, but she'd made this part of Montana her home, had a biological son with whom she'd recently been reunited, and had finally found a steady partner in Dylan O'Keefe, a man who had been in and out of her life for years.

He was back, and she felt centered for the first time in memory. Though the hole in her heart was painful, she had decided she would heal, given enough time and enough work. She worked as a cop because she loved it, and as she eyed the man seated in the interrogation room, she remembered why.

Heat flowed through the air duct overhead, whispering into the room little more than a cubicle. It was warm. Stuffy. A camera mounted in a ceiling corner recorded her conversation with Douglas Pollard, the man who had reported Sheree Cantnor missing. Slouched in the molded plastic chair on the other side of the table, he was sweating, dark circles evident beneath his sleeves, dots of perspiration dotting his high forehead.

Was he sweating from the heat?

Or a case of nerves?

Probably a little of both.

Though he had reported Sheree Cantnor missing, it wasn't inconceivable that he had killed her. Most violent crimes were committed by someone close, a "loved" one, and so Alvarez handled him carefully and wasn't going to take his story or his alibi at face value. It happened often enough that the person who murdered the victim, after he or she had come up with a solid alibi, was the one who also reported that their loved one hadn't come home. It was a tactic to throw off the police and to show innocence, but most of the time, it didn't work.

"So you and Sheree Cantnor were engaged?" Alvarez was seated at a table across from the distraught man. He was tall with a soft look about him, twenty-six years old with reddish-blond hair that was already starting to recede despite his efforts to comb it forward. His jaw was unshaven, at least for the past few days, and his eyes were a sad brown that matched his uniform. He drove a truck for a local delivery company.

"*Are* engaged. We are engaged." He frowned. "Do you know something?"

No reason to beat around the bush. "You probably heard that we found a body," Alvarez said quietly, then pushed a folder across the table.

He eyed it skeptically, not touching it, as if he expected something to jump out at him.

"We'd like you to tell us if you recognize the woman in the picture."

Biting his lip, he reached forward to flip the folder open. Two pictures of the woman in the morgue were visible. One of her face, the second of the daisy tattoo on her ankle. Pollard's color drained and his chin wobbled. Squeezing his eyes shut, he shook his head and pushed the folder away. "No . . . no."

Alvarez suspected his denial was that she was gone, not her identity, so she asked gently, "Is this your fiancée, Mr. Pollard?"

"Yes," he choked out. "It can't be true." He shuddered and when he opened his eyes, they glistened with tears. "Who did this? Huh? Who the fuck did this?"

"That's what we're trying to find out."

"We?" he repeated.

"My partner, me. Everyone in the department."

He glanced nervously at the mirror, behind which, everyone knew, was a darkened viewing room where Pescoli, the DA, and Blackwater were standing. "What do you want to know?"

"Let's start with when was the last time you saw Sheree?"

"Two days ago. In the morning. Before work." He closed his eyes and screwed up his face. "We fought."

Alvarez's ears perked up. "What about?"

"A stupid argument. Nothing really. She wanted to go visit her family. This week. Just pack up and go, but I couldn't. My job isn't that flexible. She wasn't happy about it as Janine, that's her sister, is due to deliver twins. Any minute." He paused and sighed. "She might even have had 'em by now. Anyway, we got into it and Sheree wanted to talk more, but I left. I was already late for work. We didn't . . . we didn't talk or text all day, which is weird for us, and when I got home, she wasn't there. No big deal, but then . . . she never came home that night and I figured she was just showing me how mad she was."

"She's done this before?"

"Once. Before we were engaged. About a year and a half ago."

"Can you tell me about it?"

He paused again, took in a deep breath, and launched into his story.

He and Sheree Cantnor were high school sweethearts who had grown up together in Utah, but had moved to Grizzly Falls when he'd been transferred to Missoula. They'd been excited for the move, ready to make a fresh start, away from their parents and siblings who inhabited Salt Lake City and the surrounding towns. He'd given her a ring about a year ago on Valentine's Day, and they'd moved the following June after she'd graduated from BYU in Provo. She'd found a job working as a receptionist and bookkeeper for a local insurance agency and they lived in an apartment on Boxer Bluff, located on the hillside. Their one bedroom unit had a peekaboo view of the river. Sheree's job was in a strip mall within walking distance from the apartments.

"She wanted it close by so she could walk to work," he said. "We have a cat and . . . and Sheree likes to get away from the office, you know, get a little exercise, eat lunch at home and play with Boomer. . . ." His voice lost all power as the weight of what was happening, that he'd lost his fiancée, settled over him. "Who would do this? Who?"

"Did your fiancée have any enemies?"

"None. Sweetest girl to walk God's earth." He slumped farther in his chair and eyed the folder as if it were malevolent.

"But you fought."

"Not that often. We . . . we're happy. Planned on getting married around Christmas time. In Salt Lake . . . Oh, Jesus." He seemed about to break down completely so Alvarez nudged a box of tissues closer to him, but he ignored them. "I want to see her," he announced suddenly, his face mottled and red.

"Mr. Pollard—"

"I want to see her," he insisted. "This . . . this could all be wrong." He motioned to the pictures and shook his head. "This woman. She could be like Sheree's twin."

"She had a twin?" Alvarez asked.

"No, no, but like a dead-ringer. And that tattoo. It's stock. Not a big deal." He rubbed a hand over his jaw, scraping the whiskers beginning to show on his jaw. Again he stated emphatically, "I want to see her." He was grasping at straws.

"I have a few more questions," Alvarez began, but he cut her off.

"Don't you get it? I *have* to see her. To be sure." His jaw was firm.

Alvarez saw that he was set on his plan, hoping that there had been a mistake, an error in the photography, a mix-up in the morgue, some ridiculous idea she knew she couldn't dislodge.

She said, "One more thing, then we'll take a break and drive to the morgue."

"What?"

"You said you and Sheree were engaged."

"That's right."

"Did you give her a ring?"

"Of course I gave her a ring. A *diamond* ring. Why? Why are you asking about it? Was the ring stolen?" His mouth dropped open. "Man, that thing cost a fortune. I'm still paying on it." He looked miserable.

"Did it fit her?"

"Yes."

"It wasn't too big? And might fall off?"

"No, of course not. I went to a jeweler and had it sized. It fit perfectly."

"What about her earrings?"

"I don't know. She had lots of pairs."

"Diamond studs."

"Well . . . cubic zirconia. She bought 'em herself. They're not valuable—" He cut himself off and held up both hands. "Doesn't matter. I don't give a damn about her jewelry. I need to see her. I have to." He stood then as if it were decided.

Alvarez got to her feet and glanced to the mirror, a signal to Pescoli as she ushered Pollard out the door.

CHAPTER 12

Pollard stared through the window separating him from the viewing room where the draped body had been wheeled. An attendant pulled the sheet from the victim's face and he got a clear view. His knees buckled and he leaned against the glass as Pescoli grabbed him by the arm. "It's her," he choked out in a bewildered voice.

With Alvarez's help, Pescoli guided him to one of the two chairs placed against one wall. He nearly fell onto the worn seat and dropped his face into his hands. "No no no," he said, then looked up. "Who would do this? Why, oh, God, why?"

"That's what we're trying to find out." Alvarez had found a box of tissues and handed it to him.

He fumbled for a tissue–the last one–and started wiping frantically at his eyes as his head wagged back and forth. "But she was the sweetest, the most loving, the perfect girl." His voice cracked and he buried his face in his open hands again. "Why would anyone hurt her?"

"We're going to need your help to find out," Alvarez told him.

"Mr. Pollard, do you have anyone to stay with you?" Pescoli asked. "A relative? Close friend."

"No. Sheree, she . . . she's . . . she was . . . my . . ." His voice drifted away, and he seemed lost in thought for a few seconds. When he finally blinked and returned to the moment, he said, "I just can't believe this."

Alvarez glanced at the window where the attendant was waiting near the body. With a quick nod she indicated that they were done viewing and the attendant covered the dead woman's face again and rolled the gurney though wide double doors that opened automatically upon her approach. "We'll head back to the station now."

Pollard struggled to his feet and without another glance at the window and the empty room beyond, shuffled behind them, walking as if he were closer to a hundred years old than thirty.

The drive back was almost silent as Pollard, in the rear seat, was alone with his thoughts. Neither Alvarez nor Pescoli wanted to interrupt his newfound struggle with loss and grief.

"Her parents," he said, once they were back at the sheriff's office and he was following Alvarez inside. "I'll have to call them. And her sisters . . . she's got five, you know . . . no brothers." Shuddering against the cold or his own despair, he walked to the office where both detectives showed him back into the interrogation room. Seated in the chair he'd occupied earlier, he was less reticent to talk and he readily wrote down the names of her relatives and friends as well as the cities where they lived. He was fixated on the task, in fact.

Pescoli had seen it before, a way to stave off the terrible truth that a loved one was dead.

"I just don't know all the addresses, but I have their phone numbers." Pollard added those from his contact list and said, "She didn't make a lot of friends here, y'know. Just people from work. Her boss, Alan Gilbert. He's a dick. Had the hots for her. And then Marianne Spelling, no Sprattler. Oh, I don't know her last name, something that starts with an *S*, I think. She and Vickie and Sheree, they all worked in the same room, but different cubicles, you know. They'd all go out for a drink or girl talk or whatever, every now and again. It wasn't really all that often, maybe four times since we moved here, usually like during Monday Night Football. Sheree doesn't drink that much." Pollard wrote down a couple other names of people they knew, from the church they attended sporadically, and the wife of a guy he worked with. "We went out a couple times, to dinner, but Sheree didn't like Angie much. Thought she was stuck on herself or something, but Bob, he's a good guy."

He drew a breath and shuddered.

"Tell me about the engagement ring," Alvarez urged as he finished with the list of people Sheree had known.

"I told you it's a diamond. My grandmother's."

"I thought you said you were paying on it."

"I took out a loan to buy it from my mother. She inherited it and decided that she'd probably sell it before she died and split the money between me and my brother and sisters. I told her I wanted it. I'm the youngest and my sisters already had their own rings. My brother really didn't want it. So Mom had it appraised and it came to about twenty grand. I had some money, but I had to take out a loan on my car for the rest. It was worth it, though," he added. "I surprised Sheree with it last February. Put it in a box of chocolates. She almost bit into it," he admitted, smiling before the tiny grin wobbled and he had to clear his throat.

"Do you have a picture of the ring?"

"Oh, yeah. I insured it. It's valuable." He scrabbled in his pocket for his phone, brought up the picture gallery and spying a photo of himself with Sheree, quickly found another shot of a left hand with the engagement ring visible. "Two karats," he said proudly. "And those, the smaller stones flanking the diamond? Rubies. It's an antique, you know. Sheree, she loves . . . loved it." Before he could dissolve into tears again, he asked, "You think someone killed her to rob her?"

"We don't know," Alvarez answered truthfully.

"Why wouldn't she just give it to him?" he asked. "I mean, if it was her life . . ."

"We don't know what happened," Pescoli said. "We're trying to figure that out, so any help you can give us will help."

"But I can't. Everybody loved Sheree."

"No one was unhappy that you were engaged?" Alvarez asked.

"No." He gave a quick shake of his head as if dislodging an unwanted idea.

"Maybe you had an ex-girlfriend who didn't like it."

"Sheree and I started dating when I was sixteen and she was fifteen. We . . . we were each other's firsts."

"Can you send the picture of the ring to me?" Alvarez asked, offering up her e-mail address.

"I can do it now." He typed onto the keypad of his phone, then said, "There."

"Thanks. We'll need to go over to your place, take your computer and anything of hers that might be of interest."

"Okay." His shoulders drooped wearily.

Two hours later, Pollard had finished calling Sheree's relatives and

Alvarez had coordinated information with the office so that bank, insurance, cell phone, and tax records could be accessed. Pescoli and Alvarez had not only examined the victim's living space and taken her personal computer and iPad but her fiancé's electronic gear, as well. Pollard had offered up passwords and given them Sheree's cell phone number, which he'd admitted to calling "about a hundred times" when she hadn't come home.

They were young and unmarried. There were no life insurance policies, even though she worked for an insurance agency. Just hadn't gotten to it yet, he claimed. Sheree didn't own a car, and she was a renter, so there were no other assets besides her missing ring.

As the detectives were leaving, Alvarez said to Pollard, "We're sorry for your loss."

He looked about to break down again, then stiffened his spine. "Just get the motherfucker bag who did this." He turned and walked into the apartment alone.

Next, the detectives went to Sheree Cantnor's place of business. Armed with a warrant, they approached the twenty-something behind a wide wooden desk and asked for her boss. Pescoli's eye followed a blue carpet that ran behind the receptionist and through a room bristling with cubicles. A one-sided conversation was emanating from the only office, where shades were drawn over the glass walls, but the door was ajar.

"Wait a second, Len," said the male voice inside the shaded box. "I'll call you back. I think I may have a situation I have to deal with here. No . . . no . . . give me five. No big deal."

Seconds later, hitching up his ill-fitting slacks, a man who was as wide as he was tall sauntered out of the office. "I'm Alan Gilbert," he stated, obviously the "dick" that Pollard had mentioned. Also the namesake for the Alan Gilbert Insurance Agency. He was balding and, as if to compensate, had grown a thick, neatly trimmed beard that was just beginning to fleck with gray. Frowning from behind slim glasses, he said, "Can I help you?"

"Detectives Selena Alvarez and Regan Pescoli. We're looking into the disappearance and possible homicide of Sheree Cantnor."

Behind Pescoli a woman gasped.

"Homicide?" Gilbert blinked rapidly. "Oh, holy . . . Sheree didn't show up a few days ago and we've been calling . . ." He looked as if he might actually swoon.

"We'd like to check out her work space and speak to everyone who worked with her," Alvarez said.

"What? Now? Oh . . ."

"We have a warrant," Pescoli said, handing him the document. She asked for someone to box up Sheree's personal things. "We'll also need access to her computer."

He glanced at it unseeingly, still processing. "Yes, yes. Of . . . of course. Uh, there's a conference room in the back." He waved limply at a glassed-in area behind a row of cubicles.

Pescoli glanced at it and saw four different women's heads stretched over their soundproof half walls. Every face showed shock, from the girl barely out of her teens and still wearing braces, to an older woman with a phone headset buried deep in her neat, gray curls.

"I, uh, I have to leave at three," he said, rubbing his broad forehead as if that would help him think. "This way." He walked along a path toward the conference room at the far end, passing by an empty cubicle. "This . . . this is Sheree's."

The small, boxed-in desk was neat with pencils and pens in a cup inscribed with _DOUG AND SHEREE, NOW AND FOREVER_ and a date, presumably of their engagement as they weren't yet married. Pictures of Doug adorned the cloth-covered walls along with a few of them as a couple, a calendar, and various notes and memorabilia.

"I'll be right with you," Pescoli said, stopping to look through Sheree's work space and gather what she thought might aid in the investigation. As she sorted through the personal belongings, she heard one woman softly crying and two others whispering. Sheree, it seemed, had made more friends than her fiancé knew.

By the time Pescoli met Alvarez and Gilbert in the conference room with a faux-wood table, Alvarez had already set up. A recorder was in place, a notepad at her side, and she was asking Gilbert basic questions about Sheree—how long she'd been with the agency, what kind of an employee she'd been, any odd behavior, who were her friends, and who were not.

The interview took less than thirty minutes and the same was true for the women who worked with her, all who happened to be present. After the interviews, in which the detectives learned again that everyone was convinced Sheree didn't have an enemy in the world, they crossed the parking lot to Pescoli's Jeep. Daylight had faded and dusk had begun to creep through the snowy streets. Street lights had winked on, adding a bluish illumination to the coming night, and traffic rushed by, wheels humming, engines purring, most vehicles pushing the posted speed limit of thirty miles an hour.

Once inside the car, Pescoli jabbed her keys into the ignition and threw Alvarez a disappointed look. She suddenly craved a cigarette. "We've got nothing," she said, feeling a little defeated.

"It's early. We haven't begun to dig yet. So the work place was a bust. Maybe there's something on her calendar or on her computer."

Pescoli shook her head, started the SUV, and backed out of the parking slot. She felt her stomach rumble. "Let's grab some coffee. Maybe something to eat. I'm starved."

"Fine."

Pescoli took a detour to the lower level of town located on the banks of the river, then drove to Joltz, her favorite coffee shop, with not only a walk-up but a drive-up window. A blond barista took their orders. Decaf coffee and a raspberry scone for her and just a cup of jasmine tea for Alvarez.

"I got this," Pescoli offered before her partner could dig into her wallet. As the Jeep idled beneath a wide awning covering the order pick-up area, she dug into a space meant for sunglasses where she'd wedged a change purse along with a spare set of shades. She pulled out a couple bills, then rolled the window down as the barista appeared again. Despite the shelter of the roof, a blast of cold wind managed to sneak into the car as Pescoli handed the blonde some cash in exchange for the drinks and a white paper bag presumably holding her scone. "Keep the change," she told the barista, then rolled the window up quickly and handed Alvarez her cup. "God, it's cold."

"Montana. In winter." Alvarez pulled the tab from the top of her cup and tested a sip as Pescoli took a long swallow.

She dropped her cup into its holder and eased the Jeep onto the street. "Yeah, but you know we could still do this same job in Phoenix or San Diego or El Paso or somewhere warmer."

"You'd hate Phoenix."

"Why?"

"Too dry. Too many people. Not your style. San Diego's crowded, too close to the border. El Paso?" Alvarez's eyebrows raised a fraction. "Really?"

"Maybe."

"For sure."

Pescoli rolled to a stop at the light and took another drink, the warm coffee taking off a bit of the chill as the police band crackled.

"So," Alvarez said as Pescoli turned onto the road that wound along the face of Boxer Bluff, the Jeep's wheels bouncing a little over the railroad tracks. "You're wearing your ring again."

"I'm getting married." Pescoli had put the ring on again, but she wished she hadn't.

"What's going on?"

"Oh, I don't know. . . ." Pescoli sighed. "I was talking to my kids and they're less than enthusiastic, but I'm going to marry Santana, crazy as that may be. My third time, and all. I just didn't want to talk about it, so I took the ring off."

"Okay."

"I don't mean with you," Pescoli assured her. "Just everybody else. And with Grayson's death, I just . . ."

"I know. I do," Alvarez said solemnly. "It's so damn hard."

"You got that right. Jeremy's okay with it. He's planning to move out, anyway." As they reached the station, Pescoli waited for a flatbed heading in the opposite direction to pass, then pulled into the parking lot and nosed into an empty slot, her tires slipping into the ruts from an earlier vehicle. "Bianca isn't a fan of the idea. She's made that abundantly clear."

"She'll come around."

"Hope you're right." Cutting the engine and pocketing her keys, Pescoli thought of her daughter's issues. Bianca's preoccupation with her looks, how she was trying to "diet" to fit into the bikini good old Michelle had given her for Christmas, that she was obsessive about her weight. Not good signs.

Luke and Michelle planned to take Jeremy and Bianca on a trip to Arizona or California or somewhere warm enough to sunbathe for spring break. Hence, all of Bianca's concerns about being "bikini ready." There was even talk of a spa treatment before the trip that included manicures, pedicures, facials, and waxing.

"Have you set the date yet?"

"No." Pescoli found the bag with her scone in it, dropped it into her purse, grabbed her coffee cup, and opened the door. Again, the winter weather billowed inside. *San Diego can't be* that *crowded,* she thought. As she slammed the door shut and headed into the building, she said, "It'll be a small thing, though. The wedding. Maybe just the two of us, maybe my kids. We haven't even discussed it. But I've already been to this rodeo a couple times, so it'll be low key."

"Got it." Once they were inside, Alvarez added, "I'll start with the victim's family and associates, friends, enemies—"

"She didn't have any. Remember?"

"Right."

They exchanged a look.

"I'll take the ring," Pescoli said. "It's pretty distinctive, so maybe we'll get lucky and find it in a pawn shop."

"No one has to cut off a finger to get a ring to pawn."

"Yeah, well, we're dealing with a sick bastard."

"Amen," Alvarez said. "I'll fill Blackwater in."

"Good." The less Pescoli had to deal with the new sheriff, the better. She started for her office. Halfway down the hallway, she heard the distinctive clip of mincing footsteps and a few seconds later, Joelle called out, "Detective." Pescoli glanced over her shoulder and caught the receptionist waving frantically to flag her down.

With an inward sigh, Pescoli waited in the hallway while Joelle, black leather heels tapping, ebony earrings swinging in rhythm, approached. "There's going to be a memo later, of course, but I thought you, being as you were so close, should know the memorial service for the sheriff will be a week from Saturday. I know it's a long time away, but because of all the officers from other jurisdictions who might want to attend, the family thought it would be best to wait. That way all the final tests will be performed on the body and"—she took in a deep breath, collected herself—"the service will be held at the Pinewood Center. As I said, there'll be more information on the interoffice memo via e-mail."

"The family?"

Joelle flicked a hand. "Cade and Zedediah, but of course Hattie had a hand in the decisions, too." She looked about to launch into the gossip about Hattie being married to Bart Grayson while supposedly involved with either Cade or Dan, depending on the year, but seemed to think better of it. Her polished lips, in a shade of pale pink, were pursed in disapproval as she clicked back down the hallway in her black heels. With Joelle, there really wasn't any need for e-mail or interoffice memos or even telephones. She spread the word more effectively than any technology. "Sergeant," she was calling as she tip-tapped along the hallway, her sweater billowing like a black cape behind her.

Pescoli stepped into her office, slung her jacket and holster over the hall tree, kicked out her chair, and nearly devoured the scone, which had, she guessed from its dry consistency, been sitting in the case at least one day, maybe two.

She was opening her e-mail, looking over the reports, hoping for a full autopsy on Sheree Cantnor, when she heard footsteps and a familiar voice outside the door to her office.

"You requested this?"

She looked up to find Jeremy standing in the doorway. He was carrying a worn cardboard box with a case file sticker attached that read GRAYSON, BARTHOLOMEW, a case number and dates of the investigation.

"Hi," she said, always a little surprised to see her son, whose hours at the department were few and far between. It hadn't been that many years ago that she'd been afraid he would make a wrong turn and end up working on the other side of the law. "Sure. Just set it there in the corner." She pointed to a space between the filing cabinet and her desk. Then, as he turned to go, added, "Hey, Jer, got a sec?"

He looked pained. "I guess."

"Close the door, would you?" she asked, waggling her finger at the door to the hallway.

Pushing the door shut, he leaned against it. "What?"

"I, uh, I wanted to apologize for last night."

"For what?"

Seriously? Is he that clueless? Maybe. "For what I said about you and Heidi. You've grown up in the past six months or so, seem to know what you want. If you're seeing Heidi, I'm not going to fight it. Your decision."

"It's not a big thing, Mom. I like her, yeah, and you know, we plan to go out when she comes back here or if I go visit her, but that's about it." His face was serious. "She's been through a lot, too. Her folks are splitting up and her sisters are all in college. It's just her and her mom. In a new town."

"I know," Pescoli said. "She's probably grown up a lot, too."

"Yeah, I guess. She's talking about moving out and getting married and—"

Pescoli felt the blood drain from her face just about the same time her stomach did a slow, nauseous flip.

"Oh, not to me, Mom. I mean, I don't think so. But someday she wants to—hey!"

She retched. Unable to stop herself, she grabbed the garbage pail beneath her desk, bent over, and upchucked all over the wrappers and trash already in there.

"Gross." Jeremy gazed at his mother in horror.

"Sorry," she said after spitting a couple times. She grabbed a cold cup of coffee and washed the bile out of her mouth, drinking the foul-tasting concoction down.

"What's wrong with you? I didn't say I was getting married."

"No, no, that's not it," she assured him and almost laughed aloud. "I haven't felt well all morning."

"Have you got the flu?"

"Something I ate, probably." She sensed the blood returning to her face. "I feel better now."

"But"—he motioned to the garbage pail—"God, it stinks."

"Maybe you should clean it up. Isn't that part of your job description?"

"Are you kidding?"

"You think you can look at dead bodies, blood spatter, go to an accident with people barely alive, mangled in their smashed cars, but you can't clean up a little puke?" She was shaking her head. "Better get used to it, Jer. Sometimes deputies have drunks throw up all over them, or do worse in their squad cars, defecating and all."

"I know, Mom, but, this is *my mother's* vomit!"

She did laugh at his obvious disgust. "Not in your job description?"

"No!"

"Okay, okay. I'll handle it. *This* time."

"*Any*time."

Her grin stretched wider. "I was just yanking your chain."

"Geez, Mom, *not* funny!" Swiftly, before she could change her mind, he opened the door and nearly sprang through.

She eyed the mess in her trash can. He was right. The sour odor of vomit reeked, causing her stomach to roil again. She had no choice but to haul the trash to the women's restroom and clean up the mess as best she could.

She spent most of the rest of the afternoon on the phone, calling the local pawn shops and faxing or e-mailing photos of the missing ring, hoping to get a hit. She was only partway through the list that Doug Pollard had provided of people who knew Sheree, when the calls from Utah started coming in. A torrent of them. She spoke with Sheree's distraught parents and three of her five sisters, even a cousin. The family itself was immense and the upshot was no one had left the Salt Lake City-Provo area, nor spoken to Sheree, in the last week before her disappearance. Of course, they all told Pescoli the same thing—Sheree had no enemies, no one even the least disgruntled with her as far as anyone knew. Sheree, it seemed, was an "angel," which was usually the case when someone came to a violent and unexpected end. Less usual were the remarks about Doug and how great he was. Theirs was a perfect match, except, of course, for the parents wishing they'd gotten married before they started living together, but even that ultimate sin was forgiven as Doug was so devoted, such a "good guy."

"Nobody's that great," Pescoli said under her breath before pushing back her chair and checking her e-mail again. Two of the four pawn shops within a sixty mile radius had responded. Neither one had Sheree Cantnor's missing engagement ring.

Maybe it had been fenced. Or kept for a trophy by the killer. Or was still in Sheree's attacker's pocket a thousand miles from Grizzly Falls. *It's early yet,* she told herself. If the maniac who'd done this had his wits about him, he'd wait, but if he needed money fast, for instance in order to score drugs, then he might try to get cash for the ring ASAP.

Then why leave the earrings? Did he know they weren't valuable? And why hack off her finger instead of just yanking the ring off?

Because robbery isn't the motive.

Alvarez was right. It was personal somehow. Cutting off the finger was making a statement to the victim or someone else.

Pescoli glanced down at her own engagement ring and twisted it a little, thinking hard. The earrings bothered her, but she told herself that they were just lucky the sicko hadn't sliced off the woman's ears and stolen them along with the fake diamond studs. Would he have known they were of little value? How? Not unless he was an expert or Sheree, or someone else, had told him so.

Despite the fact that Sheree was "beloved by all," Pescoli wondered who might hate her so much that they wanted to torture her before killing her. Or, had the severing of the digit been postmortem? The case was troubling, that was for sure.

From the corner of her eye, she caught a glimpse of the case file Jeremy had hauled down on Bart Grayson. "Later," she said to the box of notes and evidence reports. Hattie's wild theories about some connection between the Grayson brothers' deaths would just have to wait.

Pescoli had enough on her plate, personally and professionally, to last a couple lifetimes.

CHAPTER 13

Ryder sat in his truck, not running the heater, staring through the windshield and falling snow at the Midway Diner across the street. He'd parked in the shadows, avoiding the pools of light from the street lamps, and every once in a while he turned on the engine long enough to clear the snow from the glass.

It had taken him a few days to find her, but he'd done his homework, whittled down his options by focusing on job opportunities that didn't require too much of a background check, and rooms for rent around the area. He'd also checked out Cade Grayson, who was already involved with another woman, one who had been married to his brother Bart, a victim of a suicide. Ryder wasn't really surprised. Cade Grayson was a love 'em and leave 'em kind of guy, though taking up with his dead brother's wife seemed low, even for the likes of him. So far, it seemed Anne-Marie wasn't in the picture.

Yet.

After learning that this particular restaurant had advertised for a waitress about a week earlier and the job had been filled, Ryder started watching the place. Just today, he'd caught a glimpse of the new hire through the windows. The pudgy waitress with the blond hair and full lips didn't look much like the woman he'd known in New Orleans.

His jaw slid to the side and he had to give her mental kudos for the transformation. The new woman appeared matronly, at least ten, maybe fifteen years older than Anne-Marie Calderone.

Then again she was a mistress of disguise, something he'd

learned the hard way. It had been a slow realization on his part that the woman he was with was more fantasy than reality, but by then, he'd been caught in the pure heat of her, willing to let inaccuracies slide, uncaring that the facts didn't add up.

Idiot, he thought and flicked a glance at the rearview mirror, catching sight of his own gaze. Troubled hazel eyes glared back at him.

The restaurant was closing down. He could tell as the final patrons were leaving, the parking lot thinning out.

Lights were dimming in the diner, and the Sorry, We're Closed sign was visible. Ten minutes passed. He flipped on the wipers again, then cut the engine. Another five minutes and then he saw her, the woman he thought was Anne-Marie, as she headed to an SUV, an older model Chevy Tahoe. He watched her climb inside. The headlights flashed on, the engine sparked to life.

He waited as she drove out of the parking lot, then pulled out when another car was between them, following a couple blocks behind.

The streets of the godforsaken little town were nearly empty, only a few cars moving cautiously around corners or along the storefronts. He didn't bother with headlights until he was certain that, if she had been looking in her rearview, she wouldn't notice him joining traffic about the same time. He kept his truck behind the car between them, a Volkswagen Beetle that had seen better days. When the Bug turned a corner and only the snowy street stretched between their vehicles, he lagged back until she, too, turned off, heading out of town away from the businesses and through a residential district with widely spaced houses on large lots. At one stoplight, two vehicles turned onto the street behind her, pulling between them. One was a bulky delivery truck and he couldn't see around it for a time, but it turned onto a side street. The other was a smaller compact that didn't block his view and he could easily keep her in his sights.

Eventually the compact turned onto a residential street but Anne-Marie kept on, leaving the residential district and turning onto a county road that wound its way past farms with large snow-covered fields and into the hills where the farmland gave way to wooded foothills.

He smiled to himself. For once, rather than hide in the throng of a city where she could get lost in a crowd, Anne-Marie had chosen isolation. Her mistake. Though he had to slow down and make certain the curtain of snow between them hid his vehicle, sometimes losing sight of her, it was still better that she was away from prying eyes.

Few cars drove in the opposite direction, nor did he see a glimpse of headlights in his side mirrors. The snowfall became thicker, visibility lessening. As he crested a rise, he caught a glimpse of red taillights, burning brighter for a second, then the road dipped again and they disappeared. When he reached that next hillock, the lights were nowhere to be seen. He hit the gas and drove a little faster, hoping to close the distance, to catch another glimpse of her. As he rounded a corner, he expected to see a hint of red through the thick snow, but there was nothing. Just curves and bends making it difficult to speed in that section of the forest. Gritting his teeth, he pressed down on the accelerator, feeling his tires slip a little as the truck rounded the sharper curves. Still, no hint of her Tahoe.

He drove another four miles, but had the sinking sensation that she'd gotten away.

"Damn it," he muttered, traveling another mile even faster, his tires struggling for purchase. Finally, he realized he'd lost her. He ground his teeth. Rather than drive endlessly on the road, he turned around in a wide spot in the road and with the wipers flicking off the snow, retraced his tracks. No cars met him on the way back. The woods were dense, only a few lanes veering off the main road. He slowed when he thought he'd come near the spot where he'd seen her brake lights flash, squinting into the darkness, searching the snow pack.

The ditches on the sides of the road were buried, brush barely visible in the mounds of icy white powder. There were no mailboxes. He'd thought he'd lost her for good when he noticed a drift and then another, realizing that they were actually ruts in the snow, fresh tire tracks, with only a trace of fresh snow covering them.

Bingo, he thought but kept driving, making note of the landmarks, a split tree across the road, the snag knifing upward, and a huge boulder about a hundred feet closer. He also pressed the button on his odometer so he could track the distance to his room at the River View, then he made a note of the location on his GPS and cell phone. He'd come back once he was sure that she was at work. There was no reason to confront her now.

Not until he was certain that she was, indeed, Anne-Marie.

He had work to do.

"I really have to go," Pescoli said. She was lying in Santana's arms, his naked body spooned against hers in the downy folds of a sleeping bag in the master bedroom of their new, unfinished house. The musky scent of their recent lovemaking still hung in the air and perspiration was evaporating on her skin.

He gazed out the French doors to the night beyond. It was peaceful there. Serene. Snow falling, the lake a mirror, the world and all its problems seeming far away. "I'd argue with you, but I've tried that before."

"And?"

"I'm not saying you're mule-headed . . ."

"But," she prodded.

He chuckled deep in his chest, kissed the back of her head.

"So you *are* saying it."

"Maybe."

Twisting in the bag so that she faced him, she said, "So . . . there's something I need to tell you."

"Shoot."

His eyes, dark with the night, held hers. Unflinching. His lips had twisted into that sexy smile that had a way of burrowing into her heart.

"I'm pregnant." She let the words hang in the air and the silence was suddenly deafening.

He was still as stone. "You're kidding."

"As serious as I've been about anything in my life." Clearing her throat, she added, "I haven't been to the doctor yet, but I took an in-home test a while back and then, of course, three more. They all turned out positive. We're going to have a baby."

His gaze searched her face and she knew he still didn't believe her. They'd been lovers for years and had always been careful. Though they'd never discussed children, the unspoken understanding was that they weren't going to be parents, at least for the present. All that had changed, of course. For a second, he didn't say a word. She was aware she was holding her breath and her heart clutched.

Finally, he said tautly, "You mean it?"

"I wouldn't make this kind of bad joke. I'm having a baby; it's a fact. I know it's not ideal, but it happened. I didn't plan it, but I realize some people aren't cut out to be parents and—"

"Whoa. Wait a sec. Give me a minute to catch up. Okay?" He was staring at her in wonder. "You're for real?"

"Yes. For real. Near as I can tell, I'm due late summer, or probably early fall."

"I thought you didn't want any more kids." He pulled her into a sitting position, the sleeping bag falling open.

"I don't know how I feel. My kids are nearly grown and though it's been great, it's also been a pain and now . . . just when they're about out of the house . . . to start all over? With diapers and breast feeding and late night feedings, and then toilet training and preschool and bratty friends and snooty mothers, most of whom are fifteen years younger than me?" She shivered and pulled the sleeping bag over her bare shoulders.

He froze. "Are you saying you don't want the baby?"

"No, no, of course not! But you and I never discussed kids. You had a hard enough time getting me to say I'd marry you, and now we're talking about sleepless nights and colic and teething and bottles, then baby food. It's been so long since I've been through it, it's probably all changed."

A slow smile was spreading across his jaw, his teeth white against his skin in the half-light, his arms surrounding her more tightly. "You're sure?"

"Four pregnancy tests. *Four*. I wasn't going to tell you until I was certain."

He suddenly grabbed her shoulders and kissed her again. Hard this time. "This," he said once he lifted his head, "is the best damn news I've ever had."

"Really?"

"Yes."

She held him at arm's length. "Honestly? I just want to make sure. If you don't see yourself as a father, if this isn't what you had planned for your life . . . Raising kids is a major responsibility, and I—"

"What do I look like?" He was grinning like a fool.

Her heart soared. "Happy?"

"Very happy. God, Pescoli, I'm stoked. What do I have to do to show you, run outside naked, whooping in the snow?"

"That I'd like to see," she said.

He kissed her, his arms wrapping around her shoulders and dragging her close. Sighing, she let her worries slide away.

"We need to get married," he said. "Soon."

"Don't worry, my father's not around and I don't even know if he ever owned a shotgun. It's not as if this is the first time this happened. You'd think by now that I would know how to keep this from happening."

"You do."

"What?" She hit his chest.

"I'm just saying that at some level we both wanted this without saying so, and we became less vigilant. And I'm glad. I love you," he added gently.

"Hmmm," she said, mollified. "Wait until I'm eight months pregnant and big as a whale or when we're at a soccer game for Little Santana and they think I'm the kid's grandma."

"Football, and you'll be the sexiest damn old lady rooting on the sidelines."

"Nice," she mocked.

"I've always had a thing for older women."

"You're digging yourself a deeper and deeper hole, you know."

"Why don't we elope?" he suggested. "This weekend."

"Nope. I still have to tell my kids. Once you have your own, you'll understand. I hope. And I don't want to leave until after Grayson's funeral. That's a week from tomorrow."

"Immediately after, then. Las Vegas. No arguing."

"This isn't my first rodeo, you know. The first couple times I said 'I do' didn't turn out all that great."

"Third time's a charm."

"What an optimist." But she was smiling.

"Come on, Regan. Take a chance on me. On us. You've already said, 'yes,' and are wearing the ring again—glad to see it—so let's just do this thing." He was so sincere, her heart nearly melted.

"It's a matter of timing, that's all." She thought about the cases that were outstanding, especially Sheree Cantnor's murder, then decided she, too, deserved a life. After all, she was going to be a mother again. "Just let me get through the funeral and take care of a few things, including telling my kids, then . . . then it's a go." She said the words and felt a little trill of excitement. Or was it trepidation?

"I'm holding you to it." His grin was a devilish slash of white.

"All right, Santana," she finally agreed and he gathered her close. Nose to nose, they smiled at each other in the darkness.

The next morning, Ryder waited in the snow flurries outside the Midway Diner until he saw the Tahoe drive into the customer lot at the front of the building. The SUV bounced a little at the curb where the snow was piled high, then disappeared beyond the building to the employee parking area around back. It was early, not quite six and still dark outside, but he recognized Anne-Marie through the glass as she appeared inside the restaurant a few minutes later. Her wig was in place as was the extra padding, hiding her figure enough that she had a little trouble tying her apron around her thickened waist.

Itching to move, to sneak to her vehicle and plant a small GPS device, he forced himself to wait. He'd seen the owner, two waitresses, and a couple of cooks show up, then finally another girl who worked as a busboy. Usually a kid in a souped-up Accord was the last to arrive and Ryder wanted them all inside before he started near the Tahoe.

A few minutes later, he heard the sound of after-factory exhaust pipes ripping through the winter air as the kid wheeled into the lot, his car nearly taking flight over the berm of ice and snow, the bass from his radio so loud it throbbed.

That should be it, Ryder thought. He gave the kid five minutes to get into the parking lot. Still, he had to be careful. The security lamp was illuminated and with all of the snow, the darkness was incomplete. Nonetheless, once he caught a visual of the Honda's driver tying on an apron and working at the service counter, Ryder climbed out of his truck. Staying to the shadows, he walked down a side street, then through an alley, and landed at the Dumpster behind the restaurant.

The back door was closed, thankfully. With one eye on the building, he slipped between the parked cars and tucked the tiny device on the undercarriage of Anne-Marie's SUV.

Headlights flashed, the beams washing over the Dumpster.

He froze, his heartbeat accelerating. For a second, he thought he'd missed an employee and would get caught.

Crap. How would he explain himself?

Fortunately, the beams disappeared quickly and he realized that the flash of illumination was from a vehicle turning into the front lot, a customer who'd shown up before the diner was open.

About to leave, he took a step toward the alley when the back door of the diner opened suddenly.

Ryder ducked down, hiding behind the Dumpster, certain he'd been seen. *Damn!*

Footsteps trudged through the snow.

"Shit, fuck, damn! Goddamn bitch," a male voice growled as the lid of the trash bin creaked open. Then, a falsetto voice, "Marlon, take out the garbage. Marlon, get your butt in here. Marlon, do this. Marlon do that!" *Thud.* Something landed on the metal bottom, then the lid slammed down so forcefully it clanged and the entire Dumpster shuddered. "Fuckin' goddamn bitch," he said again.

Ryder didn't so much as move a muscle. Getting found out wouldn't be good.

"Wish I could throw your scrawny ass out with the trash!"

Noiselessly, barely breathing, Ryder waited, listening hard as snow collected on his shoulders and hat. He heard Marlon's heavy footsteps thump through the snow and fade away, then the sound of the back door creaking open to slam shut again. He held fast, mentally counting to thirty before he peeked over the top edge of the Dumpster to assure himself he was alone.

The parking area was empty and all of Midway Diner's employees appeared to be inside. Quietly, he made his way through the alley and eventually to his truck parked in the shadows.

Inside the cab, he took a deep breath as he watched another car drive into the lot. He stared at the diner's front windows, waiting for another visual of the woman he presumed was Anne-Marie. As a pickup signaled to turn into the diner's parking area, Ryder witnessed the blond waitress flipping the COME IN, WE'RE OPEN sign as the early birds, dressed in heavy jackets, boots, and caps, jonesing for their morning cup of joe, started bustling inside.

Time to make tracks.

For the next few hours, the diner would be busy with the morning rush and he'd have time to hook up equipment at the cabin in which he assumed she resided. He drove out of town and into the hills, his own GPS as his guide, until he saw the snag and boulder and on the other side of the road, a lane with obvious tire tracks. He kept going, drove to the next opening in the trees where a broken down gate with a faded PRIVATE PROPERTY, NO TRESPASSING sign had been posted. He made short work of the gate, breaking the rusted lock and pushing the creaking metal gate inward. Ignoring the warning, he drove through. There were no tracks on the snowy land, so he drove cautiously through the opening in the trees, but, of course, he had no idea how far it wound or where the residence, if there was one, was located. Also, he would be guessing that the cottage or cabin or whatever Anne-Marie was using as a hideout was about the same distance from the main road. He hoped that was the case or otherwise he would lose valuable time searching for the place.

Less than an eighth of a mile in, the trees parted to a clearing where a house had once stood. It was a shambles—the roof collapsed, charred boards visible through the snow, a river rock chimney standing but losing stones. One wall with a broken window was still upright, though listing, and the remains of a staircase, about five steps, climbed upward to end abruptly, leading nowhere. Obviously, a fire had destroyed the cabin, the singed branches of a few nearby trees in evidence. Over the rubble, snow had drifted, softening the angles, muting the blackened boards.

Ryder wasted no time. From the bed of his truck, he grabbed his cross-country skis and snapped them on to his boots. Then he clipped his snowshoes to his backpack and slid his arms through the straps. The pack held electronic gear as well as other items he might need.

As dawn broke, a gray light stealing through the trees, snow forever falling, he started moving through the trees, gliding on his skis while using the compass on his phone to make sure he was heading in the right direction. The snow was thick enough to make skiing easy and soon he came upon a fence that was in the same condition as the gate and house, totally broken down and neglected. Without any difficulty, he skied through a wide gap in the mesh. Avoiding fallen trees and sliding over a frozen stream, he wound his way toward where he thought Anne-Marie's new residence might be. It took awhile. He had to double back once but finally caught a glimpse of a cabin through the trees. Carefully, he skied to the secondary row of evergreens surrounding the building and eyed it. No smoke trailed from the chimney, but the snow was mashed in the front of the cabin, multiple sets of tracks making ruts in the snow. The curtains were drawn, but it seemed as if no one was inside. He traded the cross-countries for his snowshoes and, after breaking off a low hanging hemlock branch, he trekked across the shortest expanse of cleared area to the back of house. After dumping his backpack onto the porch, he worked quickly, using a pick to open the lock, then took off his boots, and in his stocking feet, let himself inside.

The cabin was crude. Just the barest of essentials.

Quite a come down for the princess.

The ancient cottage had none of the creature comforts she was used to. Located in this frigid section of the Bitterroots, her new, if temporary, residence was a far cry from the manicured lawns, graceful verandas and wide, magnolia flanked porches of her New Orleans home. No fancy paddle-fans that moved the warm, sultry air of Louisiana, no white pillars or brick facades of the genteel Southern manor she was familiar with.

Nuh-uh. Just bare bones, and crappy bare bones at that.

No time for comparisons, he reminded himself, so he went to work. Quickly. Efficiently. The first order of business was to rule out that she'd set up her own security system. With a trained eye, he searched for any electronic equipment but found nothing. Next, he unfolded a small plastic sheet onto which he put all the pieces of his electronic equipment so that none would get lost. Then, he went about setting up tiny cameras and recorders, hiding them expertly. His training in the Special Forces served him well. Lastly, he hid the wireless transmitter. Military grade, it would broadcast to his receiver in his room at the River View.

Less than an hour after he'd arrived, he packed up his tools, walked out of the cabin, and relocked the door behind him. He stepped into his boots and after making certain the porch looked undisturbed, backed out within his original footsteps, using the hemlock branch to sweep them away. But if she returned in the next few hours, and there wasn't enough time for the snowfall to obliterate the tracks, Anne-Marie would realize someone had been at her cabin and she'd bolt again. However, he was betting on the snowfall and her shift at the diner keeping her busy until long after his tracks had disappeared. His plan was far from foolproof, but it was the best he had.

At the edge of the woods, he traded his snowshoes for skis and again whisked away his tracks with the branch until he was a hundred yards or so into the forest. Then he took off, skiing rapidly next to his own ruts and reaching his truck quickly. He threw his gear into the bed of his Dodge, turned the pickup around, and drove to the main road where he stopped to relatch the gate. Thankfully no one drove by as he was securing the place, and he only hoped that Anne-Marie didn't miss her turn-off and happen to drive past this lane as she might notice that the snow had been disturbed.

If so, she'd run like a rabbit.

But this time, he'd be right on her tail.

CHAPTER 14

"You're getting married? Like, *soon*?" Jeremy asked, dumb-struck. He was pulling a carton of orange juice out of the re-frigerator.

"In the next couple weeks."

"Why?" Bianca had come out of her room at her mother's request and was as shell-shocked as her brother. "You can't."

"Why not?"

"But . . . but . . . is *he* going to live *here?* Because I'm not moving!" Her little face was set and she tossed her dark curls away from her face. Blue eyes thinned suspiciously. "Why *now?*"

Here came the lie. At least a partial lie. "Because life is short. That really came home to roost this past week or so."

Jeremy let the refrigerator door close. "Because of Sheriff Grayson." He took a big swallow from the carton.

"Glass, please," Pescoli said automatically.

"Don't talk about that. Too depressing," Bianca said with a shud-der. She was dressed in skinny jeans and a sweater that hung off one shoulder, showing the strap of her black bra.

"It is depressing," Pescoli agreed.

"You're getting married and he's moving in here?" Bianca flounced into a kitchen chair. "This sucks."

"No one's moving anywhere yet. Santana and I haven't even talked about that part yet. We just decided the other night. We're planning on going to Vegas in a week or so. Depending."

"Are we, like, invited?" Bianca asked, her ears perking up at the mention of Sin City.

"I haven't got that far yet."

"It's your wedding, Mom!" her daughter declared.

"My *third* wedding. Not to put too fine a point on it."

"Well, it wasn't like I could go to either one of the first two because I wasn't born yet," Bianca said. "Jeremy got to be there when you married Dad."

"He was a toddler," Pescoli said at the same time Jeremy drawled, "Like I remember it."

Bianca lifted a shoulder and had to adjust the wide neck of her sweater. "Maybe it would, you know, make it suck less, if we were there."

"I'm not going to be blackmailed into this," Pescoli said. "If I decide it's the right thing to do, then we'll work it out. As I said, we'll all move in together once the new house is ready." She thought of the construction. "It'll be awhile yet. At least a month, maybe two, but probably three. It's not as if you haven't been expecting this. Haven't I been telling you to go through your things and start thinking about moving? How far have we gotten with that?"

"I'm *not* moving there." Jeremy finished off the juice and crushed the carton in one hand. "I'll get my own place."

"Good. I'll live with you," Bianca announced.

"Yeah, right," Pescoli said dryly.

"I'm almost seventeen!"

"Precisely."

"You just don't care what I want," Bianca huffed.

Refusing to be baited, Pescoli nodded. "That's right. I've never put your needs before mine in the last sixteen years."

"You don't understand!"

"Probably not."

"Do you know you're like . . . impossible?" Bianca charged, so angry she was nearly spitting, "It really doesn't matter because I'm moving in with Dad and Michelle. *They* want me."

Pescoli just looked at her daughter. They'd had this argument before. Dozens of times, Bianca had angrily threatened to move out and live with Lucky and his second wife. Though the hot argument always ripped out Pescoli's heart, she'd learned to play it cool and keep her reactions to a minimum. "I think you should give living with Santana and me a chance. You could love it."

Bianca rolled her eyes. "Mom, I don't like him and I never will, okay? So don't get this super romantic idea that we're going to live like some big loving, *blended* family."

Pescoli slid a look at her son, who was leaning against the breakfast bar that separated the kitchen from the eating area. "I thought you might want to live in the apartment over the garage. Well, it's not really an apartment with all the bells and whistles, but it's big, kind of a bonus room with its own bath. If you wanted, you could take in a microwave and minifridge. It even has its own separate entrance."

Jeremy asked, "That's cool with Santana?"

"It will be."

"I thought you said it was going to be his office."

Pescoli lifted a shoulder because she wasn't really certain. "We can move things around. Besides, it wouldn't be forever."

"If Jer doesn't want it, I'll take it," Bianca said, seizing what she perceived as a prime opportunity to assert her independence.

"How would that work? You'd commute from Lucky and Michelle's?" Pescoli asked.

Bianca glared at her mother. "I'd live there, as you well know. In the apartment over the garage."

Pescoli shook her head. "But not for a few years."

"That's just not fair!" Bianca actually stomped a bare foot and marched back to her room, slamming her door behind her.

"Sixteen going on twelve," Pescoli muttered.

"Give her a break," Jeremy said, opening the refrigerator again and finding some deli meat. He sniffed it, deigned it good enough to eat, and slapped it on a slice of bread that he'd left on the counter. "It's not easy, you know."

"I know. It's not easy for me, either, but it's going to happen. I want it to happen."

"Okay." Jeremy dug deeper into the fridge and pulled out a jar of mayo. He quickly slathered one slice of bread, then squirted a thick dollop of some kind of hot sauce onto the meat. "It'll be cool."

She eyed her son as he grabbed a butcher knife from the block near the stove and sliced his sandwich into two thick halves. "Yeah?"

"Uh-huh."

"Wish I could believe you," she said on a sigh.

"You can."

"What, are you suddenly clairvoyant?"

"Yeah, me and what's her name? The nutcase who talks to ghosts."

"Grace Perchant, and we don't call her a nutcase."

"Since when?" He eyed his mother, almost daring her to argue.

"Plate!" she yelled and he rolled his eyes, but pulled a plate from the already-opened cupboard and transferred the sloppy sandwich onto it. "What about some vegetables on that."

"Mom . . ."

She lifted her hands in surrender. She knew she was one of the worst offenders when it came to nutrition, although that was going to have to change, too.

"Give Bianca some space. Y'know? She'll come around." He picked up a thick, dripping half. "If she doesn't and moves in with Lucky and Michelle, who cares? It's not the end of the world. Isn't that what you always say?" He smiled as he threw her words back at her, then took an impossibly large bite.

She didn't argue, because he was right, even though it burned her to think of Michelle parenting her daughter. But she'd given her kids a lot to swallow, so she bit her tongue. She figured it was time to let the news of her impending marriage settle in and Jeremy and Bianca find a way to deal with it.

Jessica's feet throbbed, her back ached, and she was fighting the pounding in her head as she drove along the mountain road to her newfound home. Working a double shift was well worth it in tips, but her body was rebelling. She envisioned a magnolia scented bath, thick towels, luxurious shampoo, and the open doors to a shaded veranda where a pitcher of iced tea was waiting.

In another lifetime.

She checked the rearview of her Tahoe, but the street was empty aside from the ever-falling snow. Would it never let up? Enough of the icy flakes had fallen and piled by her drive that it was nearly impossible to see her tracks and she almost missed the turn-off. Again.

One last look in the mirror, then she cranked on the wheel and guided her Chevy through the trees to the clearing and the little ramshackle cabin. Wearily, she locked the SUV and unlocked the house that was dark and nearly as cold inside as out. Closing the door behind her, she stood in the living room for a second, listening. She left the rooms in darkness for a second, hearing the drip of a faucet and the whistle of the outside air as it swirled down the chimney and rattled the window panes. Normal sounds. Noises she'd gotten used to.

She snapped on the lights, one room after another, checking to see that the house was still secure, assuring herself that she was, at least for the moment, safe.

So why did she have the nagging feeling that something wasn't right? That there was a disturbance in the air?

Because nothing is right. Nothing has been for a long time. Why else would you be on the run, hiding out in this isolated cabin? How long are you going to keep running?

As she'd dragged herself from the banks of that muddy river months before, she'd told herself that she just needed a little time to pull herself together, to go back and face the music, to end this.

Before he found her.

God, what a mess. Yanking off the wig, she dropped it onto the couch, then clicked her dental appliance from her mouth. Stretching the muscles of her face, she unpinned her hair and shook it free, then started working on the dress and padding. When she was naked, her clothes folded, she took a quick shower, never really getting rid of the chill as the water was lukewarm at best.

She toweled off and pulled on fresh underwear and sweats. Tomorrow, in between her shifts, she'd need to drive into town to the Laundromat she'd used once before to clean her uniforms and to take care of other errands.

Then, she determined, she would finally look up Cade Grayson. From the gossip in the restaurant she'd pieced together that the sheriff's funeral was still a week in the future and she couldn't wait any longer. Not when she felt as if she still wasn't safe.

You're paranoid.

He won't find you here. He can't. . . .

But she wasn't convinced. There were still rumors about the corpse of the woman found on the O'Halleran farm, a woman named Sheree Cantnor, being mutilated in some way. That in and of itself wasn't enough to convince her that he'd found her, but then she knew him and also knew what he was capable of. For the love of God, she'd fancied herself in love with him once upon a time. Even gone so far as to marry him.

Naive fool. He'd never loved her, had only been after her money, but still believed he'd possessed her. That she had no longer wanted him, had no longer wanted to be one of his possessions, had brought out his rage, the depth of his depravity and cruelty.

Her stomach quivered at the thought.

She had trouble believing that he would go so far as to murder an innocent woman. The idea was beyond far-fetched. Surely he wouldn't kill someone else just to terrorize her. No no no. That didn't make any sense.

It's not about you. That woman, Sheree Cantnor, is the one who suffered. Don't turn this around.

Still, Jessica's skin crawled and she felt unseen eyes upon her, as if he were watching her. She double-checked the locks and latches, making certain any possible way into the cabin was secure. She adjusted the shades and curtains, blocking out the chance that anyone could see into the small rooms.

You can't keep running. You can't go on hiding. You have to go to the police.

And tell them what? They'll only think you're crazy. Even you doubt your own sanity at times. They will not keep you safe. No one can.

Disgusted, she flopped back onto the poor excuse of a couch.

Somehow, someway, the madness had to stop.

This place is no-damn-where.

Calypso Pope drove through the frigid streets of Grizzly Falls and wished she'd never taken the detour off the freeway. On her way to Missoula, her coffee had kicked in and not only was she a little hyped up on caffeine, her bladder was stretched to its fullest, which was such a pain. She drove past the brick courthouse and noted that the buildings along the waterfront were at least a hundred years old and the parking spaces weren't only narrow, but nearly nonexistent. It seemed everyone in the hick town must be out for the night.

"Come on, come on, come *on*!" she muttered, shutting off the radio in irritation as the song she'd been listening to faded out into a cluster of static. She considered heading back to the main artery into town when she spied a neon sign for a restaurant called, oh so quaintly, Wild Wills. "Ugh."

She saw a parking spot on the street. Unfortunately, so did the driver of a huge Hummer or whatever they were called, some long-ass rig that hung out into the street and nearly swiped the cars on either side of him.

"Bastard," she muttered under her breath, circling the block to come upon a street that led to the edge of the river, an alley almost, and two blocks down found an area under a bridge that was posted NO PARKING.

Oh, hell. Who cares? She'd just run into the damn restaurant, use the bathroom, and get something to go, if that. Maybe another coffee.

She nearly slipped getting out of her Mercedes and had to catch herself. Swearing silently, she tucked her purse under her arm, remotely locked the car, and hurried carefully along the dimly lit alley to Wild Wills.

Once inside, she nearly peed herself when she came face-to-face with a huge grizzly bear, standing upright, its long teeth pulled back in a snarl, its glass eyes glittering angrily. It was stuffed and dressed in a ridiculous Cupid outfit complete with glittery wings and a quiver filled with arrows that had red hearts rather than feathers stuck into the shafts. Worse yet, the huge creature was swaddled in a pink diaper and a bow had been propped into one clawed paw.

Whose dim idea was that? "Your bathroom?" she asked a tall girl with a ponytail and a sour expression who was standing at the hostess station.

"It's just for customers."

"I plan on being one. And, if you don't want me to pee all over your floor in front of that ridiculous creature"—Calypso jabbed a long finger at the bear—"you'll point me in the direction." At that moment, she saw the sign with the little cut out woman in the dress indicating the women's room. She didn't bother explaining further and barreled down the short hallway, with the pissy-faced hostess calling after her.

"Hey! Wait!"

Calypso ignored her. *Please don't let it be occupied,* she thought, pushing against the broad panels. She breathed a sigh of relief as the door swung inward and, just in time, she dashed into one of the two empty stalls. "Thank-you, God," she whispered as she yanked down her jeans and thong in one swift movement, then relieved herself.

She almost sighed in ecstasy as the sensation was as close to orgasmic as she'd ever want to feel in a public restroom.

Once she'd cleaned up and regained some of her dignity, she walked back into the foyer where the damn bear seemed to be leering at her.

"As I said before, I'm a customer, and now I'd like dinner," she said with a haughty lift of her chin.

"Right this way." The hostess led her to a table in a cavernous room where stuffed animals abounded. A moose head and a stalking puma graced one wall; antelope and deer faces glared down at her from another. A porcupine was balanced on a shelf to her right, while wagon wheel chandeliers and paddle fans hung from the wide expanse of ceiling.

"This place is beyond rustic and weird as hell," she observed, sliding into a booth. She was relieved to see that no family with a raft of little children was seated anywhere near her. "I mean, seriously, dead, dusty stuffed animals don't exactly spark one's appetite."

"People seem to like them," the hostess said as she slid a menu onto the table.

"No one from PETA, I bet."

The girl looked lost. "From where?"

"Never mind."

"Would you like to hear the specials?"

"Sure," Calypso said and slid her reading glasses out of her purse to scan the menu quickly while half-listening as the girl mentioned something about monkfish and wild trout and . . . *God, did she actually say* reindeer? A shiver ran through Calypso.

Scowling as she read the menu, she was about to say something about the taxidermy and putting dead animals on display being so nineteenth century and totally un-PC, but the hostess had disappeared. "How rude," she muttered under her breath, then checked her cell phone, searching for a message from that jerk Reggie.

Another girl, one with a smile plastered to her young face which indicated she, at least, had learned the valuable lesson about customers and tips, slid a water glass onto her table. "Did Tiffany tell you about the specials?" she asked.

"If Tiffany was that sour-faced hostess, then, yes, she did, but I'm not interested in reindeer for God's sake. What's wrong with you people?" Calypso asked, setting her phone down after one last peek. "And this," she indicated the menu with a flip of her wrist to point at the plastic-covered sheets. "You're a little heavy here on the meat, aren't you?" She gazed over the half lenses of her glasses. "I mean, do you have anything remotely vegetarian or whole grain or healthy? Or gluten-free? Something that won't send my cholesterol into the stratosphere?"

The girl opened her mouth, closed it, and finally said, "All . . . all of our entrees are—"

"Oh, forget it. Just get me a cup of coffee. Black. Wait. Is it Starbucks?"

"No. I'm sorry, we use—"

"Doesn't matter," Calypso said, sighing through her nose. "Just bring me some skim milk with it. None of that powdered shi—stuff, okay? That's nothing but chemicals, and I won't drink it. I'm talking real milk. Make sure it's not one percent!" She thought about ordering her usual, a house salad with balsamic vinegar dressing, but it didn't sound appealing in the least, despite her need to always diet. Oh, what she wouldn't do for a slight case of bulimia, slight being the operative word.

She glanced around the room at the stuffed beasts again, noticing a long-whiskered bobcat posed on a ledge as if ready to pounce on a ring-necked pheasant. *Oh, God, soooo barbaric!* Then she saw the slowly spinning pie case located on the counter and her stomach nearly rumbled. Chocolate. Strawberry. Key lime. She couldn't resist. "And a piece of the lemon meringue pie." She needed to indulge. Just a little. "Oh. Wait. Is it fresh? Made with real lemons?"

"Baked this morning," the smiling waitress said. Her name tag read TERI with one *R*.

"Organic, though? Yes?"

"I-I don't know."

Well, at least the twit was honest. Calypso pursed her lips, then reminded herself not to, that she was just begging for those nasty little wrinkles around her mouth. That was the main reason she'd given up smoking. God, she missed that guilty little pleasure. She caught the waitress staring at her. "Oh, okay. The pie will do, I suppose."

"Nothing else?"

"Just the coffee. With skim? Remember?" Then Calypso pointed at her watch. "And I'm in a bit of a hurry."

The girl hurried off and Calypso leaned against the back of the booth to close her eyes for a second. She was fighting a headache again and knew she should eat something more substantial, but really, was that even possible in this den of death? The weird meats that were on the menu, rabbit and pheasant and bison, were probably laced with salmonella or E. coli or God knew what else. She probably shouldn't have any more coffee considering that it was the overwhelming urge to relieve herself that had brought her to this place. Usually, though, she had a bladder of steel and she needed to stay awake for the rest of the drive. It was already pushing eleven. That's why the dining area was shutting down, she realized, though there were still a few straggling customers scattered within the restaurant, most of them lingering over a drink or a cup of coffee and the remains of their meals.

She probably should find a room for the night. She'd been driving for hours as it was and it really didn't matter if she landed in Spokane later tonight or early in the morning, but the thought of searching out a decent, clean, safe hotel in this little burg was daunting. She checked her cell phone for local hotels. *Decent* hotels. Or even damn motels. Maybe she could make it as far as Missoula and then—

"Here ya go." The waitress was back with a cup of coffee, tiny pitcher of milk, and a thick wedge of lemon pie topped with three inches of meringue that Calypso would have loved to plunge her face into as she was suddenly starving.

"Anything else?"

"Not right now," Calypso said and the girl, grin intact, stepped backward, leaving her with a few minutes of heaven as she poured the skim milk slowly into her cup, took a sip and then dug into the scrumptious dessert. "Mmm." She couldn't help sighing, then caught herself as a text message came in. Reggie.

She felt a warming jolt of satisfaction, but thought, *No thanks.*

Reginald Larue didn't know it yet, but they were o-v-e-r.

His text, a sloppy apology for standing her up twice in one week, pissed her off, so she deleted it and turned her phone off so that she could concentrate on the pie. "Sorry, my ass," she said under her breath then put Reggie—*oh, excuse me. Reginald A. Larue III*—where he belonged. Completely out of her mind.

Well, almost.

There was a part of her that wanted to see him grovel, to twist and turn in utter despair over losing her, crawl on his knees to beg her forgiveness. Not that she'd give him another chance. No-effin'-way. She was thirty-six for Christ's sake and though she ignored the tick, tick, tick of her biological clock, she still wanted to get married and have someone else take care of her. She couldn't keep up this pace forever. Yes, she was a corporate attorney and a damn good one, but smart as she was, she wasn't into working sixteen hours out of twenty-four. She'd hoped, actually planned, to find Mr. Right in law school or in the firm she joined in Seattle, but so far it hadn't worked out that way.

She glanced down at her left hand where her grandmother's engagement ring with its huge diamond glittered under the cheesy wagon-wheel lights. She always wore the ring when she was out and, the funny thing was, it didn't appear to discourage men from hitting on her in bars. In fact, sometimes it seemed as if she posed a challenge.

That's how she'd met stupid, two-timing Reggie. Figured. He was probably stepping out on someone else when he'd tried to pick her up. She'd played hard to get until she'd checked him out and found that he was set to inherit a fortune from oil wells. But she knew he would never settle down with one woman, and when she got married, that lucky son of a bitch who claimed her as his bride had goddamn better be faithful. Or she'd have to cut off his balls.

She blinked and realized that she'd been daydreaming again. She'd nearly finished her pie without even savoring every bite. All because of Reggie. She studied the last morsel but pushed her plate aside, then finished her coffee in one gulp. She lifted her hand and signed to the smiley-faced waitress that she wanted her check, then sent a lingering look at the last bit of pie. But no. She always left at least one bite on her plate, no matter how hungry she thought she was. It was a matter of mind over matter.

"Would you like anything else?" Teri asked.

"No. Just the check. I think I mentioned I'm in a hurry."

The girl whipped out the folder with a piece of paper and a pen inside and Calypso handed her a credit card with a mere glance at the bill.

Two minutes later the transaction was finished, and Calypso was heading outside to the wintry streets of Grizzly Falls once more. *Pathetic town,* she thought, winding her scarf more tightly around her neck as the snow fell. She headed back the way she'd come and for the first time since parking illegally hoped beyond hope that her car hadn't been towed. The sidewalk was uneven, her boots slipping a little as she walked, head bent against an icy wind that chilled her to the bone.

Maybe a hotel wasn't such a bad idea after all. Cinching the belt of her wool coat a little tighter, she tried not to notice that the trail of mashed down snow was a little eerie, the back side of the ancient buildings dark, the loading bays empty. Only a few lights from apartments on the upper stories were visible. One streetlight hadn't illuminated and another was fading slowly in and out as if it were soon to die. No other pedestrians were out at this time of night, not even some idiot walking his dog in the damn snow.

Jesus, it's cold.

Following a wrought-iron fence that separated the pedestrian path and the sheer drop-off to the river below, she shivered against a wind that drove icy snow pellets right into her face, stinging her cheeks.

That decided it. She would find a place to stay, a motel close to the freeway. Hadn't she seen one on the way into this funky little town? A Holiday Inn or Motel 6? She'd backtrack in her car, follow the route she'd taken into town, find that motel, grab a room, then take off early in the morning after a hot shower, a few hours rest, and a cup of crappy motel coffee. That would be the smart thing to do.

Another bitter gust.

"God, it's cold." *And nerve-wracking.*

Even the tread of the pathway she was following was beginning to be covered with a thick layer of snow. Worse yet, between the whoosh of the wind and the rushing sound of the damn falls, she couldn't hear anything. Not really a surprise as her aching ears felt as if they were nearly frozen solid. It was as if she were the only person in the arctic world.

Just get to the damn car.

She stepped a little quicker, though she reminded herself there was nothing to be freaked out about. *So I'm alone? So it's weirdly dark? So what?*

Squinting against the harsh wind, she caught a glimpse of her Mercedes parked where she'd left it under the bridge.

Things were looking up.

She hit the unlock button on her remote key and her car's headlights flashed, though, if the lock had dinged, she couldn't hear it. Didn't matter. She just had a few more feet and—

Thump! Thump! Thump!

Her heart nearly stopped.

What was that? What the hell was that?

Footsteps?

Looking over her shoulder, she saw nothing but swirling snow.

Get over yourself!

She was nearly at the bridge.

Thump! Thump!

Adrenaline pumped through her blood and she broke into a jog.

For the love of Christ!

Just a few more steps!

Bam!

Someone torpedoed her from the back!

Her feet slid wildly in the snow and she fell forward, desperately trying to keep her balance.

Impossible. He was too heavy.

His weight slammed her forward. Down she went.

Crack!

Her knees slammed into the icy pavement, pain jarring through her body, her purse and keys sailing into the darkness.

No. Oh, God no!

This couldn't be happening. "Get off me!"

A gloved hand clamped over her mouth and she bit hard, struggling, kicking, fighting the weight upon her back. *Oh, Jesus, he's so heavy!* He drove her face into the snow. Pain ripped through her and she had trouble breathing.

No way! No way was she going to let this fucker harm her!

Wrenching her body, she struggled. Where the hell was another pedestrian, or a business owner locking up or a goddamn *cop*? Her lungs were burning and she thought she might pass out. *No no no!* Twisting, she tried to get a glimpse of him, but all she saw was a huge figure dressed in black, snow dancing around him, his body pinning her mercilessly. "Bastard!" she tried to scream, but her voice was muffled.

"Let me go!" she yelled. Again her plea was only a muted mumble. Fear spurted through her. This jerk wad wasn't giving up. *Oh, God, is he going to kill me? Shit, no!* She struggled, but his thumb pinched her nostrils together, his body pressing her flatter onto the path. Her lungs were beginning to burn. She whipped around, trying to force air through her nasal passage, but it was impossible. *No no no!*

Panic took over, but she was losing strength, her flailing arms more sluggish. It occurred to her that she might actually perish in this godforsaken town with a psycho squeezing the life out of her.

She fought valiantly until the blackness pulled her deep, her arms and legs becoming sluggish and clumsy, not obeying her mind. Her eyes rolled upward and she was vaguely aware of her body growing limp, her appendages useless. The last thing she remembered was being rolled onto her back and seeing the monster above her. In one hand he held something . . . a knife? Before she could make one last attempt to struggle, he grabbed her by the throat again and slowly, deliberately squeezed and squeezed and squeezed.

CHAPTER 15

"We might have caught a break," Alvarez said to Pescoli the minute she walked into her office. Her hair was pulled back into a knot at her nape, gold hoops dangling from her earlobes, and she was carrying two steaming cups. "Decaf." She set that one on the corner of Pescoli's desk.

"Thanks. What break?"

"The autopsy report is back. You've got a copy in your e-mail. Strangulation. Hyoid bone crushed. Not much water or foam in the airways." Alvarez took a sip from her cup. "She was definitely killed first, then tossed into the stream."

Pescoli hung up her jacket and unwound the scarf at her neck. "Not a surprise. And not exactly a 'break.'"

"There's something else."

"Yeah?" she picked up her cup, took a sip, found the coffee hot even if it didn't have a kick.

"Half a mile downstream on the Barstow property, the farmer found a shoe nearly covered by snow. Wedged between some roots."

"You think it's our victim's?"

"Woman's red heel. Covered with prints."

Pescoli was interested. "Sheree Cantnor's?"

"All except one partial which has been run with no hits. But it's something. There's a crew out scouring the area, hoping to find the other shoe, her purse, phone." She rolled a palm upward. "Whatever."

"Maybe a finger and a ring."

"Those, I think he kept."

Pescoli agreed. "Trophies."

"Uh-huh."

She took another sip of the decaf and heard Blackwater walk into his office. *His* office. Not Dan Grayson's. Funny how she'd started thinking in those terms already, funny and sad. "We got anything else?"

"Not really. I did find out that despite Doug Pollard's insistence that he and Sheree were high school sweethearts and their life was all hearts, flowers, and romance, there was an instance where she took up with another guy for a while. She and Doug had their one breakup, I guess. Then that guy landed in prison."

Pescoli looked up sharply, but Alvarez shook her head. "For a B and E. The guy's still doing time in Utah. I double-checked."

Breaking and entering was a far cry from homicide and the guy was incarcerated to boot. "So we're back to the unknown assailant." Pescoli sighed.

"Looks like." Alvarez started walking out of the office but stopped short.

Blackwater filled the hallway just outside the door. His face was set and hard, lips compressed. "Got a call from a deputy at the waterfront. They're pulling a body out of the river, just below the old bridge. A woman." His dark gaze moved from Alvarez to Pescoli. "Looks like you two are up."

"Suicide?" Pescoli asked. Every once in a while, someone took a leap from the bridge, in summer kids who dared each other jumped or dived into the river under the falls despite the postings, and sometimes, when someone decided to end it all, they took that same plunge.

"Unknown." He backed up a step as Alvarez made her way into the hall. "Maybe. Units are already in place, but it sounds like we've already got a crowd, people stopping to rubberneck. Check it out. Report back to me."

A phone rang nearby and Blackwater marched to his office.

"He should have a field day with this," Pescoli said to Alvarez, who was still standing in the hall. "Big splash, you know. Pardon the pun." Pescoli kicked out her chair and reached for her jacket again. "No rest for the wicked. Meet you at the Jeep? I'll drive."

"Yep." Alvarez disappeared into her office to get her coat and within minutes they were in Pescoli's vehicle and heading down the road that cut across the face of Boxer Bluff to the lower part of town. The snow had quit falling, but nearly ten inches had piled up overnight, so the plows were out and traffic was a snarl. They followed a school bus over the tracks before they turned onto the street that bisected the older area of Grizzly Falls. Despite the fact that she'd turned on the flashers and hit the siren, they had trouble making headway due to the traffic snarls. She pulled into the courthouse and parked in a spot reserved for a judge.

"You're going to hear about that," Alvarez said.

"Yeah." They walked the three blocks and threaded their way through the crowd. A television news crew was already on the scene despite the clog of vehicles and pedestrians. Traffic was being detoured around from the old arched bridge, constructed before nineteen hundred. Access to the river's crossing had been cordoned off, two miles farther downstream.

Alvarez showed her badge to an officer as they reached the perimeter of the area beneath the bridge and he motioned them through. Several vehicles were parked along the alley.

Probably from workers who had arrived before the police, Pescoli thought, *or had been left overnight by someone who had consumed one or two too many at one of the nearby taverns.*

There were other cars in the parking lots that serviced the rear entrances of the buildings positioned on the main street—a couple city cop cars, along with those from employees who had already started their shifts. From the back doors of those businesses a number of people were loitering, some smoking, all watching the action as it unfolded. An ambulance had gotten through and it stood by, lights flashing.

"What've we got?" Alvarez asked Jan Spitzer, the deputy who was obviously in charge.

Short, a little pudgy and smart as a whip, Spitzer looked tired, as if she'd put in her shift and was well into overtime. "Female. Caucasian. Already fished out. Thirty-five or so, looks like. Not long in the water. No decomp and, you know, the river's close to freezing over, so the body would be, too, but no fish or whatever had started taking nibbles."

Pescoli looked up to the underside of the bridge, where in warmer weather birds and bats probably roosted. "ID?"

"None on her."

"Distinguishing marks?" Alvarez asked.

"Surgical scar on her abdomen, another on the inside of her left arm, and a couple tattoos—a tramp stamp of hearts and butterflies. You know, the usual. And some kind of tiny hummingbird on her right shoulder, but that's not what's interesting." Spitzer glanced at Pescoli. "Our Jane Doe is missing a finger."

Pescoli's stomach dropped.

Spitzer continued. "Ring finger. Left hand. Sliced clean off."

"Shit." Pescoli exchanged glances with her partner. "So, it's another psycho?"

How many could one town the size of Grizzly Falls have?

Alvarez said, "Let's see."

"Right this way, ladies." Spitzer walked them over to the ME's van where a body bag, blocked from the crowd's view by the bulky vehicle, lay atop a gurney. As Spitzer unzipped the heavy bag, Pescoli felt her queasy stomach give a lurch and she fought a rising tide of nausea.

With a flip of the flap, the dead woman was exposed, supine, fully clothed, water collecting around her.

Pescoli forced back the urge to retch as she stared at the victim. Where there had been makeup were now only smudges. She was thin with a square face and her skin was tinged the bluish-gray hue of death. Her blue eyes were open and seeming to stare upward, her short, streaked hair wet and flattened to her head.

"Doesn't look much like Sheree Cantnor," Alvarez said as if she'd read Pescoli's thoughts.

The victim's hands were already bagged. Hopefully there had been a struggle and there was DNA evidence lodged beneath her nails.

"Any obvious areas where the attack occurred?" Pescoli asked as she looked toward the distant mountains, inhaling and exhaling slowly. Thankfully, her stomach was settling down.

"Near the bridge, it looks like. We found a couple tubes of lipstick and a case for eyeglasses by that section of fence." She pointed to an area not quite under the bridge's span, where snow had drifted near the tall pickets.

"Who called it in?" Pescoli asked.

"Over there." Spitzer, whose walkie-talkie began to crackle, pointed to a sheriff's cruiser.

For the first time, Pescoli and Alvarez saw Grace Perchant, the nutcase who claimed to talk with ghosts and predict the future among her many talents. Pale as a corpse herself, Grace was dressed in a long white coat, gloves, and tan boots. Her graying blond hair was anchored by a knit cap but whispered around her face. At her side were a pair of dogs, both half-wolf, one black, the other silvery gray. On slack leashes, each animal watched the approaching detectives with intelligent, if wary, eyes.

"Hello, Grace," Pescoli said. "Mind if we ask you a few questions?"

"Not at all." Grace gave some unspoken command and both dogs sat, obviously more relaxed.

"You found the body?"

"Yes. I was taking the dogs out. Sometimes we come down here, walk across the bridge. Sheena and Bane love the river, so this morning, just before dawn, I parked across the river, and we walked over the bridge. I didn't notice anything on the way over, probably because I was on the far side of the span. Then, we walked into town and around several blocks down here." She motioned behind her, past the buildings and their loading zones to indicate part of the city between the river and the high cliffs of Boxer Bluff.

"I wanted to take the steps up to the overlook," she said, mentioning a concrete staircase of nearly a thousand steps that wound up the hillside to a point above the river where one could get a bird's eye view of Grizzly Falls. "But it was so cold, we just went a few blocks down here and headed back. The dogs were a little whiny, they both kept trying to look over the railing and then I felt it. You know, a disturbance."

"Disturbance?" Pescoli repeated.

Both detectives had dealt with Grace numerous times in the past. With her dire predictions, she was a frequent visitor to the sheriff's department. Was she accurate in foretelling the future? Probably about fifty percent of the time. But she had made personal predictions about Pescoli and Alvarez that had been surprisingly on the mark—chillingly so. Neither detective could completely discount the self-proclaimed psychic's abilities.

"When I was returning to the car and recrossing the bridge, I was on the other side of the road, on the falls' side of the span. The dogs began acting up. You know, pulling at their leashes and whining, noses into the wind. Bane"—she indicated the bigger dog with the lighter coat—"was all over the railing, trying to get over. I looked then and noticed something floating down by the rocks. It wasn't quite light yet, but I thought it was a body and called 9-1-1." She shrugged, her pale green eyes unreadable.

There was something about the woman that made Pescoli uneasy. Maybe it was Grace's infinite calm despite her predictions of disaster and death, or maybe the aura of peace that she insisted surrounded her. Or maybe it was the fact that she lived alone with two wolf-dogs in the middle of the forest.

You live with two dogs, she reminded herself. *You're often alone now that your kids are always looking for ways to escape. You live and breathe your job and are as isolated as she is in many ways. Yet, you're not weird. Right?*

"I waited," Grace was saying, "And now, here we are."

And where is that? Pescoli wondered, staring at the arch of the bridge backlit by the rising sun, then watching as the body bag was loaded into the ME's van. *Just where the hell is that?*

The buzz in the diner was all about the body that had been pulled from the river this morning, customers chattering and gossiping, bits of information floating in the din of the dining room. Over the clatter of forks, rattle of ice cubes, and gurgle of the espresso machine, the conversation was centered on a second body found in so short a time.

"It just never seems to end," Misty confided to Jessica when both were at the serving counter, picking up orders. "Hey, Armando, this omelet's supposed to come with guac!"

"*Sì, sì!*" he snapped, irritated. He found a dish of guacamole and placed it on the platter. "Where is Denise? I cannot do this by my-self!"

Denise Burns was a fry cook sous-chef. And she was over an hour late.

"She called Nell. Got caught in that mess of traffic near the bridge." Misty surveyed her two platters, then pulled them from the counter. To Jessica, she said, "We've already had one psycho this season and now this."

"You think there's a madman running around?" Jessica asked, eyeing a platter that Armando slid onto the counter. "Wheat toast," she said to the head cook, "not sourdough."

"*Dios!* I cannot work like this!" Armando grumbled just as Denise, in a gust of cold air, walked through the back door.

"Sorry, sorry, sorry!" she said, holding up her hands as if she expected Armando to open fire. "It's impossible to get through town right now. The damn bridge I usually use is closed and all the roads are backed up." She was stripping off her jacket as she came inside and threw her purse, scarf, and phone into her locker. It banged shut as she reappeared, wrapping an apron around her slim waist. "Bring me up to speed," she said to Armando as she twisted her hair into a net and began washing her hands.

After slapping a stack of wheat toast onto the counter, he began reading off the orders to her, rapid-fire.

Jessica carried her platters to a table near the windows where a mother of three kids under six was trying to convince her three-year-old daughter to eat "one more bite" of a barely touched waffle. The baby was picking at Cheerios on the high chair tray, and the third child, around five, was plucking the blueberries out of his pancakes.

"Sorry for the delay," Jessica said, finally delivering the parents their breakfasts.

The mom said, "No problem," though it sounded as if it really was a major inconvenience. The dad didn't look up from his cell phone.

"Can I get you anything else?"

"Catsup," the mother said as her husband eyed his small screen.

"The body they pulled out of the river today was a woman," he told his wife. "There's talk that she might've been murdered."

Jessica's heart lurched.

"We moved here to get away from all of that, George!" the mom hissed. "Isn't that what you said? If we leave the city, life will be safer. Slower paced?"

"Who gots murdered?" the three-year-old asked.

"Nobody. I mean nobody we know." The mom shushed her.

Jessica moved out of earshot, wending her way through the tables, telling herself this latest murder had nothing to do with her. Nothing. It was just partial stories, bad information, gossip.

But throughout the morning shift and into lunchtime she heard more and more about the woman found in the Grizzly River, supposedly first seen by a woman who owned wolves and cast spells, a witch of sorts, if the gossip could be believed. Table after table of patrons speculated about the identity of the woman and if, as Misty had mentioned earlier, another madman was in their midst.

Around ten, a big man came into the diner and though Jessica was certain she'd never seen him before, there was something familiar about him. Within minutes, she realized he was Zedediah, "Big Zed," Grayson, Cade and the fallen sheriff's brother. She steeled herself, wondering if Cade would join the large man, but thankfully that wasn't the case. He was seated in Misty's section, so she didn't have to deal with him.

Others did, however, including Nell, who deigned to come out of the office to offer condolences. She'd been tallying receipts from the day before, balancing them with the payments received. "So sorry for your loss."

"Oh, Zed, a shame about Dan. Such a good man," a seventyish woman with a red beret pinned to her shiny gray hair offered up, her friend nodding solemnly.

"We're gonna miss Dan. Helluva man," a farmer-type put in.

"The town will never be the same," declared another man in a suit.

And so it went for the hour that Zed occupied his chair. He was alone, an unread newspaper spread on the table. He scooped up his paper as soon as he was finished eating, squared his hat onto his large head and, after paying his bill, strode quickly out of the building.

Misty sidled over to Jessica and confided, "That's one of the dead sheriff's brothers. You know, there's a strange thing about him. He doesn't quite seem to fit with the others. Dan was a handsome man, as was his brother Bart, the one who offed himself in the barn. You heard about that?"

Jessica nodded, though she didn't admit she'd heard about the suicide from Cade, years before. Luckily, Misty didn't ask.

"Well, that Bart, he was a looker, too. And Cade . . ." Misty made a big show of fanning herself. "Hot, let me tell you. That cowboy can park his boots under my bed any day of the week. *Any* day. But Zed," she said, watching through the window as the big man made his way to a huge king cab. "He's different. Not just in size being that he's a head taller and got seventy pounds or so on his brothers, but he keeps more to himself. Not as friendly. Almost . . . oh, I don't know, darker somehow. Someone you wouldn't want to meet at night in a deserted alley, you know what I mean?"

Jessica watched Zed put his truck into gear and drive off.

"Oh, maybe I'm all wet. I mean, Zed's done nothing to make me think there's anything wrong with him. It's just that he's so damn different from his brothers." Misty shrugged. "But it takes all kinds, now, doesn't it? Say, would you cover for me for a minute? I need to take five." She was already reaching for the pack of cigarettes in her apron pocket and heading for the back door before Jessica could agree.

Near noon, Jessica learned that Sheriff Blackwater had held a press conference. According to the customers who had smart phones and Nell, who caught it on the office TV, he'd stood on the steps of the department and made a public statement. She'd been too busy to watch the report, but from what she could gather from the customers who'd caught the news, the acting sheriff's speech had been short and concise without any room for questions. The sheriff's department wasn't giving out much information other than that the woman's death was being investigated as a homicide. Her name wasn't being released, pending notification of next of kin.

Jessica went cold inside.

Another woman fished out of a body of water.

Talk of mutilation.

Has he followed me?

She nearly dropped a tray of drinks, she was so distracted.

Quicksilver memories slid through her brain—seeing him for the first time at her parents' home near the river, the smell of magnolia in the air, spring air clear, the cloudless sky a cerulean blue, the murmur of guests as they'd wandered the grounds. His gaze had found hers and she'd sensed then that he was a rogue, a handsome man whose civility was probably only skin deep, that there was more to him to explore.

He'd wooed her easily, his laughter infectious, his kisses promising so much more, his hands on her body exciting and a little rough, but she'd wanted something that would crack the veneer of her family's genteel and oh, so fake civility.

The summer had swept by in dark moonlight nights, hours of pent-up passion, and quick decisions that, in hindsight, had proved deadly—a wedding on the broad lawn under a hot August sun. Sultry air and thick clouds, a storm brewing that had been, as she looked upon it now, a warning she hadn't heeded.

"Jessica?" Misty's harsh voice broke into her reverie. "I think table seven might want those." She nodded her head at the tray of burgers Jessica had been holding, the one that shook in her trembling hands. "Hey, you all right?"

"Fine," she said, swiftly returning to the harsh lights and noisy din of the diner. She didn't bother to explain. Couldn't. She just set about her work, listening hard to the bits of conversation that buzzed through the diner and telling herself that she couldn't take a chance any longer. Whether the woman who had been found under the falls was the victim of his cruelty or not, it was time to take action.

CHAPTER 16

Pescoli eyed her ring, the diamond glittering brightly under the failing fluorescent tubes humming above Blackwater's head in the meeting room attached to his office. Blackwater was presiding over a hastily convened gathering and she'd taken her usual chair, the spot where she'd sat so many times while Grayson had spoken to them. A small group had been called in for a briefing and discussion of the case uppermost on the minds of the citizens of Grizzly Falls. The windowless room felt close.

"Okay, looks like we've got ourselves a serial killer," Blackwater said, standing at the head of the long cafeteria-style table where everyone else was seated.

"Another one," Brett Gage interjected. As the chief criminal detective, he oversaw all cases, and, like Dan Grayson who had been his boss, he gave those under him free rein. At forty, he was only slightly older than Pescoli. A runner who was in great shape, a father of two who had completed four or five marathons—maybe more than that.

"Yes, another one." Blackwater nodded curtly. "And that's not making the mayor very happy. She called this morning and reminded me of the fact that our little corner of the state seems to be a hotbed for homicide. I couldn't argue. She's worried about a mass exodus of citizens and I don't blame her. When we actually confirm that these two victims were killed here in Grizzly Falls by the same person, all hell will break out."

"Again," Gage said, and Blackwater sent him a quick, hard look. Everyone in the department knew that Gage was angling for the vacant under-sheriff job and, apparently, he was determined to make his mark at this meeting. Politics. In the middle of a homicide investigation.

"Right, again. My point." Blackwater wasn't backing down. "So, it's early, I know, but what have we got?"

Alvarez, seated next to Pescoli, said, "We're a little ahead of the game on this one. We know the victim died last night. Sometime between ten and two is the best guess, taking into account the temperature of the water. This makes sense as so far, no one saw or heard anything."

"In the middle of town? Before the bars closed?" Blackwater asked.

"I said, 'so far,' " Alvarez repeated. "Deputies are still checking with the establishments open last night. We also think we might have an ID. There were several cars left down by the waterfront, but one, a late model Mercedes, has Washington plates and is the only vehicle not registered to a local. We checked with Washington DMV. The car is registered to a Calypso April Pope."

"Seriously?" Pete Watershed said, chewing his Nicorette gum with a vengeance. He was the only deputy in the room, called in for some reason only Blackwater understood. "Calypso? Who would name a kid that? Calypso April Pope? Jesus!"

Pescoli shot him an *oh-just-shut-up* look which he ignored.

Alvarez barely missed a beat. "That's the name on her license and the picture looks like our victim."

"Calypso danced her last dance," Watershed said.

Blackwater glared, reminding him, "You're here by invitation. And next time?" His face was set in disapproval, his irritation palpable. "Lose the gum."

Watershed's jaw quit moving and he swallowed hard, his chosen way to dispose of the gum, as Blackwater explained, "Deputy Watershed thought he saw the victim's car earlier, pushing the speed limit around ten last night, but he'd already pulled someone else over for DUI, so . . ."

That cleared up the reason for Watershed's appearance. It wasn't a major connection, but something. Still the deputy, handsome and always thinking he was God's gift to women, bugged Pescoli. She'd been on the butt end of his jokes one too many times.

Alvarez said, "We're trying to find out more about Ms. Pope. So far, no missing persons report has been filed. We're attempting to find any connection between victim one and victim two, assuming they were both killed by the same person."

The meeting went on with plans to call in the Washington State Patrol and, of course, inform the FBI, as it appeared as if they had a serial killer on their hands. There was discussion about procedure and autopsy reports and other details of the crime before the short meeting was adjourned with Blackwater saying, "Let's find this guy. If we can do it without the feds, all the better." Before anyone could protest, he held up a hand. "Hey, if we need them, yeah, work with them. They have access to manpower, equipment, you name it. The important thing is to get our man." With that he scraped his chair back and everyone filed out of the room.

Pescoli was two steps down the hallway when Watershed caught up with her. "So, are congratulations in order?"

"What?" she looked up sharply, her mind zeroing in on her pregnancy.

"Noticed the ring," he said, nodding to it.

She braced herself. Watershed and his ilk were the reasons she'd taken the ring off for a while.

"You gettin' married again?" he asked.

"Yeah."

"To Santana? Jesus, Pescoli, don't you ever learn? A cop, a trucker, and now what? Some goddamn horse whisperer dude? You know, your track record is—"

"My business. Keep your nose out of it and shove it up your ass where it feels at home," she snapped.

"Wow. Touchy."

"Yeah, I am, so maybe you should back off a bit. It's legal for me to carry a firearm, remember."

"Someone's having a bad day. That time of the month?"

If you only knew, she thought angrily. Why did stupid guys always go *there*? She jabbed a finger at his chest. "If you haven't noticed, dickhead, things aren't all that great around here. Not only have we lost one of the best lawmen in the history of the state, but since he's been gone, two women have been killed and we've probably got a brand new sicko running around. Keep your adolescent remarks to yourself and stay out of my way."

"Sheeeit," he said as Joelle came clipping down the hallway, her eyebrows raised over the tops of her reading glasses at the exchange.

"Children, children, children," she chided.

Pescoli growled under her breath, stormed into her office, and started to slam the door, but Alvarez caught it, holding it open. "Why do you let him get to you?" she asked. "He's just a loser who loves baiting women. Don't go there."

"I usually don't."

"Stress of getting married again? Because this stuff"—Alvarez motioned to the piles of paperwork on the desk—"is always here, at some level."

"I guess it is the idea of walking down the aisle again," Pescoli lied. "But Watershed's right, damn it. I'm not all that great at picking husbands." She dropped into her desk chair. "But I'm right, too. It's none of his damn business what I do."

"Amen."

"What a tool." She scowled at the door, then determined she was going to shake it off. "Let's get to work."

Rather than drive all the way home, Jessica peeled off her work clothes in the small bathroom at the Midway Diner after her shift ended at two. She wasn't due back to work until four-thirty, for the early-bird dinner crowd, so she decided to make good on her vow to become proactive.

After changing into jeans and a sweater, then replacing her work shoes with boots, she found her jacket, threw it on, and made her way to her SUV where frost had collected on the windshield. The sun was actually out, beams glistening on the snow, the sky a clear, Montana blue, the day so bright she had to slip a pair of sunglasses onto the bridge of her nose. If circumstances had been different, she might have felt lighthearted; as it was, a deep sense of dread clung to her.

She made one stop at the cleaners located in a strip mall on the outskirts of town. A smiling girl in braces worked behind the counter. After counting and gathering up Jessica's uniforms, she promised to have them ready the next day. "No problem."

Jessica left and slid behind the wheel of her Tahoe again, steeling herself. Facing Cade wouldn't be easy, but lately, what had been?

"Nothing," she whispered as she waited for a slow stream of traffic, four cars behind an older Cadillac that inched through the streets, as if it were rolling through glue.

Finally, she was able to turn down a side street before making her way to the county road leading out of town. Now that she had made her decision to face Cade again, she pushed the speed limit, afraid she might chicken out.

It wasn't all that hard to locate the Grayson ranch. Nearly everyone who had come into the diner had talked about the sheriff's death and how hard it was on a family that had been in the area for generations. Misty, always a fountain of gossip and information, had told her where the Grayson spread was located and Jessica had double-checked on the Internet and the white pages.

As the sunlight bounced off snow-covered fields, she followed the directions on her GPS to the address where an old mailbox confirmed that she'd found the Grayson homestead.

"Here goes nothing," she whispered as she cranked on the wheel and eased her SUV along the long lane that had, at one point, been cleared of snow, piles of the white stuff lining the drive, tracks visible in a newly-fallen layer. Jessica's heart was thudding, her stomach in knots as she considered how Cade would react to seeing her as they hadn't parted on the best of terms. "Too bad," she reminded herself.

Wide fields flanked the lane as it rose to the heart of the ranch where a sprawling ranch house had a three hundred and sixty degree view of the surrounding property. Half a dozen outbuildings had sprouted around the residence, but Jessica zeroed in on a garage, the doors open, one bay empty, another filled with a pickup that was facing outward. Thankfully, Big Zed was gone, or at least his truck was. She needed to talk to Cade alone.

"Now or never," she said, eyeing the rearview mirror and catching the reflection of her oversized shades in the glass as she parked near a path winding to the front door. She cut the engine in a parking area where the snow had been mashed by various vehicles and pocketed her keys.

She hiked her way toward the three front steps that had been cleared of snow, and climbed them to a broad porch where a dying wreath was mounted upon a massive door.

She rapped loudly. Three sharp knocks. From inside, a dog began barking wildly as if his sudden rash of loud woofs made up for the fact that he'd been asleep at the switch, not hearing that a stranger had arrived.

"Shad. Enough!" a male voice, Cade's voice, ordered.

Jessica's heart fluttered. *Oh, dear God, what am I doing?*

The door opened suddenly and Cade, in faded jeans and a flannel shirt that he used as a jacket over a black T-shirt, stood on the other side. He was unshaven and his hair was rumpled, uncombed. He had that outdoorsy *I-don't-give-a-damn* look that she'd always found far too sexy, but she ignored it. Whatever they'd once had, that white-hot spark of years ago, had been extinguished by lies. Her lies.

"Yes?" he said.

A speckled hound, his gait uneven, rushed out. Rather than snarl and growl, it wiggled and wormed around her feet, begging to be petted as he balanced himself on three legs.

"Hello, Cade," she said and saw his eyes darken for a second before she leaned down and gave the dog a couple pats on the head. To the animal, she said, "I'm guessing you're Shad."

"You know me?" Cade asked.

"Yeah, I do." Straightening, she pulled her sunglasses from her face.

"You sure? Oh. Jesus! Wait a second." Cade's face hardened. "You look like—"

"I know." She yanked out her dental appliance, the one that changed the shape of her teeth, and the other that plumped her cheeks. As he stared, she next removed her wig, letting down her hair.

"For the love of Christ." His eyebrows slammed together. "Anne-Marie?"

"In the flesh." She patted her stomach. "Well, more than just flesh. I'm wearing a little extra, you know, to complete the look."

"Holy shit." Dumbstruck, he filled the doorway, a tall, rangy man who was glaring at her as if she were Satan incarnate.

"Can I come in?"

He hesitated.

"It's important, Cade. You know it is. Otherwise, I wouldn't be here."

His jaw slid to the side and his gaze narrowed suspiciously. "Okay," he finally agreed, stepping back and swinging the door wide. "But what the hell's going on? What's with the getup?" The dog streaked back into the house and before she could follow, he said, "Wait. Don't tell me. You're in a little bit of trouble again."

"More than a little," she admitted as he closed the door behind her and she remembered all too vividly what it felt like to kiss this love 'em and leave 'em cowboy. "This time, Cade," she admitted, "it's a matter of life and death."

"You can talk to Teri, she's the waitress who served her," Sandi, the owner of Wild Wills said when Pescoli and Alvarez showed up at the restaurant.

One of the deputies who had helped canvas the area had shown Calypso Pope's picture to Sandi and she'd remembered one of her last customers from the night before. The detectives were following up, trying to figure out anything they could about the victim.

"I know she's dead, and I'm sorry, but let me tell you, that woman," Sandi said, standing at the hostess podium, "was a real pain in the butt. Came in late, almost closing, and didn't like Grizz." She pointed to the mascot of the establishment, the huge stuffed grizzly bear that, with the changing holidays, was dressed in appropriate or not-so-appropriate attire, depending on how one viewed it.

Pescoli had seen Grizz wearing an angel costume for Christmas, a red, white, and blue Uncle Sam outfit for Independence Day, and a Pilgrim hat and collar for Thanksgiving. At his place of honor in the vestibule, Grizz currently was dressed as Cupid in honor of Valentine's Day, his snarl at odds with the cute little sparkling wings strapped to his broad, shaggy back.

"Odd to think she didn't see the humor," she said.

"A real sourpuss. Tried to go all organic and vegan, which is fine, but not here. This is Grizzly Falls, Montana, and it's wild out here." Sandi, a known animal lover who had three rescue dogs and two cats at last count, was clearly deeply irked. "It's not as if I killed all these animals, for God's sake. They came with the place when you-know-who and I originally bought it." You-know-who was Sandi's ex-husband; he who could not be named, apparently. They'd been through a bitter divorce and Sandi had ended up with the restaurant, only to make it thrive under her management. "She ended up with her nose in her iPhone—a lot of that going around these days—and ordered just pie and coffee, and left a miserable tip."

Pescoli asked, "Was she with anyone?"

"Nope. Alone. I saw, you know, 'cause I'm always close. As far as I could tell, she didn't speak to anyone."

"We'd like to talk with Teri. Is she here?"

"Just came on an hour ago. You can use the office if you want some privacy."

Sandi led them into a crowded office with a desk and one chair, files piled to the high ceiling. She cleared off a stack of invoices and then found Teri. Wary, it turned out she was unable to tell them any more than Sandi had. Calypso Pope had arrived close to eleven and left at eleven thirty-two, according to the credit card receipt she'd signed.

"Lousy tipper," the waitress grumbled, almost as if getting killed served Calypso Pope right for being so cheap. Then she heard herself and straightened as if caught in some nefarious act. "Not that I would wish anyone dead."

"Was she wearing a ring?" Pescoli asked.

"Oh, yeah, one with *major* diamonds. But no wedding band. Just like an engagement ring."

"You noticed there wasn't a second ring?" Alvarez asked.

"Oh, yeah." Teri's head was bopping up and down. "I pay attention. Me and my boyfriend, we've been looking at rings 'cause we're coming up on our one year anniversary, and I think it's time."

"How old are you?" Pescoli asked.

"Nineteen."

"Give it a year or two," she said and saw the girl's eyes cloud. "Sorry. None of my business. Anything else you can tell us about the woman?"

"Other than that she was in a real bad mood? I don't know if that's her normal personality or not, but if it is, she really needs an attitude adjustment. That's what my dad always tells my mom when she's in one of her bitch moods. Oops." She placed her fingers over her lips. "Sorry. That just slipped out."

"No problem," Pescoli said, thinking of the language she'd heard from her own kids.

They ran some more questions but didn't learn anything more as no one else in the place had been on duty or remembered the one customer.

As they walked back to the Jeep, Alvarez found her sunglasses and slipped them on. "We're already waiting for the security cameras from the buildings along the river. Maybe we'll catch a break and one of them will show something."

"Or the Spokane PD will find something in her home," Pescoli thought aloud as they knew the victim's address, but she wasn't holding her breath. So far, they knew little about the woman other than where she lived. They'd found no connection between the two victims, other than they'd both been killed and had their ring fingers, complete with diamond rings, sliced off their left hands.

"This guy got a thing against engagement?" Alvarez thought aloud as they crossed the street and got into Pescoli's rig.

"Or marriage. But that's half the male population."

"And then there's the missing fingers."

"What the hell do you think he does with those?" Pescoli asked.

"Hmmm . . ." Alvarez shook her head in disgust. As they reached the base of Boxer Buff her cell phone went off. "Alvarez," she answered. "Yeah . . . where? You're sure?"

Pescoli glanced over at her partner.

Yeah . . . okay. We'll be right there." Alvarez hung up and said, "We got lucky."

"What?"

"Calypso Pope's purse. Found by a teenager on the rocks near the falls. All her ID intact. Credit cards, too, or so it seems on first inspection. No cash. Anyway, he turned it in at the station. It's at the lab already and they're processing it, checking for trace evidence, fingerprints."

"Needle in a haystack."

"Maybe, but it's something."

"Yeah."

"Lars Bender, the kid who found it, claims there wasn't a dime in it," Alvarez said. "He's already asking about a reward."

"Figures." Pescoli cranked on the wheel and turned up the hill behind a tow truck with a crumpled mid-sized sedan on its bed. "You never go wrong being disappointed in human nature."

With his gaze on the GPS monitor, Ryder followed the woman he was certain was Anne-Marie Calderone. He drove a mile or two behind her outside of town, past a smattering of houses on the fringe of Grizzly Falls, and into the rolling hills of farmland. The road was getting chewed up from traffic, but the pastures that spread beyond the fences were still covered in a white, pristine mantle, sunlight bouncing off the icy crystals of snow so that he was forced to squint and finally find an old pair of sunglasses he kept in the glove box.

Slipping on the polarized lenses, he kept driving, meeting a few other vehicles, checking his mileage and finally guessing where she was heading. Sure enough, he passed a long driveway and saw from the small monitor's screen that she'd turned into the lane. No surprise the oversized mailbox had the name GRAYSON written across it.

Some things never change.

He told himself it didn't matter, but he couldn't help wondering why she'd decided to go to Cade Grayson. Was he the real reason she'd taken this winding path from Louisiana to Montana? The end piece of her game? Ryder drove past the place and turned around about a mile up the road. Then he waited, wondering what she was doing, thinking that after meeting with Grayson she might take off again.

He'd have some time, though. She hadn't packed up.

Yet.

He'd been watching, feeling every bit the voyeur as he'd sat in his dive of a motel room, sipping beer and staring at the monitor of one of his laptops, the one that had been hooked up as a receiver to the wireless transmitter he'd left on her property. The second one he used for research and communication.

He'd nearly collected enough evidence, and after today, it would be time to execute phase two of his plan.

His lips twisted a little at that thought.

Seeing Anne-Marie face-to-face for the first time in months would give him a small degree of satisfaction. But then telling her what he was going to do with her, that was going to be difficult because like it or not, he still felt a connection to her, that same old attraction that hadn't quite let go, despite everything.

She deserves what she's getting he told himself. *It's only right that it comes at my hand. This will all be over soon.* He took heart that once the job was finished, he could forget about Anne-Marie Calderone forever.

Never in a million years would Cade have expected Anne-Marie to be standing on his doorstep, on the ranch in Montana. "A long way from New Orleans," he said, rubbing his chin and eyeing her from across the room. He'd offered her a seat in the living room that didn't get used much and was still filled with memorabilia and furniture from the days over a decade earlier when his mother had still been alive.

"I know. Cade, I'm sorry about your brother."

She appeared sincere, but he didn't trust his instincts around her. They'd always been off a bit. She'd come to his home in a disguise, and he couldn't read her eyes as they'd been darkened with contact lenses. She was still wearing some kind of padding. Her body didn't fit her head now that she'd removed whatever it was that had changed the contour of her cheeks and the look of her teeth. That she'd shown up out of the blue with no word for years, her beauty intently played down, wasn't a good sign.

"I doubt you came all the way up here to give me your condolences."

"No," she admitted, clearly nervous. She glanced away for a second, and he wondered if she was concocting her story, trying to think of a way to make it plausible. "That's not why I'm here."

"You said it was life or death."

"I think so, yes." Though she was nodding as she balanced on the edge of the dusty couch, she didn't seem so sure of herself. It was as if she were suddenly second-guessing her arrival on his doorstep.

He decided that was just desserts. He owed her nothing.

"Look, Cade," she said, one hand nervously plucking at a bit of fabric on the couch. "Years ago, you said if I was ever in trouble . . . you know, with the law, that I could count on your brother, that . . . he would help."

"You came up here to talk with Dan?"

"Yes," she admitted weakly, "and then, well, I heard that he'd passed."

"Killed," Cade corrected. "He was murdered in cold blood. A bastard he knew and trusted laid in wait and pulled the goddamn trigger. That's what happened."

"I'm sorry."

"So you said." He closed his eyes for a second and tried like hell to tamp down the rage that overtook him every time he thought of his brother's death. That the son of a bitch who'd taken Dan's life was still alive pissed him off. Forcing his eyes open, he stared at her and asked, "What is it?"

"I think," she started as if unsure of herself, "he's followed me here. I think he might be behind the attacks on the other women who were killed. I don't know, but . . ." She let out her breath slowly.

"Who?" he asked, but he felt it, that chill of premonition that warned him that bad news was coming his way.

"My husband," she whispered softly. "I think he followed me here."

CHAPTER 17

"**Y**our husband?" Cade repeated, his expression guarded, suspicion visible in his eyes as Shad settled into a dog bed near the fireplace.

Too late, Jessica realized she'd made a big mistake in going there, in hoping he might be able to help her. But she was in too deep to backtrack. "I've been hiding from him."

"Here? In Grizzly Falls?"

"Yes. That's why I'm dressed like this." She made a sweeping gesture to include her whole body. "When I drove here, I didn't know about Dan, about what had happened to him. I was just desperate. You'd said once that if I were ever in serious trouble that your brother was someone I could trust, a fair officer of the law. And I thought, hoped, that I could explain to him what happened and . . . and that he would believe me and trust me and help me."

"You think your husband is out to kill you?" Cade asked dubiously.

"I know he is," she said, shivering inwardly. "He tried once, thought he'd gotten rid of me, but I managed to survive. And now he has to make sure."

He regarded her suspiciously. "You have family."

"Who have disowned me."

"And why is that?"

She didn't answer. Didn't have to. They both knew why. "Look, Cade, even if I contacted them and told them my story, they wouldn't believe me. Because . . . because . . ."

"Because you've cried wolf one too many times."

"Essentially." She was nodding. "Yeah, that's about it."

"Let's just tell it like it is. You're a liar, Anne-Marie. You lied to your family, you lied to me, hell, you probably lied to your damn husband. Christ, I *know* you did. So now you're on the run and you wind up here and you expect me . . . *me* . . . to believe you and do what? Take you in? Hide you out from some *imagined* threat? Start something up again."

"No!"

Obviously, he wasn't buying it. "Jesus H. Christ. You're unbelievable. And you can take that literally."

"I'm telling you the truth."

"That's the trouble with compulsive liars; they start believing their own shit."

"Cade. Trust me, I'm not—"

"Trust you?" he threw back at her. "That's a laugh. You expect *me* to trust *you.*" He was angry, his jaw hard, but it wasn't the raw, passionate fury she'd witnessed in him before. No, this was cold and deep, the kind of wrath that has had time to burrow and fester. It was obvious he wasn't buying her desperate pleas and she knew that he had good reason.

"I made a mistake coming here."

"You got that right," he said, his glare cutting through her. "I don't know what you're involved in and I don't care. If you seriously believe someone is out to kill you, whether it's your husband or someone else, then you need to go to the police. Immediately. No matter how wild a tale you spin, they'll look into it."

"I'd planned to, but then—"

"I know. Dan died. Jesus, don't you know I'm painfully aware of that fact," he said.

She shrank back. "I didn't mean—"

He waved off her apology. "Whatever it is you think you're involved in, it has nothing to do with me." A muscle worked in his jaw as if he were trying and failing to rein in his anger. "Just go down to the station and tell your tale. They'll ask you some questions and that'll be it. Maybe they can sort out what's real and what's all in your head."

"I'm not making this up." She was on her feet. "You think I drove all the way from New Orleans to seek you out because of some convoluted, sick fantasy? Have you noticed women are being *killed*?"

"I don't really see how they're connected to you. Did you know them? The first girl's been IDed, some woman from Utah, I think, and the second one"—he shrugged—"I haven't heard."

"You're the only person I knew in Grizzly Falls before I came here. But I think he followed me somehow."

"As I said, tell it to the police. I don't know the new sheriff or much about him, but someone thought he was fit for the job, so go and tell him your tale."

"I don't think that's a good idea," Anne-Marie said.

"Why not?"

She remembered the acting sheriff, how when she'd spilled coffee on him, he'd turned his attention on her like a laser.

"If you're serious about this. If you really think that you being here in Montana has cost two women their lives, you have to go to the police. It's your moral obligation."

She felt her back go up. "Moral obligation? You're a fine one to lecture me on morals."

"I wasn't the one who was married," he said.

She saw in his eyes that he was daring her to tread farther, into dangerous emotional territory which, she knew, would be unwise. "Okay. I get it," she said, deciding it was time to leave just as she heard the muted rumble of an engine. Shad was on his three feet in an instant, howling and barking and running into the kitchen.

She glanced through the window and saw a massive pickup had pulled into the empty bay of the garage. Zed's truck. Her heart sank as she watched the Grayson brother climb out of his king cab.

"I should leave," she said, reaching up to twist and pin her hair onto her head. Quickly she donned her wig again, uncaring that it wasn't on perfectly. Then, she slid her sunglasses onto the bridge of her nose. She started for the front door but looked over her shoulder. "I know it's a lot to ask. And God knows you don't owe me any favors, but please . . . don't give me away until I talk to the police."

"You're going there?"

"I will . . . just not right now." She drew in a long breath.

"When?" he asked as she noticed Big Zed squinting at her car as he walked toward the back of the house.

"This week."

"And if you don't?"

"You won't have to worry about me. I'll be gone and . . . and he'll follow."

"To kill again," he said, lifting an eyebrow. "That's what you're try-ing to get me to believe."

She let out a nearly inaudible sigh and opened the door. "Believe whatever you want, Cade." She heard another door open and didn't wait any longer. She didn't want to explain herself to Zed or anyone else, yet.

She followed her earlier tracks across the front yard to her car and wondered if Cade were watching her or if Zed was asking questions. Well, so be it.

She should never have shown her hand, never have driven there and tried to drag Cade into it.

Her hopes for help from anyone named Grayson had died with the sheriff.

It was time to come up with Plan B.

"Who was that?" Zed asked as he walked into the house and found Cade staring out the living room window.

"No one."

"Like hell."

"Okay. Someone I knew a long time ago." He watched Anne-Marie drive off and thought, *Good riddance*. It surprised him that she'd tracked him down, but it didn't surprise him that she'd shown up with some wild-ass story. She'd always been slightly off, one wheel not quite on the track. Yes, she'd been his lover and he still remembered how passionate she was in the bedroom, but he also recalled what a crazy and bona fide liar she was. The kind of woman best left alone. He didn't know why she was in Grizzly Falls, but if it was to start something up again, he'd shut her down. Fast. It was over, and for the first time in his life, he wasn't interested. He was with Hattie and had her daughters to consider. He'd be a fool to risk losing his family, and he wasn't about to do it with Anne-Marie Calderone.

"A woman." There was a sneer in Zed's voice.

Cade turned and faced his older brother. "Yep."

"Women are always getting you into trouble."

That much was true. Sex had always been Cade's downfall. He liked women. All women. Lots of women. And he'd never been one to shy away from danger, especially if it involved a slightly over the top woman, the operative word being *slightly*. At least that's how he'd reacted until recently, but Anne-Marie had been trouble from the get-go. He'd wondered then, as he wondered now, if she was missing a few vital screws. She'd always been attractive and sexy, but mentally a little unbalanced. And there was the lying thing; he hadn't been kidding when he'd called her compulsive. It was as if she just couldn't stop.

"She's just a friend."

"No such thing. Not with you."

"Believe me," Cade said.

"So how do you know that waitress from the diner?" Zed asked. To Cade's look, he said, "That's who it was. I saw her there."

For a reason Cade couldn't name, he felt suddenly protective of a woman he'd sworn to abhor. "Long story. Long time ago. Long over."

Zed's eyes thinned and he took a look out the window, but Anne-Marie's car had disappeared. "Okay," he said as if he didn't quite believe Cade, but was willing to move on. "I was just at the funeral home. Everything's a go for the service."

Cade grunted. He didn't want to think about Anne-Marie, true enough, but he also didn't want to dwell on the fact that the brother he'd looked up to was gone. "Can you handle the night's feeding?" he asked Zed.

"S'pose. Where you goin'?"

"Into town to have dinner with Hattie and the girls." The darkness in his soul dissolved a little when he thought of Mallory and McKenzie, the twins he'd recently found out were not sired by his brother Bart, but by Cade himself. Had it changed how he felt about them? Not much. Since Bart's death he'd thought of the girls as his, anyway. The new biological information had been a shock, but not an unpleasant one. Truth be known, it was a possibility he'd considered a couple times but had tossed aside while his brother had been alive.

"Hattie." Zed snorted again. "She's no good, y'know. I don't know what your deal is, or was, with the waitress from the diner, but it sure as hell has to be a lot less complicated than the thing you've got going with Bart's wife."

"Ex-wife."

"Or maybe even an excuse. The reason she was his ex might well be because of you."

Every muscle in Cade's body clenched. He was super-sensitive in that area. Hell, maybe they both were. "Let's not go there, Zed. We've already lost two brothers. Now it's just you and me."

"And Hattie."

And your whores, the one-night stands that don't encumber you.
"And Hattie," Cade said, thinking of the woman he loved. Theirs was a complicated relationship and always had been.

"So why the fuck don't you just up and marry her? That's where this is all heading, isn't it? To make it legal? That little thing you had going with your brother's wife."

Cade grabbed a piece of Zed's work shirt in his fist and yanked. "I never touched Hattie while she was married and you know it."

"I don't know a damn thing," Zed said, his eyes blazing, his lips barely moving.

"That's the first thing you said that's right."

Zed punched him. Hard. In the ribs.

"Jesus!" Cade's fingers released and he fell backward, barely catching himself.

Zed, his face red, warned, "Don't you ever put your hands on me again."

"Then stop all this shit-talking about Hattie, you got that? She's the mother of my kids."

"That's the goddamn problem," Zed growled. His hands balled into fists and he looked as if he were about to launch at Cade as they had when they were young bucks, always fighting. Kicking, punching, knocking holes in the walls, the four boys had all possessed hot tempers and become the hellions of town, much to their mother's dismay. Though they'd grown out of their testosterone-charged teen years, that sibling rivalry always simmered just beneath the surface. They'd fight like hell for each other in public, then turn brother against brother when they were home, either fueled by alcohol or spurred by jealousy over a woman.

"You don't want to take me on, Zed," Cade warned.

"Don't I?"

"You're bigger, but I'm smarter."

"Fuck you!" Zed lunged and Cade rolled deftly away as the big man landed face-first into their mother's couch in the very spot Anne-Marie had so recently vacated. The sofa skidded into the wall with the window, panes rattling, a lamp teetering on an end table, to fall and crash, its bulb shattering, the shade ripping. Shad, who had been on a nearby chair, let out a startled yip, then began barking and hopping around on his three legs.

"Told ya."

"You got lucky."

"Luck had nothing to do with it," Cade said but felt little satisfaction in the statement. Zed was a pain, yeah, but he was the only damn brother he had left. "Just be sure to feed the damn cattle and horses, would ya? And Shad, too."

As Zed struggled to his feet, Cade walked into the kitchen to the anteroom near the back door where his boots sat under a bench and his jacket hung on a peg. There was no use arguing with Zed when he was in one of his dark moods, which seemed to be all the time. Not that Cade could blame him much. Ever since a sniper had taken shots at Dan, Cade too had been tough to live with.

Gingerly, he shrugged into his jacket, his ribs aching. Jesus, were they cracked? That would be a helluva thing. The fights with Zed had been increasing lately though it was the first time they'd gotten physical.

Not a good sign.

Maybe it would be best for everyone concerned if he moved out, found a place, tried living with Hattie and the girls. It wouldn't be so bad. Hattie had admitted her mother, who'd been diagnosed with cancer, was losing that hard-fought battle. Hattie could use a little help with the girls. Yeah, that part would be more than all right. But, he wasn't ready for marriage yet. They had too many things to iron out, but there was a chance, someday in the not too distant future, he might be ready to finally settle down.

Then again, maybe not.

The darkness was complete.

Whichever way she looked, she saw no one, heard nothing. But he was here. She sensed his presence.

Creeaak!

A door opened and she whipped around, her gaze scouring the blackness. No shaft of light appeared. There was no indication from which direction the sound had come.

Think, Jessica, think. You know this place. You know him! *You can escape.*

She started moving, inching backward, afraid that at any second she might stumble and fall, and he would pounce on her.

Her throat was dry as dust in fear. The night, so black and cold, seemed to wrap around her, its talons piercing her skin, an icy fear infusing her blood.

There was no way out. No walls, no windows, no doorway that she could sense. Backward, step by step, bracing herself for the inevitable—

Bam!

The gun went off though no flash of light burst from its muzzle. Anne-Marie stumbled backward, farther into the darkness.

Bang! Another hit! She felt no pain, but when she clutched her stomach, then lifted her hand, she saw the blood. Dark red stains running down her palm.

Why? she mouthed, staring at her attacker. *Why?*

"Because you deserve it," he sneered, his voice deep and accusing. "Because of what you did."

"I'm sorry!" she cried, staring into the void.

"I loved you, Stacey. That's what you go by now, isn't it? Stacey Donahue."

"Y-yes, I'm Stacey," she admitted, though that didn't sound right. *No, wait!* "You've got the wrong person," she said desperately. "I'm Jessica. Jessica Williams. Yes, Jessica Williams!"

"Are you?" he said, toying with her. "Last I heard you were Stacey Donahue."

"No! You're wrong."

"While you were in Colorado," he reminded her. "Denver."

She was confused, still stumbling backward, her skin crawling as she felt him getting closer. "I'm . . . I'm from Louisiana," she said, then realized her mistake. "I mean Nebraska!" Oh, God was that right? She couldn't remember.

"Anne-Marie is from New Orleans." His voice was cold. Empty. And he was getting closer. Squinting, she tried to see him, even just a glimmer of his shadow, or the glow of his eyes, or *any*thing, but she saw nothing but blackness.

"I'm Jessica. Jessica Williams. I live in Montana. Yes. That's right. I'm Jessica and I live in Montana—"

"Not for long."

Oh, God, he was going to kill her!

The bullet into her gut wasn't enough. And then she saw it. Rising silver in a slow arc, a knife with a glinting blade.

"No!"

Recoiling, she stumbled and fell backward, tumbling and flailing. Trying to get her grip, she descended into the darkness. Downward, farther and farther until she splashed into the water, piercing the surface of a slow moving river. The water covered her and she began kicking, trying to swim to the surface, but the harder she struggled, the farther down she slid, the water sucking her into a slow-turning but deadly whirlpool. Downward she spun, trying to scream, to breathe, as the vicious eddy funneled far from the surface. In the darkness, she spied a plume, blood red and swirling around her, enveloping. Thrashing, she tried to breathe, couldn't suck in any air, gasped wildly. Desperately she fought.

Bang!

She shot upward, throwing off her pillow and sitting straight up in bed. Her tiny pistol tumbled to the floor and landed with a sharp thud. For a second, she didn't know where she was, couldn't find her bearings. Her heart was drumming and she was breathing hard from the feeling of suffocation, her own damn pillow having covered her face.

Oh, Lord. She dropped her face into her hands and tried to cast off the dream, the fear, the feeling of desperation.

It had been so real. No, so surreal, but she was still cold, the flesh on her arms rising in tiny goose pimples despite her sweatshirt. She pulled the sleeping bag over her shoulders for warmth.

Bang!

She nearly shrieked, scrambled on the floor for her gun, then realized the noise was the wind buffeting the cabin, its gusts causing something, probably a tree limb, to pound against the roof. In her dream, the rush of the wind whistling down the chimney had been the sound of the river and the thud of that branch had become the report of a gun, nothing more.

She let out her breath slowly, then threw off the covers and walked to the window where she peered outside to the darkness beyond.

Is this how you want to live the rest of your life?

Alone?

Isolated?

In fear?

Always looking over your shoulder?

Forever thinking you're being chased?

Almost believing that others are harmed because of your damn sins?

"No," she said aloud, squinting through the dirty glass. Outside, the snow-laden branches were moving with the stiff breeze, the whiteness of the ground in stark contrast to the black, unforgiving sky.

It had to end.

She could no longer live in fear.

With a shiver, she remembered the fights, the shattered dishes, the balled fists, the pain she'd endured far too long. Trusting that he would be able to control his temper, that he loved her, that he truly was sorry after each of their fights, she'd stayed with him, never reporting what had happened. Because of the shame. Because she'd stupidly believed that no one would believe her. Who would take *her* word—a spoiled woman who had her own emotional issues—against a man well regarded in the community, a smooth talker and outwardly, a do-gooder whose rage few had witnessed? Outwardly cool and in control, his demeanor had changed behind closed doors, just little things at first and then . . . oh, God, and then . . .

If I could only go home, she thought for the millionth time.

But she'd burned those bridges long ago. For all intents and purposes, she was dead to Talbert and Jeanette Favier, all because of *him*.

Well, not entirely, her wayward mind reminded her. *You carry your own burden here. You are far from blameless. Cade Grayson is proof enough of that. And he's not the only one. Some of your heartache and your fear can be placed on your own damn shoulders.*

With no one to turn to and no one to trust, she'd run.

Away from her home. Away from wealth. Away from privilege.

Her family didn't believe her then; they wouldn't now.

She was painfully aware of that horrid little fact.

Nonetheless, the running, which had seemed her only option a few months back, had to stop.

"Tomorrow," she whispered. After her morning shift. Then she realized that it would be Friday come morning and she'd be working most of the day. No, she needed a clear head to come clean with the police.

Saturday was the funeral for Dan Grayson.

Sunday was another full day at work and she didn't want to try and track down the sheriff or the appropriate detective over the weekend.

Excuses, excuses, her mind chided and she wondered if she'd chicken out altogether. Cade's assessment of her hadn't been that far off. But he was right. If innocent women were dying because of her, then she had to go to the police.

If not, she still needed help in straightening out the whole mess. Just because the cops in New Orleans were dirty didn't mean the same held true in this little town. Most officers of the law were heroes and worked for the common good: To protect and serve. Just because Dan Grayson was no longer the sheriff didn't mean that the man who'd taken his place wouldn't be just as good, nor that he wouldn't uphold the law.

And therein lies the problem, yes? Because you are guilty, aren't you? It's not as if you're pure as the driven snow.

She felt that same sense of doom nip at her heels again, the one that had been chasing her since leaving Louisiana. God, she'd made a mess of things.

No matter what the consequences, she would try to face the music and right her wrongs, if possible.

On Monday.

Come hell or high water, she'd march into the Pinewood Sheriff's Department and tell her story.

If she didn't turn tail and run again. Crossing her fingers, she told herself she needed to do it. Before anyone else ended up dead.

CHAPTER 18

Alvarez stood and stretched, using her desk chair for support. She hadn't been to the gym for the better part of a week, nor had she had time for her usual daily run. That would have to change as all of her muscles were tight and her brain was clogged with dozens of questions about the murdered women. Fortunately, the other active cases had been closed.

Ralph Haskins had taken his life. He'd left a good-bye note blaming his mother for his depression and his wife for their bankruptcy. The position of his Magnum as it had fallen from his hand as he'd collapsed after putting a bullet in his brain, and the fact that gunshot residue was all over his hands, had made the case pretty cut and dried. End of story.

She raised an arm over her head and stretched as if she were reaching for the overhead light fixture. Then she did the same with her other arm before rotating her neck and finally, leaning over from her hips, allowing her arms to fall free.

The latest domestic abuse accusation in a long series had been dropped. Again. Jimbo Amstead's wife, Gail, had changed her mind for the fourth time in half as many years. Though the DA wanted to prosecute the bastard for "slapping the bitch around" as he'd told a friend, bragging after a few too many at the Black Horse Saloon, that good ol' boy refused to testify, said he'd probably been mistaken, heard wrong in the loud bar. Besides, he'd been drunk at the time. Since Gail Amstead refused to speak ill of her husband, even though she was recovering from her sixth black eye in three years, the DA was powerless to prosecute. Gail swore she'd been mistaken about the fight and had run into a door once again.

"You know how many times I've 'run into a door' in my lifetime?" Pescoli had asked Alvarez when they'd heard the decision. "Exactly zero." She'd slid her partner a look. "How about you?"

"The same."

"So in our combined seventy plus years, not one door and yet Gail, who's not quite fifty, has done it three times that she's reported. In the last couple years or so. Either she's a damn klutz, or lives in a house with attacking woodwork, or . . . she's a liar and lives with a bastard who beats the shit out of her. Take your pick."

Alvarez's mouth had been a thin line. She had so wanted to nail Jimbo to the wall. Big, with a swagger and yellowed teeth from too many years of chewing tobacco, the guy leered at every woman he passed, then beat the one woman who had agreed to be his wife.

Alvarez would have loved to see him wearing a prison suit for the rest of his life.

She finished stretching, checked her e-mail and concentrated on the most pressing case, that of the homicide victims who had been strangled, then mutilated. The autopsy on Calypso Pope had been given top priority, and damn if she hadn't died the same way Sheree Cantnor had. Strangled, then tossed into a body of water, though it seemed Sheree had been strangled somewhere else, probably snagged while walking home for lunch or dinner, and left in the creek that wound through the O'Halleran property. They had come up with no further evidence after the one shoe. Odd that. What had happened to the other?

She was about to walk to Pescoli's office when Joelle, clicking briskly down the hall, showed a middle-aged woman into the room. In one arm, the woman clutched her purse so close against her body it seemed as if she expected it to be snatched out of her arms right there in the station. The fingers of her other hand were curled around the upper arm of a pimply-faced boy of about fourteen. Grasping his arm so tightly as to crush the fabric of his ski jacket in her iron grip, she looked as if she could spit nails.

"Detective Alvarez?" Joelle said, silver crosses swinging from her earlobes. "This is Mrs. Bender and her son, Lars. They would like to speak to you if you have the time."

"Lars Bender?" Alvarez said, recognizing the name of the kid who'd located Calypso Pope's purse on the rocks below Grizzly Falls. As Joelle made her way out of the tight office, Alvarez asked the boy, "You found the purse belonging to Ms. Pope?"

Scrawny in his oversized jacket, the kid didn't meet her eyes but gave a short nod.

"Answer her. Where are your manners?" his mother asked impatiently. "I'm Elaine, by the way," she said extending her hand across the desk, then retrieving it quickly.

"Please, have a seat." Alvarez settled back into her chair as mother and son sat down across from her.

"Lars has something to tell you." The severity of Elaine's expression was matched by the harsh lines of her haircut, which probably was supposed to bring a youthful hipness to dull brown locks that were beginning to gray. Stick-straight, her hair was whacked sharply at the point of her chin. Straight cut bangs ended nearly an inch above round owlish glasses that only emphasized the sharp angles of a face that looked as if it was fixed in a perpetual state of being perturbed.

"What is it, Lars?" Alvarez asked.

"Go on. Tell her!" Elaine said as she dug into the prized purse and came out with a ziplock bag holding a cell phone.

"I found it," the boy said.

"Where?" the mother prodded, handing the bag over to Alvarez as if it might burn her fingers. "Where did you find it, Lars?"

"In the bag," the kid mumbled, looking down at his hands.

"The purse we turned in earlier, the one from that woman who was killed," Elaine explained in clipped words. "That's the bag he was talking about. I didn't find anything else, but he found it and went through it first and he kept that phone." She jabbed a long, accusing finger at the smart phone. "He was going to sell it or something. Lars is acting out, you know. Because his dad and I split up, like it was my fault." Lips pursed even further, she added, "Jeff, that's his father, had an affair. Wants to marry this . . . this *woman*. Met her in the church where he's a part-time youth minister. It's no wonder that Lars is on the wrong path."

She sent a pointed look to her son. "What kind of an example is that? A youth minister!" She let out a shaky breath and shivered, her severely chopped hair shaking in her rage. "I don't know if Lars took anything else. He says not. But he came up with a new video game this morning," She flung her son another condemning glare. "How'd you pay for that, huh?"

He shrugged.

"Answer me, Lars!"

"Money from Christmas!" he spat out. "From *Dad!* Geez."

Mrs. Bender rolled her eyes and looked across the desk to Alvarez as if silently saying, *Do you see what I have to deal with?*

Alvarez focused on the son. "Okay. Lars, why don't you tell me everything about finding the purse? Was there anything else in it or around it?"

"No." He caught a warning glance from his mother. "No."

"God hears everything," she reminded him. "He sees *every*thing."

Lars swallowed, his prominent Adam's apple bobbing nervously. "Okay, maybe there were a couple bucks inside." His head actually seemed to shrink into his neck.

"A couple?" his mother sneered. "How much is a couple?"

"I dunno. Sixty . . . maybe eighty."

"Oh my God!" His mother's hands fell onto her lap. To Alvarez, she said, "Can you believe it?" Before Alvarez could answer, Elaine turned on her son again. "So, what was it, Lars? How much did you steal? And from a dead woman!"

Lars's head snapped up. "I didn't know she was dead! Not then!"

She wasn't derailed. "So, was it sixty or eighty, or maybe a hundred?"

"Eighty," the kid answered quickly.

Alvarez suspected he'd shaved the amount and that Lars was smart enough to hide the extent of his theft, giving his mother a large enough amount to make it believable, but less than what he'd really pocketed.

"You'll have to tell your father and work off the debt. You'll pay the family back or if they don't want it, give it to the church, after you tell Preacher Miller what you've done. You can start by shoveling the snow off the walkway, which you should do for free anyway!" She folded her hands over the long skirt that covered her legs. "There are lots of projects Lars can tackle. We can't stay in the house, anyway. It's much too expensive now that I'm a single mother."

Before Mrs. Bender could launch into another diatribe about the sins of her ex, Alvarez cut her off. "Let me ask Lars a few questions," she suggested, then turned to the boy. "Tell me about finding the purse and this phone. Other than picking it up, did you touch it? Use it?"

He looked absolutely miserable. "Maybe."

"Answer her with the truth!" his mother almost screeched.

Alvarez held up a hand. "Please, Mrs. Bender."

The detective had a teenaged son who lived with his adoptive parents. Even though she'd just recently reconnected with Gabe, she understood that the boy was far from perfect and had already had a brush or two with the law. The same, it seemed, held true for Lars, but thoughtless teenaged stunts were not always a precursor to a life of crime.

"Let Lars speak."

The kid did. The fingers of one hand working over the fist of another, he answered her questions one by one. She found out that he'd swiped the phone and the cash out of the purse. He'd found nothing else inside or around the bag and seen nothing that would help. Yes, he'd made a call or two on the phone, tried to download an app, but was unable without Calypso Pope's user ID and password, and he'd gone on the Internet where he'd entered some chat rooms and surfed a bit.

By the time his mother had marshaled him out of the office, Alvarez had learned little, but since she knew the approximate time of death, and when the purse had presumably been lost, she would be able to figure out who was the last person Calypso called or texted.

Grabbing her jacket, she walked to Pescoli's office where she found her partner at her desk reading an old case file, the box on the floor open, the lid propped against the wall.

"What's that?"

"I told you about Hattie Grayson and her insistence that Bart's death wasn't a suicide."

Alvarez asked, "Don't you have enough to do?"

Pescoli snorted. "I should have never told Hattie I'd look into it, but I did, and now I can't just ignore the file or she'll be calling every day." She set the file on her messy desk.

How Pescoli could ever find anything on a work surface cluttered with notes, cups, pens, and papers Alvarez didn't understand.

"I imagine I'll run into Hattie at the funeral on Saturday, and she'll be asking me about Bart's suicide and make some ridiculous connection to Dan's murder. I thought I'd better read over the old reports, you know, get my ducks in a row." Pescoli rolled back her chair. "Anything new?"

Alvarez held up the cell phone in its plastic bag. "The kid who found it seems to have a little bit of larceny in his blood and his God-fearing mother is having nothing of it."

"Good thing," Pescoli said.

"Yeah, I'm glad to have the phone, but the mother——" Alvarez shook her head. "Let's just call Elaine Bender a piece of work and leave it at that." She brought her partner up to speed as Pescoli donned a pair of gloves and took out the phone.

She looked into the recent activity, the calls and texts and e-mail connections that had gone in and out, and said, "Looks like we'd better check out someone named Reggie."

Jessica's shift was over at nine that night. Dead tired, her lower back aching from hours on her feet, her brain was exhausted from the mental strain of a double-shift and not sleeping due to her wild dreams. She'd been dragging all day.

Misty had even seen fit to comment, "Not our usual Miss Merry Sunshine today, are we?"

Jessica had wanted to tell her to shove it, but had held her tongue.

She was tired, cranky, and hungry. She hadn't been able to choke down any of the leftovers that had been congealing on the counter for the better part of the evening. They'd consisted of an order of fries proclaimed "too salty" by a customer, and a wilted salad that had been topped by French dressing when the patron had insisted she'd said, "dressing on the side." As was the custom at the Midway Diner, orders that were returned to the kitchen weren't immediately thrown out, but left for the staff, should they be interested, before they were tossed into the trash.

"Waste not, want not," Nell had professed to them enough times that it had become a standing joke behind the boss's back. The trouble was that Marlon took Nell's suggestion to heart and somehow, in between clearing and resetting tables, washing dishes, and even swabbing the floors for spills, he was able to inhale anything that was placed in the return area of the counter. Hamburgers, chicken strips,

Diet Cokes that were supposed to have been the real thing and desserts that were just "too rich" or "not what I thought" or "really, I said coconut cream, not banana," somehow got gobbled up while he was on the job. So all that was left were the unappealing cold fries and wilted lettuce.

She didn't waste any time leaving and was glad Misty and Marlon were handling the few stragglers who might wander in. She just wanted to get home.

As if that cold, dark cabin could ever be considered anything close to what she would think of as her home.

Inside the Tahoe, she flipped on the engine and the wipers as desultory flakes of snow were drifting from the heavens. Her stomach rumbled and though it seemed ridiculous after working around food in a diner for most of the day, she decided to stop at the local pizza parlor that she'd spied earlier in the week.

Within ten minutes, she was pulling into a parking spot on the street one block away from Dino's Italian Pizzeria. She hurried inside and the sharp smells of tomato sauce and oregano hit her in a warm, welcoming wave. The crowd was thinning out, and it didn't take long to reach the counter and order a small pizza to go. As she waited, she sat at a table in the corner and watched people coming and going, attacked by more than one pang of desperation. Here were people, all involved in their personal lives—teenagers goofing around with friends, even blowing the papers off straws at each other; a frazzled mother trying to corral three stair-step toddlers all of whom made a beeline to the ice cream counter; other tweens playing video games in an arcade; a twentysomething couple who held hands as they decided on what kind of pizza to order. Everyday people. Ordinary lives. With the common stresses and worries of normal living.

No one running for his or her life.

No one concerned that a crazed husband was intent on killing her.

"Pizza to go for Williams," a teenager behind the counter called and she was out of her chair in an instant. She collected her order and carried the box outside. Snow was still threatening, a few solitary flakes drifting from the sky, catching in the lamplight. Cars rolled by on the quiet streets and she couldn't shake the feeling that someone was watching her.

Don't be a fool. No one's followed you.

But she kept up her pace and sensed her heartbeat beginning to increase, her pulse pounding. Last night's dream crawled through her brain in a frightening memory that she struggled to shake off.

The street was deserted, nothing to worry about, not a soul on the icy sidewalks, no car moving slowly along the snowy asphalt.

You're fine. Nothing to worry about.

A figure rounded the corner in front of her and she nearly jumped out of her skin.

But it was nothing, just a woman walking her dogs. Jessica let out her breath slowly and was about to step into the street when the woman called her name. "You're Jessica," she said in a voice that was cold as the night.

Jessica hesitated. The knife in her bra would be hard to reach because of her coat, and the pistol was tucked under the seat of the SUV. "Yes," she said. "Do I know you?"

"I've seen you," the woman said, advancing slowly in her long, white hooded coat. Her dogs were large and shaggy, their heads lowered, their gold eyes looking upward to hers. Though not on leashes, they kept pace with their mistress, noiselessly moving forward, staying close to her side. "You visited my dreams, Anne-Marie. You worry me."

"What did you say?" Jessica stopped. Aside from Cade, no one in this town knew her real name. "I'm sorry, you're mistaken."

"Am I?" The woman was so serene, almost ghostly.

Realization flashed. She must be Grace Perchant with her wolf-dogs and claims of talking with the dead.

"You're in danger." Still Grace approached.

"From whom? Or what?" Jessica asked, poised for flight. Where the hell were all the people? It wasn't *that* late. Why wasn't someone coming out of Dino's or the pub down the street?

The woman closed the distance between them. Under the lamplight, Jessica saw that her eyes were light green and piercing, her pale blond hair mixed with gray, strands blowing around her face where it escaped her hood. Her skin was so white it appeared almost bloodless.

"From him," the odd woman clarified in that same emotionless voice.

"Who?"

"You know, Anne-Marie." The pale woman seemed so certain of herself.

"I don't know what you're talking about," Jessica lied.

Grace's lips twisted into a disbelieving smile, but she didn't argue. Instead, in a voice without inflection, she said, "You're no longer safe. Trust no one."

"Lady—" Jessica began in protest.

Grace struck as quickly as a snake, her hand streaking forward, her fingers wrapping over Jessica's forearm.

Jessica gasped and dropped the box holding her pizza. "Let go of me!"

"No one," Grace repeated then released her grasp.

Neither dog so much as glanced at the cardboard container though the lid had popped open, pizza slices jumbling together.

Freak, Jessica thought. *Weirdo!* Her pulse raced, fear and adrenaline pumping through her blood as she picked up the ruined pizza.

She glanced back as Grace added, "Remember. Not a soul."

Jessica stood up, shaken. "Okay."

To the dogs, Grace ordered softly, "Sheena. Bane. Come." Then she walked across the street and disappeared into the darkness of an alley.

Her appetite gone, Jessica hurried to her vehicle. She tossed the box onto the passenger seat. *How did that woman know my name and what the hell was she prattling on about danger? How could she know? How the hell could she know?*

Fingers shaking, nerves stretched to the breaking point, Jessica hustled into the driver's seat and started the Chevy. The smell of pepperoni, garlic, and onion was nearly overpowering.

Now, of course, she saw others on the street—two guys hanging out by the pub, smoking near the doorway; the couple she'd seen in the pizzeria huddling close together as they made their way to a sedan parked just around the corner from Dino's; a Prius cruising past in electric mode. Where had they been during her exchange with Grace?

She started to pull onto the street and was rewarded with a blast of a loud horn. She jumped, hit the brakes, and watched as a Jeep painted in camouflage nearly clipped her. The driver with a shaved head and a furious glare looked across the passenger seat and flipped up his palm as if to say, *Stupid woman driver! Watch out!*

Once the Jeep had passed, she pulled out and drove, checking her rearview mirror every five seconds, trying not to be rattled, telling herself that no one was following her. Yet, despite all her internal pep talks, the weird woman's warning echoed through her brain.

Trust no one.

CHAPTER 19

"**I** found her." Lying on his bed in his room at the River View, his cell phone pressed against his ear, Ryder stared at his computer monitor. The grainy black and white image was clear enough to observe Anne-Marie as she slept restlessly on the old couch in her cabin. He watched as "Jessica," or, really, Anne-Marie, tossed and turned, her pistol tucked under her pillow, her sleep broken and tortured. He felt more than one niggle of guilt for observing her every move, but he reminded himself it was just a job, nothing more.

At least, that's the level to which it had dissolved.

"You're sure it's her?" the voice on the other end asked, the slight Louisianan accent discernible.

"Oh, yeah." Shifting, the back of his head moving against the stacked pillows, Ryder nodded as if the SOB on the other end of the wireless connection could actually see him.

"Why haven't you finished the job?"

Good question. "I had to be certain. Now I am."

"Then get to it."

"I will, when the time is right. She should have a day or two off work."

"She works?" A sneer in the voice.

"She's a waitress."

"My, my." A clucking of the tongue. "How the mighty have fallen." Satisfaction oozed through the phone.

Ryder wondered again why he'd ever agreed to do this job. The answer was stone-cold simple. He'd wanted to chase her down. He wanted to face her. He wanted her to know that it was he who had found her.

"So what's the problem?"

"As I said, I'm waiting for her to not be expected at her job so I can get a head start before anyone gets wise and realizes she's missing."

"Won't they just think she took off? No one really knows her."

"I can't take a chance. The extra twenty-four, maybe forty-eight hours, will give me a head start."

"I don't understand." Obvious irritation came through the phone.

"We don't need any interference from the police," Ryder pointed out.

A pause.

He could almost hear the gears turning in the head nearly a thousand miles away.

"Just don't screw this up."

"I won't."

"Good. Because it's been a while. I've been patient. Either she's been extremely elusive or you've fucked up. Or maybe a little of both."

"I said I'd handle it." Ryder's eyes focused on the screen where Anne-Marie was still sleeping. He was reminded of waking up next to her, the smell of her hair mixed with the odor of recent sex causing him to second-guess his need to run her to the ground.

Again.

He witnessed her shift again. One arm stretched over her head, her eyebrows drew together, and his guts wrenched.

"Just end this," he was advised, then the connection was severed.

The woman on the screen opened her eyes wide, startled, instantly awake as if through some invisible cosmic connection, she'd heard the conversation and was ready to bolt.

"You'd better get down here," Alvarez said as Pescoli groggily answered her cell. She'd spent the night with Santana in the new house again, the sun already up and shining, beams streaming through the windows.

"Why?" she asked, sitting up and pulling the sleeping bag over her naked breasts as she tried to shake the cobwebs from her brain. Beside her, a disturbed Santana rolled closer to her, one arm circling her waist.

Alvarez said, "Could be a break. The lab found a print on Calypso Pope's bag and get this. It looks like it matches the partial found on Sheree Cantnor's shoe."

As if the missing digit and ring weren't enough to tie the two victims together, but at least it was physical evidence.

"I'm on my way." Pescoli pushed her mussed hair from her eyes as she reached for her clothes.

Santana opened a bleary eye.

"Gotta run," she explained, yanking on her underwear and jeans, then reaching for her bra. "Possible big break in the case."

He didn't argue, didn't so much as mention that it was the weekend as he'd learned long ago that Pescoli's work took precedence over her free time. "What about today?"

"How 'bout I meet you at the funeral?" she suggested. "I'll go with Alvarez and the officers from the station, and you and I can hook up with the kids then. Jeremy is supposed to pick up Bianca at Luke's place and they'll peel off after the service."

"Works for me," Santana said, for once not trying to lure her back into the bed, which was really just sleeping bags thrown on the floor. He flung off the covers, got to his feet, and walked naked to the French doors where he looked through the clear panes to the grounds and lake. "Good day."

Pulling her sweater over her head, she said, "For a funeral?"

"For anything."

She forced her arms down the sleeves and pulled her hair through the cowl neckline. She glanced at Santana. He was looking away from her and she sighed inwardly. The sight of his wide, muscular shoulders and smooth back that narrowed into a slim waist and taut buttocks, the cheeks of which might have had a few marks from her fingernails, made her blush a little at the memory of their lovemaking. She imagined their hungry, primal sex would last until her pregnancy got in the way or until it became routine. Stolen as their time alone was, the kissing and touching and stripping of clothes was almost frantic, their desire heightened by so much time spent apart.

Would it change once they were married?

Probably. It always did.

But for some, that physical connection never completely abated, and they kept their desire hot while their emotional bond deepened.

Maybe this time, she thought, searching for a missing boot, *I'll get lucky*. She certainly hoped so. "I'll call you later if there's a change in plans," she said, zipping up her boots and reaching for her jacket, which had been tossed carelessly over a ladder that stood near the top of the stairs.

"Do," he said. "Hey, wait! You're forgetting something."

"What?" She smiled, certain that he was going to give her a kiss. To her surprise he scooped up the cell phone she'd dropped into the folds of the sleeping bag when she'd hung up.

"This."

"Oh." She extended her palm.

He dropped it into her outstretched hand and, slightly disappointed, she turned toward the stairs.

Strong fingers clasped over her wrist and he spun her back against him. "And this." He kissed her then. Hard. Determined. His tongue slid past her teeth as she responded, opening her mouth and leaning into him. Memories of the night before and their heated lovemaking in the cold room flooded her head. Her heart cracked a little and she realized just how much she loved this man, the cowboy who worked with horses that she swore she'd never fall for. What an idiot she'd been, and probably still was.

When he finally lifted his head, a cocksure smile twisting his lips, she said, "That's better."

"Not better," he returned as she started down the plywood steps. "The best."

"If you say so."

"I *know* so."

"Egomaniac," she called up the unfinished staircase and hurried outside where the sun was blazing, the snow a shimmering white, and her Jeep damn near frozen solid.

Montana in winter.

Glorious.

"What the hell's wrong with you?" Alvarez demanded an hour later as Pescoli suddenly rushed to the bathroom from Alvarez's office where the two partners had been going over new information on the case.

Upon her return, Alvarez eyed her closely. "You coming down with something?"

Pescoli, white faced, shook her head. "Santana and I celebrated a little too much last night," she lied.

"What about the other times? All of a sudden you can't view dead bodies without losing your lunch? Is it the flu? What—"

"I'm pregnant, okay?" Pescoli said through her teeth. She went to Alvarez's office door and pushed it shut.

"Holy moly." Alvarez stared at her.

"I know. My kids are grown. I could be a grandmother in a few years. I'm only telling you because we spend so much time together. I haven't even confided in my kids yet. So far, just Santana knows. Now, you. It wasn't planned. I wasn't convinced that I'd even have another baby. Not with Santana. Not with anyone. My kids . . . are going to be dumbstruck. Worse than even you are."

Alvarez shook her head. "Wow. You're sure?"

"I took a bunch of in-home tests and they all turned out positive. I'm late, and feeling like crap, emotional as hell and tossing my cookies in the morning, so yeah, I'm pregnant. I go to the doctor next week."

"Well . . . congratulations."

"Thanks. You'll keep this to yourself?"

"Of course."

"Good."

"No wonder you've been all over Blackwater."

"What do you mean?" Pescoli bristled.

"You're pregnant. Emotional. Grayson's death, and Blackwater stepping in. You're not handling it well."

"Like you are?"

"I don't like Blackwater, but I *deal* with him. He's the boss, and unless I think he's handling things all wrong or crooked or neglectful, I'll keep dealing with him. Do I miss Dan Grayson? You bet. Do I wish he was still alive, still running this department? Every damn day. But that's not the way it is, and me having my own personal snit fit about it isn't going to change it."

"I haven't been having snit fits," Pescoli snapped.

"I just gave you a pass for being pregnant. Let's leave it at that."

"Snit fits . . ." she muttered.

Alvarez almost laughed. "Are you going to stay on the force? You were thinking about cutting back, but now . . . ?"

"I don't know. I'm still dealing with the news," Pescoli admitted. "I just told Santana this week, and as I said, my kids are still in the dark. Santana wants to move up the wedding to like, yesterday, but"—she turned both palms upward, toward the ceiling—"there's a lot to figure out and it's not like I'm not buried here."

"You have to have a life. We *both* have to have lives."

"I was going to talk my hours over with Grayson when . . ." Closing her eyes for a second, she drew in a long breath. "Well, you know. Anyway, we've got this case we need to figure out."

Alvarez nodded.

"Let's just get through today. It's going to be a rough one, right?"

It was a rhetorical question that didn't require an answer. A funeral was never easy. This one, not only for a fallen officer but for a mentor as well, would be especially tough. Grayson had been an officer who had epitomized everything Alvarez believed was the essence of a true lawman. He had also been the person she'd fallen for, the one who had taught her to trust again. And that was the truth of it . . . until Dylan O'Keefe had reentered her life and shown her what real love could be. Nonetheless, the service was going to be emotionally ravaging. Already, she felt that awful pang deep in her heart again, the one reserved for Sheriff Dan Grayson.

She took a deep breath and put the conversation back on track. "We should get an answer from AFIS soon about the prints, if the killer is in the system." The Automated Fingerprint Identification System was usually fairly quick. Now that they had a full print, there might be a match in the database that held millions of prints on file.

Pescoli said, "Let's hope." There was a chance that the prints only matched each other, that the culprit had never been printed, and therefore couldn't be identified. If so, they were back to square one.

"I got hold of Reggie," Alvarez told her. "Actually Reginald Larue the Third. He lives in Spokane and admitted to dating Calypso. Nearly fell into a million pieces when I mentioned that we found a body we think could be hers. Couldn't get off the phone fast enough and is even now on his way to ID the body. He sounded shocked and very upset. He claims both of her parents are already dead and she has no siblings. No kids, no ex-husband, at least that she told him about. As far as he knows, he's the closest thing to family she has."

"What about a job?"

"She was a consultant. An engineer. Worked with road crews. Again, on her own. A one woman show."

"The Teflon woman. No one sticks to her."

"At least according to Reggie. I checked the call log and text log on her phone. He was the last one who tried to contact her at two twenty-three in the morning. That's when the last text was sent, all of them more and more pleading, asking her to call him and forgive him. Here they are, printed out." Alvarez slid the pages to Pescoli. "I double-checked with his cell phone carrier. His phone was in Spokane when he sent them. I thought there was a chance he might be trying to call or text her after she was dead to throw us off, but the phone, at least, was in Spokane, or so it seems. I can't say that he was actually there."

"No alibi?"

"He's got one and it's pretty interesting. A woman."

"Another woman was with him that night?" Pescoli asked. "As in *all* night?"

"So they both claim."

"But now he's in a million pieces about Calypso?"

"Seemed real, but I'll find out. I'm meeting him at the morgue before the funeral. There's enough time for questions, I think."

"Should be interesting," Pescoli said.

They discussed the case a little while longer, then each went their separate ways. Pescoli was all about getting her kids ready for the sad event while Alvarez returned to her condo to meet Dylan. He would be her rock during the service.

At least with him at her side, she could get through the event without completely falling apart . . . she hoped. Usually, she was the cool, level-headed detective and kept her emotions under tight rein.

Dan Grayson's death had changed all that.

CHAPTER 20

Pescoli had dreaded this day from the minute she heard the sheriff had died.

She was dressed in full uniform, Sturgis with her. The idea had been Joelle Fisher's, and for once, Pescoli had agreed with the receptionist that Sturgis's presence would be fitting as the dog had been constantly at Grayson's side, in or out of the office. Sturgis was part of the department, too, and he always behaved himself.

With a quick look around the crowded auditorium of Pinewood Center, she located her children standing together in the center of one section of chairs. Santana wasn't with them, but that was no surprise as they weren't yet a family. In fact, she wondered if there ever would be a time where they existed cohesively . . . and doubted it. She finally found him amidst the standing room only throng, near enough to the wide set of double doors at the back to satisfy the fire marshal.

She moved to the section reserved for law enforcement, where she and her fellow officers would stand during the service.

Though there had been a hum of conversation rising to the tall ceiling before the funeral got underway, a hush fell over the mourners as Blackwater approached the podium and introduced himself. Without any fanfare, he gave the opening remarks about the dedication and service of Dan Grayson. He was sincere and true, without any self-promotion and his remarks were surprisingly spot-on without the usual aggrandizing of the dead's accomplishments. No flowery phrases. No inordinate sentimentality. He called Grayson a straight shooter who was respected by his peers and those who worked for him, and stated that the sheriff was embraced by the community that had elected him. Blackwater summed up by saying that Sheriff Daniel Grayson would be missed by those he worked with and those he worked for, and that the community had lost an honest, kind, and dedicated officer of the law.

Pescoli grudgingly had to admit Grayson would have approved of the acting sheriff's remarks.

Flanked by flags of the United States and the State of Montana, a huge picture of the sheriff hung from a wall of navy-blue draping in the front of the hall. In the headshot, Grayson wasn't smiling, his stern expression offering none of the warmth that had epitomized the man. His sense of humor, his calm hand in running the department, the love he had for the dog at her side weren't evident.

Considering Pescoli's emotional state, it was probably a good thing. She, like so many others jammed into the large room, remembered him for the level-headed and kind man he was.

Officers from other jurisdictions as well as the Pinewood County Sheriff's Department, the city of Grizzly Falls' Police Department, and the Montana State Police were in attendance. Friends and family, townspeople, and neighbors filled the large hall to overflowing.

As she listened to the eulogy given by the chaplain, Pescoli caught glimpses of the wives and husbands of the officers, as well as Trace O'Halleran and Dr. Kacey Lambert along with Grace Perchant and Ivor Hicks. For once, Hicks was quiet, not causing a scene. She hoped he could maintain as much for the duration of the service.

Pescoli noticed Manny Douglas, the reporter for the local paper, taking notes. *God, the guy has no couth.*

Sandi from Wild Wills was in attendance, as was the owner of Dino's, the local pizza parlor. Pescoli recognized the local veterinarian and the pharmacist. There were several hundred people she didn't know along with more than a sprinkling of familiar faces.

The Grayson family was seated front and center, everyone dressed in black, each member grim-faced. Dan's brothers Cade and big Zed were seated with Hattie, Bart's ex-wife. She was fighting a losing battle with tears, a tissue wadded in her fist. Her girls were also part of the group.

Nearby, both of Dan's ex-wives, neither of which Pescoli cared much for, sat ramrod straight. Akina Bellows, seated next to her current husband, Rick, remained dry-eyed, but sober. Their one-year-old daughter, squirming slightly, was seated on Akina's lap.

Dan Grayson's first wife, Cara, a petite woman who was related to Hattie—Pescoli frowned. *Maybe a half sister or something?*—sat stiffly next to her husband, Nolan Banks. Their daughter, Allison, who was a little younger than Bianca, sat between her father and brothers and was fiddling with her cell phone despite what appeared to be several reprimands from her father. Nolan's jaw tightened and finally he rolled his palm toward the ceiling and wiggled his fingers, silently indicating she should hand over the phone. The girl, ever-petulant, slid the offensive cell into a small clutch purse.

Pescoli suspected Allison was her own kind of trouble. Ezekiel and Isaiah, Nolan's sons from a previous marriage, were leaning forward, elbows on their knees. Both boys, around college age, looked uncomfortable as they whispered and pulled at their collars and ties.

It seemed as if everyone in town had come to pay their respects. The chairs were all full, mourners spilling out into the hallway and anteroom.

After the chaplain, Cade and Zed approached the podium. While Zed didn't say a word, Cade offered up some anecdotes about Dan Grayson, the man and the brother. Cade's voice broke as he admitted he'd looked up to Dan, who had often been his ideal and sometimes even a father figure. Dan could get mad enough, but he'd always been able to see the clear path and had helped his hellion of a brother find his way, too.

After a prayer, there was a solo of "Amazing Grace" by Frannie Hendrickson, who led a choir at the Methodist church on Sundays and was known for her purple wig and karaoke renditions at the Tin Roof Saloon in Missoula on Saturday nights. Today, her hair was black, as were her dress and heels, her voice a clear and pure soprano that rose to the rafters.

Once again, Pescoli felt teary. She patted Sturgis's head and the damn dog licked her hand, then leaned against her. At that moment, she knew that she'd keep the black lab until his dying day. Until then, she'd thought one of Dan's brothers might want the dog, but it no longer mattered. Sturgis was hers and would be a living reminder of the sheriff. She caught Santana's eye just before the last prayer and he gave her an encouraging smile and small wink that somehow made her heart swell despite her sadness. Her throat clogged at how suddenly grateful she was to be marrying him.

With the back of one finger she swiped away her tears and mentally reminded herself to toughen up, that if the chaplain were to be believed, Dan Grayson was in "a better place." She wasn't certain about that, but it was a nice idea and she liked to think it was true even if she didn't quite believe it.

Once the service had concluded with another quiet prayer, the flag-draped coffin was wheeled out of the hall by the pallbearers—Grayson's brothers and four officers from the department.

Pescoli, the dog in tow, left the hall and found her kids outside. They were standing close together, talking, their breath visible in the air as they waited by Jeremy's pickup, which was parked in the side lot. She and Sturgis made their way to the truck.

"Thanks for coming. It means a lot to me."

" 'Course," Jeremy said. He'd even dressed for the occasion in a long-sleeved striped shirt and slacks that could've stood a pressing, but hey, a vast improvement over his sweats or jeans and sloppy football jersey. He'd found an old suit coat of his father's that was a little short in the sleeves and slightly faded, but at least he'd taken the time to appear presentable. Bianca, starting to think of herself as a fashionista, was dressed in a short charcoal gray dress with matching leggings and a black coat that hit her at the knees, just an inch above her boots.

"Are you coming to the cemetery?" Pescoli asked them.

"No," Bianca said quickly.

"Yes, we are," Jeremy disagreed. He shot his sister a look that suggested she not argue.

"I don't see why." Bianca started to go into her petulant routine.

"Because Mom worked for him, and so did I and like, duh"—Jeremy motioned toward Sturgis—"we've got his dog." He was firm as he strode to the driver's side of his truck. "We're going, Bianca. Get in."

Bianca's shoulders slumped as if she were an eight-year-old being punished and sent to her room.

Pescoli said, "I think it's a good idea. Respectful. Dan Grayson was good to all of us."

"Let's go," Jeremy yelled from behind the wheel and fired the engine before slamming his door shut.

"Great," Bianca grumbled but climbed into her brother's rig as Pescoli made her way to her own Jeep.

Santana was waiting for her. "Trouble in paradise?" he asked, hitching his chin toward Jeremy's truck as it wheeled out of the lot.

"Nothing serious." She didn't want to go into it.

Santana picked up on it. "You want to ride to the cemetery together?"

"Yes. Please. That would be great." It felt good to let someone else take charge, if only for a little while. "But there's three of us," she said, indicating Sturgis.

Santana's dark eyes sparkled in the sun. "I'm used to that. Come on." He walked her to the passenger side. She handed him her keys and slid into the Jeep. Sturgis hopped inside.

They drove to the cemetery in a long procession and Pescoli stared out the window. Once they were through the city with its plowed streets and piles of graying snow, they passed by broad fields spangled beneath the bright sun. The cemetery was located on a hill outside the city limits that angled softly upward and offered a view of the valley and the town sprawled below. Tombstones half buried in snow sprouted from the frozen ground and two roads bisected the graves. Ahead was a fresh plot—dark earth turned over in the snow, an oblong hole in the ground surrounded by several floral sprays, a small tent, and fake grass.

Fewer people had made the trek to the cemetery, though a bevy of vehicles were parked and mourners trudged through six inches of frigid powder to stand at Dan Grayson's final resting spot. The chaplain said a few more words and led another prayer. The Grayson family sat in a sober group near the grave.

Pescoli's stomach knotted at the finality of it all. When the guns were fired in salute, she fought a fresh spate of tears. Sturgis didn't so much as whimper as the rifles blasted and afterward the dog, head down, followed Pescoli obediently to Santana's truck.

It was over.

For everyone.

Sheriff Dan Grayson had been laid to rest.

Jessica woke Sunday morning feeling tired all over, and at work, the diner was a madhouse. While Saturday had been a little slow, the crowd had returned for Sunday breakfast, brunch, lunch, and then later for dinner.

Nell was beside herself, delighted that the receipts were keeping the register busy. "This is just what we needed," she said, grinning.

Misty was quick on her feet, and obviously thrilled with the tips. "Maybe I will take that winter vacation to Puerto Vallarta after all. My cousin's got a place down there, ya know. Always asking me to come down, but the airfare's out of my league. However, with a couple more days like this, I can see myself sitting on a beach and sipping a margarita from some hottie in a Speedo."

Armando rolled his eyes and muttered something in Spanish under his breath. He and Denise had worked harder than ever getting the orders cooked and plated at a breakneck pace. Though Denise was handling the extra work effortlessly, Armando was at his rope's end, griping that they were running out of staples and that too many of the orders came in with changes. Jessica, grateful for the fast pace, didn't have time to think about the fact that she'd promised herself to go to the sheriff's office the next morning.

But as the shift wound down and the last customers drifted out of the diner, her stomach once again knotted. Could she go through with it?

It was a little before eleven when Misty said, "You run on home. I'll close."

Jessica nodded. She was dead tired and told herself to get a decent night's sleep, then face the music. When she drove out of the lot, she found the city streets nearly deserted, the town of Grizzly Falls seemingly folded in on itself and closed up for the cold winter's night.

She told herself again that she wasn't being followed, that the headlights she'd seen in her rearview mirror weren't zeroed in on her. As she had before, she considered all of her options. She could wait for the bastard to find her, stand her ground, and try to blow him away herself, but then she'd end up in a trial and possibly prison or the mental hospital. Again.

No, thank-you.

Fleeing or turning herself in to the police were her options.

If she ran again, she was only putting off the inevitable. Buying a little frantic time. Putting more people in danger. Again, she'd pass.

That left going to the police, telling them her story, and hoping they would believe her, trust her, go against all the evidence.

She turned onto the county road and the streetlights gave way to darkness. No car seemed to be following her and the more distance she put between herself and Grizzly Falls, the more she told herself to relax. She had only one more night on the run, then, come morning, her life would take another turn and change.

Forever.

"So be it," she said, the beams from her headlights cutting through the deep night. A few snowflakes drifted lazily from the night sky to catch in the light. As she left the city behind she should have felt calm, but instead, she was still uneasy. Restless. She fiddled with the radio and heard an old Johnny Cash song on a country station that kept cutting out. She thought of her family and a bitter taste rose in her throat. Would they come to Montana? Would she be sent to Louisiana where she would face them again through iron bars or through thick glass where they could only speak through phones mounted in the walls? Or would they abandon her?

Did she even care? Those ties had been severed a while back, their frayed ends unable to be stitched back together.

She had, of course, not only betrayed and embarrassed them, she'd renounced them publicly, a sin for which she would never be forgiven. Her mother and father lived by a very stiff and archaic set of standards. A public life that was, to all who looked at it, picture-perfect. No cracks to be seen. But once the doors were closed, their private life was very different and very guarded.

She'd known the rules growing up.

She'd not only broken them, she'd done so in a very public way.

She remembered the day she'd first confronted her mother.

Outside on a lounge chair, her mother was reading a paperback. Wearing a sundress and dark glasses, she'd positioned herself on the porch in the shade of the overhanging oak tree, leaving only her legs exposed to the sunlight.

Though it was barely nine in the morning, the summer heat was sweltering, the day sultry, almost sticky, a haze in the blue Louisiana sky. An Olympic-sized pool, her father's prized possession, abutted the veranda of her parents' home outside New Orleans. It shimmered as it stretched far into the tended backyard.

"Mom?" Anne-Marie called, gathering her nerves.

Jeanette looked up and set her paperback onto her lap. A glass of sweet tea was sweating on the small table beside the lounge chair. A smaller glass of ice and a clear liquid, most likely gin, sat near a pack of long cigarettes by the ashtray and a lighter. Paddle fans, as always, were softly whirling overhead. Butterflies with orange and black wings flitted through the heavily blossomed bougainvillea flanking the yard.

"This is a surprise." Jeanette smiled, but Anne-Marie knew it was false. Jeanette Favier had never been a warm person.

"I have something to tell you."

"Oh." Nothing more. Just the hint of disappointment from dealing with a daughter who had continually disappointed and bothered her.

"It's about . . . him."

"Again?" Her mother sighed, her smile falling away. "Why you have such a problem with your husband, I'll never understand. Marriage isn't easy, and given your . . . condition, you're lucky he wanted you."

"My condition. You mean because I was a little wild?" Anne-Marie challenged.

Her mother sighed through her nose. "Your brothers were 'a little wild,' but you pushed the boundaries, got yourself in that accident and—" She stopped. "Oh, well."

"Go ahead. Say it. I've never been the same since. Isn't that what you were going to tell me? You blame me for falling off a damn horse and hitting my head and think that's the cause of every bad thing that's happened to me since."

"You were in a coma for days, but of course, you don't remember that. When you finally woke up"—Jeanette shook slightly—"you were . . . different."

"With a condition."

"You went from bad to worse. I'd thought . . . no, I'd hoped . . . when you finally decided to get married that you would settle down, make a decent life for yourself. But that's not the way it ever is with you."

"He's not the man I thought he was."

"No one is. We all have girlhood dreams of white knights and thunderous steeds and chivalrous men who pledge their lives to us, but in the end, they are all just men." Jeanette let out a long breath and shook her head. "Have you forgotten the 'for better or worse' part of your vows?"

"He hit me, Mom."

Jeanette looked up sharply. "Oh, Anne-Marie," she said as if she didn't believe her, as if Anne-Marie were spinning another lie.

"I'm serious, Mom," she insisted and witnessed the cords in her mother's neck tightening, the way they always did when Jeanette was forced to deal with her wayward, rule-breaking daughter's problems.

"Okay. So he shoved you," she finally said, finding a way to make the statement more palatable. "Why don't you just, you know, keep quiet about it?" Jeanette Favier's type of motherly advice. "That's what we do, you know." She reached for her cigarettes, then her fingers scrabbled over the glass top of the table, nearly knocking over her iced tea before she clenched the soft pack.

Anne-Marie stood her ground. "He beat me!" she repeated, her fists clenching at her sides. "That's assault, Mom."

"Hush!" Her mother sat up quickly, then glanced furtively over her shoulder toward the inside of the huge plantation-style home. "For the love of God, Anne-Marie, keep your voice down. The cleaning people are here and your father's in his study." She pointed overhead to the area in the general direction of Talbert Favier's private office.

"You don't care that he hit me?"

"Of course I care." Jeanette tried to shake a cigarette out of the crumpled pack.

"You should, because he hit me over and over again. I thought . . . I thought he would crack my ribs."

"But he didn't, did he?" Jeanette managed to shake out a cigarette and light up despite the fact that it was slightly bent. Her hands were trembling.

Anne-Marie stared down at her mother. "Not yet. But he will."

"No, no. You don't know that."

"He's going to really hurt me."

"Now, look, Anne-Marie," Jeanette said, sighing in a cloud of smoke. "This is not good. But you knew he had a temper before you married him."

"Not like this. I didn't know he was violent."

Lifting up her sunglasses, Jeanette squinted at her daughter through a thin tendril of smoke. "So what do you want to do?"

"Go to the police."

"What? Oh, Lord!" She shook her head at the thought, then set her cigarette in the ashtray. "No way. You have to leave the police out of it."

"He beat me, Mother. What part of that don't you get?" To prove her point, Anne-Marie took off her own shades to display the red in her eye, the bruise surrounding her eye socket.

"Oh . . . oh, dear." Jeanette winced.

Not stopping with the damage to her face, Anne-Marie lifted her T-shirt to show the black, blue, and sickly green discoloration across her abdomen.

Her mother sucked in a swift breath. "I'm so, so sorry." In an act so foreign to her mother that Anne-Marie was stunned, Jeanette grabbed a towel draped over a nearby chair and dipped one corner into the pool. "Sit," she said, indicating the end of the chaise and then, smelling of smoke and her signature perfume, she gently dabbed at her daughter's injuries.

Anne-Marie sucked in her breath as her mother touched her face, pressing the cold towel against her cheek.

"I think you'll live," Jeanette pronounced.

"This time."

"It's not that bad." She took her time folding the towel.

"He attacked me, Mother. Beat me. Then raped me." Anne-Marie was trembling inside, the memory of the vicious attack fresh and brutal. She needed her mother to understand, to be her champion.

"Oh, darling," her mother said softly.

For an instant, Anne-Marie believed Jeanette's hard exterior had cracked with empathy and love for her only daughter, but that hopeful impression was short-lived as the older woman asked gently, "Whatever did you do to provoke him so?"

"What? Didn't you hear me? He assaulted me, gave me these." Once more, Anne-Marie lifted her T-shirt to display her bruises. She hurt inside, was as emotionally beat-up as she was physically. But it was at the hands of her own damn mother, the woman whom she'd hoped would believe her and protect her.

"Oh, I heard you, sweetheart," Jeanette said as she leaned over the table and took a final puff of her cigarette before putting it out in a series of nervous taps until the filter tip was mashed in the ashtray. Then she turned to grab her daughter by the shoulders. "I know you're sore. It's obvious, but . . . but your husband's a good man, maybe a little rough around the edges in private, but you just have to try to please him."

"How can you say that?" Anne-Marie nearly screamed. "These aren't the dark ages for God's sake! Mother, listen to yourself. Do you really think I should stay with a man who does this to me?" She held her T-shirt higher, where bite marks were visible on her breasts over the top of her bra.

"Honey." Her mother picked up the towel again, and, looking as if she really had no idea what to do, tried to dab at the contusion on Anne-Marie's cheek again.

Anne-Marie dropped the hem of her T-shirt and grabbed her mother's wrist, stopping her. "He's an animal," she hissed. So angry she was nearly spitting, she shoved her face close to her mother's so that their noses nearly touched. She saw the tiny imperfections in the older woman's face, the pores that were a little larger on her nostrils and the telltale web of red lines running across her nose to her cheeks. Minuscule threads lurking beneath the surface, they were evidence of far too many gin and tonics by the pool that were stubbornly resisting an ever-thickening layer of makeup.

Anne-Marie said, "I will not be used as a human punching bag."

Jeanette backed up. "You married the man."

"I didn't know."

"Listen to me, Anne-Marie. There is no divorce in our family. You might see that as archaic, but that's the way it is. Your father is an elder in the church, a respected businessman. And your grandfather's a preacher. Do you hear me? My father preached from the Good Book. Your brothers have problems with their wives and kids and they're working it out. You haven't been easy, my dear. Not at all. Not with the craziness you spew. But," she said and then repeated, "but . . . we are proud, genteel people, expected to set an example for the community."

"You would sacrifice me? For the sake of . . . what? Some ridiculous and antiquated notion of what a marriage is? Your precious reputation?"

Slap!

Her mother's palm struck fast and hard, leaving a red mark over Anne-Marie's already bruised cheek. "Sacrifice is a part of life, a path to heaven. And marriage is sacred. Don't you ever forget it. And as for divorce? In this family, it's out of the question." She yanked her arm back.

Anne-Marie let it go. "You can't tell me what to do. I'm a grown woman."

"Then act like one." Disgusted, Jeanette added tautly, "Do your duty, Anne-Marie."

"Are you kidding?"

"You're a wife. His wife. Your choice. And, let's face it, you haven't been a very good one, have you?"

Anne-Marie didn't answer.

"I didn't think so." With a frown, Jeanette said, "Look into a mirror. Think about what you've done. You're not the victim here."

"He hit me."

"Then deal with it. But, please, don't come running to me!" She started for the inside of the house.

"I'm divorcing the son of a bitch."

Her mother hesitated at the French doors leading to the kitchen. With one hand on the doorknob, she glanced over her shoulder. "Then you're divorcing all of us, Anne-Marie. You won't be welcome here again."

Anne-Marie's stomach tightened and she'd fought the urge to run to her mother and beg her forgiveness, but she stood firm.

"I trust you can show yourself out," were the last words her mother said to her.

CHAPTER 21

Jessica shoved thoughts of her family aside as she drove through the night. They would not be any help. Never had been. Even her grandmother on her mother's side, Marcella, who had adored her only granddaughter, wouldn't come to her aid.

Not any longer.

That, of course, was her own fault. The effect of stealing from someone who loved and trusted her.

Would the police be able to protect her?

She doubted it. She had too many strikes against her—a mental patient as well as a thief and a known liar. No, she didn't really believe the cops would help her, at least not the cops in New Orleans. She'd pinned her hopes on Dan Grayson. But even if he'd still been alive, chances were he wouldn't have come to her rescue, either.

"Face it," she said to the disguised woman in the mirror, "you're on your own."

Then again, hadn't she always been?

The snow began to fall a little more heavily, collecting on the windshield, and she remembered the storm that had been predicted, a blizzard moving south from Canada, the biggest of the winter. *Great,* she thought sarcastically. Just what she needed. She flipped on the wipers and from the corner of her eye, caught a flash of headlights shining through the night, a vehicle somewhere behind her.

You're not the only one who lives out here, she reminded herself.

"But almost," she said, her gloved hands tightening over the steering wheel. Again, she looked back. Again she saw lights.

She swallowed hard and wondered where the hell all of her bravado had gone. It was as if her courage had dissolved in the time, over a year, since that conversation with her mother.

It's nothing. Don't be paranoid. Get a damn grip.

Her heart was pounding like crazy. Despite the cold, her fingers began to sweat in her gloves as she clenched the wheel.

Another look in the mirror.

The lights had disappeared.

Probably turned off at that last junction. She let out her breath.

It was nothing. See? For God's sake pull yourself together. You have to keep a level head.

She saw the lane leading to her cabin and started to turn in when two eyes caught in the headlights. "Oh, God!" She slammed on the brakes and the SUV skidded, back end fishtailing as the deer leaped nimbly into the surrounding trees.

She sat for a second, waiting for her rollicking heart to return to normal as snow drifted down, falling steadily, piling on the ground.

It was a damn deer. Nothing more.

She pressed on the gas pedal. Wheels spinning, she whispered, "Come on, come on," as the back end slid some more. Finally, the front wheels caught, the Tahoe lurched forward, and she drove along the ruts to the cabin, a tiny dark abode in the middle of nowhere.

She'd been foolish to come to Grizzly Falls, she realized, propelled by fear and confusion and, yes, paranoia. But, come the daylight, she would make things right.

The rest of the drive down the winding length of the lane was uneventful. She parked, hurried into the cabin, then went through her usual routine of replacing firewood, then stoking the flames, and double-checking all the locks on the doors and latches on the windows before making certain that every curtain or shade was pulled tight.

After twisting on the shower to get the warm water running, she took off the pieces of her disguise. She hung her wig and padding on a hook behind the bathroom door then secured her dental appliance in a ziplock plastic bag that she left on the counter. Cold to the bone, she showered quickly, then dried off, tossing her towel over a hook near the window. She cracked the window just enough to clear the room of what little steam had collected. Shivering, she pulled on her sweats, grabbed her uniform and underclothes, then hurried back to the living room where the fire was burning more brightly, some heat emanating from the grate.

Yeah, this place is miserable, she thought. Hardly a haven.

By habit, she folded her work clothes then placed them on the table at one end of her makeshift bed. Finally, she settled in by the fire and turned on her computer to catch up on the day's news and watch some mind-numbing television. Currently, she found no more information about the two women who had been killed in Grizzly Falls and she prayed that they hadn't been targeted because of her.

No way.

That was impossible, right?

Creeeaaak.

Her heart stilled as she listened.

Had she been mistaken, or had a floorboard squeaked somewhere in her house?

Waiting, not moving a muscle, she listened hard.

Nothing.

There's no one here. No one. You know it.

But there had been a noise. She was sure of it. And it sounded as if it had emanated from *inside* the house.

Swallowing back her fear, she stayed motionless, her ears straining as she listened, but she heard nothing other than the sound of dry tinder popping and moss hissing as they caught fire, the sound of the wind outside the cabin, and the damn drip of the bathroom faucet.

Get over yourself.

Still, she held her breath, then slowly retrieved her tiny pistol and, moving slowly, carefully went through the house to investigate. Cautiously she moved through the small rooms. Over the internal clamoring of her heart, she listened for any sound that was out of the ordinary while searching the nooks and crannies, every shadow, for someone or something that was trapped inside.

An animal. That's it. A squirrel or rat or rabbit. Or God forbid, a skunk might have found its way inside. Right? Or do they hibernate? She didn't really know. Just hoped that whatever it was, it wasn't human.

Her throat was dry as sand.

Fear pulsed through her.

The living area was clear, no one inside. The kitchen alcove was empty, too, and cold, a bit of air seeping from the area around the window over the sink. On bare feet, she made her way to the back door and lifted the shade where she could peek outside to the small porch.

The snow was falling faster. The predicted blizzard had arrived. She worried her lower lip and wondered if she'd be trapped, her plans of telling her wild tale to the police thwarted.

You're not backing out of this. Too many times you've turned tail and run. Tomorrow, come hell or high water . . .

She forcibly steeled herself. For months, she'd been a coward, but no longer. She had a four-wheel-drive vehicle and would make it to the police station . . . if she got through this last, lonely night.

Trying to see through the thickening veil of snow, she saw no one. Nothing sinister seemed to be peering from the shadows. Narrowing her eyes, she studied each of the trees closest to the house and the back of the old garage and the small pump house. She waited, antic-ipating movement, but nothing moved other than the flurries of snow that swirled past frantically, the wind increasing.

Give it up, Anne-Marie or Jessica or whoever it is you're calling yourself now.

Her fingers clutched fiercely over the pistol's grip, because some-thing didn't seem right outside. Everything looked peaceful, even serene and yet . . . what was it?

Then she knew. It wasn't that she saw anyone, but the snow be-hind the house seemed uneven rather than smooth. Were those footprints on the landscape, large impressions in the icy powder that she hadn't created?

She looked harder, but, of course, she couldn't be certain as it was so dark, and really, who would be skulking around the cabin? Who knew she was there?

No one.

Well, besides Cade. And maybe Big Zed as he had to have seen her SUV parked in the driveway, but they wouldn't be a problem. No one would come. And it was her last night in the cabin.

She hoped.

Staring into the night, she saw no movement other than the sway of branches and swirl of snow. The impressions she thought were footprints could have been caused by the irregular terrain behind the house—dirt clods or boulders or brush. Surely there was no clear trail, no path that someone had broken in the snow, no clear print on the thin snow of the back step. No, no, she was just letting her wild imagination get the better of her.

Still convincing herself that she was safe, that no one was lurking in the frigid shadows outside, she backed away from the door, letting the shade drop. She moved silently to the bathroom, slowly pushing open the door a bit with the muzzle of the gun so that the weak light of the living area could permeate the darkness. She started to step inside and—

No!

Her heart jolted at the sight of a dark figure in the reflection of the cracked mirror.

She bit back a scream, stepped back, and pointed her pistol at the doorway. "Drop your weapon!" she ordered, taking another step back, gun aimed, ready to fire.

Nothing.

No movement.

No response.

"Drop your weapon! Step out! Hands over your head!"

Again no response.

Just the keen of the wind and somewhere a branch banging against the side of the house.

"I mean it. I'll shoot!"

She was breathing hard, nearly hyperventilating. The gun beginning to wobble. She considered firing a warning shot, but was afraid of the ricochet. "Come out. Now!"

Damn. He wasn't responding. In fact, he hadn't so much as moved a muscle.

Cautiously, her finger on the trigger, she moved forward to the side of the door in case he should jump into the bathroom and start firing.

But that wasn't his style, was it?

"Who the hell are you?" she cried and then, ever so cautiously looked into the bathroom, to the mirror.

He was still in the same position. Crouching. Hiding halfway behind the door. His eyes were guarded, but his hair was visible. She swung her straight arm around the edge of the door. "I said 'Drop!' " she cried.

Not a whisper.

Trembling, she repeated, "I said—" But the command died in her throat and she felt all the strength seep out of her. "For the love of God."

As she looked more closely, first in the mirror, and then around the door to the wall itself, she realized she wasn't looking at some sinister cloaked figure ready to do her bodily harm. The "figure" wasn't a person at all. What she'd seen in the distorted image of the broken mirror was her own disguise, the padding and wig suspended from a hook in the wall behind the door. Just where she'd left it not an hour earlier.

"Idiot," she muttered, leaning against the vanity. Her knees were jelly and she felt herself flush in embarrassment. What was wrong with her? She was letting her paranoia get the better of her.

You keep this up and you'll end up in the mental hospital again. Is that what you want? For God's sake, get a damn grip, would ya?

She studied her image in the cracked mirror and thought it was ironically symbolic that her face was disfigured and warped.

So so true.

As her heart rate eventually slowed, she collected her wits and yanked the window shut tight, latching it securely.

Why would anyone, even a maniac as malicious as her husband, harm an innocent person? She'd leaped to the wrong conclusion. Again.

Still, she felt as if someone were watching her, following her, tracking her. The feeling never left her. From the moment she awoke, all through her days at the diner, on the road, and even in the cabin, it was the same. She glanced around the room and wondered about bugs—the kind with tiny microphones and itsy little cameras—and even her own computer. It had a camera in it. Could someone even now, be looking through—

Stop it! No one's been here. No one's planting listening devices, for God's sake. You don't even talk to anyone. And as for cameras—really? Why would anyone on God's green earth go to all that trouble? Why not just come in and kill you in your sleep? Get over your crazy self!

Whether there was reason or not, she did a quick sweep with her flashlight of the obvious places, and double-checked her stashes that she'd hidden to make certain her money and fake licenses and passports that had cost her so much were in place. Using the cash she'd stolen, she'd purchased them from a sketchy friend of a sketchy friend of a sketchy friend. She and the contact had met twice, once in an alley behind a crowded bar in the wee hours and the second time when she'd actually been handed the perfect-appearing documents on the waterfront of the slow-moving Mississippi in New Orleans in the dead of night. With the noise and lights of the French Quarter not far away, they'd made the exchange. Being that close to the river alone had made her skin crawl, and dealing with the skinny sharp-nosed man who didn't hide the fact that he was carrying a weapon, had been nerve-wracking. The pictures on her ID were far from perfect, of course, but so far, she hadn't been asked to show her driver's license anywhere. That would change when she told her story, of course.

Oh, God, she hoped the officer she connected with would believe her.

Don't freak out. You're safe. You'll go into the sheriff's department in the morning and demand protection, explain yourself. Everything will be fine.

That of course was a lie, but she swallowed back her fear, forced her heartbeat to slow, and found a way to become calm again. Tomorrow, come what may, she would be done running.

The fire crackled and hissed. Warmth radiated through the small room. She closed her eyes on the couch and touched the underside of her pillow, making certain the pistol was back where she'd placed it.

As nervous as she was, she felt too wound up to fall asleep and the minutes ticked by in the dark. She heard the wind screaming through the mountains and that damn limb bang against the house. The drip in the faucet, too, was audible, but it had become a part of her environment and eventually, as the fire began to die, exhaustion finally took over and she drifted off.

She didn't know how long she'd slept, but awoke slowly. *Today is the day,* her mind nagged, but she pulled the sleeping bag tighter around her to fend off the cold. She didn't open her eyes, didn't want to wake up. Not yet. Who knew what the day would bring? After all, it wasn't as if she'd gotten a full night's rest. It had been late when she'd fallen asleep and her recurring nightmare of drowning in blood had been peppered with the noises of the cabin. Images of glowing eyes watching her as she'd frantically tried to swim had been accompanied by a keening laughter and the steady clap of her attacker's hands. The wind screaming, the window panes rattling, the pounding of the branch against the house all added to her unrest. She'd even half-woken once, certain she wasn't alone, that someone was near enough that she felt his warm breath against her neck, but after blinking her eyes open and seeing nothing, she'd rolled over and settled back into fretful sleep.

Hours later, her back aching from her uncomfortable position on the old couch, a crick in her neck, Jessica rolled over without opening her eyes. It felt as if she hadn't slept a wink. Thankfully, she had a couple days off so she could sleep in.

And put off the inevitable? Isn't that what you're doing? Get up! Get going! Face the damn music. It's time to get on with the rest of your life.

"No," she said aloud and shivered, pulling up the sleeping bag as the temperature in the cabin had fallen overnight. She needed to get up and stoke the fire. Try to make herself presentable. Get her story straight.

What story? For once you'd better tell the truth.

That thought was foreign. Unappealing.

"Oh, God," she whispered. Throwing off the covers, she opened her eyes.

The cabin was nearly dark, of course, though she discerned from the bits of gray light filtering through the shades or cracks in the curtains that dawn had broken. *Good.* It was time to stoke the fire and get moving, face the damn music.

Finally, the waiting, and, oh God, the running, were nearly over.

She flung her legs off the couch and, stretching her arms over her head, yawned as she tried to wake up. Rotating the tightness from her neck, she felt it—that sizzling, heart-stopping sensation that something wasn't right.

Don't be silly.

Then she heard a scrape of leather against old floorboards.

Instinctively she rolled off the couch, her arm shooting forward under the pillow, her fingers searching for the hard steel of her pistol.

Nothing.

What? No!

"It's not there," a deep voice said.

Turning to look over her shoulder, she saw him then, the huge dark figure standing against the door.

Oh, God!

He'd found her.

CHAPTER 22

Pescoli had half-expected the atmosphere around the department to be different after Grayson's funeral, but when she got to work on Monday it didn't feel that way. Stomping snow from her boots, she felt a wall of heat greet her along with that same sense of somberness. Everyone who'd worked for Grayson may have gotten some closure from the ceremony, but it was going to take a while until it was business as usual again.

Winter had returned full force, a mother of a storm blowing in from Canada that had dumped nearly a foot of snow in the area and wasn't done yet. The wind was gusting and brutal, the temperature plunging to below freezing. Currently, most of the roads were clogged, some closed, maintenance crews working overtime. Deputies from the department had been called in early to deal with traffic snarls. Parts of the county were reporting electrical outages. Frozen pipes might be next, and the homeless population needed more shelter.

All that along with their current whack job—one who liked fingers and rings and dead women.

Pescoli, who had always claimed to have hated all the folderol over celebrations from New Year's to Christmas, found she missed the lightheartedness of Joelle's attempts to decorate the office, or at least her chance to poke fun at it. It was going to take a while until denial slowly morphed into reality and people got back into routine.

She had gotten up early and it was still predawn outside, not her norm by a long shot. She'd been unable to sleep, so she'd come to the station earlier than usual, ready to get back to the job, even though she was working for a man she didn't much like.

As she unwound her scarf, she told herself it was time for a personal attitude adjustment. She didn't like Blackwater, and she was pretty sure he didn't like her. So what? It was a time to get along, at least as long as she was employed in the department. Considering her current state—engaged, pregnant, the mother of teenagers who still needed her words of wisdom and guidance—it might be time to pack it in.

But not quite yet.

She still needed to find who'd killed Sheree Cantnor and Calypso Pope. That part—solving the mysteries of homicides, catching the culprits, and slamming their asses behind bars—she would miss. As for the particular freak they were currently chasing, she wanted him behind bars and fast. She and Alvarez needed to wrap it up.

Unzipping her outer coat as she walked by Blackwater's office, she caught a glimpse of him on the floor doing a slow, determined set of push-ups. "Detective?" he called before she could move past. "I'd like to have a word."

She paused. Backed up a step. Stood in the open doorway.

"Glad you're in early."

His face was away from her and as far as she could tell he hadn't even looked in her direction, which was a little disconcerting. She hadn't spoken, wasn't usually in before eight, and didn't think her footsteps were all that unique, yet there was no doubt he'd known it was she who was passing by his door.

"Come on in." He lifted one arm, still balancing himself off the floor with the other as he waved her inside.

Was he showing off? For her? She could have told him it wasn't going to work.

She stepped inside the small room that had once held a dog bed and hat rack. Both were gone, as were all of Grayson's personal belongings. Then again, his memorabilia had been missing for a while because Blackwater wasn't the first person to claim this office after Grayson had been shot; another man had sat in his chair, wielding his own brand of distorted power for a very short period.

"What can I do for you?" she asked him.

Dressed in uniform, his sleeves rolled up, his body straight as a board, not so much as breaking a sweat, Blackwater did three more slow, perfect push-ups, holding his body rigidly off the floor.

"You look busy," she said, looking longingly toward her office door.

"Nope. Finished. For now." In one swift, athletic motion he hopped to his feet and straightened, his face only slightly flushed. "Have a seat," he said, and she thought better of arguing, even though she was still wearing her jacket and hadn't even spent a second at her desk. "I'd like your take on the Cantnor and Pope homicides. Bring me up to speed."

"I thought Alvarez talked to you." Pescoli was pretty sure Blackwater had all the information they did.

"She did. As did Gage. But I'd like to hear what you think." He was staring at her intently, almost as if he were trying to read her mind.

So, he wants a recitation. Fine. "Well, I think we've got ourselves another nutcase." She perched stiffly on the chair she'd occupied so often when Grayson was alive.

Some kind of classical music was playing softly, Blackwater's computer was at the ready, the monitor glowing with the logo for the department on display, and every book, file, pen, or note pad was placed neatly on the desk or the surrounding cases, his awards mounted precisely on the walls. The whole "neat as a pin" feel gave Pescoli a bad feeling—kind of like Alvarez's office on steroids. It was all part and parcel of Blackwater's consistent military style.

"I think the murders are linked. That's the obvious conclusion, and I think it's the right one. We've got one sick jerk-off who gets his jollies by slicing off the victim's ring finger. I've got no real idea who's behind the deeds yet." She almost lost her train of thought, he was staring at her so intently, but she went through all the facts again as they knew them, finally returning to, "The big connection so far is the missing fingers and rings, and that fingerprint. We only hope we'll come up with a hit and be able to ID whoever picked up Sheree Cantnor's shoe and Calypso Pope's bag."

His eyebrows pinched together. "Not one suspect so far?"

He knew that, too, but apparently wanted her to reiterate. "No. At least not until we identify the print found on Cantnor's shoe and Pope's bag. Or, if our killer is dumb enough to try and pawn the rings and give himself away."

Blackwater picked a pencil out of the holder and leaning back in his chair, fiddled with it. "Odd case."

"We get our share around here."

"And then some," he agreed.

"Must be the water, or the hard winters. Makes people crazy."

He didn't so much as crack a smile. So much for a little levity.

"You got anything else?" he asked.

"We're still looking for a connection between the two women, old schools or boyfriends or friends, even friends of friends, but as near as we can tell at this point, the two victims didn't know each other."

"Random?"

"Or possibly each woman knew the killer, but not each other. If this were a TV show, it would turn out that the female victims happened to share the same bad-boy lover who maybe went to prison and hired some lunatic to off them or something like that. So far, we haven't been lucky enough to find any connection between the victims and Montana's version of a modern day Jerry Brudos."

When Blackwater didn't immediately respond, she elucidated. "The guy in Oregon who had a fetish for shoes and cut off body parts and kept 'em in the freezer. Back in the sixties, I think. My folks told me about it. Our guy has a thing for fingers and rings."

Listening, Blackwater asked, "You think the killer will strike again? Here?" He pointed to the office floor, but she knew he meant in the general area of Grizzly Falls.

"I would have said 'probably not' after the first victim. I mean, who knew what was going on? I thought the Cantnor woman's killer might just be a pissed off ex-boyfriend. But after Pope that doesn't make as much sense now. Maybe he's setting up for another kill, or maybe he was just passing through, did his business here, twice that we know of, then moved on. For all we know, there could be more bodies of earlier victims that have been killed and dumped somewhere else, and not yet discovered."

"He could have had other victims. Cases before ours."

"We're double-checking that, as well as the names of all of the women who've gone missing in the past month."

"Do you think he's moved on?" Blackwater asked.

Pescoli slowly shook her head. "Just a gut feeling, but no. Our doer seems to know the area pretty well. Either that, or he's been extremely fortunate, as we can't find a link between the women, and we have no video footage or pictures of anyone near the victims in their last moments. Somehow, he avoided any cameras on that stretch of the waterfront when he attacked Calypso Pope. The same goes for Sheree Cantnor, yet these days everyone has a camera phone in their purse or pocket. People are always taking pictures and posting them on social media sites. And most businesses keep security cameras running twenty-four seven. So, how's our guy been so lucky unless he's really aware of the area?"

As if realizing he was fiddling with the pencil, Blackwater replaced it. "Why the rings? The fingers?"

"Trophies? You know, to relive the moment. Again, like our friend Brudos. Or maybe some kind of personal statement about the rings, or marriage? Maybe both?" She shook her head. "Hard to know what kind of psychosis the doer's dealing with."

"You think he's insane?"

"Without a doubt, but, hey, I'm not giving the killer a defense. I'm just saying he's not what most of us would call normal."

Blackwater nodded. "Rings with fingers. A weird fetish."

"Name a fetish that isn't abnormal," she suggested and realized that for the first time since Blackwater had taken over they seemed to be on the same page.

His phone rang and he ended the meeting abruptly with, "Okay. Just wanted your thoughts. Keep me posted."

"Will do." She rose, then couldn't help herself from asking, "So, what's with the push-ups?"

"Keeps the blood flowing. Any kind of exercise. I do something every two hours, makes my brain clearer."

"Oh."

"You should try it."

"I should," she said equably.

He actually smiled, seeing through her. "And Pescoli?"

"Hmmm?"

"Just for the record, I know what happened. Out in the woods that day when you'd chased down Grayson's killer."

"Oh, yeah?" *Where is this going?*

"I'm glad your son saved your life and shot the son of a bitch who was trying to kill you." His hand was poised over the phone which was on its third ring, but his gaze was locked with hers.

Surprised, she said, "Umm. Me, too."

"You're lucky." Then he added, "Jeremy's a good kid." Blackwater actually flashed a quick smile, straight white teeth against bronzed skin. "And fortunately a damn good shot."

"Thanks," she said, then started down the hall to her office. She still wasn't fond of the man, but it seemed like he was at least trying harder. Unless he was just blowing hot air up her skirt because he sensed she neither trusted nor liked him. He was smart enough to pull that off, she knew.

As she reached the door to her office, she heard him answer, "Sheriff Blackwater," and the muscles in the back of her neck clenched. She had to remind herself to get over it. The office was his. Whether she trusted him or not, he was her boss. Until someone else was elected, or she quit, she'd just have to deal with him.

End of story.

Her hand searched frantically beneath the pillow, but her damn gun was missing!

Terrified, Anne Marie sat bolt upright, her eyes narrowing, her mind racing. It was a dream. That was it. A very real nightmare.

"I've got it." His voice was a raspy whisper over the wind screaming outside.

She blinked. Knew it was no dream. It was happening. *He'd* found her. Somehow. Someway. Her heart pounded, her courage flagged, and she wanted to melt into the couch.

You're still alive. He's got the gun, but you're still alive. Maybe he doesn't want to kill you . . .

And then she knew. Not kill. Torture. Maim.

Fight, damn it. Don't give up.

How had he found her? How had he broken in and she not heard? How the hell had he plucked the gun from under her head without her waking? She licked suddenly dry lips and remembered her dreams, the hot breath against her neck, the waking and thinking someone was inside, then convincing herself otherwise. Had he been right beside her? Within touching distance? If so, why hadn't he just killed her then, if that was his intent?

Her insides curdled at the thought of him watching her sleep while she lay unaware. While her heart was hammering wildly, she tried to think, to plot out her escape. But there was nowhere to run in the storm. If she tried to leave, he'd catch her fast. Still, her gaze slid to the window, so near the door where he stood, blocking any chance of escape. If she flung herself over the back of the couch and tried to make it across the room and through the kitchen to the back door, no doubt he would be on her in less than a second.

No no no! Even if she was able to run outside, how far would she get barefoot in the snow, in the raging wind and driving storm?

Unless she made it to her SUV.

She could drive to the sheriff's office. . . . Wait! Her phone! If she could somehow get away from him and call 9-1-1, she might have a chance.

A very slim one.

Or she could try to reason with him.

Oh, yeah. Right. Like that had ever worked.

"What are you doing here?" she finally demanded when she had her wits about her. Fear had driven any lingering vestige of sleep from her mind. As her eyes adjusted to the dim light, she tried to see him more clearly, still in the same position at the door. She tried to make out his features, to read his expression.

"Come on, Anne-Marie," he said, his voice a little clearer, his faint Texas drawl perceptible. "Is that any way to greet your husband?"

CHAPTER 23

Grabbing a cup of decaf from the carafe in the lunchroom, Pescoli settled down at her desk. Though it was still early, the department was starting to come alive. Officers, talking, laughing, and shaking off the cold, were drifting into the building with the change of shifts. Phones rang and a common printer positioned off the hallway near Joelle's desk hummed and clacked while the beast of a furnace wheezed as if it was on its last breath.

She sipped her weak-ass coffee and scanned her e-mail. Though she wouldn't admit it to Blackwater, she'd spent a lot of her free time on Sunday going over the Bart Grayson suicide file, as much for Dan as for Hattie. She felt it was an exercise in futility, but it had seemed fitting somehow, almost cathartic. With her kids at Luke's for the weekend, and Santana working on the new house, she'd put in some serious hours reviewing the years-old case and had tried to look at it with a new eye. But she'd found no hard evidence in the old reports that indicated Bartholomew Grayson had died by anything other than his own hand. Even though there was no suicide note left at the scene, nor message found in his belongings, nor conversation with a close friend or family member about taking his life, it still added up to the same conclusion. Friends and family alike had admitted how despondent Bart had been over the breakup of his marriage to Hattie. Apart from his widow, they, like the authorities, believed he'd ended it all. He'd died from suffocation by hanging himself in the barn, which was where his brother Cade had found him.

Bart Grayson's death had been a tragedy, of course. Unfortunate.

And probably preventable. He'd been a young, strapping man with two kids who, it seemed, had so much to live for.

Pescoli was certain everyone in the Grayson family, Dan included, had beat themselves up for not seeing the signs of Bart's depression. No one had been aware of how deep his despair had run.

Still, the bare facts of the case all pointed to the man taking his own life.

She would have to call Hattie and tell her as much. No doubt Bart's ex-wife still wouldn't accept the truth. In Pescoli's opinion, Hattie had been grappling with guilt ever since hearing the sad news about her ex and it was probably the root cause of her obsession with proving the suicide was really a murder. She fervently believed Bart would never willingly leave his daughters, that his love for them would have stopped him from taking his own life.

Pescoli wondered about the whole tangled web of Hattie Dorsey and the Grayson brothers. As rumor had it, Hattie's love for Bart hadn't exactly trumped her interest in the other men in his family. Then there was Cara, Dan's first ex-wife, whom Pescoli had learned at the funeral was Hattie's half sister. That was the family connection. It was all so intertwined, but hey, who was she to judge? Hattie had always had a fascination with all things Grayson.

Another aspect of the case was the insurance money. Bart had taken out two substantial policies with Hattie Grayson and her daughters listed as the beneficiaries. As it was, those benefits had never been paid, not because Bart had changed them, nor because he and Hattie had been divorced at the time of his death, but because Bart had taken his own life, thereby nullifying the payment. The insurance companies had been within their legal rights to refuse to pay. The upshot was that Hattie and her daughters had inherited Bart's portion of the Grayson ranch, but they'd been cut out of several hundred thousand dollars that would have been theirs if Bart's death was declared a murder.

Therein lay the problem. Hattie Grayson was not a rich woman and could really use the money. A single mom, she worked in her own catering business in order to support her children, no doubt struggling at times to make ends meet. She could probably sell her part of the Grayson ranch to the remaining brothers, but she hadn't done that yet.

Money, in the form of insurance benefits, could be another reason beyond basic guilt that Bart's ex and beneficiary was so stubbornly insistent that he hadn't killed himself.

"The facts are the facts," Pescoli said to herself, satisfied that Bart Grayson's death was neither a mystery nor a homicide. The man took his own life.

She replaced the reports in the box Jeremy had brought in a few days earlier, then unzipped her bag to retrieve a banana.

God, she was hungry. Always, it seemed. So she'd eat, then, not half an hour later, puke.

Taking her first bite, she heard quick footsteps in the hallway and half-expected Joelle to appear. Instead, Alvarez nearly slid as she rounded the sharp corner into Pescoli's office.

"Guess what?" Alvarez said.

"Not in the mood for twenty-questions."

Alvarez actually flashed a smile, the first Pescoli had witnessed since Dan Grayson had been shot, and she was energized for the first time in weeks. "We got a hit."

"A hit?" Pescoli repeated, and for a second or two, she forgot the hunger pangs that had been so overpowering only seconds before. "On the fingerprint?"

"Yeah." Dark eyes sparking, Alvarez nodded. "It's from a missing person from New Orleans."

"New Orleans?"

"Yep. A missing heiress who was disowned by her family. They filed the report, uncertain if she were alive or dead, but, I'd say from the prints we found, she's very much alive. And deadly. Her name is Anne-Marie Calderone."

"How do you know this already? It's barely eight in the damn morning."

"It's earlier in New Orleans, so I've been in contact with them already. Been here since five."

"Good God," Pescoli said, aghast.

"Look, I couldn't sleep. O'Keefe's not here. The animals wanted to get up early, so the dog and I tried to go for a run, but it was too nasty. Nearly impossible, so I gave it up. Anyway, I had too much on my mind to sleep in," she admitted. "Like you, right? You're in earlier than usual."

"Not at five friggin' a.m."

Alvarez's smile faded a bit, and she glanced over her shoulder to the open doorway as if she thought someone might overhear. "It's weird, you know," she admitted over the rumbling of the furnace and the hard tread in the hallway as two deputies passed by the open door. "I thought that after the funeral, I'd be able to put everything in perspective. Get back to business here and make sure my personal life was on track, kind of sort things out, but . . ." She shrugged, her black hair shining nearly blue under the fluorescent fixtures on the ceiling.

Pescoli nodded. Sometimes it was eerie how Alvarez's thoughts echoed her own feelings. "At least we have a lead now. Though, I gotta admit, I didn't figure the killer for a woman. The strangulation and then the pre- or postmortem mutilation? It just seems too brutal, too physical."

"Women can be violent," Alvarez countered, though she, too, sounded a little dubious.

"I know, I know, but . . . it's hard for me to get my head around it."

"Well, that's the way it's looking."

"How was she careless enough to leave a print at each crime scene? Who the hell is Anne-Marie Calderone?"

"You're *not* my husband," Anne-Marie said, her fear bleeding into anger at the realization that the man standing in front of her had the nerve, the unmitigated gall to hold her at gunpoint and say he was her husband when they both knew it wasn't true. He wasn't the maniac she'd expected, the butcher from whom she'd been running. The man by the door was Troy-damn-Ryder.

"And whose fault is that?" he drawled in the damnably sexy West Texas drawl she'd once found so intriguing.

She decided to duck that particular, painful question. "What the hell are you doing here?" she demanded, her heart trip-hammering. A million emotions, none of them good, swirled inside her.

Troy was no killer. Or not that she knew of. Okay, he was rough around the edges and the law had never been something he'd worried about too much, but he wasn't the brutal psychopath she'd thought was chasing her down, the person she'd thought had killed at least two women as some kind of warning to her. How could she have been so foolish to think those poor women who had been murdered had anything to do with her? Was she that much of an egomaniac? If she could jump to such conclusions, maybe she really was ready for the loony bin again, just as her husband had claimed.

And this damn cowboy in front of her, the one she'd tried, and failed, to marry . . . *what is he doing here?*

In the shadowy interior of her cabin, she struggled to see his features, to read his expression, but failed.

"Isn't that what husbands do when their wives just take off? Track them down?"

"But you're not my husband," she repeated. "You know you're not my husband."

"Oh, yeah, that's right. When you said 'I do' at that little chapel in Vegas, you were still married."

That much was true. "I didn't know," she said, but even as the words passed her lips, they sounded lame.

"How could you not know?"

"It was an assumption on my part. A mistake. We've been over this." She felt the chill of his gaze cutting through the dark atmosphere, and for a second, she regretted what she'd done, how she'd led him on, not that she'd meant to. "You know I thought my ex had signed the papers and—"

"He wasn't your ex."

"Okay, okay. Not officially."

"Not legally," Ryder bit out, irritated. "Kind of important."

"Oh, forget it." She threw up her hands in surrender. "Saying I'm sorry now doesn't cut it. I know that. I screwed up."

"Big time."

"*Yes*. Yes." When he didn't respond, she said, "I can't believe that you hunted me down, in this . . . in this damn blizzard in Montana to steal my gun and argue about the past. You *scared* me." It felt like a dream, a remnant of the terrors that had invaded her brain during the night and made her think she'd woken up when she was really still asleep, everything taking on a weird twist. But that was only wishful thinking. She was very much awake, beyond alert, and she was in the cold, dark, smelly cabin with the wild-ass cowboy she'd fallen for so hard that she, like him, had ignored the details of the law.

"I get it that you're pissed. You should be. But that was over a year ago and . . . and since when are you such a stickler for legalities?"

'When it comes to my damn wife." He strode closer to her. "You're impossible, you know."

"I'm not the one pointing a gun at the person I once swore I loved." Folding her arms over her chest, she squinted up at him, trying to see his features, read the expression in his eyes. "But why? Why go to all these lengths? I thought we understood each other."

He muttered furiously under his breath, but just said, "I came to get you."

For the briefest of instants, her heart tripped, a tiny bit of hope soared, but she tamped it down quickly. She wasn't that foolish anymore. She didn't trust him blindly. Nor did he trust her. And then, there was the matter of the weapon. "Well, okay, but most men who come for a woman, don't hold her at gunpoint."

"It probably happens more often than you think. I never understood until now. But I didn't come here to patch things up."

"You couldn't," she said, cringing inwardly at the bit of a lie. The truth was, she'd never completely gotten over him. Not one hundred percent. There was a part of her, a tiny very feminine part of her, that still fantasized about him, but she tamped that emotion down, wishing she could kill it.

"Just for the record, this"—he moved his hand, displaying her pistol—"is a pathetic excuse for a gun."

"Thank-you so much. That's so helpful," she shot out, then wished she'd held her tongue. That was the trouble with Ryder. Her blood ran hot around him, her emotions volatile. "It might be small, but you're still aiming it at me."

"You're lucky I don't just pull the trigger."

"You didn't come all this way just to shoot me. You could have done that and been halfway back to Louisiana by now."

"Well, darlin', at least you're starting to get it."

"What?"

"It's time to go. The reason that I'm pointing this gun at you is because I want you to grab your things and get moving. I figured you might not be all that keen on the idea, so your pistol came in handy. So, get up. Now."

* * *

"I'm just not buying it," Pescoli said from her desk chair. She was still processing the information her partner had given her and trying to see a woman as their doer. "I know a lot of women who have jewelry envy. They're all about who has the biggest rock as some kind of validation of love or something. Even my daughter went crazy over my ring when she first saw it. But I've never heard of one who would kill for a ring by cutting the damn finger off."

"Women kill," Alvarez said. "If it isn't for a justifiable cause like protecting their children, then it's over a man. Usually a loser of a man."

"Yeah, that's true," Pescoli admitted.

"You ever watch *Judge Judy*?"

"No. You do? You have time for reality TV in the middle of the day?"

"I record it."

That surprised Pescoli as she'd pegged Alvarez as a workaholic.

"O'Keefe got me started on it, and once in a while I tune in. If the litigants are complaining about loans and gifts or rent and broken leases, it's usually some woman all up in arms that her friend slept with her boyfriend or husband or whatever. The weird thing is that to a one, they blame the other woman as if it was all that woman's fault and their poor, dumb husband couldn't resist. That he was just the patsy in the Jezebel's lurid, malicious trap, and that's why he couldn't keep it in his pants."

"No one on *Judge Judy* is a killer," Pescoli pointed out.

"I'm just saying it's not impossible. We've run in our share of women who've killed. You know it."

"But to cut off a finger—"

"What about those women who kill a pregnant woman and cut open her uterus because they want the baby or have somehow convinced themselves that the baby inside is really theirs?"

"Those women are mentally deranged." Pescoli fought an overpowering need to place her hands protectively over her own midsection and failed.

"Sorry," Alvarez said, pulling herself up short. "But our killer's mentally deranged, too. Taking a finger wouldn't be past a woman. That's all I'm saying."

Pescoli glanced at the autopsy report on Calypso Pope, a copy of which lay atop another file on her desk. "A crushed hyoid bone. In both cases. That takes strength."

"Strength, but not necessarily size. And know-how. Maybe martial arts?"

Pescoli tossed the remains of her banana in the trash. "So you think this Anne-Marie Calderone is our killer?"

"That's the avenue I'm taking."

"Doesn't it seem a little too obvious? To leave a print on the one piece of evidence that's located? There's not a second shoe, and that's the only print on Pope's Mercedes. Lots of other prints all over that car," she corrected herself. She was thinking aloud. "The Cantnor woman's purse wasn't located, but the second victim's bag was found fairly easily and it had that identifying print."

"But any way you look at it, this woman is at the top of the suspect list. Right now, she's all we've got. She's obviously involved, we just don't know how. I've got a call in to the New Orleans PD and Zoller is checking all the newspaper and police databases, looking for information about Calderone." Sage Zoller was a junior detective with the department. Tiny and fit, she ran marathons, mentored at-risk teens and was a techno wiz kid. A dynamo. "She'll report back to us."

"Good."

At that moment, Alvarez's cell phone rang. She answered, "Detective Alvarez," then held up a finger. "Thanks for calling back, Detective Montoya. We've got a situation up here—a couple homicides—and we found the same fingerprint at both scenes. Looks like it belongs to Anne-Marie Calderone. I was hoping you could supply me with a little more information about her as she's just become a person of interest up here."

She nodded at Pescoli and headed out of the office.

Pescoli rolled her chair closer to the desk, where she brought up the basic information on Anne-Marie Favier Calderone from New Orleans. The woman's driver's license picture and information appeared on the screen and though, more often than not, the photo taken at the DMV was usually pretty damn bad, this woman was stunning with her large eyes, easy smile, and oval face. Her hair was a deep brown with red highlights, shoulder-length and thick, her height and weight consistent with someone who kept herself in shape.

Pescoli stared long and hard at the photo. Was she looking into the face of a cold-blooded killer? A woman who took satisfaction, even joy, in cutting off fingers and diamonds?

She found herself playing with her own ring and stopped. This was insane. Or was it?

"No way," she said aloud, but, of course, she couldn't argue the facts. Anne Marie Calderone was connected to the dead women. Pescoli just had to figure out how.

CHAPTER 24

Shivering, the cold of the morning seeping into her bones, Anne-Marie said, "I'm not going back to New Orleans." She stared pointedly at the man in shadow. "Gun or no gun." But she did climb off the couch, her bare feet touching the floor. "Come on in. You don't have to guard the damn door. Where do you think I'm going in this?"

As if to add emphasis to her words, the wind squealed around the house and the damn limb started banging against the exterior wall again. Ignoring him, she walked the few steps to the fireplace and went to work, grabbing chunks of split wood she'd hauled inside the night before, prodding at the charred logs with the poker, searching for an ember glowing red beneath the ash. When she had success, she blew on the coals so that they burned brighter, a flame sparking against the moss and dry hemlock as the wood caught fire.

Settling back on her heels, she watched as the flames began to grow, crackling as they devoured the fuel. Her fingers tightened over the poker still in her right hand. She didn't want to harm Ryder, but she wasn't going back to Louisiana with him. No way. She never wanted to see her family again and there was a chance that *he* would find her there. Now that she felt a new security, that she realized it was Ryder who had been following her rather than the monster who had tossed her into the Mississippi, she could finally feel some sort of relief and believe that she did have a chance for a new life for herself. A life without any ties to the past and that included Troy Ryder.

"Drop it," he ordered.

Still crouching near the grate, she looked over her shoulder to see that he still had the gun pointed at her. For the love of God, did he really think she believed for a second that he would shoot her? She didn't let go of the poker, but stared at him over her shoulder. He was still near the door, about eight feet from her. If she sprang and swung, she might be able to hit him hard. She needed to take his advantage away and somehow, remove his gun. She had the poker, and her little switchblade was hidden in the folds of the clothes she'd piled near the couch.

Maybe there was some way to disarm him, gain the upper hand. As the fire burned brighter and hotter, the room lightened. Finally she saw his face, no longer in complete shadow and her heart twisted again. His was a rugged visage. His features were oversized—his jaw strong, big eyes deep in his sockets, a nose that had been broken a couple times, a hard line of a mouth, and a square jaw covered in a couple of days' worth of stubble.

"I said, 'drop it,' Anne-Marie. Don't even think about it."

Her grip tightened.

"Jesus, are you serious? You think you're going to get the better of me with a poker?"

"You won't shoot me. I'm not going back to New Orleans. Not ever." The fire popped then and her muscles jumped. Then, as if he'd been reading her thoughts all along, she saw him reach into his pocket with his free hand only to withdraw a stick of some kind . . .

Click! Her switchblade snapped open in his hand, its spring-loaded blade suddenly reflecting the shifting light from the fire.

"How—?" Inadvertently, her gaze slid to the stack of folded clothes where she was certain she'd hidden the deadly knife. She didn't finish the sentence. Her mind spinning, she wondered how the hell he'd known she had it, how he'd found it as well as the gun. She'd assumed he'd guessed she had hidden a weapon under her pillow, but the knife from her clothes? Had he rifled through her things while looking for the pistol and found the switchblade first, then continued his stealthy search while she'd been restlessly sleeping unaware or had he . . .

"You *spied* on me?" she charged, astounded, her mind taking hold of the idea and churning wildly. "You were in here before and planted devices and *spied* on me?" That was a big leap, a major vault, but he didn't immediately deny it. She remembered feeling as if she were being watched, that though the shades had been drawn, the doors locked tightly, that there had been hidden eyes following her every move. "What is wrong with you?"

"I had to make certain that Jessica Williams was really Anne-Marie Calderone. And that my leads were right, that Jessica was also the same person as Stacey Donahue in Denver and Heather Brown earlier on."

Dear God, how long had he been following her? He knew *all of it.*

"I wasn't going to barge in on the wrong person, so I had to make sure."

She shook her head, disbelieving, not even understanding how he, a damn half-broke rodeo rider, could understand about high tech electronics. It suddenly occurred to her that because their romance had been so white-hot and rushed and she'd decided to marry him after knowing him only a few weeks, there was much more to the cowboy from somewhere in West Texas than met the eye. She hadn't known him and his secrets any better than he'd known her and the lies that were the bones of her past.

But now she wanted to.

"Who *are* you?"

After hanging up from Detective Montoya, Alvarez coordinated the information he'd given her with what was known about the crimes in Montana. Zoller had e-mailed some information on Anne-Marie Calderone and was checking to see if there had been any similar killings in the last year in other parts of the country. So far, the department hadn't heard of women who had been murdered, the ring fingers of their left hands severed, nor had they found any other crimes where the Calderone woman's fingerprints had shown up.

But, she told herself, *it is still early.*

The Pinewood Sheriff Department might be on the track of one of the most deadly female serial killers in history.

I'm getting ahead of myself, she thought, leaning back in her desk chair and taking a sip of her tea that she'd gotten from the break room. It was stone-cold, the tea bag still steeping in it, the orange-spice so strong she nearly gagged. Setting her cup aside, she concentrated on her computer screen, reminding herself that most likely there were no other identical crimes anywhere close by or she would have already found mention of it. Because of computers and communication systems, like crimes were more quickly identified.

She glanced at her e-mail, searching for more reports and heard a text come into her cell phone. One look and she smiled.

The short missive was from Gabriel, her biological son with whom she'd recently reconnected. No school!!! Along with the two words he'd attached a winking smiley face.

She quickly texted back, Have fun. See you soon.

Her heart swelled at the thought of him, the teenager who'd been raised by Aggie and Dave Reeve. Aggie was Dylan O'Keefe's cousin and not all that happy that her son had discovered his birth mother, but the two women were working things out. Alvarez kept her distance as she didn't want to intimidate the woman who had spent all of Gabe's life caring for him, raising him, teaching him right from wrong.

She added a smiley face to her text despite the fact that she loathed all the emoticons. *But when in teenaged Rome . . .* She hit SEND.

She turned her attention back to the matter at hand—running Anne-Marie Calderone to the ground. Whether the woman who'd left her fingerprint on the belongings recovered from the victims was the actual killer or an accessory, or something else, she had some explaining to do. Some serious explaining.

Taking a swing at him wouldn't help, so Anne-Marie let loose of the poker, stood, and dusted her hands.

"Who am *I?*" Ryder repeated. "I'm not the one with myriad disguises, a series of fake IDs, and multiple aliases."

"But you were spying on me. I don't remember you being some kind of techno geek who could bug rooms. Where the hell are they?" she demanded and turned around in a tight circle, searching in the dark corners, the lamps, wherever.

"You never bothered to find out that I was in the Special Forces and specialized in communications, did you?" When she looked at him as if he were mad, he admitted, "Afghanistan. Nothing I really want to dwell on."

"Was this pre- or post-cowboy?"

"Between," he admitted, snapping the switchblade closed and putting it, along with her gun, into a pocket.

Now that it was light, she could see that pocket was already bulging. "Wait a minute. You have your own damn gun?"

He smiled then. That reckless, roguish smile she'd found so irresistible. "You didn't think I'd come in here unarmed."

"But you stole my gun."

"Didn't feel like having you use it on me."

"I wouldn't have . . . well, if I'd known it was you, anyway."

Apparently satisfied that she wasn't going to flee or attack him, he started stripping small microphones and cameras from the tiniest of places around the room—a crack in the fireplace, a dark corner of the bookcase, even the damn wood box.

"Really?" she said, watching in disbelief and suddenly feeling bare and vulnerable, all of her worst fears coming to the fore. He'd been observing her every move, whether she'd been awake or asleep. He'd seen her break down or flop in despair or rail at the heavens. "I can't believe you would do all this—"

"Believe," he said without emotion.

She was trying to make sense of it all but couldn't. She'd thought, once they'd broken up, she would never see him again. He'd been so furious with her that she'd thought he might strangle her. He'd said as much. "Go to hell, Anne-Marie," he'd said, "and don't look over your shoulder."

So, why would he be there now, dissecting her life . . . no, injecting himself back into it . . . trying to force her to retrace her steps and return to a city she'd sworn she'd never set foot in again?

"I don't understand why you want me to go back to New Orleans," she said.

"I've actually got a couple reasons," he admitted. "The first is that after you and your husband disappeared—"

"Me and my husband?" she interrupted.

"Yes, after—"

"He left, too?" The dread that had temporarily abated came flooding back.

"You know that."

"No." She shook her head and swallowed with difficulty. Dear God, she was back to where she'd started. "Why would he leave?"

"You two had a major fight. The neighbors heard it."

Her knees went suddenly weak at the memory and cold terror slipped through her veins. She dropped back onto the mussed sleeping bag covering the couch.

"My name came up," Ryder said.

Of course. Oh. Sweet. Jesus.

"So, you both go missing and guess who's left holding the emotional bag? Yours truly."

"But you had nothing to do with it."

"As I tried to explain, but the police had a different idea. A guy by the name of Detective Montoya? He's pretty sure that somehow I'm involved in both disappearances."

"What? No!" She couldn't believe it. "But that's insane."

"Insanity to you and me. *Motive* to the police. The theory is that I might have been so damn pissed about the affair blowing up in my face the way it did, that I went into a jealous rage and got rid of you both."

"You're lying."

"That's your department, darlin'." Ryder's voice was cold. "The police are grasping at straws, and I told them that. But my alibi of being on the road that night didn't hold any water with them. That hotheaded homicide detective? Montoya? He's a real piece of work and he never quite believed my story. The only good news was that he didn't have a body, not even one . . . with two people missing, so they couldn't build a case against me. Not that he isn't trying. So, it would be a big favor to me, if you'd go prove that you're not dead."

"That still leaves my husband," she whispered.

"Your problem. Not mine."

"Oh, God," she whispered, believing Ryder's story, knowing she'd left a mess behind her when she'd worked so hard to disappear. And the mess kept following her. The only good news was that she was more convinced than ever that the two women who'd been recently killed around Grizzly Falls had nothing to do with her.

"So pack up because we're leaving."

"There's a storm outside," she reminded.

"Always a storm of one kind or another, always a road block." He cast a glance in her direction. "We'll take our chances."

"That's nuts."

"All relative, especially where you're concerned." He pocketed yet another camera, then walked into the kitchen and small bath.

He'd even seen her showering or on the toilet or . . . "You're a pervert, Ryder," she yelled, but her eyes were on the front door. She only needed her keys and she could race to the Tahoe and peel out of there. Or—*Crap!* Why hadn't she thought of it before? Her cell phone. It was . . .

In the pile of clothes where her switchblade had been hidden. She quickly tossed her jeans and sweater aside, but, of course, the tiny phone wasn't where she'd left it. Her keys . . . no, they were gone, too.

"Son of a bitch," she hissed just as he returned from the bathroom. "You really are a bastard, aren't you?" She was standing in the middle of the living room, trying to come up with some kind of option because no matter what he thought, she was not returning to Louisiana.

"You know, I try my level best."

At the news of a potential suspect in the Cantnor and Pope homicides, Blackwater wanted an up-to-the-minute report on everything the department knew about the new suspect. If the lead panned out, he would order a BOLO—Be On The Lookout—bulletin for the woman.

He called in Alvarez and Pescoli, Zoller, the junior detective in charge of the Internet research, Deputy Winger as he trusted her advice, and Brett Gage, the chief criminal deputy.

Joelle Fisher, of course, couldn't let a meeting go without bringing in a tray with two kinds of coffee, cups along with napkins, creamers and sweeteners.

Blackwater finally understood that, especially with the receptionist, there was a certain amount of decorum that had to be followed, tradition, if you will. He could appreciate Joelle's single-mindedness when it came to a task, but worrying over who drank decaf or avoided artificial sweeteners or that the platter had a damn paper doily covering it, weren't his top priorities. He wished Joelle would dial it back, just a notch or two, and he'd said as much.

She'd complied, but he sensed it was only temporary. Decorations and baked goods, celebrations of all kinds were part of her DNA, just like her throwback beehive hairstyle.

"Thank-you," he said as she left the meeting room, each step reverberating quickly against the tile floor.

"Let's get to it," he said as the invitees took spots around the table.

Other than Gage, no one bothered filling a cup. Alvarez and Zoller each had electronic notebooks, Gage and Pescoli notepads and pens. Blackwater had both at his fingertips. "I know about the prints and the connection, but what do we know about this person, Anne-Marie Calderone? You talked to someone in New Orleans, right?"

"Detective Montoya, yes," Alvarez said, taking the lead in the discussion and passing out two pages, one with the picture from the suspect's Louisiana driver's license, the other a sheet of facts about the woman in question. "Anne-Marie Favier Calderone. She's thirty years old and, according to Montoya, been missing for several months. He's sending us the files and a timeline, but the long and the short of it is that she was married to Bruce Calderone, a medical doctor who, until recently, worked at a private hospital in New Orleans. Once connected to the Catholic church, it's now run by lay people. He was a surgeon."

"Was?" Blackwater interrupted, feeling his eyebrows slam together.

"He seemed to have disappeared, as well. Both he and his wife. From the interviews Montoya did with friends and family, it appears the marriage wasn't stable, with accusations of affairs on both sides. Though there were never any charges filed, there were rumors of abuse."

Alvarez continued on, saying that Anne-Marie Favier had grown up a daughter of privilege. The Faviers had once had family money, at least during Anne-Marie's youth. According to her parents' sworn statements, she was headstrong and brilliant but a little unbalanced. In high school, she spent three months in a mental hospital for undisclosed issues. Montoya had said the records were sealed as she'd been a minor at the time. Later, she'd not only finished a four year program but also held an MA in philosophy from Tulane University.

The trouble started after her marriage to Bruce Calderone, a medical student whom she'd helped through school. There followed breakups and reconciliations, even some long separations, which included the last one. She and Calderone had been separated and she'd filed for divorce. She'd signed, but Calderone had balked.

She'd ignored that little fact when she'd married her latest fling, a cowboy by the name of Troy Ryder in a tiny chapel in Las Vegas. When that relationship apparently soured, she returned to New Orleans sans the new groom, but when Calderone learned about the second marriage he'd blown a gasket. Though, again, not reported to the police at the time, the neighbors had heard screaming and yelling which ended abruptly around ten or ten-thirty. The next day, they were gone. Both of them. All of their worldly possessions left behind. It was, according to Montoya, as if they'd each just fallen off the face of the earth.

No cars taken, no credit cards used, no cell phones answered or turned on so the cops could locate them.

"That's basically it, except for one interesting fact," Alvarez said. "Though Anne-Marie wasn't close to either of her parents, she was adored by her grandmother. The grandfather died years earlier, but the weekend Anne-Marie and her husband went missing, the grandmother was robbed. She claimed she had fifty thousand dollars in her safe and no one, other than her granddaughter and her daughter, knew the combination, though they of course could have told others. Montoya thinks the mother is in the clear and that leaves Anne-Marie."

"She would steal from the one person she loved?" Pescoli asked.

Alvarez paused. "Maybe she was desperate. According to her parents, Montoya notes, that despite all of her education, their daughter never made any serious money or pursued a career in her field of interest. She held odd jobs all through school. Worked as a clerk or a waitress even after she graduated."

"While her husband finished medical school?" Blackwater asked.

Alvarez studied her screen. "Uh-huh. What little Anne-Marie made, coupled with his student loans, kept them afloat."

Blackwater asked, "Either of them ever steal before?"

"Neither had a criminal record. So if they had, they were never caught. But if they had the grandmother's cash to finance their disappearance, and maybe new identities, it could explain why we can't find either one of them."

He rubbed his chin and shook his head as he thought. "They hated each other, so it's unlikely they were on the run together, and if he had a thriving medical practice—"

"Not thriving." Alvarez shook her head. "In fact, Dr. Calderone not only worked at the hospital but was a partner in a clinic. The business was going bankrupt, though his partners think he was not only syphoning off money but prescription drugs, as well. After he disappeared, a couple women came forward and reported that he'd been inappropriate with them. They're suing his practice as well as him personally, and as such, his wife."

"Because she had money?"

"Her family had money, *at one time*, but according to the New Orleans PD, Mr. and Mrs. Talbert Favier are teetering on the verge of bankruptcy. It's kind of a case of everyone believing everyone else had huge piles of dough stashed somewhere, but the Faviers had invested in real estate and their own business and it was all hit hard during the recession. The only person with any money left is Grandma Favier."

Blackwater frowned at the flat image of the woman who seemed to be staring up at him from her driver's license photo. "Do we have any more pictures?"

"Montoya's sending them through e-mail." Alvarez checked her iPad. "Oh, here we go. Let me hook this up." She spent a few seconds connecting her device to a large monitor on the wall and clicked through a series of images of a beautiful woman in her twenties, laughing and mugging for the camera. "Some of these are from her Facebook account. No activity of course since they disappeared. Nothing on any social media platforms. And here." She flipped through another series. "This is the husband, Bruce Calderone."

They all leaned forward to look at the picture. Calderone was a big man with even teeth and an easy smile. He was dressed in a lab coat.

"And one more. Anne Marie Calderone's love interest. Troy Ryder." Another image filled the screen, a man of thirty odd years with tanned skin, crow's feet, and eyes set deep in his skull.

Blackwater looked from Alvarez to Pescoli, who'd let her partner do all the talking. Pescoli's mouth was stubbornly set as if she didn't agree with what was going on.

He glanced back at the picture. "So, now we've got a love triangle, a robbed grandmother, two missing people from New Orleans, and our two dead victims with the severed fingers dumped here in Grizzly Falls." He glanced around the table. "Am I missing anything else?"

"Just one more thing," Alvarez said. "There was talk about her being involved at one time with Cade Grayson."

"Another boyfriend?"

"Long before Ryder. Cade's a person who could be her connection to Grizzly Falls, maybe why she ended up here."

"That woman really gets around," Gage observed.

"Two boyfriends, one husband," Pescoli said. "Not so much getting around."

"More like two husbands, one boyfriend," Gage rejoined. "She seems to have a little trouble with her marriage vows."

"Lot of that going around," Pescoli said.

Blackwater interrupted. "Someone needs to talk to him. See if Grayson's seen her."

Alvarez said, "Already on it."

"Good. Now, is there anything else?"

Gage shrugged and Alvarez shook her head. Zoller and Winger were both busily taking notes. He focused on Pescoli. "What do you think, Detective?"

"Fingerprint or no fingerprint, I have trouble believing our doer's a woman."

Blackwater felt impatient, but whether he liked the rogue detective or not, he grudgingly respected her gut instincts.

"I think it's damn convenient that we have her prints, no, make that *print*, singular. One at each scene," Pescoli went on. "Doesn't anyone else find that convenient?"

Gage gave another shrug. "Maybe odd."

Blackwater regarded Pescoli for a moment, then said, "Since we can't find hide nor hair of Mr. or Mrs. Calderone, maybe we should be looking for Ryder. Unless he's hiding, too, and they're all involved in this thing together, which I don't believe, there should be records of him. Credit card receipts and cell phone records?"

"Montoya's already on it," Alvarez said, reading from her device. "Looks like he was recently in Denver, but he did buy gas in Casper, Wyoming and Billings, Montana and finally, a few days ago, made a purchase right here in Grizzly Falls at Corky's Gas and Go."

Blackwater said, "And I assume we have a make and model of his vehicle?"

Alvarez glanced up from her computer while Winger broke down and poured herself a cup of coffee. "We do."

"Then I suggest you start at the gas station with pictures of Ryder. Take the others as well, just in case he's traveling with either of them, then check the local motels. He probably doesn't think anyone's looking for him, so he might be registered under his own name. Let's bird-dog him." Blackwater felt a warm spot deep in his gut. Maybe this case would break under his watch, the culprits of a scandalous crime spree that stretched from the deep South to Grizzly Falls brought to justice. "Don't forget Cade Grayson. The two on the run might be in disguise, so let's work with the computer guys, do some enhancements, Photoshop a little, play with the images." He grinned at his team. That's right, *his* team. "Who knows, the missing Calderones might be hiding in plain sight right under our noses."

CHAPTER 25

Anne-Marie was through being bullied. She jabbed an angry finger straight at Ryder. "I'm never going back to Louisiana, but I was willing to turn myself in here."

"Because of Cade Grayson?"

She'd picked up her jeans and was reaching for her sweater but stopped to look at him in surprise.

"I knew about him. And when your coworkers in Denver mentioned you were hooking up with an old boyfriend, he came to mind."

"What happened between Cade and me was a long time ago."

"But you came here."

"I was going to meet with his brother. Dan was the sheriff. Cade had sworn he was fair and would look at all sides of an issue. I knew I had to turn myself in, that I couldn't keep running, but I didn't trust anyone in New Orleans. My father golfs with judges and lawyers and . . . and he thought I'd made a big mistake. That no matter what, I should stick with Bruce. He would rather believe I was lying." She bristled at that thought, that her own parents had sided with the man who had beaten her.

"So, what made you finally run?" Ryder asked, a tenderness in his voice.

It made her heart soften though she knew it was stupid. He didn't care for her, possibly never had. After the whole bigamy thing, he could never trust or think kindly of her again. Yet there was a note in his words that pierced beneath the shield she'd built around her heart.

She sat on one arm of the couch and pulled on her jeans. The fire was burning bright and finally casting some heat into the room. "We'd had one of our classic fights. The last one, I'd hoped. It was on the phone and I'd decided, once and for all, it was over. I was strong enough to leave him forever.

"I'd never moved back into the house once you and I . . . well, ever since Las Vegas. I didn't love him. Probably never had. I was done. I wanted out. If I never saw him again, that would have been fine. I knew he'd never forgive me, but I made a major mistake. I still had things at his house where I used to live, and so . . . I knew he was working at his office, so I went back to our townhouse intent on loading up the rest of my things and leaving town."

She clenched her teeth at the memory, and heard once again in her mind, the downstairs door opening when she'd been on the upper floor in the master bedroom.

She had already stripped out the closet. Her clothes were strewn across the king-sized bed she'd come to hate. Barely able to breathe, she prayed he had just come home for a quick bite, that he hadn't seen her car parked out back.

And then she heard his footsteps on the stairs, his tread swift and determined as he mounted the steps to the second floor. She cowered in the closet, but it was no use. He threw open the bedroom door, looked at the mess on the bed, and zeroed in on the closet. As he opened the door, a shaft of light pierced the messy interior where she was hiding between his suits and shirts.

"What do you think you're doing?" he roared, though her intent was painfully obvious. "Leaving? Leaving me? You think you can do that? Leave me for some cheap cowboy? Steal away like a common whore in the middle of the night?" His face, the contours of which she'd once found so handsome, twisted in rage. Nostrils flared, skin flushed, cords in his neck pronounced, he grabbed her by the hair and pulled her forcibly from the interior of the closet.

She swung at him hard, connected with his ribs, and then saw the hypodermic needle in his free hand. Oh God, she thought, he knew she'd returned and was ready for her.

She felt the jab of the needle in her arm and, as the room began to swim, saw him pick up the rings she'd put on the night stand—the engagement ring and wedding band that he'd given her—that she shouldn't have ever let him see again.

"Are you fucking kidding me? This isn't over until I say it's over." The diamonds winked in his hand and then he closed his fist around the clear stones. His lips were curled in rage.

Still swinging her arms and flailing wildly, she gratefully passed out at that moment.

Anne-Marie shook her head. From that point, she remembered nothing at all until she became groggily aware. It all came back.

She felt cold air on her bare skin and a dull throb in her hand, something slick beneath her, the smell of dank earth in her nostrils. Before she could fully revive, she was kicked hard, sent spinning and rolling. The plastic tarp whipped from under her body as she careened down a berm and splashed into the murky water where she woke with the first gulp of silty water.

She knew she had to play dead, to let the slow-moving current carry her on its path. She caught glimpses of moonlight through scudding clouds, saw the ghostly roots of cypress trees rising above the water line, and knew she wasn't alone in the sluggish water, that alligators waited, hunting. Yet she managed to slip slowly downriver, around a wide curve, and deeper into the woods, undisturbed.

She eased her way to the bank, praying that she didn't disturb a nest of gators or step on a snake as she dragged her naked body out of the water by grabbing on to a thick, bleached root. She made her way through the soupy ground to a shack that was boarded over. She broke through a small window and found clothing three sizes too large, but dry. She quickly dressed and stumbled out to the road.

She made her way to the outskirts of New Orleans, hitching a ride with some teenagers high on marijuana.

"Anne-Marie?"

She heard and snapped back to reality and the dilapidated cabin where Ryder was still waiting for an answer. There was more to her story, of course. The most pivotal part that she hated to think about.

He was standing by the fire, warming the backs of his legs.

"I ran because he beat me, Ryder. That's why I ran." She closed her eyes at the admission, and though she knew she shouldn't be ashamed, it was difficult to admit the hateful truth. How could someone who'd sworn to love her, to protect her, had vowed to be her husband for all their lives, been able to raise his hand to her, to beat her with a viciousness that could only be described as hatred?

"I put up with it for a while, believed him when he claimed to love me, begged me to come back, and promised that he would never hurt me again. He cried, and I wanted to believe him. At least in the beginning." She saw the unasked questions in Ryder's eyes, listened to them ricochet off the walls of her brain because she'd asked herself the same things—*Why did you stay? Why didn't you walk away the first time? Why didn't you call the police? Why in the world did you let it happen more than one damn time?*

"You didn't tell me any of this."

"I didn't want you to know." She couldn't read what he was thinking, so she just went on. "I finally realized that he would never change so we split up. He wasn't happy about it, but I was through being his punching bag. It wasn't about love, it was about ownership. I was his, and though he really didn't want me anymore, he sure as hell didn't want anyone else to have me." Her fists clenched at the memory. "So, I filed for divorce, met you . . . and it felt so good to laugh again, to fall in love, to . . . oh, hell, I don't know . . . to *live* again without fear. I wanted it to work out with you and me. Wanted it so much."

She blinked back tears. Refused to cry. She knew that she'd thrown herself into her affair with Ryder far too fast and her enthusiasm had more to do with breaking free of her old life than of starting a new one with him. She hadn't really known him and had kidded herself about finding true love with a happy-ever-after ending.

Forcing her balled fists to unclench, she said, "I thought he'd sign the divorce papers, but I should have known better. Bruce Calderone doesn't lose. Especially to his wife. My leaving meant that I'd won. At least to him. I was naive enough to think that with time, he'd cool off, see that our marriage was a big mistake from the get-go. I convinced myself that he would calm down and accept that we shouldn't be together."

Ryder was frowning hard, but he let her continue without comment.

"I made the mistake of returning to the house after we'd been separated for over a year to pick up some of my things. And . . . and he beat me within an inch of my life."

Ryder's jaw slid to one side, a muscle working under his temple. "So, what happened to him?"

"Don't know. Don't care."

"He's still your husband."

Her insides shriveled at the thought. She didn't want to think about it anymore. Something Ryder had mentioned earlier still bothered her. "You said that there were two reasons you wanted to haul me back to Louisiana, the first being to clear your name as that detective down there . . . what's his name?"

"Montoya."

"He thought you were involved in my disappearance." She pulled her sweater from the pile of clothes she'd gathered on her lap and drew it over her head. "What was the second?"

Ryder was still standing by the fireplace. He'd scarcely moved a muscle.

"What's the other reason?" she asked again. "You've made it abundantly clear that it isn't because you missed my company."

He was quiet, as if he didn't want to admit to his reasons.

Though she'd sworn she didn't care, she felt a niggle of disappointment. She'd kidded herself that he was different, that he wasn't interested in her because of her looks, or her charm, or the fact that her family had money and someday she would inherit a small fortune. No, Troy Ryder had been different from the others, more into her as a person than anyone, including Bruce Calderone and Cade Grayson, had been.

She saw he wasn't all that different, after all. And then, like a tidal wave that's drawn far out to sea only to turn, she realized the truth in a crashing, drowning blow. "Let me guess," she said, hating the thought. "You're here because you think I have money."

"Close." His jaw was hard.

"You think my family will pay for me? You're going to hold me for ransom?"

"Gettin' warmer," he said but didn't seem to have any pride in his statement. And the drawl she'd once found so endearing actually grated.

"What the hell is that supposed to mean?"

"It's not a ransom," he said shortly. It was clear he was having some difficulty explaining himself.

Why would he chase her down, then spend these last months searching for her? Then she knew. "It's a bounty. My damn family offered you money to bring me home and you accepted." She let out a disgusted sigh and folded her arms across her chest, staring at him. "How disappointing."

That actually looked like it penetrated, but she wasn't going to let her romantic side believe something that wasn't true any longer. "I can't believe they even care," she said bitterly. "How much am I worth, if I dare ask?"

It took him a moment or two, but then he bit out, "One hundred thousand dollars."

"Cade Grayson's still not answering," Alvarez said from the passenger seat of Pescoli's Jeep after calling twice. She'd left two messages for him to call her back.

"He might not have his phone with him." Pescoli was driving, her wipers slapping off the snow. "He doesn't seem the type to keep his cell with him twenty-four seven, and I don't see him texting." She turned off of the road leading down Boxer Bluff. "He's probably pretty busy with his livestock in a storm like this. It's not a picnic. If we have to, we'll drive out there."

Alvarez said dryly, "Conditions couldn't be better."

Ever since the meeting at the station less than half an hour earlier, Pescoli had been anxious, more anxious than usual. Her fingers tapped on the steering wheel as she followed three cars all creeping through town. Her mind was on the case, running through the new-found information about Anne-Marie Calderone. She felt a sense of urgency, as if time were her enemy and she had to keep moving— which was damn difficult as traffic was crawling more than ever, just inching along.

"Why don't these people stay home?" she muttered when the lead car finally pulled into the parking lot of a pharmacy. The guy, ninety if he was a day, cruised slowly into a handicapped spot, his front tires running against the berm in front of the sidewalk.

"People still need their meds."

"Then they should learn to drive in the frickin' snow."

Alvarez shot her a look and Pescoli gripped the wheel a little harder. She was tired, cranky, hungry, and had no use for anyone out driving in the bad weather who didn't know how. No, strike that. She had no use for anyone driving and getting in her way.

Finally, the gas station mini-mart came into view. At the first entrance, she pulled into the parking area of Corky's Gas and Go, the very station where her son worked off and on, and wheeled into an empty parking space. "Let's do this," she said, and she and Alvarez climbed from the vehicle.

Inside, a girl in her early twenties with huge eyes rimmed thickly in mascara was manning the cash register. The detectives flashed their badges, introduced themselves, showed a picture of Troy Ryder, and asked if she'd seen him.

"Oh, yeah," the clerk said, nodding her head so rapidly the twist of hair that had been pinned on her crown threatened to slide off. "He came in last week, I think it was, bought a few things, gas and beer, maybe. He saw the Help Wanted sign in the window and was, like, asking about a job."

"A job," Alvarez repeated. Bells rang indicating another car had pulled into the pumps.

"Yeah. He, um, got turned off when I told him Corky, that's the boss, insists on background checks and drug tests." The clerk pulled a face. "Funny thing, y'know. He didn't look like a druggie." She lifted a shoulder. "But then everyone smokes weed these days. Oh. Sorry," she added quickly, having forgotten she was talking to cops. "Not me. I don't. I couldn't. Corky would fire me. Corky, he's not into that. Not just for the liability. He just don't like any drug stuff. Won't even sell papers for rolling your own."

Good for him, Pescoli thought, wondering how her son had held a job here because she suspected that Jeremy, if not a habitual user, had dabbled with weed more than a time or two. However, it seemed he'd grown out of that phase of his life, or somehow managed to hide it from her.

"Do you remember this guy's vehicle?" Alvarez asked, pointing to the picture of Ryder.

"Beat up old pickup, maybe? It had out of state plates, I think. I kinda noticed that because sometimes it gets a little boooring around here, if ya know what I mean. But it didn't have any special marks or bumper stickers or anything on it, that I noticed. It was kinda like the type everyone else around here drives." She glanced out the plate glass window as a man in ski gear filled the tank of his sedan.

She slid her gaze back to the picture of Ryder on the counter. "With him though it fit, y'know. He looked like a cowboy type. Well, again, like everyone else around here." She rolled her expressive, mascara-laden eyes and then thought of something. "Wait a minute." Her gaze zeroed in on Pescoli. "Aren't you Jeremy's mom? Jeremy Strand? I think I read about you in the paper awhile back. He, like, saved your life, shot a guy who was trying to kill you."

Pescoli nodded. She was proud of Jeremy, how responsible he'd become, and she did owe him her life.

"Tell him 'hi,' from Jodi," the girl said as a big bear of a man walked into the convenience store, a gust of freezing wind and snow following after him. "Brrr. It's soooo cold."

"Do you remember anything else about the guy in the picture?" Alvarez asked.

Jodi shook her head and the top knot wobbled precariously again. "He was in here for, like, half a second."

She was about to turn her attention to the next person in line when Pescoli said, "Hold on a sec." She took two steps to the candy counter and returned with an oversized package of Peanut M&M's. "I'll take these. You want anything?" she asked Alvarez and when her partner declined, paid for the bag. "I don't need a receipt."

Jodi rang up the sale, then turned her attention to the older man with the silvery stubble, rimless glasses, and a baseball cap with a John Deere logo. He was fishing in his back pocket for his wallet so that he could pay for gas, a pack of Rolos, and some chewing tobacco.

"For my grandson," he said, half-flirting with the clerk.

"Oh, I like Rolos, too," the girl said as Alvarez opened the door and Pescoli opened her bag of candy with her teeth.

"The Rolos? Those are for me." The old geezer winked at Jodi and started pulling bills from a slot in the well-used wallet. "The tobacco? That's for Josh."

Perfect, Pescoli thought as the bag popped open and peanuts threatened to spill out every which way. She managed to corral them and thought, *Way to go, Gramps. Get the kid hooked. Great idea.*

Maybe it was a joke, the old guy's way of flirting. Pescoli hoped so as she winced against the bitter cold, plopping a couple candy-coated chocolate peanuts into her mouth. Together, she and Alvarez half-sprinted past the gas pumps, where two cars were being refueled, to the spot where her Jeep was parked, already collecting snow.

"Want some?" she asked again as they climbed inside and she held the open bag toward her partner where Alvarez was dutifully snapping on her seat belt.

"No."

"God, they're great," Pescoli threw a few more into her mouth, then tossed an empty coffee cup onto the floor in front of the back seat and dropped the open bag into her vacant cup holder.

"Maybe to ten-year-olds or pregnant women."

"*Especially* ten-year-olds and pregnant women. But trust me, they're for everybody." Pescoli jammed her key into the ignition and sent her partner a *don't-even-go-there* stare which Alvarez ignored as her cell phone rang sharply.

Plugging one ear to block out the ambient noise of the Jeep's engine, she answered, "Alvarez."

Pescoli strapped her seat belt into place, cranked the heat to the maximum, then slammed the gearshift into reverse and backed out of the gas station.

"Yeah . . . yeah . . . Okay, I got it," Alvarez said. "We're on our way." She hung up. "Looks like we're going to the River View Motel. One of the deputies on the search found out where Ryder's been staying. The River View is on—"

"I know where it is. Just down the road." Pescoli wouldn't admit it to Alvarez, of course, but a few years earlier when she'd first started her affair with Santana, they'd sometimes stayed in little out of the way no-tell motels where they would have complete privacy. Away from her family. Away from her job. Away from Brady Long, the rich pain in the ass Santana used to work for. The River View, as well as a few other motels scattered around the outskirts of town, had been a great little rendezvous spot.

"We're too late. He's already checked out."

"Damn." Pescoli pulled into traffic which, because of the storm, was light. "Always a day late and a dollar short. But maybe he left something behind."

"Maybe."

Her partner didn't sound too convinced or even hopeful, but surely something would break in the case. It damn well had to.

"It's time to go," Ryder said, packing up the last of the electronic equipment. "We've wasted too much time already."

If Anne-Marie had hoped he would change his mind, that he'd hear her tale of battery and pain and give up the outrageous bounty placed on her head by her family, she'd been sadly mistaken. Yes, his eyes had reflected some empathy and a fierce anger as she'd explained about her husband's abuse, but in the end, once she'd finished talking, he'd said nothing for a second, then had clipped out, "I didn't know what you went through."

She realized that, overall, he didn't sound all that moved by her story. Instead, he was staring at her coolly as if she were some interesting, maybe dangerous, specimen. She suddenly understood that he was second-guessing her, wondering if she were lying again. Of course.

She walked to the window and flipped open the blinds. It was daylight and she saw both vehicles parked outside. Hers with more snow piled upon it near the sagging building she thought had once been used as a garage, his truck parked a few yards back, probably where he'd slid to a stop without headlights so as not to wake her. He'd parked carefully, wedging his pickup between two trees, guarding the lane so that no other vehicle could pass and she couldn't get away.

She didn't bother asking him how he'd sneaked in on her as he'd obviously been in the place once before to plant his electronic equipment, so he'd no doubt used his same breaking-and-entering skills.

Snow was still falling and the tracks of both vehicles were covered, his less so as it was parked beneath a canopy of branches and had been stationary for a shorter amount of time. Was she really trapped? If she couldn't convince him to let her go, would she really be forced to return to New Orleans with him?

Thinking of reuniting with her family, of the disappointment carved on her father's face, the disgrace in her mother's eyes, and the hurt on her grandmother's proud visage, she knew she couldn't return to Louisiana. Ever. Even if she could face the condemnation and shame, there was her husband, who seemed to have vanished, as well. No doubt she would be a suspect in his disappearance, or, worse yet, if he should suddenly show up in New Orleans again, she would have to look him in the eye and see him smirk at her fear.

Her stomach turned over at the thought of him. No. She'd never go back. Ryder wasn't going to take her. He just didn't know it yet. Mind turning with thoughts of escape, she started to close the blinds, then stopped. Had she seen something outside the window, some movement that she'd caught from the corner of her eye? She squinted hard, staring through the shifting veil of flakes, but whatever it was had disappeared.

Another deer perhaps.

Or, more likely, a figment of her imagination.

She told herself it was nothing, but couldn't quite shake the feeling that something outside wasn't right. Then again, nothing inside the dilapidated cabin was right, either.

"You can see why I can't go back," she tried.

"If you're telling the truth."

She knew it. The bastard didn't believe her. "Come on, Ryder. You think I made that story up?"

"What I know is you're a liar, Anne-Marie, and a good one, if I recall."

"Everything I said to you was the God's honest truth. Who would make up something so . . . so brutal?"

"Who would rob their damn grandmother?"

Anne-Marie was dying inside. She'd bared her soul to him. Stupidly.

"You told me how much she meant to you. So, it's not making a whole lot of sense to me that instead of running to her and confiding in her, asking for her help and protection, or insisting she take you to the police, you decided to steal from her. From the one woman you swore you adored."

Anne-Marie's throat clogged and she fought tears. The biggest regret in her life had been sneaking in the back door when she'd known her grandmother was sleeping in the next room and with nervous fingers opening the safe that was hidden behind a shelf in the pantry. But she had. When the safe had opened, she'd scooped up the bills that had been stacked so neatly within, money she'd used to escape, to buy her vehicle, to purchase her new identity, to visit a dentist for appliances and a costume store for the extra padding and wigs. And for the doctor in Oklahoma City. "I can't go back," she said again.

His expression hardened. "Maybe not willingly," he said, crossing the room.

"Not ever." She met his uncompromising glare with one of her own. "You'll have to shoot me. Your gun. My gun. It doesn't matter, but I won't go."

"Fine."

To her horror, he dragged a pair of handcuffs from his pocket and before she could move, he reached her and snapped them over her wrists. "We're goin', darlin', and we're goin' right now."

CHAPTER 26

The wipers weren't keeping up with the falling snow, so Pescoli tried to turn them up, to increase their speed, but they were maxed out. The storm was just that fierce. "Global warming, my ass," she muttered as the sign for the River View appeared through the thick, swirling flakes.

"Actually these storms and all the weird weather patterns we've been experiencing are the direct result of climate change." Sometimes Alvarez could really be a buzz-kill.

Pescoli cranked the wheel and her Jeep slid a bit before they drove into the lot of the motel and parked under the broad portico that was, according to several signs posted near the front doors, reserved for guests of the facility.

Pescoli really didn't give a rat's ass what the protocol was.

Inside the brightly lit reception area of the motel, they waited as a hippy woman in a uniform finished a phone call, her fingers flying over the keys of a computer. The lobby was small and smelled of day-old coffee. One faux leather couch that had seen better days was situated near a stand of brochures describing highlights of the area.

"That does it," the receptionist said with a smile wide enough to show off a gold molar. "So what can I do ya for?"

They introduced themselves, showing badges, and asked about Troy Ryder.

"A deputy was in earlier," said the woman whose name tag read CARLA SIMMS. "I told them everything I knew."

"I know, but we'd like to see for ourselves the room he stayed in," Pescoli said.

"Ooookay." The hippy woman checked her computer monitor again. "As I told the deputy, Mr. Ryder was in a king room with a view for a little over a week and didn't bother anyone. If he had company, I didn't see it. Truthfully, we here at the River View respect our guests' privacy."

"I'm sure," Pescoli said, knowing first-hand about the policy.

"It's already been cleaned. We're quick about that, you know." Carla was obviously proud of her work at the River View, as if this dive of a motel was a five-star hotel. She swept a walkie-talkie off the desk, hit a button, and said, "Can you send someone down to the reception?"

She'd barely hung up when a tiny woman appeared. She wore a puffy coat and a knit cap pulled low enough to brush the top of a red scarf wound around her neck. She couldn't have been five feet tall and even in the heavy coat, she seemed diminutive. Pescoli felt like an Amazon next to her.

"Rhonda," Carla said. "This is Detective Pescoli and . . . wait, I'm sorry—?"

"Alvarez," Pescoli's partner supplied.

"Yes, yes. Detective Alvarez. Would you please show the officers to room thirteen? It's been cleaned, right?"

Rhonda nodded her head and began fiddling with a key ring as she led the officers outside and along a covered walkway to room thirteen, which supposedly had one of the sought-after river views.

To Pescoli's way of thinking, it was all false advertising. The place was known to be clean and reasonable, nothing more. The old carpeting, and drapes that matched the bedspread, had to be from the nineties. Unfortunately, the receptionist hadn't been mistaken and the tacky room had been cleaned, no trash, no bit of visible evidence left behind.

"Clean as a whistle." Disappointed, Pescoli leaned down and looked under the bed while Alvarez checked the adjoining bath, then opened the sliding door to the small patio beyond.

"Same here," Alvarez agreed.

The room looked tired and dated, but there was nothing to indicate that Troy Ryder or any other person had ever resided there.

"We'll need to look through the trash," she said. "It hasn't been picked up yet?"

"Thursday." The maid walked them outside where the snow had covered the parking lot and the few cars parked in front of the motel. The empty spot in front of room thirteen, where Ryder's truck had been parked, had accumulated only a few inches over the asphalt. One other slot had the same level of snow. It had recently been vacated, only a thin layer covering the pavement.

"Mr. Ryder left early this morning," Rhonda said. "I'm on the early shift and he was already gone, so I got the notice to clean his room first thing." She tested the knob to make certain that the room was secure. "The same with his friend."

"Friend?" Alvarez asked, exchanging looks with Pescoli. "What friend?"

"The guest in twenty-five. I don't know his name. But he was always asking about Mr. Ryder." She stopped talking abruptly as if she realized she was giving out too much information about customers who guarded their privacy.

Alvarez clarified, "A single man?"

"Yes. No one was with him," the maid assured them, finding her voice again.

"And he hung out with Ryder?" Alvarez made a swirling motion with her finger. "You saw them together."

Shaking her head, the petite woman wagged her head thoughtfully side to side. "I don't know, but I never saw them together. They were both very private, holed up in their rooms. And the guest in room thirteen? Mr. Ryder? He never asked about the man in twenty-five, or anyone else that I know of." She raised and lowered her shoulders. "I wouldn't know. I was only here during my shifts and I was busy, you know."

"But the other man checked out this morning?" Pescoli said. "What time?"

Rhonda said, "I don't really know. He didn't stop at the desk. Just left."

Room twenty-five was around the corner from room thirteen, and offered a bird's-eye view of Ryder's activity. The parking area for that room had only a little snow in front of it, about the same level as thirteen.

"Has room twenty-five been cleaned yet?" Alvarez asked.

The maid shook her head. "I don't think so."

"Hmph." Alvarez eyed the parking lot. "Mind if we look inside?"

"Okay." The maid led the way along the long concrete porch and unlocked the room that was identical to the one Ryder had occupied.

Whoever had resided there had left in a hurry. The bill was still under the door. The bed was a tumble of blankets, and towels and hangers littered the floor. Trash was still in and around the waste baskets—newspapers and fast food wrappers, water bottles, paper cups, plastic packaging for some kind of headphones, and wadded up receipts from local stores.

"Didn't he ever have the room cleaned?" Alvarez asked.

"No. Both he and the man in number thirteen asked for no service. I talked to each of them and they refused." Rhonda shrugged in a *what're-you-gonna-do* manner. "The management doesn't like it, but the guest's wishes are always granted."

"We're going to want to seal both rooms. We don't want either of them cleaned any more," Pescoli said.

Alvarez was looking at the billing that had been left. "I assume your guests have to register their vehicles at the front desk?"

"Yes. Always."

"Good," Alvarez said. "We need to see the registration for"—she met Pescoli's gaze—"Mr. . . . Bryan Smith. I saw cameras outside. Does the motel keep the tapes?"

Rhonda shook her head. "The outside cameras are all for show. All they are is a red light to make it look like they're filming. Just like the security signs about a company that is monitoring the place. It's all just to make people think twice about stealing or loitering or whatever. The only cameras that work are in the lobby."

Alvarez said, "Then we'll need to see the lobby tapes."

They left the room.

Arms wrapped around her, shoulders hunched against the cold, Rhonda led them toward the main building. "You'll have to talk to Carla about that. She's the manager."

"We will," Pescoli said as she tightened her scarf and wondered about Ryder's "friend" in room twenty-five. She had a bad feeling about Bryan Smith. It didn't make sense. Did the two men know each other? She doubted it. Could the maid have been wrong about a possible connection? Probably not. "Just seal the room, make certain it's not cleaned." She recalled Blackwater's comment about Bruce Calderone, Anne-Marie Calderone, and Troy Ryder being in the plot together. Far-fetched, she'd thought, but maybe some part of it was true?

Rhonda was already on a walkie-talkie, speaking in rapid-fire Spanish.

Alvarez whipped out her cell phone. "I'll get officers over here ASAP," she told Pescoli as they headed back to the reception area.

Looking over the registration information in the River View's lobby, they added a 1998 Ford Explorer with Texas plates to the APB they'd sent out earlier for Ryder's Dodge pickup and asked for any and all security tapes from the motel's archives, which, Carla told them proudly, were kept for a month.

As they walked back to the Jeep, Alvarez's phone rang again

"Do you have those head shots yet?" Blackwater asked, finding Zoller at her desk, her fingers on the keyboard of her computer. As a junior detective, she shared an open space with several other detectives, each desk area divided by half walls to create a cubicle.

"Yes, sir," she said, hitting a few keys. Within seconds, a slide show of images appeared on her monitor, each essentially the same face and expression. The features were different in each, changing as they would look if artificially manipulated or permanently altered with surgery. The hairstyles were different, the cut and color changing, glasses added, contacts used to alter eye color, makeup to change the shadows of the cheekbones, eyebrows plucked or thickened, lips made fuller or thinned out, and the aging process factored in, just in case Anne-Marie Calderone had decided to disappear into middle-age. Twenty-five different shots rolled slowly by and with each one, Blackwater became more frustrated.

He was certain he'd seen her before. Would have sworn to it. Something about her eyes and shape of her face caused a memory to tug at his brain. He was good with faces, to the point that he never forgot one, so why then did he sense he'd met her but couldn't quite recall?

One image swept by and he asked Zoller to freeze it. In the shot, the woman looked a good ten or fifteen years older. Her brown hair was short, her glasses rimless, her lips thin. "Can you make her blond? Not like before." There had been several blondes in the lineup. "But this particular hairstyle."

"Sure." With a keystroke, the head shot was of a woman with pale hair.

Blackwater nodded. That seemed better. "And give this one the full lips."

Again, Zoller altered the shot.

God, he *knew* he'd seen her. But where? He concentrated. It was important on a lot of levels. If Anne-Marie Calderone was found under his watch, and the detectives managed to prove a case against her, his job as sheriff would be secure. Solving the bizarre crime would attract lots of media attention. It was already happening, and it wasn't just the local press. Papers and news agencies from as far away as Spokane and Boise were calling. If Anne-Marie Calderone, involved in bigamy and murder, were captured in Grizzly Falls, he might be hailed as a national hero . . . And if his team stopped a serial killer's rampage? Though that kind of spotlight had never been his goal, he would take any means to become the next sheriff of Pinewood County. Any political ambitions after that would have to wait.

But first things first. They still needed to locate and capture Calderone.

"Anything else?" Zoller asked, looking up at him with her hands poised over the keyboard.

He heard footsteps in the hallway and turned to find the receptionist craning her neck around the corner. "Sheriff," Joelle said with a tentative smile. "I don't want to bother you, but Manny Douglas of the *Mountain Reporter* phoned for the third time this morning and I told him you'd call him back. If he calls again, I could refer him to the public information officer, but I've dealt with him before and he doesn't seem to take the hint, if you know what I mean." Her glossy red lips pursed. "The last time he called, less than two minutes ago, he said he was on his way to the station and was only five minutes away."

Blackwater held back his initial annoyance and said, "I'll phone him as soon as I'm done here. If he's already here, give him coffee and let me know. I'll talk to him. In my office." The last thing he wanted to do at this point in his career was piss off a reporter.

She handed him a WHILE-YOU-WERE OUT memo with Douglas's name and number, then hurried off as a phone started ringing down the hallway.

As he folded the note and tucked it into his pocket, Blackwater swung his attention back to the screen. The break in his attention had given him a fresh perspective. As his eyes narrowed on the image, he felt a little sizzle of anticipation, and realized what was wrong, what had to change. To Zoller, he said, "Is it possible for you to change her teeth? Or her jawline? Give her more jowls?"

Concentrating so hard she bit into her lower lip, Zoller actually was able to draw on the screen with her mouse, the computer filling in the gaps or shaving off what she took off. She was able to change the contour of the face and add in some more crooked teeth so that in a matter of minutes, he was no longer staring at the face of Anne-Marie Calderone as pictured on her driver's license. Instead, he was looking at a much dowdier, older appearing woman that he was certain he'd seen before.

"Darken her eyes." He knew before Zoller had finished the change that he would be staring into the face of the waitress from the Midway Diner. Her name tag had read JESSICA, he remembered, but he would bet his badge she was the missing heiress, Anne-Marie Calderone.

Pescoli had already gotten a text from Bianca that there was no school today and, of course, her daughter was ecstatic, saying she was going back to bed for a while, then hoping to get a ride to a friend's later. Driving back to the station, Pescoli hoped her daughter stayed put. As far as she knew, Jeremy was at home, probably still fast asleep and would be for a while. *Good.* At least for the morning, she needed not to worry about either of them.

She wheeled into the station's parking lot and spied a spot in the thickening snow. "If this keeps up, Blackwater will have us all shoveling," she said, cutting the engine. "I can see it now, part of his new military regimen to keep his officers in shape. Did I tell you I caught him in full uniform doing push-ups in his office? Told me it kept the blood flowing."

"It does," Alvarez said as she unbuckled her seat belt.

"Yeah, well, once up and showered, I'm not interested in getting my blood flowing," Pescoli grumbled, climbing out of the car and spying Cade Grayson just parking his pickup in the visitor's lot not far from the pole where the flag was still positioned at half-mast, Old Glory billowing in the falling snow. "Take a look."

"Let's see what he has to say."

He wasn't alone. As he hopped out of one side of the truck, his brother Zed, several inches taller and at least fifty pounds heavier, stepped his size fourteen boots into six inches of icy powder. Both men were dressed in thick outerwear and cowboy hats, the wide brims collecting a white dusting as they made their way to the officers.

"Got your message," Cade said to Alvarez. "We were already in town, picking up supplies, so I thought it might be best to talk face-to-face."

"Let's go inside." Alvarez led the way, and within minutes, they were seated at the conference table, hats removed, jackets unzipped, faces stern, coffee supplied by Joelle on the table, untouched. Alvarez had taken time to dash into her office to retrieve her files and Pescoli, as was her custom these days, had made a quick trip to the bathroom.

The brothers were obviously uncomfortable, whether it was because Cade was being questioned, or due to the fact that they were seated in the sheriff's department, a door away from what had been Dan's office.

"Is this about Bart?" Zed asked, bushy eyebrows pulling together. "We all know that Hattie won't let that one go." He sent his brother a glance that was unreadable, one that Cade tried to ignore.

"I did look through the case files on your brother's suicide," Pescoli said, taking in both brothers as they were seated across from her. "But I can't find any reason to reopen the case. It looks to me that Bart took his own life. I'm sorry."

"Not unexpected," Zed said, his lips twisting down.

More, Pescoli thought, *in disapproval of his ex-sister-in-law, than in disappointment about his brother's cause of death.*

"Hattie's had a bug up her butt about it from the first but hell . . . we all just have to accept what happened. We may not like it, but it's time to move on." Pointedly, he glanced at the door leading to the office once occupied by his brother.

Cade's gaze zeroed in on Alvarez. "Why did you call? You seemed to think it was pretty damn important."

"It is," she said, her tablet firing up in front of her. "I've been in contact with Detective Montoya of the New Orleans Police Department."

"New Orleans?" Zed said. "What the hell's this all about? We've got a ranch to run and a helluva snowstorm to deal with." He shot a disgusted look at Cade. "I told you we should've just called."

"What about New Orleans?" Cade asked, deathly solemn, but not surprised.

"Montoya says you were involved with a woman from there, a woman by the name of Anne-Marie Calderone, or possibly, at that time she might have told you her name was Anne-Marie Favier, though she was married."

He didn't respond, so Alvarez attempted to jog his memory. "You were in Texas at a rodeo, took a side trip to Louisiana, and met her there?" She slid a copy of the woman in question's driver's license across the table.

The edges of Cade's lips turned white as he let his gaze skate over the image on the license before he found Alvarez's eyes again. "What about her?"

"For the love of Christ," Zed said. "You and your goddamn women!" He snorted through his nose and shook his head.

"We're investigating a couple homicides here in Grizzly Falls. You've no doubt heard of them. We think there's a connection to Ms. Calderone, and we think she's here. Has she contacted you?"

"You think there's a connection between Anne-Marie and those murders?" Cade sounded poleaxed.

"Shit, *that* woman? The waitress?" Zed said in a huff of disgust. "I knew she was trouble."

"Slow down," Pescoli advised. "So, she is here in Grizzly Falls?"

Alvarez asked, "A waitress?"

"I don't know all the details, but she admitted she was in trouble, that she thought—" Cade closed his eyes for a second, then clenched his jaw and spit out, "Shit-fire," as if he were on the horns of a dilemma.

"She thought what?" Alvarez pressed.

When Cade remained silent for a few moments, clearly trying to get his head around what he'd just heard, Zed jumped into the fray. "She came to the ranch." He flung an angry glare at his brother. "Whatever you think you're doin' by holdin' back, like you're saving her or something, or keeping some damn confidence, it's over. They're on to her."

A muscle worked in Cade's jaw.

"Mr. Grayson," Alvarez urged.

Cade scowled, angry with his brother and quite possibly himself. "She dropped by a few days ago. Said she was in trouble, that it had something to do with those women who'd been found. I don't know how, but she was afraid."

"About what? Being caught?" Pescoli asked.

"That she was in danger. For her life, or something. She'd wanted to talk to Dan about what was going on, but of course that didn't happen. I turned her away. I thought . . . hell, I'd hoped she was going to talk to you."

"She works down at the Midway Diner," Zed stated flatly.

"Did she say what she was afraid of?" Alvarez was making notes, but Pescoli was ready to shoot out of her chair and drive like a maniac to the diner. It was time to end this.

"Yeah." Cade leaned back in his chair and exhaled heavily. "She did, but I didn't believe her. She . . . well, she has a history of lying."

Zed swore under his breath.

Cade straightened. "The thing is, she told me she was afraid of her own damn husband."

"You can't do this!" Anne-Marie spat, trying to worm her way out of the handcuffs he'd slapped on her wrists.

"You had the option. You wouldn't leave on your own."

"You really are a bastard." She was furious, nearly spitting as, to her horror, he walked unerringly to the area along the baseboard where she'd stashed her important documents, her extra cash, her passports. "Don't! You can't!"

Ignoring her, he withdrew her switchblade from his pocket, clicked it open, and bent down to pry the board off to expose her niche. "We'll have to wait until the fire dies a little for the other spot," he said over his shoulder. He was serious. He was actually going to force her back to New Orleans.

He dug out the baseboard, then pulled her papers from their hiding spot. As he straightened, he snapped the knife closed and looked over the documents. "This must've cost you," he said, opening one passport after another, his eyebrows rising in appreciation. "Or your grandmother."

"I had to do it," Anne-Marie said, desperate to change his mind. "If I went back, he would've killed me."

"The police would have protected you."

She gave a short, dry laugh. "I don't think so."

"You should've—"

"I should've nothing," she cut him off. She'd had enough. Taken enough.

With a sudden yank, she removed the ring she wore, the fat piece of costume jewelry that hid her joint. Then quickly, with little effort, she grabbed her left hand with her right and removed the lifelike prosthesis to reveal the stump of her left ring finger, all that remained after the butcher she'd been married to had cleaved off the very finger on which he'd slipped her engagement ring years earlier.

CHAPTER 27

"The Midway Diner?" Pescoli said after the Grayson brothers had left the sheriff's department. She and Alvarez were still in the conference room, picking up their things. "It's almost lunchtime and maybe we'll get lucky. She'll be there, or we can get information from her boss or coworkers." Pescoli's stomach was rumbling again. *Close enough for a meal,* she decided. Even if it was one on the run. They hadn't learned much from the Grayson brothers.

Zed Grayson had been certain he'd spied Anne Marie Calderone in her job as a waitress at the diner, though the one time Cade had seen her had been at his home when she had come to visit him, desperate, it appeared. He'd suggested she turn herself in and tell her story to the police. So far, she hadn't taken his advice. Pescoli only hoped that Anne-Marie hadn't run again. That woman had about half a million questions to answer, though Pescoli still wasn't convinced she was a killer, fingerprint or no.

During the interview, Alvarez had pulled up the most recent photos of Troy Ryder and Bruce Calderone, sent to her by Montoya in New Orleans. She showed Zed and Cade several shots of the men in question. Besides his Texas driver's license photo, there was another picture of Troy Ryder from his rodeo days. As for Calderone, his driver's license photo issued by the state of Louisiana was tucked between two posed shots, one in a business suit, the other of the man in a lab coat, a stethoscope visible in his pocket. Both men were good-looking and about the same height and weight if the information on their licenses was to be believed. Troy Ryder was a little more rough and tumble looking, an outdoorsy type with tanned skin, light brown hair, and a cocksure grin. Dr. Bruce Calderone, dark hair combed neatly, chin lifted in authority, smile forced, did appear more polished and sophisticated, at least according to the shots, but that was how the photographer had staged the pictures, how the man wanted to be portrayed.

The Grayson brothers hadn't recognized either of the two men who had said "I do" to Anne-Marie.

"Let's go." Alvarez was sliding her iPad into its case. "Maybe one of Anne-Marie's coworkers has gotten close to her and knows where we can find her."

Keys in hand, Pescoli said, "Don't count on it." She was already at the door to the hallway when the other door of the conference room, the one leading directly to the sheriff's office, opened.

Blackwater took one step into the conference room. "Detectives," he said, motioning them into his office. "We need to talk. I want you to bring me up to speed, but before you brief me on what you've learned, I think you should know that Anne-Marie Calderone is in Grizzly Falls."

Alvarez gave a swift nod. "We just heard."

"From Cade Grayson?" Blackwater's eyes narrowed.

"Zed thinks he saw her at the Midway Diner, and she showed up at the ranch to visit Cade," Pescoli said. "Neither of them has any idea where she lives, but Zed said she's driving an older model Chevy Tahoe. Silver or gray or light blue, he thought. Colorado plates. Neither brother got the number."

"They still involved? She and Cade?" Blackwater asked. "Or . . . Zed?"

"They both say not." Pescoli shook her head.

"Come into the office and brief me. I know about the Midway Diner. Already talked to the owner." He stepped out of the doorway and they filed in.

Waving them into chairs, he said, "She's e-mailing me information about Jessica Williams—the alias Anne-Marie Calderone is using— her employment application, tax info, and cell number. I asked Zoller to get in touch with the cell phone company who issued the phone, but of course, it's one of those pre-paid things that requires little or no info." His dark eyes sparked and Pescoli recognized the look—a cop hot on the trail of a suspect. "Still, we don't have a physical address for her. Yet. She did pick up mail at a local postal annex, you know, where the box is the 'suite' number?" He made air quotes and added, "I've already sent deputies over there checking her application."

"You're taking over the case now?" Pescoli asked, trying and failing to mask her irritation. He was the boss, yeah, but this was their case and she was a little bristly about it . . . well, about most things these days.

"No. No way." He held up a hand, fingers splayed. "It's all yours. All yours." He glanced from one detective to the other. "But we're a team here, all work together, and so I want you to report to me. I wanted to get some answers pronto and I didn't want to interrupt your meeting with the Graysons. Time is crucial on this one; I thought it best if we get moving. Anne-Marie Calderone has a history of slipping away."

Bugged, Pescoli, for once, didn't argue. "Okay. Anything else? How did you find her?"

"Computer enhancement of her driver's license photo." He actually smiled a bit. "I had Zoller tweak it because I was certain I recognized her. It's amazing what Photoshop can do."

So he thought he'd broken the case wide open on his own. Pescoli got it. No doubt that bit of information would be leaked to the press.

"Okay, so now," he encouraged, "tell me what you learned from the brothers Grayson."

Pescoli took a back seat while Alvarez summarized their morning. "We think Troy Ryder is a party of interest in this case, as well, though we don't know how he's currently involved with Calderone or the homicides." With that as a lead-in, she launched into what they'd discovered about Ryder, the unknown person of interest in room twenty-five of the River View, and Cade Grayson's admission of actually talking to Anne-Marie Calderone, including her fear of her husband.

Blackwater listened thoughtfully.

Beneath some of his bravado, his eagerness to have things his way, Pescoli saw a glimmer of the lawman who had worked his way through the ranks, a good cop who had inherited Grayson's position through ambition and hard work.

She still didn't like him; didn't care for his style, but she grudgingly accepted that he might not be as bad as he initially seemed. He preened too much to the cameras for her taste, and she wasn't completely convinced his motives were what they should be, but maybe she could work with him.

At least for a while.

Possibly even the length of her pregnancy.

Alvarez was talking about the possibility of Bruce Calderone having landed in Grizzly Falls.

Blackwater was listening, just not convinced. He picked up a pencil from the holder on his too tidy desk. "But he's not with his wife."

"Not according to Grayson. He thinks she's running scared."

Blackwater asked the same damn question that had been plaguing Pescoli, "So where is he?"

"Don't know. But there is a possibility that he stayed at the River View Motel, registered as Bryan Smith. He was either in touch with or observing Troy Ryder. According to the maid, he kept tabs on Ryder. We've got security tapes from the motel for all the dates that Ryder was a guest. Smith should be there too as he showed up the day after Ryder checked in and left soon after Ryder checked out. We've got his vehicle description and plates, this time from Texas. Plates and vehicle don't match. Already issued BOLOs on both Ryder's vehicle and Bryan Smith's."

"Good." Blackwater was nodding, agreeing with his own thoughts as he tapped the eraser end of the pencil on his desk. "The trouble with this is that it's getting more complicated as we get closer. Anne-Marie Calderone sighted," he thought aloud, "now, possibly both husbands." Dropping the pencil into its holder, he looked from Alvarez to Pescoli. "Looks like we're searching for three people instead of just one. Let's do it."

Ryder stared at the stump where Anne-Marie's finger had been. His stomach turned sour, bile rising up his throat as he stood in front of the dying fire. "He did that to you?" A new rage burned through him and he felt his back teeth grind together. Yes, Anne-Marie was a liar. A major liar. The best he'd ever come across and that was saying something, but for the first time, he wondered if she could possibly be telling the truth. He didn't want to believe her, didn't trust her as far as he could throw her, but who would make up such a grotesque story?

"Of course he did!" she said, her teeth drawing back in anger. "Look!" She held up her hand, fingers spread wide. "Do you want to know what he did after? Huh?" She didn't wait for an answer. "He kicked me, Ryder. Like so much trash, he kicked my naked body into the river and hoped to hell that alligators would finish me off, eat me alive, to get rid of the evidence."

Ryder's insides curled in repulsion.

She inched her chin up defiantly. "I'd made the ultimate mistake. Of walking away from him."

As they stood inches apart, she unburdened herself, letting go of her secret. She stood toe-to-toe with him and told him about going to the townhouse to get her things, and being discovered by Calderone. How he'd drugged her and jammed her rings on her finger before taking her somewhere deep into the Louisiana swampland. How, while she was starting to rouse, he'd sliced off her finger, rings and all, with the skill of the surgeon he was. As a final act, he'd kicked her, rolling her into the murky water.

Ryder listened, but didn't say a word.

"So"—she stared up at him with her wide eyes—"just so you understand. I'll never go back." She blinked once, then whispered, "Never. I'd rather die first."

He found his voice and dug deep for his resolve. "If what you're saying is true—"

"If?" she repeated as a blast of wind slammed against the cabin, the walls shuddering. "*If?* Oh, my God, what do you think, Ryder, that I cut off my own damn finger?"

"No." He knew a sane person wouldn't mutilate themselves so. And he didn't think Anne-Marie was insane, just . . . self-serving to the max.

"Then take off these frickin' cuffs!" She glared at him as the fire sizzled, dying in the grate.

He almost reached for the key. He'd told himself that no matter what, he was going to haul her back to New Orleans, that no matter what kind of lies she spun, he was going to stand strong, never believe her. Yet there he was in the dilapidated cabin, his determination crumbling. His faith in her had been destroyed long ago. Her lies; her fault. But he found it impossible to believe that she would go to such incredible, grotesque lengths.

She'd do anything to save her own skin. You know it. You lived it. The woman has no scruples. None. Zero. Zilch. Don't be tricked, Ryder. Yes, she's beautiful and seductive and even charming, but

*she's a twisting, diabolical snake and you know it. Once bitten, re-
member? Twice shy? Twice fucking shy!*

Her hands bound together, she brushed her hair out of her eyes
and frowned, a bit of pain registering in her green eyes. "You don't
believe me."

"I don't know what to believe," he said honestly.

"I hurt you that badly?"

"You're just so into your own lies that you believe them yourself,"
he said. "You don't seem to know the difference between real truth
and your own skewed fantasy."

Sighing, she glanced down at the floor, bit her lip, and shook her
head as if finally understanding she couldn't convince him of her
twisted reality. "Fine," she whispered under her breath. "As I said, I'd
rather die first."

"Not gonna happen," he said as she thrust out her chin. Defiant to
the end.

"Then let's go," she bit out, furious. "But give me a moment,
okay? I need to use the bathroom."

He wanted to argue, didn't think it was a good idea to let her out
of his sight. "Five minutes," he said, feeling like an idiot, telling himself not to give her an inch.

But where could she go? Where could she run? The storm was still
raging and it was even doubtful that the two of them in his truck
would be able to make it out of the mountains, let alone through
Montana and south.

But he didn't chase her all the way up there to give up.

"Leave the door open," he said and turned to the fireplace where
he started searching for the niche near the firebox. He'd watched her
on the screen he'd set up in his hotel room stash more of her valuables there. He wanted everything with him when he returned to the
Crescent City.

"You really are a son of a bitch," she threw at him as she walked to
the bathroom and left the door cracked.

He felt a bit of satisfaction that she'd followed his order, but experienced a pang of regret and wondered how hard and callous he'd
become.

*Because of her, Ryder. This is all her fault. You don't trust her. Of
course you don't. And the reason is directly because of her actions.*

He heard water running and the shuffle of footsteps.

After tossing the tiny leather pouch of papers he'd found in her hiding spot, he grabbed his cell phone and flipped open the blinds to survey the weather. "Anne-Marie?" he called.

"You said five minutes! It hasn't been two."

So she was inside. Good. He stepped onto the tiny porch, then closed the door and looked back through the window to make certain she didn't try to escape, walk out of the bathroom and take a hard right for the back door.

Everything inside the darkened interior remained the same, the fire offering up enough light that he could make out the door to the bathroom.

Quickly, he dialed the phone and turned up the collar of his jacket as it rang. Once. Twice. The wind rushed across the porch, scattering the few dry leaves that weren't already covered in snow.

"Hello?" A man's voice. Rough. Irritated.

"Yeah, it's me. Ryder."

"I see that. Modern technology you know. Where the hell are you?"

"Still in Montana."

"What? I thought you'd be on your way by now! What the hell's taking so long?"

"I've got her."

"Then why the fuck are you still in Montana?"

"Big storm," Ryder explained.

"Big storm? Big deal. You should have prepared for bad weather. Christ, you knew where you were going, what you were doing."

"I know. I did."

"Then, what's the problem?"

What was the problem? Ryder stared through the window into the darkened interior. He felt the wind battering the tiny, falling-down cabin in the middle of the Bitterroot Mountains, a ramshackle abode no rational person would try to make their home. Unless she was desperate. Unless she didn't want to be found.

He thought about the passports he'd riffled through, remembering the different photographs, the changed names, the altered looks. He considered Anne-Marie Favier Calderone. She was a gorgeous girl who'd grown up in wealth and seemingly a princess-like existence who was frantic enough to change her good looks and adopt different personas to hide herself, a woman on the run who had eventually wound up in the middle of the mountains, isolated and alone, in a damn cabin with thin walls, no heat, and barely running water.

Why? he wondered again.

Why would she go to all the trouble? Why would she willingly propel herself into all this hardship? How desperate was she to try and disappear off the face of the earth? What had been the reason that she would tumble to such depths as to steal from her grandmother, the one woman she'd sworn she adored?

It didn't make sense.

Unless she was scared out of her mind.

Unless her bravado was a mask.

Unless her damnably stubborn attitude was propelled by sheer terror.

"Hello?" called the voice on the phone, but he ignored it.

With snow falling all around him, Ryder remembered her vanity. How she'd known how beautiful she was, how sexy and alluring she could be, and she'd reveled in her good looks and charm, in her sensuality. She would never have sliced off her own finger and no accident would have been so clean. As if it had been cleaved by a butcher. Or a surgeon. Or one man who had been both—the monster that she'd married.

"Shit," he whispered, realizing he was making a huge, irreversible mistake—one it might already be too late to rectify.

"Hello? For Christ's sake, Ryder? Are you there? Fuck!"

His boots ringing, Ryder stepped to the far end of the porch and took a quick look down the side of the cabin to the bathroom window, just to make certain she hadn't done anything foolish like squeezing herself through the tiny window and dropping to the ground to escape. As far as he could see, the window wasn't open and the snow below it was undisturbed.

Still, he was uneasy.

And then he saw a shadow. Just a faint image of something beyond the veil of snow. His gut clenched and he reached into his pocket, his fingers curling over the butt of his gun, but the image vanished as quickly as it had appeared and he told himself it was nothing.

Right?

Squinting, he decided it was a trick of light.

"Hello? Are you there?" demanded the voice on the other end of the line. "I asked you when you will get back here?"

"Never," Ryder replied, finally responding.

"What? I can't hear you. Are you outside? I asked when you were coming back!"

The wind screamed as it raced around the corner of the house and the icy, snow-laden branches of the trees danced, shedding pieces of their white mantles.

"And I said 'never!'" he repeated, a little more loudly. Then added, "Oh, and by the way?"

"Yeah?"

"Go fuck yourself."

CHAPTER 28

"The cell phone company should get back to us soon," Alvarez said as she stood. She and Pescoli were still in Blackwater's office, getting ready to hit the road again. "Hopefully they'll have information on Ryder's position."

"If his phone isn't turned off," Pescoli reminded her.

"My guess is, he's made some calls, and if he has, we'll have a place to start," Alvarez said. "We'll take the position of the last ping, wherever it comes from, and work from there. Maybe we'll get lucky."

"Maybe," Pescoli said, not willing to bet on it as she recognized the quick staccato tap of Joelle's high heels in the hallway. From the sound of it, the receptionist was nearly sprinting and stopped abruptly at Blackwater's office.

"Sorry," she said, sticking her head inside, her heart-shaped earrings still swinging in her earlobes. "But I've got a news crew here from KMJC. And Nia Del Ray, the reporter, is being very insistent that someone make a statement. To her." Clutching the doorframe in one hand, Joelle let her gaze skate over the detectives to land on Blackwater. "Apparently someone over at the station heard that you already talked to the *Mountain Reporter,* and now she wants equal time. At least, I think that's how she put it. Any way around it, she's in the reception area and not budging."

"You talked to Manny Douglas?" Pescoli asked her boss. She had no use for the wormy little reporter for the local newspaper. The guy was always crawling around, poking his pointy nose in where it didn't belong, getting himself and the department into trouble.

"I did. It was a good move." Blackwater was making no apologies. "The public might be able to help us locate Anne-Marie Calderone, and now, the others involved in the case. We can use the press to our advantage."

"Or your advantage," Pescoli said, and caught a warning glare from Alvarez.

Blackwater said softly, "My decision." He looked to Joelle, still waiting in the doorway. "Tell her to hold tight. I'll talk to the public information officer, and we'll organize a press conference later today."

"Today?" Pescoli repeated. "You're not going out with what we've got, are you?" She was horrified. "We have to hold all this close, or we could spook Calderone and Ryder, maybe compromise the case."

"I said, 'later.'" He was firm.

Pescoli said, "This is a bad idea."

"Maybe, but mine." Even seated at his desk while she was standing, Blackwater still held the upper hand, was still in command. "Just wrap it up, Detective."

So there it was. Obviously, he couldn't give up another shot at the spotlight.

Joelle clarified. "You want me to ask Nia Del Ray to wait for the press conference."

"She can damn well cool her jets," Pescoli said.

But Blackwater held up a hand to silence her. "I'll speak to Ms. Del Ray," he said to Joelle. "Give me five minutes, then send her in."

It was all Pescoli could do to hold her tongue.

"I'm not going to tell her anything about the case," Blackwater assured the detectives as he pushed his chair back and stood. "I just want to assure her that we're not holding anything back and, as I said, see if the press can help us." With one eye on the mirror, he reached for his jacket. "Keep me up to the minute, Detectives," he ordered and waited as they walked out of his office.

Pescoli seethed.

"Don't let him get to you," Alvarez whispered. "Don't. It won't end well."

"No?" Pescoli threw back. "You know me. Here I was believing in happy endings."

Something was wrong.

Ryder sensed it the minute he stepped inside the cabin again. It was too quiet. Too damn quiet. "Hey!" he called, crossing the living room. "It's been five minutes."

Still nothing. "Anne-Marie?"

No response, just the soft thunk of one of the blackened logs in the fireplace splitting, causing a few sparks to rise and the reddish embers to glow bright. He told himself to relax, that he was starting to jump at shadows. Hadn't he conjured up someone lurking through the veil of snow around the cabin a few minutes ago? Being cooped up, listening to her lies . . . hell, believing them . . . was making him edgy. "Anne?" he yelled again. "Let's go!"

Nothing.

Not one damn sound.

In a heartbeat, he knew what had happened. "Shit!"

Somehow, though he'd watched the interior during his phone call, even checked the grounds near the little cottage, she'd managed to escape, either by lucking out and running to the back door while he was surveying the snowy landscape near the side of the house, or somehow she'd crawled through that tiny window in the bathroom and dropped outside, hiding her tracks.

He flashed on the shadow he'd witnessed.

Crap! It had been her. Of course!

Damn it all to hell, I've been an idiot, he thought, crossing the small space.

He'd been careless, believing the stupid window was too damn small. But without all the extra padding, Anne-Marie was a slim, athletic woman. And she had a purpose. Hadn't she told him over and over that she wouldn't go back, that she'd rather die than . . .

Jaw clenched, he flung the cracked door open wide. "Anne— Oh, God!"

His voice died in his throat as he looked into the small interior. There, crumpled on the floor, blood pooling beneath her on the dirty old linoleum, she lay.

A pair of long-bladed shears, the kind used by hairdressers, were still clutched in her right hand. Despite her wrists being handcuffed, she'd been able to open the blades and slash at her wrists. Jagged red scratches, blood still oozing, ran lengthwise down the inside of her forearms.

Her eyes were closed.

And she seemed peaceful.

As if she'd accepted death all too willingly.

Pescoli and Alvarez stared at the images Zoller brought up on the computer screen. She had copies of the security tapes from the motel. They'd been on their way to the diner when the junior detective had asked them to step into her cubicle.

"I thought you'd want to see this," Zoller said. "I had the lab send me a digital copy."

"They've already done that?" Alvarez asked.

"I told them it was a rush. I, uh, I might have invoked Sheriff Blackwater's name."

"Better than God's," Pescoli observed, then shut up as Alvarez sent her another sharp look. Her partner was right. If she wanted to keep her job, she needed to keep the peace. You attract more flies with honey than vinegar. Wasn't that the old saying? *Well, it sucks,* she thought.

"So here it is." Zoller freeze-framed the tape. "This is Bryan Smith as he checked in."

Pescoli recognized the registration desk, the same brochures on the stand nearby, the coffeepot, and old couch. Carla, the heavyset manager of the River View Motel was standing on the business side of the counter, her gold tooth catching the light. A tall man stood on the other side, leaning over to fill out the card. He was handsome, fit, with dark hair and the very visage of Dr. Bruce Effin' Calderone.

Heart in his throat, Ryder fell to his knees beside Anne-Marie's pale unmoving body. "Oh, Jesus," he whispered. "Anne, goddamn it, Anne-Marie!" Warm blood seeped through his jeans. "Anne-Marie? Can you hear me? Oh, come on, come on!"

He felt for a pulse and found it, heard the soft sound of her breathing. He felt a bit of relief. It wasn't too late. She was still alive. "Hang in there. You . . . hang in there."

Yanking the phone from his pocket, he dialed 9-1-1, but it was a futile call. They were too far out of town to wait for an ambulance and no helicopter could fly in the storm. "Come on," he said to Anne-Marie as the operator answered.

"9-1-1. What is the nature of—"

"Listen! I have a woman near death. Dying. Her wrists slashed. I need help!" Ryder didn't hesitate.

"Is the woman alive?"

"Yes! Yes! I said so."

"Sir, I need your name and your location."

"We're off a county road in the mountains, twenty miles north of Grizzly Falls, maybe fifteen miles west of Missoula, I'm not sure, but I'm bringing her in. To the hospital in Missoula. Northern General." *God, this is taking too much time.*

All the while Anne-Marie was bleeding out.

He set the phone down and found a roll of gauze in an emergency first aid kit, probably Anne's, and probably where she'd kept the damn scissors she'd used to try and end her life. Heart thudding, operator yelling at him, he quickly unlocked her cuffs, stuffed them into his pocket, then pried her blood-stained hands apart. As he'd learned in the Army, he wrapped the wounds, binding them, hoping to staunch the flow of blood as the 9-1-1 operator still yelled at him, her voice squawking instructions as he worked.

"Sir!" she yelled. "Are you still there? Keep this line open. Officers are dispatched and—"

He ignored her instructions. "Come on, Anne-Marie," he said, forcing himself to remain calm, to go into that zone he'd learned long ago. But it wasn't working. Not with her, the only woman he'd married no matter how false it had been. "Hang in there, honey." His voice cracked a little.

Why hadn't he paid attention to her desperation?

Hadn't she said she'd rather die?

She was on the brink of death by her own hand, her choice, because he'd run her to the ground. Guilt tore at him as he looked at her, the woman who had been so full of life, such a brilliant, careless liar, the only woman he'd ever met who could hold her own with him in a verbal sparring match or while making love. His damn heart wrenched and he realized he'd been kidding himself. It had been a lie when he'd convinced himself that he didn't care for her and never had. She'd gotten to him, burrowed under his skin and into his damn soul.

The reason he'd agreed with her bastard of a father to bring her back to New Orleans wasn't about justice or even money. It was about seeing her again, having his day of reckoning.

Well he was having it.

In spades.

As for her old man, the devil with whom he'd partnered, Talbert was nearly broke. No way would Ryder have gotten paid. He'd known that from the get-go. Had done a little research. The old man had probably hoped that with his notorious daughter's return, he could somehow capitalize on her capture, figure out a way to make some big cash. Maybe a tell-all book? A movie of the week? Or even a reality television series. Who knew? The man had grandiose opinions of himself.

Stupidly, Ryder had wanted to see Anne-Marie again and yes, to take her back to New Orleans to clear up the mystery. He had outwardly been Talbert's willing pawn.

Ryder had told himself he had to be the one to bring Anne-Marie to justice, to make her face her sins. Oh, yes, his own motives had been far from altruistic.

Well, no longer.

That whole returning to New Orleans thing was over. At least for him.

He would take Anne-Marie to the hospital and hope beyond hope that she survived. That was all that mattered. How they dealt with the rest of their lives was of little concern. Once she was healthy again, he would help her prove that she was innocent of any crimes and that her husband, the bastard of a doctor who had severed her finger, was the true ungodly culprit.

What was it she'd said? That she'd worried the women killed recently in Grizzly Falls had been targeted because of her? Killed to terrorize her.

That, of course, had to be her own fears taking flight.

Right?

But the thought gnawed at him as he worked over her, and he wondered if it was possible. Was she crazy? Or singularly perceptive where Bruce Calderone was involved? As he tucked the final end of the gauze strip around her bandaged arm, she moaned. Gently he tried to rouse her. "Anne-Marie? Honey. Anne? Come on. Hang in there. We've got to go now."

The white strips of gauze covering her arms were already turning scarlet.

Time was running out.

And the damn 9-1-1 operator was still yammering, advising him to stay on the line when he slid his arms under Anne-Marie and gently lifted her, his heart hammering at the urgency. Would he make it in time? Or would she die on the way?

Either way, guilt would be his lifelong companion.

"We've got a hit," Alvarez said, checking her phone as they were leaving Zoller's cubicle. "Ryder's cell phone."

"Already?"

"Today's technology."

"Let me get my coat." Pescoli grabbed her jacket, sidearm, purse, and another energy bar as they'd never made it to the diner. Her stomach had started growling again, the hunger pangs only subsiding by the shot of adrenaline that pumped through her bloodstream at the thought of catching one of the key players in the homicide cases.

Once she and Alvarez met in the hall again, walking rapidly to the back door, Alvarez explained. "Not only is Ryder's location being triangulated by the cell phone company and our department, but, get this, he's on the line now with 9-1-1."

"Are you kidding me?"

"Nope. The call is being traced, emergency vehicles dispatched."

"What's the emergency?" It didn't sound good. People on the run didn't tend to call the police unless something unexpected and dire, usually life-threatening, had gone down.

"Don't know for certain. He said something about a possible suicide attempt."

"By whom?"

"A woman."

"Shit. It's Anne-Marie Calderone. Suicide attempt, my ass."

"He claims he's at a cabin in the Bitterroots off the county road. The triangulation confirms the location. A cabin owned by someone who lives out of state."

"He's there? With her? You mean, they're there?"

"It's sketchy. He's not responding to the operator though he hasn't hung up."

"Ominous," Pescoli thought aloud as she scrabbled into the side pocket of her purse for her key ring. Side-stepping around Pete Watershed, who was heading in the opposite direction, Pescoli tried to piece it all together. "Maybe he tracked her down and they got into some kind of lover's quarrel. She did do the bogus marriage thing with him. That's gotta sting. Big rodeo rider. Probably a macho guy. Maybe he tried to kill her and has remorse."

"Who knows?"

"It's just unbelievable that after all this time of chasing shadows, we get a goddamn call for help from one of the suspects."

"Person of interest," Alvarez pointed out. "Not a suspect."

"There you go again, semantics." Pushing open the back door, Pescoli caught a blast as the arctic air slapped her full in the face. "You know, just once, just damn once, it would be nice if one of our local serial killers decided to do his business in the summer." She hit the button on the remote lock, and the Jeep's lights flickered, its horn giving a soft beep. "Yeah, wouldn't that be the ticket."

"Careful what you wish for," Alvarez said. "Summer brings heat, rotting flesh, maggots, flies, stench, you name it."

"Still—" Pescoli's breath formed clouds as she talked.

Alvarez turned the conversation back to the case. "Even though emergency vehicles have been dispatched, Ryder's claiming he's taking the victim to a hospital in Missoula. Northwest General."

Where Dan Grayson had died. Pescoli didn't like the reminder.

At the county vehicle, Alvarez opened the door to the passenger seat. "Oh. I've already advised Blackwater."

Perfect. Pescoli slid behind the wheel and remembered the new sheriff showing up at the O'Halleran ranch where the first victim had been discovered. The two doors closed simultaneously. "Isn't Blackwater already driving to the location? Trying to grab a little glory?"

"You're awful."

"So I've heard." Pescoli started the Jeep, flipped on the wipers, and backed out of the parking spot.

Alvarez actually grinned. "I don't know if the sheriff will show up. He was still eyeball deep in a conversation with Nia Del Ray. I had to text him the info. Didn't want to break up his moment to shine with the press."

"Then, no," Pescoli said, answering her own question. Ramming the Jeep into gear, she nosed out of the lot. "He wouldn't pass up the opportunity for a sound bite."

"Even for capturing a serial killer?"

"Eh." Pescoli tipped a gloved hand up and down. "Maybe. Maybe not." She checked the street, then gunned the engine and cut in front of a slow-moving van of some kind.

Alvarez hung on. "Slow down, Detective. Remember, we don't know that we're going to find Calderone and even if we do and she survives, we still don't have proof other than one lousy fingerprint that she's the killer."

Pescoli flipped on the overhead lights and siren. No time to waste.

Ryder didn't bother gathering his things. He had to get Anne-Marie to the hospital. Nothing else mattered. Though she was a dead weight in his arms, he kicked open the door and carried her to the truck, trying like hell not to jar her, but feeling the clock ticking. Once at the pickup, he set her on the worn cushions then laid the passenger seat back as far into a reclining position as it would go. "Anne," he called to her. "Anne-Marie? Darlin', come on, now. Stay with me."

Her eyes fluttered and he felt hope swell in his heart.

"We're goin' now," he told her but her eyes didn't track. "Hang on." He closed the side door, then rounded the truck and climbed in, his keys already out of his pocket. Double-checking that the rig was in four-wheel drive, he flipped on the starter. The old engine fired. He found reverse and started to back up past the trees that had flanked the lane. The snow was deep, but his Dodge moved easily, cutting tracks through the powder to the wide spot in the lane a little farther back, an open space where he could turn his vehicle around and head to the main road. Hopefully, it had been plowed.

If so, within twenty minutes or so, he would be able to get Anne-Marie to the hospital. "Hang in there," he said again, squinting through the snow. His back window was fogged and it was hard to see. He used his mirrors, trying to keep his truck on track. Almost at the place he hoped to swing the back end around, he caught a glimpse of something that appeared through the veil, a huge shadow looming behind him.

"What the hell?" He looked in the rearview mirror, and God

Almighty, if there wasn't another vehicle behind him, blocking his path. A grayish Ford Explorer. Older model.

Like the one he'd seen at the River View.

His heart nearly stopped. He thought of the shadow he'd seen earlier. Squinting, he didn't see anyone inside the Explorer, but the interior was impossible to clearly discern through the snowfall. He glanced around the area. Was the vehicle there because of them or had it been parked by someone going cross-country skiing or snow-shoeing or even poaching?

The hairs on the back of his neck rose and he thought about his pistol, hidden deep in the pocket of his jacket, just behind the passenger seat.

It didn't matter. He just had to get around the thing.

He didn't like it, but he had to deal with it.

He thought he could squeeze around one side, but he'd have to back around the Ford; there just wasn't enough room between the trees to rotate his truck. "Son of a bitch," he muttered, his attention on the Explorer.

He didn't notice her move.

Didn't see it coming.

All of a sudden, quick as a rattler striking, Anne-Marie sat bolt upright, reached forward, and grabbed the handcuffs from his pocket. As he jerked, she managed to click one over his wrist. With a snap, the other was locked over the steering wheel.

"What the hell?" he said, pulling back, trying to release the lock.

As if she'd done it a thousand times, she slid his Glock from his jacket pocket, cut the engine, then opened the side door.

"Hey!"

"I told you I wasn't going back, Ryder."

"Wait! No! Anne-Marie! For the love of God! I was taking you to the frickin' hospital!"

"Sure. Give me a break!" She slammed the door shut and took off running, racing along the tracks he'd just cut, hurrying back to the cabin.

Furious with himself, with his damn gullibility where she was concerned, he pounded the wheel. *Damn.*

He'd been a fool. Not just once, but again! He swore and pulled at the cuffs, but they were locked solid. "Shit!" he yelled. "Shit, shit. Shit! Anne!"

But she was gone. Through the windshield and falling snow, he watched her leap over the step, not slowing an inch, her self-inflicted injuries all part of her disguise. In the blink of an eye, she disappeared into the cabin.

God. Damn. It.

With a sickening sense of what was happening, he realized that he'd been duped. She was never in any real danger of dying. Her whole suicide attempt had been a ruse. And he'd fallen for it, hook, line, and sinker.

CHAPTER 29

Anne-Marie worked fast. There wasn't much time. She found Ryder's phone in the bathroom where the stupid 9-1-1 operator was still bleating out instructions. She turned the phone off, severing the connection, then disabled it completely, ignoring the smeared blood on the bathroom floor—her blood.

Heart thumping, hating herself for her deception, she changed quickly, but didn't remove the damn bandages. She was still bleeding a little bit but wasn't worried. She hadn't cut an artery or even a major vein, just sliced the surface over and over again, a trick, considering the restrictions of those damn handcuffs, but one she'd researched on the Internet long ago. She had become a master of disguise and deception, two traits of which she wasn't all that proud, but sure as hell came in handy.

She thought of Ryder trapped in the truck.

It wouldn't be for long.

The damn cops were on their way.

So she couldn't waste a second. She changed quickly, tucked Ryder's Glock into the back of her jeans, the waistband holding it snug against her back. "Here we go," she said and started loading her SUV.

"Anne!" Ryder yelled. "Anne-Marie!" *Shit! Fuck! Damn!* "Anne! Oh, for the love of . . ." Pissed beyond pissed, he yanked at the handcuffs holding him fast to the steering wheel.

Wait a second!

The key!

"Where the hell is the key for the cuffs?" He'd put it on the ring . . .

then he saw the tiny notched piece of metal dangling from the key ring still in the truck's ignition.

He couldn't believe his good luck. Tantalizingly close, he reached for it, but it hung just out of his reach. No matter how he strained, leaned, and twisted, he just couldn't get it.

His mind started spinning with options, none of them possible. As cold as it was, he started to sweat with his efforts. He'd been such a fool to let her, a known criminal, a major liar, and a master of deception, get the drop on him. Letting his breath out in frustration, he glanced in the rearview again to that damn SUV blocking his escape. No doubt it was part of Anne-Marie's plan.

How had I been so stupid?

How had I let her lie to me?

He took another swipe at the keys and swore when his fingertip brushed the bottom of the ring. But that was it. Not good enough. Too far away by less than an inch. If he could just reach the key ring, if he could slide the handcuffs up the steering wheel to give him just a bit more leeway, then maybe he could . . . *Crap.* The steering wheel wasn't an unbroken circle, of course. The braces holding the wheel to the column prevented him from sliding around it completely. He stretched, trying to reach the keys with his free hand, but the most he could do was tick the key with the tip of his middle finger.

"Son of a bitch." He strained, the cords of his neck distending, his muscles stretching to their limits, but no go. Through the fogging windshield, he watched as she loaded her SUV with essentials and her bag. Even a wig was tossed into the back seat. Swiftly. Efficiently. Something black and bulky was tucked into the belt of her jeans at her back and he realized it was a gun—his damn Glock. She never once looked in his direction, just packed her truck with singular efficiency and climbed behind the wheel.

Damn her.

Where did she think she could go? How could she drive around his truck and that damn vehicle parked behind him? And where was the driver of the truck? The bad feeling that had been with Ryder when he first saw the Explorer blocking the lane burrowed a little deeper in his soul. Though he told himself he was imagining things, that the truck was just a coincidence, he didn't quite believe it.

He felt the weight of her tiny pistol in his pocket, a practically useless weapon, but a weapon nonetheless. Of course, it was lodged deep on the opposite side of his body as his free hand but, just to be on the safe side, he decided it was worth the effort to retrieve it and her damn switchblade. But of course, he was thwarted. The weapons in that pocket, like the keys dangling in the ignition, were just out of reach. No matter how he twisted and contorted his body, he couldn't slide his free hand near the pocket. However, he could, just maybe, shrug out of the coat, at least on the side of his body that wasn't clamped to the wheel. If he got his shoulder free and slid the jacket down his back, partially off his cuffed arm, he might be able to twist the fabric enough to be able to reach the gun. Then, at least, he'd be armed. Trapped, but armed.

But it wasn't going to happen.

Try as he might, all he could do was free up his left arm, the padded sleeve of his jacket no longer binding, which gave him a little more wiggle room. Not much. But he didn't need more than another half an inch. He reached for the keys again, finally able to touch part of his house key.

Maybe he wasn't trapped after all.

Maybe he could—

Through the snow collecting over the windshield, he saw the very same kind of shadow he'd viewed from the porch only minutes earlier. He squinted and his heart stopped.

The shadow was a man. A tall man.

And in his hand, he held a gun.

"We've got a little more info," Alvarez told her partner as Pescoli hit the gas and sped around a dawdling minivan that thankfully pulled to the side of the road. With the Jeep's light bar lit menacingly and the siren screaming a warning for the slow-moving traffic to get out of her way, she was able to push the speed limit despite the storm.

As she drove into the hills, she slid around a flatbed truck that was inching up an incline, her red and blue lights reflecting off the snow.

Alvarez was staring at the small screen of her phone.

"What?" Pescoli asked.

"It's on Ryder's phone. Apparently, he didn't think he was doing anything worrisome, because his last call, the one before the hospital, was to an unlisted number in Louisiana. Private cell. Zoller called

Montoya, who's in the loop, and he was able to come up with the owner of the phone."

"Let me guess. Bruce Calderone."

"Not even close." Alvarez slid a glance at her partner. "The phone is listed to Favier Industries. Specifically Talbert Favier."

"Anne-Marie's father?" Pescoli asked. "He's in cahoots with the illegal second husband?"

"Seems so."

"I wonder what the hell that's all about."

"We should find out soon," Alvarez said, checking her GPS. "We'll be there within ten. Deputies and an ambulance are probably arriving."

"If anyone's still there. By now, Ryder was supposed to be taking her to the hospital, isn't that what you said?"

"Yeah." Alvarez was still staring at the screen. "We've got officers waiting at Northern General?"

"And the other hospitals in the area in case that was a ruse to throw us off."

"Good."

Pescoli smiled as she took a corner a little too fast and the Jeep slid a second before the wheels caught. "This is all going down. Finally."

Anne-Marie stepped onto the porch.

Ryder witnessed the assassin raise his gun and aim. "No!"

Shit! With a supreme effort, Ryder reached for the keys again, his fingers touching the end of his dangling house key. No longer did he care about the handcuffs. No, he had another plan in mind . . . if the bastard would just stay put.

And he had enough time.

God, help him. He felt the cold metal brush against his fingers.

Once.

Twice.

And then he grabbed the truck key, still engaged. All he had to do was throw his weight into it and then . . .

Anne-Marie stopped dead in her tracks.

Her heart hit the ground as she recognized her husband, her first and only legal husband standing behind her SUV, a huge pistol aimed straight at her heart.

"Bruce," she said, going cold inside, her worst fears crystalizing.

"Going somewhere?" he asked in that voice she found so hateful.

"What're you doing here?" she said, trying to stay cool when she was beyond freaked. She needed to buy time. She had a weapon, too, a large pistol, but it would take a second or two to reach behind her.

"You've been hard to find."

She moved to one side, and the muzzle of his huge gun followed her. Sick inside, she realized that once again, she was at his mercy, the little wife of the outwardly handsome, inwardly insidious monster of a husband. Only this time, she knew she was doomed. If he'd gone through all the trouble of tracking her down, he wouldn't just let her be.

"I-I thought you'd disappeared," she said, thinking hard, looking for some means of escape. If she could just buy some time . . .

"Like you."

"You left me for dead."

"I did," he admitted with a mock-disgusted smile. "And damn it, I made a mistake, thinking the alligators would finish you off." All humor faded from his voice. "Trust me, this time I won't."

She didn't doubt it. But the gun. If she could just get to the gun. "How did you find me?" she asked, though it didn't matter. She was just putting off the inevitable.

"Simple. I didn't have to look for you." Again, he was pleased with himself, thought he was so damn clever, was glad to rub her nose in it. "I just followed Ryder."

She felt sick inside at the thought that she, even inadvertently, had dragged Ryder into this.

"He was pretty dogged you know. Seems as if he had as much of a bone to pick with you as I do." Calderone chuckled humorlessly. "Husbands. They can be such a problem. Especially when you have more than one at a time."

"That was a mistake. I know it now," she said, wondering if there was a chance that she could reason with him and desperate enough to try. It wasn't just her skin she had to worry about, but Ryder's as well. Handcuffed as he was, Ryder was a sitting duck.

"Look," she said, inching up slightly to the open door of the cabin but splaying her hands to keep his attention off her feet. She saw him

stare at his handiwork. Her stump—the finger he'd cut off as a reminder of how she'd abused her wedding vows. "It's over. You and
me. We both know it and we knew it a long time ago. So, don't do
anything foolish. You're a doctor for God's sake, you're young. Go
and live your life. Leave me alone."

She was rambling, she knew, but still, he hadn't shot her. Not
yet. Though she was panicking inside, still intending to shoot him if
she had the chance, she forced her voice to remain calm. "Go away,
Bruce. So far, you're not a killer and you could leave me . . ." Her voice
faded away as reality hit her and she thought of the two women who
had been killed recently.

"Too late for that. Sacrifices had to be made."

"Sacrifices? I don't under—" But she did. Her stomach turned
over. She thought she might throw up. God, how she hated this
man. How, how, how had she ever remotely thought she loved him?
Why in the world did she marry him? Because her own home life
hadn't been the picture-perfect postcard everyone had believed. And
she'd been duped by him. If given the chance, she'd blow him away
and not think twice about it.

"They needed to die, so that you would be blamed."

"Me? But how? I had nothing to do with them."

"Didn't you?"

"Of course not." She inched backward, still trying to figure out
how to save Ryder, save herself. "I didn't even know them."

"Oh, but Anne-Marie, there's the problem." Calderone wagged
the gun a little and her eyes were fixed on the muzzle. Was it her
imagination or over the whistle of the wind did she hear the faint
shriek of sirens?

The police!

Ryder had called 9-1-1!

Had they come up with the right location?

Hurry, hurry, hurry!

"You can't prove it though, can you? That you'd not met those
women," Calderone was saying, so caught up in his own story, in his
bragging, that he hadn't heard the sirens as he stood confidently behind her SUV.

He couldn't prove it—yet. But he would. He wouldn't be so outwardly cocky if he hadn't made certain of that fact. Oh, how her fingers itched to grab Ryder's Glock.

"You know, it looks very suspicious that those women happened to die just about the time you arrived in town, don't you think? And then, oh dear, evidence points to you."

'What do you mean?"

"Your fingerprint, Anne-Marie. Your fucking telltale print showed up on the victims' personal effects."

"But I never—"

"I guess you just got careless."

"What? No! You're bluffing," she accused. But she knew him too well to believe her own words.

The glint of satisfaction in his eyes, and his cold, cold smile convinced her he wasn't lying. To prove his point, he kept the gun trained on her with one hand, while with the other, he unzipped his jacket to expose a chain that he lifted and she saw something withered and dark and . . .

Her stomach dropped and she retched, fighting the urge to throw up. "Oh, God."

"That's right. A little keepsake from my dear whore of a wife."

"You shit!"

His eyes flared. "So let's end this," he said harshly.

The sirens were getting closer, but Calderone didn't seem to notice the noise over the wind, so intent was he on killing her. "Go ahead and try for the gun," he said smoothly. Confidently. Always the supercilious egomaniac. "I know you've got one, but, trust me, Annie-girl, you'll never reach it, aim it, and fire before you're dead."

So much for the element of surprise. She saw him level the gun straight at her heart and threw herself backward into the open doorway.

Blam! Calderone fired.

Wood splintered.

She hit the floor, rolled over, reached around her back.

A big engine roared to life.

What the hell?

Blam! Another shot, the bullet whizzing into the cabin.

The engine raced louder, a truck spinning its tires in the snow.

Looking through the doorway, she saw Calderone turn, his face a mask of horror. Suddenly his aim was no longer on her or the open doorway, but on the huge truck, Ryder's Dodge, churning forward, gathering speed, heading straight at him.

Blam! Calderone fired again.

The Dodge's windshield shattered.

Ryder's body jerked.

Blood sprayed.

The horn blared.

"Nooooo!" Anne-Marie screamed, rolling to her feet, yanking out her weapon from the back of her jeans and swinging her arm around. "No! No! No!" She started firing wildly, all of her pent-up rage forced into pulling the trigger.

But the truck didn't stop.

Calderone stepped back, a bullet grazing his shoulder. For a second, he forgot the truck. When he looked up again, it was too late. The Dodge slammed into him, pinning him against the back of her SUV. In a mash of shattering bones and crumpling metal, he howled in agony. His voice rose to the heavens. Writhing. Screaming. To no avail. Calderone dropped the gun and frantically pushed on the hood of Ryder's truck as if he could shove it off him. But the wheels kept grinding, churning in the snow, mangling him, twisting the lower half of his body into a pulp of bone and tissue and blood.

"Oh, God!" Horrified, Anne-Marie threw herself off the porch and ran to the truck. Snow was blowing inside the cab. She yanked open the door as the engine continued to turn over, trying to drive the Dodge's spinning wheels forward, still crushing the man pinned in the contorted metal.

"Troy. Ryder!"

His body spilled into her waiting arms, blood everywhere.

"Don't die," she said to him, though he was obviously unconscious. "Don't you dare die on me!" With all her effort, she reached across him and yanked out the keys. The engine died, the wheels stopping suddenly.

Tears filled her eyes and she didn't bother dashing them, just fumbled with the damn key ring until she found the smallest key and unlocked the cuffs. As the cuff sprang open, he slithered out of the truck and his weight pulled them both onto the frozen ground.

Blood spilled, and she tried frantically to stanch it.

She had done this. It was her fault that he lay dying in her arms.

For a second, everything seemed to go quiet. The engine no longer ground and Calderone's voice had been stilled, probably forever. She felt that in that one suspended second, she and Ryder were alone in the universe.

"Don't you die on me," she said to him again, sobbing, holding him close. Blood covered her hands, smearing on her clothes. So wrapped up in saving him, she barely heard the sirens or the wind or the sound of anxious shouts. "Do you hear me, Ryder? Don't you dare die on me." She heard him expel a rattling breath.

Then he opened one eye. Looking up at her, his lips barely moved as he said, "Wouldn't dream of it, darlin'. Wouldn't dream of . . . it."

Epilogue

Las Vegas, Nevada
February

Never in her life would Pescoli have dreamed that she would be standing next to Santana, saying "I do" in a tiny chapel in Las Vegas, but here she was, her kids at her side, witnessing their mother getting married again.

Surprisingly, it felt right.

As if she'd been destined for this moment for all of her life.

Okay, she knew that was the stuff of romantic dreams she didn't believe in, but just for the day, wearing an off-white dress that almost touched her knees, Santana looking handsome as as hell in a black suit, she went with the fantasy.

It wasn't February fourteen, but the day after. Bianca and Jeremy, if not thrilled at the hasty marriage, went with it. Santana had promised to take Jeremy target shooting in the next few days and Bianca was able to sunbathe in the bikini she'd received from her father and stepmother last Christmas. So it was a win-win situation, or as much as it could be, considering.

Less than two weeks ago, she and Alvarez had wrapped up the Anne-Marie Calderone case. Bruce Calderone had died at the scene. No big loss there. The finger found dangling from his neck matched the prints they'd found on Calypso Pope's purse and Sheree Cantnor's shoe and was the ring finger he'd sliced off his wife's left hand, the proof of which she bore as a stump on her hand.

Troy Ryder had survived a bullet wound to the neck, though he'd lost enough blood to kill a lesser man. However, he was out of the hospital and in New Orleans where he, Anne-Marie, and Detective Montoya were sorting things out.

The last Pescoli had heard, Anne-Marie's grandmother wasn't pressing charges, but that was just the first and foremost of Anne-Marie's crimes, now that she'd been cleared of murder. She had other nasty details, like false passports and IDs, to deal with.

Again, Pescoli was glad that was all part of the New Orleans Police Department's problems. She had heard that Anne-Marie's parents were filing bankruptcy and had disowned her after being exposed as trying to profit from their daughter's notoriety.

The true killer of Sheree Cantnor and Calypso Pope had been exposed, all part of Calderone's twisted plan to get back at his wife. Sometimes, marriages weren't exactly made in heaven, which was a weird thing to think on her wedding day. Then again, it was her third time down the aisle, so she could be a little cynical.

She wasn't going to think about the whole Calderone mess another minute.

That case was closed.

At least for her.

And from this moment forward, she was a bride. Again. God knew what the future had in store for her. Bianca, in a short pink dress, the maid of honor, blinked back tears. Jeremy stood tall and solemn, a man who had given his mother away to a new man he didn't quite trust. In a suit, he resembled his father on that long ago day when Pescoli had married Joe Strand.

But that was the past. Santana was the future.

As she held Santana's hand and thought of the baby that was growing inside her, the infant her other children knew nothing about, she felt a wellspring of hope that was unlike her. The pseudo clergyman, grinning widely, proclaimed them man and wife and Santana leaned down to kiss her.

"Just one thing," she whispered before his lips met hers. "I'm not changing my name. I've done that enough."

"You think you might have mentioned that a little earlier?"

"Probably."

He winked at her, and she wondered how it was possible to love someone this much, especially a man she'd once considered just a fling. "It's fine," he assured her.

"Really? You don't care?"

"Don't you know me by now?" His dark eyes flashed in that sexy way that always made her throat catch and she couldn't help but grin. "I'll take you any way I can get you, Regan Pescoli. Any damn way you want." And then, to seal the deal, he kissed her so hard, she nearly swooned.

Yes, she thought, *this time I finally got it right.*

HOME

Along the shores of Oregon's wild Columbia River, the Victorian mansion where Sarah McAdams grew up is as foreboding as she remembers. The moment she and her two daughters, Jade and Gracie, pull up the isolated drive, Sarah is beset by uneasy memories—of her cold, distant mother, of the half-sister who vanished without a trace, and of a long-ago night when Sarah was found on the widow's walk, feverish and delirious.

IS WHERE

But Sarah has vowed to make a fresh start and renovate the old place. Between tending to her girls and the rundown property, she has little time to dwell on the past. . . . Until a new, more urgent menace enters the picture.

THE FEAR IS

One by one, teenage girls are disappearing. Frantic for her daughters' safety, Sarah feels the house's walls closing in on her again. Somewhere deep in her memory is the key to a very real and terrifying danger. And only by confronting her most terrifying fears can she stop the nightmare roaring back to life once more . . .

Please turn the page for an exciting sneak peek of

Lisa Jackson's

CLOSE TO HOME

on sale in September 2014 wherever print and e-books are sold!

CHAPTER I

October 15, 2014
Blue Peacock Manor

"God, Mom, you've got to be kidding!" Jade said from the passenger seat of the Explorer as Sarah drove along the once-gravel lane.

"Not kidding," Sarah responded. "You know that." Winding through thick stands of pine, fir, and cedar, the twin ruts were weed-choked and filled with potholes that had become puddles with the recent rain.

"You can't actually think that we can live here!" Catching glimpses of the huge house through the trees, Jade, seventeen, was clearly horrified and, as usual, wasn't afraid to voice her opinion.

"Mom's serious," Gracie said from the backseat, where she was crammed between piles of blankets, and mounds of comforters, sleeping bags, and the other bedding they were moving from Vancouver. "She told us."

Jade shot a glance over her shoulder. "I know. But it's worse than I thought."

"That's impossible," Gracie said.

"No one asked your opinion!"

Sarah's hands tightened over the steering wheel. She'd already heard how she was ruining her kids' lives by packing them up and returning to the old homestead where she'd been born and raised. To hear them tell it, she was the worst mother in the world. The word "hate" had been thrown around, aimed at her, the move, and their miserable lives in general.

Single motherhood. It wasn't for the faint-hearted, she'd decided long ago. So her kids were still angry with her. Too bad. Sarah needed a fresh start.

And though Jade and Gracie didn't know it, they did too.

"It's like we're in another solar system," Jade said as the thickets of trees gave way to a wide clearing high above the Columbia River.

Gracie agreed, "In a land far, far away."

"Oh, stop it. It's not that bad," Sarah said. Her girls had lived most of their lives in Vancouver, Washington, right across the river from Portland, Oregon. Theirs had been a city life. Out here, in Stewart's Crossing, things would be different, and even more so at Sarah's childhood home of Blue Peacock Manor.

Perched high on the cliffs overlooking the Columbia River, the massive house where Sarah had been raised rose in three stories of cedar and stone. Built in the Queen Anne style of a Victorian home, its gables and chimneys knifed upward into a somber gray sky, and from her vantage point Sarah could now see the glass cupola that opened onto the widow's walk. For a second, she felt a frisson of dread slide down her spine, but she pushed it aside.

"Oh. My. God." Jade's jaw dropped open as she stared at the house. "It looks like something straight out of *The Addams Family*."

"Let me see!" In the backseat, Gracie unhooked her seat belt and leaned forward for a better view. "She's right." For once Gracie agreed with her older sister.

"Oh, come on," Sarah said, but Jade's opinion wasn't that far off. With a broad, sagging porch and crumbling chimneys, the once-grand house that in the past the locals had called the Jewel of the Columbia was in worse shape than she remembered.

"Are you blind? This place is a disaster!" Jade was staring through the windshield and slowly shaking her head, as if she couldn't believe the horrid turn her life had just taken. Driving closer to the garage, they passed another building that was falling into total disrepair. "Mom. Seriously. We can't live here." She turned her wide, mascara-laden eyes on her mother as if Sarah had gone completely out of her mind.

"We can and we will. Eventually." Sarah cranked on the wheel to swing the car around and parked near the walkway leading to the entrance of the main house. The decorative rusted gate was falling off its hinges, the arbor long gone, the roses flanking the flagstone path leggy and gone to seed. "We're going to camp out in the main house until the work on the guesthouse is finished, probably next week. That's where we'll hang out until the house is done, but that will take . . . months, maybe up to a year."

"The guest . . . Oh my God, is that it?" Jade pointed a black-tipped nail at the smaller structure located across a wide stone courtyard from its immense counterpart. The guesthouse was in much the same shape as the main house and outbuildings. Shingles were missing, the gutters were rusted, and most of the downspouts were disconnected or missing altogether. Many of the windows were boarded over as well, and the few that remained were cracked and yellowed.

"Charming." Jade let out a disgusted breath. "I can't wait."

"I thought you'd feel that way," Sarah said with a faint smile.

"Funny," Jade mocked.

"Come on. Buck up. It's just for a little while. Eventually we'll move into the main house for good, if we don't sell it."

Gracie said, "You should sell it now!"

"It's not just mine, remember? My brothers and sister own part of it. What we do with it will be a group decision."

"Doesn't anyone have a lighter?" Jade suggested, almost kidding. "You could burn it down and collect the insurance money."

"How do you know about . . . ?" But she didn't finish the question as she cut the engine. Jade, along with her newfound love of the macabre, was also into every kind of police or detective show that aired on television. Recently she'd discovered true crime as well, the kind of shows in which B-grade actors reenacted grisly murders and the like. Jade's interests, which seemed to coincide with those of her current boyfriend, disturbed Sarah, but she tried to keep from haranguing her daughter about them. In this case, less was more.

"You should sell out your part of it. Leave it to Aunt Dee Linn and Uncle Joe and Jake to renovate," Jade said. "Get out while you can. God, Mom, this is just so nuts that *we're* here. Not only is this house like something out of a bad horror movie, but it's in the middle of nowhere."

She wasn't that far off. The house and grounds were at least five miles from the nearest town of Stewart's Crossing, the surrounding neighbors' farms hidden by stands of fir and cedar. Sarah cut the engine and glanced toward Willow Creek, the natural divide between this property and the next, which had belonged to the Walsh family for more than a hundred years. For a split second she thought about Clint, the last of the Walsh line, who according to Dee Linn and Aunt Marge, was still living in the homestead. She reminded herself sternly that he was not the reason she'd pushed so hard to move back to Stewart's Crossing.

"Why don't you just take me back to get my car?" Jade said as Sarah swung the Explorer around to park near the garage.

"Because it won't be ready for a couple of days. You heard Hal." They'd left Jade's Honda with a mechanic in town; it was scheduled to get a new set of tires and much-needed brakes, and Hal was going to figure out why the Civic was leaking some kind of fluid.

"Oh, right, Hal the master mechanic." Jade was disparaging.

"Best in town," Sarah said, tossing her keys into her bag. "My dad used him."

"Only mechanic in town. And Grandpa's been gone a long time, so it must've been eons ago!"

Sarah actually smiled. "Okay, you got me there. But the place was updated from the last time I was there. Lots of electronic equipment and a couple of new mechanics on staff."

To her amazement, Jade's lips twitched as well, reminding Sarah of the younger, more innocent girl she'd been such a short while ago. "And a lot of customers."

"Must be bad car karma right now," Sarah agreed. There had been an older woman with her little dog and two men, all having problems with their vehicles; the little group had filled the small reception area of the garage.

"Is there ever such a thing as good car karma?" Jade asked, but she seemed resigned to her fate of being without wheels for a while. Good.

Until recently, Jade had been a stellar student. She had a high IQ and had had a keen interest in school; in fact, she had breezed through any number of accelerated classes. Then, about a year ago, she'd discovered boys, and her grades had begun to slip. Now, despite the fact that it might be a bit passé, Jade was into all things Goth and wildly in love with her boyfriend, an older kid who'd barely graduated from high school and didn't seem to give a damn about anything but music, marijuana, and, most likely, sex. A pseudo-intellectual, he'd dropped out of college and loved to argue politics.

Jade thought the sun rose and set on Cody Russell.

Sarah was pretty sure it didn't.

"Come on, let's go," she told her daughters.

Jade wasn't budging. She dragged her cell phone from her purse. "Do I have to?"

"Yes."

"She's such a pain," Gracie said in a whisper. At twelve, she was only starting to show some interest in boys, and still preferred animals, books, and all things paranormal to the opposite sex, so far at least. Blessed with an overactive imagination and, again, keen intelligence, Gracie too was out of step with her peers.

"I heard that." Jade messed with her phone.

"It is kinda creepy, though," Gracie admitted, leaning forward as the first drops of rain splashed against the windshield.

"Beyond creepy!" Jade wasn't one to hold back. "And . . . Oh, God, don't tell me we don't get cell service here." Her face registered complete mortification.

"It's spotty," Sarah said.

"God, Mom, what is this? The Dark Ages? This place is . . . it's horrible. Blue Peacock Manor, my ass."

"Hey!" Sarah reprimanded sharply. "No swearing. Remember? Zero."

"But, Jesus, Mom—"

"Again?" Sarah snapped. "I just said no."

"Okay!" Jade flung back, then added, a little more calmly, "Come on, Mom. Admit it. Blue Peacock is a dumb name. It even sounds kind of dirty."

"Where is this coming from?" Sarah demanded.

"Just sayin'." Jade dropped her phone into her bag. "And Becky told me the house is haunted."

"So now you're listening to Becky?" Sarah set the parking brake and reached for the handle of the door. The day was quickly going from bad to worse. "I didn't think you liked her."

"I don't." Jade sighed theatrically. "I'm just telling you what she said." Becky was Jade's cousin, the daughter of Sarah's older sister, Dee Linn. "But it's not like I have a zillion friends here, is it?"

"Okay. Got it." In Sarah's opinion, Becky wasn't to be trusted; she was one of those teenaged girls who loved to gossip and stir things up a bit, gleeful to cause a little trouble, especially for someone else. Becky cut a wide swath through everyone else's social life. Just like her mother. No doubt Becky'd heard from Dee Linn the tales that Blue Peacock Manor harbored its own special ghosts. That kind of gossip, swirling so close to home, just barely touching her life but not ruining it, was right up Dee Linn's alley.

Gracie said, "I think the house looks kinda cool. Creepy cool."

Jade snorted. "What would you know about cool?"

"Hey . . . ," Sarah warned her oldest.

Used to her older sister's barbs, Gracie pulled the passive-aggressive card and acted as if she hadn't heard the nasty ring to her sister's question. As her seat belt clicked open, she changed the conversation back to her favorite topic. "Can we get a dog, Mom?" Before Sarah could respond, she added quickly, "You said we could. Remember? Once we moved here, you said we'd look for a dog."

"I believe I said 'I'll think about it.' "

"Jade got a car," Gracie pointed out.

From the front seat, Jade said, "That's different."

"No, it's not." To her mother, Gracie threw back Sarah's own words, " 'A promise is a promise.' That's what you always say." Gracie regarded her mother coolly as she clambered out of the backseat.

"I know." How could Sarah possibly forget the argument that had existed since her youngest had turned five? Gracie was nuts about all animals, and she'd been lobbying for a pet forever.

Once her younger daughter was out of earshot, Sarah said to Jade, "It wouldn't kill you to be nice to your sister."

Jade threw her mother a disbelieving look and declared, "This is so gonna suck!"

"Only if you let it." Sarah was tired of the ongoing argument that had started the second she'd announced the move two weeks ago. She'd waited until the real estate deal with her siblings was completed and she had hired a crew to start working before breaking the news to her kids. "This is a chance for all of us to have a new start."

"I don't care. The 'new start' thing? That's on you. For you. And maybe her," she added, hitching her chin toward the windshield

Sarah followed her gaze and watched Gracie hike up the broken flagstone path, where dandelions and moss had replaced the mortar years before. A tangle of leggy, gone-to-seed rosebushes were a reminder of how long the house had been neglected. Once upon a time, Sarah's mother had tended the gardens and orchard to the point of obsession, but that had been years ago. Now a solitary crow flapped to a perch in a skeletal cherry tree near the guesthouse, then pulled its head in tight, against the rain.

"Come on, Jade. Give me a break," Sarah said.

"You give me one." Jade rolled her eyes and unbuckled her seat belt, digging out her cell phone and attempting to text. "Smartphone, my ass—er, butt."

"Again, watch the language." Sarah pocketed her keys and tried not to let her temper get control of her tongue. "Grab your stuff, Jade. Like it or not, we're home."

"I can *not* believe this is my life."

"Believe it." Sarah shoved open the driver's side door, then walked to the rear of the vehicle to pull her computer and suitcase from the cargo area.

Of course, she too had doubts about moving here. The project she planned to tackle—renovating the place to its former grandeur before selling it—was daunting, perhaps impossible. Even when she'd been living here with all her siblings, the huge house had been sinking into disrepair. Since her father had died, things had really gone downhill. Paint was peeling from the siding, and many of the shiplap boards were warped. The wide porch that ran along the front of the house seemed to be listing, rails missing, and there were holes in the roof where there had once been shingles.

"It looks evil, you know," Jade threw over her shoulder before hauling her rolling bag out of the cargo space and reluctantly trudging after her sister. "I've always hated it."

Sarah managed to hold back a hot retort. The last time she'd brought her children here, she and her own mother, Arlene, had gotten into a fight, a blistering battle of words that precipitated their final, painful rift. Though Gracie was probably too small to remember, Jade certainly did.

Gracie was nearly at the steps when she stopped suddenly to stare upward at the house. "What the . . . ?"

"Come on," Jade said to her younger sister, but Gracie didn't move, even when Sarah joined her daughters and a big black crow landed on one of the rusted gutters.

"Something wrong?" Sarah asked.

Jade was quick to say, "Oh, no, Mom, everything's just perfect. You get into a fight with that perv at your job and decide we all have to move." She snapped her fingers. "And bam! It's done. Just like that. You rent out the condo in Vancouver and tell us we have to move here to a falling-down old farm with a grotesque house that looks like Stephen King dreamed it up. Yeah, everything's just cool." Jade reached for her phone again. "And there's got to be some cell phone service here or I'm out, Mom. Really. No service is like . . . archaic and . . . and . . . inhumane!"

"You'll survive."

Gracie whispered, "Someone's in there."

"What?" Sarah said. "No. The house has been empty for years."

Gracie blinked. "But . . . but, I saw her."

"You saw who?" Sarah asked and tried to ignore a tiny flare of fear knotting her stomach.

With one hand still on the handle of her rolling bag, she shrugged. "A girl."

Sarah caught an I-told-you-so look from her older daughter.

"A girl? Where?" Jade demanded.

"She was standing up there." Gracie pointed upward, to the third story and the room at the northwest corner of the house, just under the cupola. "In the window."

Theresa's room. The bedroom that had been off-limits to Sarah as a child. The knot in Sarah's gut tightened. Jade again caught her mother's eyes in a look that silently invoked Sarah to bring Gracie back to reality.

"Maybe it's a ghost," Jade mocked. "I hear there are lots of them around here." She leaned closer to her sister. "And not just from Becky. You told me you'd been doing some 'research' and you found out the first woman who lived here was killed, her body never found, her spirit roaming the hallways of Blue Peacock Manor forever."

Gracie shot her mom a look. "Well . . . yeah . . ."

"Oh, please," Jade snorted. "The second you step foot here, you see a ghost."

"Angelique Le Duc did die here!" Gracie flared.

"You mean, Angelique Stewart," Jade corrected. "She was married to our crazy, homicidal, great-great-great-not-so-great-grandfather or something. That's what you said."

"I read it on the Internet," Gracie responded, her mouth tight at being corrected.

"So then it must be true," Jade said. She turned her attention to her mother. "The minute you told us we were moving, she started in on all this ghost stuff. Checking out books from the library, surfing the Net, chatting with other people who think they see ghosts. And she didn't find out about just Angelique Le Duc—oh, no. There were others too. This place"—she gestured to the house and grounds—"is just littered with the spirits who've come to a bad end at Blue Peacock Manor!" Jade's hair caught in the wind as the rain picked up. "Do you see how ridiculous this all is, Mom? Now she's believing all this paranormal shi . . . stuff and thinking we're going to be living with a bunch of the undead!"

"Jade—" Sarah started.

"Shut up!" Gracie warned.

"You sound like a lunatic," Jade went right on, then turned heatedly to Sarah. "You have to put an end to this, Mom. It's for her own good. If she goes spouting off about ghosts and spirits and demons—"

"Demons!" Gracie snapped in disgust. "Who said anything—"

"It's all a load of crap," Jade declared. "She's going to be laughed out of school!"

"Enough!" Sarah yelled, though for once Jade seemed to be concerned for her sister. But Sarah had enough of their constant bickering. Forcing a calm she didn't feel, she said, "We're going inside now."

"You don't believe me," Gracie said, hurt. She looked up at the window again.

Sarah had already glanced at the window of the room where she knew, deep in her soul, dark deeds had occurred. But no image appeared behind the dirty, cracked glass. No apparition flitted past the panes. No otherworldly figure was evident. There was no "girl" hiding behind the grime, just some tattered curtains that seemed to shift in the dreary afternoon.

"I saw her," Gracie insisted. A line of consternation had formed between her brows.

"It could have been a reflection or a shadow," Sarah said as the crow cawed loudly. Deep inside she knew she was lying.

Gracie turned on Jade. "*You* scared her away!"

"Oh, right. Of course it's my fault. Give me an effing break."

"She'll punish you, you know." Gracie's eyes narrowed. "The woman in the window, she'll get even."

"Gracie!" Sarah's mouth dropped open.

."Then you'll see," Gracie declared, turning to the front entrance and effectively ending the conversation.

"Here's the latest," Rhea announced as she stepped through the door of Clint's cramped office in the small quarters that made up Stewart Crossing's City Hall. As city building inspector, he checked on all the jobs currently being constructed or renovated within the city limits and beyond, and contracted with the county for the outlying areas. "You might find one particularly interesting." She raised her thinly plucked eyebrows high enough that they arched over the frames of her glasses. "A neighbor."

"Don't tell me. The Stewart place."

"The Jewel of the Columbia?" she said dryly, shaking her head, her short, red hair unmoving.

His insides clenched a bit. "Maybe Doug wants to take this one."

"I thought you hated Doug."

"Hate's a strong word," Clint said. "He just wouldn't be my first choice to become my replacement." He wasn't sure why he didn't trust Doug Knowles, but the guy he was training to take over his job seemed too green, too eager, too damned hungry, to give each job its proper attention. There was something a little secretive about him as well, and Clint had a suspicion that Doug would take the easy way out, maybe let some of the little details slide on a job. "On second thought, I'll handle the Stewart project."

"Figured," she said, her red lips twisting a bit. "Oh, and wait!" She hurried out of the room and returned a few seconds later with a candy dish that she set on the corner of his desk. "Halloween candy for your clients with sweet tooths, er, teeth."

"I don't need these."

"Of course you do. It's that time of year. Don't be such a Grinch."

"I believe he's associated with Christmas."

"Or whatever holiday you want. In this case, Halloween." She unwrapped a tiny Three Musketeers bar and plopped it onto her tongue.

"Okay, so I'm a Grinch. Don't hate me."

Laughing, she gave him a wink as she turned and headed through the door to the reception area of the building that housed all the city offices. Built in the middle of the last century, the structure was constructed of glass and narrow, blond bricks; it had a flat roof and half a dozen offices opening into the central reception area. The ceilings were low, of "soundproof" tile, the lights fluorescent, the floors covered in a linoleum that had been popular during the 1960s. Now, it was showing decades of wear. "Just take a look." Rhea clipped away on high heels as a phone started jangling. She leaned over her desk and snagged the receiver before the second ring. She did it on purpose, he suspected, knowing he was still watching her as she gave him a quick glimpse of the skirt tightening over her hips.

"Stewart Crossing City Hall," she answered sweetly. "This is Rhea Hernandez."

She had a nice butt, he'd give her that, but he wasn't interested.

Attractive and smart, Rhea had been married and divorced three times, and was looking for husband number four at the ripe old age of forty-two.

It wasn't going to be Clint, and he suspected she knew it. Rhea's flirting was more out of habit than sincerity.

". . . I'm sorry, the mayor isn't in. Can I take a message, or, if you'd like, you can e-mail her directly," Rhea was saying as she stretched the cord around the desk and took her seat, disappearing from view. He heard her start rattling off Mayor Leslie Imholt's e-mail address.

Clint picked up the stack of papers she'd dropped into his inbox. Plans for the complete renovation of Blue Peacock Manor, the historic home set on property that backed up to his own ranch, was the first request. No surprise there, as he'd heard Sarah was returning to do a complete renovation of the Stewart family home. The preliminary drawings were already with the city engineer for approval; these had to be renovations to the original plans. A helluva job, that, he knew, and to think that Sarah was taking it on and returning to a place she'd wanted so desperately to leave. He eyed the specs and noted that he needed to see what work had already been accomplished on the smaller residence on the property—the guesthouse, as the Stewart family had called it.

Until the mayor had hired Doug Knowles, Clint had been the only inspector in this part of the county and had checked all the work himself. Now he could hand jobs off to Doug if he wanted. Clint had already decided that was generally a bad idea. It certainly would be in this case, he thought.

But if he took on Blue Peacock Manor, no doubt he would see Sarah again.

Frowning, he grabbed one of the damned bits of candy, and unwrapping a tiny Kit Kat bar, leaned back in his chair. He and Sarah hadn't seen each other for years, and if he were honest with himself, he knew that their split hadn't been on the best of terms. He tossed the candy into his mouth, then wadded up the wrapper and threw it at the waste can.

High school romance, he thought. So intense, but in the larger scheme of things, so meaningless, really.

Why, then, did the memory of it seem as fresh now as it had half a lifetime ago?

His desk phone jangled, and he reached for it willingly, pushing thoughts of Sarah Stewart and their ill-fated romance to the far, far corners of his mind.

CHAPTER 2

"That's it. I'm outta here," Rosalie Jamison said as she stripped off her apron and tossed it into a bin with the other soiled towels, aprons, jackets, and rags that would be cleaned overnight, ready for the morning shift at the three-star diner. She slipped her work shoes onto a shelf and laced up her Nikes, new and reflective, for the walk home. "I'll see you all later."

Located a few blocks from the river, the restaurant had been dubbed the Columbia Diner about a million years ago by some hick with no imagination. It was located at one end of the truck stop about a half mile out of Stewart's Crossing. Rosalie had spent the past six months here, waiting tables for the regulars and the customers just passing through. She hated the hours and the smell of grease and spices that clung to her until she spent at least twenty minutes under the shower, but it was a job, one of the few in this useless backwoods town.

For now it would do, until she had enough money saved so she could leave Stewart's Crossing for good. She couldn't wait.

"Wait!" Gloria, a woman who was in her fifties and perpetually smelled of cigarettes, caught up with Rosalie before she got out the door, and Gloria stuffed a few dollars and some change into Rosalie's hand. "Never forget your share of the tips," she said with a wink. She continued, "They keep me in all my diamonds and furs."

"Yeah, right." Rosalie had to smile. Gloria was cool, even if she continually talked about how long it would be before she collected Medicare and Social Security and all that boring stuff. A frustrated hairdresser, she changed her hair color, cut, or style every month or so and had taken Rosalie under her wing when a couple of boys, classmates from high school, had come in and started to hassle her with obscene comments and gestures. Gloria had refused to serve them and sent them out the door with their tails between their legs. The whole scene had only made things ugly at school, but Rosalie had solved that by cutting classes or ditching out completely.

"If you wait a half hour, I'll give you a ride home," Gloria said, sliding a fresh cigarette from her pack as she peered outside and into the darkness. "I just have to clean up a bit."

Rosalie hesitated. It would take her at least twenty minutes to walk home on the service road that ran parallel to the interstate, but Gloria's half hours usually stretched into an hour or two, and Rosalie just wanted to go home, sneak up the stairs, flop on her bed, and catch an episode of *Big Brother* or *Keeping Up with the Kardashians* or whatever else she could find on her crappy little TV. Besides, Gloria always lit up the second she was behind the wheel, and it was too cold to roll down the windows of her old Dodge. "I'd better get going. Thanks."

Gloria frowned. "I don't like you walking home alone in the dark."

"It's just for a little while longer," Rosalie reminded her, holding up her tips before stuffing the cash into the pocket of her jacket, which she'd retrieved from a peg near the open back door. "I'm gonna buy my uncle's Toyota. He's saving it for me. I just need another three hundred."

"It's starting to rain."

"I'm okay. Really."

"You be careful, then." Gloria's brows drew together beneath straw-colored bangs. "I don't like this, y'know."

"It's okay." Rosalie zipped up her jacket and stepped into the night before Gloria could argue with her. As the diner's door shut behind her, she heard Gloria saying to the Barry, the cook, "I don't know *what* her mother is thinking letting that girl walk alone this late at night."

Sharon wasn't thinking. That was the problem. Her mom wasn't thinking of Rosalie at all because of crappy Mel, her current husband, a burly, gruff man Rosalie just thought of as Number Four. He was a loser like the others in her mother's string of husbands. But Sharon, as usual, had deemed Mel "the one" and had referred to him as her soul mate, which was such a pile of crap. No one in her right mind would consider overweight, beer-slogging, TV-watching Mel Updike a soul mate unless they were completely brainless. He owned a kinda cool motorcycle that she could never ride, and that was the only okay thing about him. The fact that Mel leered at Rosalie with a knowing glint in his eye didn't make it any better. He'd already fathered five kids with ex-wives and girlfriends that were scattered from LA to Seattle. Rosalie had experienced the dubious pleasure of meeting most of them and had hated every one on sight. They were all "Little Mels," losers like their big, hairy-bellied father. Geez, didn't the guy know about waxing? Or man-scaping or, for that matter, not belching at the table?

Soul mate? Bull-effin'-shit!

Sharon had to be out of her mind!

Rosalie shoved her hands deep into her pockets and felt the other cash that she'd squirreled away in the lining of her hooded jacket, a gift from her real dad. The jacket was never out of her sight, and she'd tucked nearly nine hundred dollars deep inside it. She had to be careful. Either Mel or one of his sticky-fingered kids might make off with the cash she was saving for a car. Until she could pay for the Toyota outright, as well as license and insure it for six months, she was forbidden to own one.

All around, it sucked.

Her whole damn life *sucked.*

As rain began to pelt, striking her cheeks, splashing in puddles, peppering the gravel crunching beneath her feet, she began to wish she'd waited for Gloria. Putting up with a little cigarette smoke was better than slogging through cold rain.

She couldn't wait to get out of this hole-in-the-wall of a town where her mother, chasing the ever-slippery Mel, had dragged her. Kicking at the pebbles on the shoulder, she envied the people driving the cars that streaked by on the interstate, their headlights cutting through the dark night, their tires humming against the wet pavement, their lives going full throttle while she was stuck in idle.

But once she had her car, look out! She'd turn eighteen and leave Sharon and hairy Mel and head to Denver, where her dad and the boyfriend she'd met on the Internet were waiting.

Three hundred more dollars and five months.

That was all.

A gust of wind blasted her again, and she shuddered. Maybe she should turn back and take Gloria up on that ride. She glanced over her shoulder, but the neon lights of the diner were out of sight. She was nearly halfway home.

She started to jog.

A lone car had turned onto the road and was catching up to her, its headlights glowing bright. She stepped farther off the shoulder, her Nikes slipping a little. The roar of a large engine was audible over the rain, and she realized it wasn't a car, but a truck behind her. No big deal. There were hundreds of them around Stewart's Crossing. She expected the pickup to fly by her with a spray of road wash, but as it passed her, it slowed.

Just go on, she thought. She slowed to a walk, but kept moving until she saw the brake lights glow bright.

Now what?

She kept walking, intent on going around the dark truck, keeping her pace steady, hoping it was only a coincidence that the guy had stopped. No such luck. The window on the passenger side slid down.

"Rosie?" a voice that was vaguely familiar called from the darkened cab. "That you?"

Keep walking.

She didn't look up.

"Hey, it's me." The cab's interior light blinked on, and she recognized the driver, a tall man who was a regular at the diner and who now leaned across the seat to talk to her. "You need a ride?"

"No, it's only a little farther."

"You're soaked to the skin," he said, concerned.

"It's okay."

"Oh, come on. Hop in, I'll drive you." Without waiting for an answer, he opened the door.

"I don't—"

"Your call, but I'm drivin' right by your house."

"You know where I live?" That was weird.

"Only that you said you're on Umpqua."

Had she mentioned it? Maybe. "I don't know." Shaking her head, she felt the cold rain drizzling down her neck. She stared at the open door of the pickup. Clean. Warm. Dry. The strains of some Western song playing softly on the radio.

"You'll be home in three minutes."

Don't do it!

The wind blasted again, and she pushed down her misgivings. She knew the guy, had been waiting on him ever since she took the job. He was one of the better-looking regulars. He always had a compliment and a smile and left a good-sized tip.

"Okay."

"That-a-girl."

Climbing into the truck, she felt the warm air from the heater against her skin and recognized the Randy Travis song wafting through the speakers. She yanked the door shut, but the lock didn't quite latch.

"Here, let me get that," he said. "Damned thing." Leaning across her, he fiddled with the door. "Give it a tug, will ya?"

"Okay." The second she pulled on the door handle, she felt something cold and metallic click around her wrist. "Hey! What the hell do you think you're doing?" she demanded, fear spreading through her bloodstream as she jerked her hand up and realized she'd been cuffed to the door handle.

"Just calm down."

"The hell I will! What is this?" She was furious and scared and tried to open her door, but it was locked. "Let me out, you son of a bitch!"

He slapped her then. Quick and hard, a sharp backhand across her mouth.

She let out a little scream.

"There'll be no swearin'," he warned her.

"What? No what?" She swung her free hand at him, across the cab, but he caught her wrist.

"Ah-ah-ah, honey. You've got a lot to learn." Then, holding her free wrist in one hand, he gunned the engine and drove toward the entrance to the Interstate.

"Let me out!" she screamed, kicking at the dash and throwing her body back and forth, screaming at the top of her lungs. The heel of her shoe hit the preset buttons of the radio and an advertisement filled the interior.

Dear God, what was this? What did he plan to do to her?

Panicked, she tried to think of a way out of this. Any way. "I—I have money," she said, thinking of the cash in her pocket, all the while struggling and twisting, to no avail. His grip was just so damned strong.

"It's not your money I want," he said in that smooth, confident tone she now found absolutely chilling. His smile was as cold as the wind shrieking down the Columbia River Gorge. "It's you."

Not ready for the thrills to end?

Hunt down more killers in chilly Montana with Detectives
Selena Alvarez and Regan Pescoli

LEFT TO DIE

Four people have already been left to die in the cruel
Montana winter, and detectives Selena Alvarez and Regan
Pescoli are trying to make sense of a nightmare. With
nothing but a killer's cryptic notes and their unsettling
conviction that there is worse to come . . .

CHOSEN TO DIE

Pescoli and Alvarez have spent months searching for the
Star Crossed Killer, never imagining one of their own will
be captured by the madman they have been hunting . . .
Time is running out and the only way to save Regan is to
get inside the killer's twisted mind . . .

BORN TO DIE

At first, Kacey Lambert thinks it's a strange coincidence
when two women with an amazing resemblance to her die
suddenly. But then Selena Alvarez learns that the autopsy
shows traces of poison in one of the victims . . .

AFRAID TO DIE

Montana is in the grip of a hard winter when the first two
bodies are found. Selena Alvarez knows both victims . . .
and both of them are wearing a piece of her jewellery . . .
The secrets of her past are coming to the surface, one by
one, and soon a madman bent on revenge will show her
just how much she has to lose

READY TO DIE

Sheriff Dan Grayson is at death's door when a prominent
judge's body is found. Regan Pescoli and Selena Alvarez
head the search for the killer, not realising they are hunting
a monster who has had them in his sights all along . . .

You've turned the last page.

But it doesn't have to end there . . .

If you're looking for more first-class, action-packed, nail-biting suspense, join us at **Facebook.com/MulhollandUncovered** for news, competitions, and behind-the-scenes access to Mulholland Books.

For regular updates about our books and authors as well as what's going on in the world of crime and thrillers, follow us on **Twitter@MulhollandUK**.

There are many more twists to come.

MULHOLLAND:
You never know what's coming around the curve.